Echoes of Fendamor

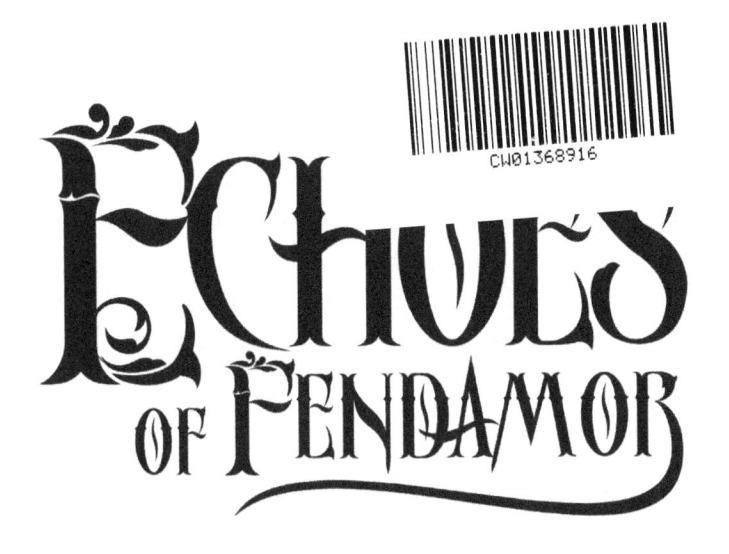

R MAISEY

Copyright © 2020 Robert Maisey.

All rights reserved. No part of the publication maybe reproduced, distributed, or transmitted in any form or by any means, including photocopying, recording, or other electronic or mechanical methods, without the prior written permission of the publisher, except in the case of brief quotations embodied in critical reviews and certain other non-commercial uses permitted by copyright law.

Any references to historical events, real people, or real places are used fictitiously. Names, characters, and places are products of the author's imagination.
First printing edition 2020.

ONE

ARRIVAL

The gulls were the first to greet Umishi as she climbed up to the deck of the *Queen's Memory*. Her digitigrade legs rendered the ascent awkward and uncomfortable, struggling to distribute her weight in a way that would not land her face down on the floor. In the company of those more familiar with her kind, she would tackle such staircases on all fours. However, she was aware of the eyes upon her, all too ready to look down on her. While under the scrutiny of other races, walking on two legs had become second nature to her; she did it without thinking most of the time. This was not one of those occasions.

Umishi's remaining large, red eye peered through the wilds of pale, white hair that masked most of the scars on her face. She found twelve sailors on deck, their attention fixed on her, drinking in the rare sighting of their elusive passenger. They had spent the entire voyage trying to catch glimpses of her, and in return, she had spent most of the three weeks out of their sight. It was no great feat to be undetectable to such blind fools. However, she could avoid it no more; she was forced into the light, under their gaze. Taking the measure of each of their stupid, grinning faces, she tried to predict which of her inhuman characteristics would gain the most laughs when recounted in their tavern tales. Would they mock her childlike size, her tail, or maybe her pale blue skin? In that moment she hated them, detested each of their transfixed eyes and poisonous smiles. Were her will a sword, all aboard the ship would have been slain the second she set foot on the deck. A spiteful wind blew against the sails, waking them from their slumber and forcing more of the sun's merciless light onto her. She raked her hair further over the ruined left side of her face as her mind fired wordless curses at the sky.

With some effort, she pushed the sailors' stares to the back of her mind and focused her attention on the land. It was so changed that, at first, she thought there had been a mistake; that these liquored up fools had somehow managed to fail at the only task she expected them to be capable of. She thought that, somehow, they had gotten lost at sea, and washed up in some thrice damned kingdom at the arse end of nowhere. *This* was not the Domvalkia that turned her memories cold and plagued her long nights with terrifying dreams.

The docks of this alien place were filled with curious things: lamps aglow with something that was not fire, carriages made of steel and not pulled by any beast, but guided on iron poles which lay upon the stone floor. The city's absences were also strange: no plants, grass and trees, as though some great calamity had drained the life from this place, leaving nothing but stone in its wake.

The dock itself offered further questions. It seemed unfit for purpose, barely able to contain a large fishing boat, let alone the *Queen's Memory*. It wasn't nearly adequate for a city so large. The dock's size was not due to a lack of seafront. No, back when she fled the island there were piers and ships lined further than the eye could see. It was clear that the new regime was sending a message. If the limited dock was not enough to convey that message, then the great battleship docked in the only sizeable berth was roaring it out, like an angry dog, eager to be unleashed.

Another set of eyes irritated the back of Umishi's neck: the captain had arrived on deck. If the heaviness of his steps hadn't revealed his identity, then the overpowering smell of whatever alcohol he had taken a fancy to would have. With a sigh, Umishi turned to greet him, a hand subconsciously rising again to her hair.

This was not the captain she had hired in Vandrel Pines. After three weeks away from land, this once respectable human had transformed into a drunken fool. His shirt was open and stained with something yellow, his leather breeches were noticeably too small for him and his once groomed facial hair had become wild and unkempt.

'My lady,' he said, in a voice whose elegance no longer matched his appearance. 'We shall be docking shortly. They signalled us in a few moments ago.'

Umishi only nodded in response, afraid that were she to unseal her lips, she would be intoxicated by the gasses that his mouth emitted.

'Must be strange, being back, I mean. No doubt a smack to the jaw seeing how much the place has changed. It's the same with my wife, I swear someone is playing a joke on me and swapping her with a different, more hideous, beast each time I return home.'

Umishi offered him nothing but a sideways glance for his crude attempt at humour.

'Will you be requiring any of my boys to help you with your belongings?' he asked in a cheery tone, oblivious to her scorn.

Umishi wanted him to be silent. There was clearly no reason to have summoned her so early, save to waste her time. However, Umishi did give the offer some thought. While she had only brought a single sack of belongings, with the amount the voyage had cost, the least they could do was take it to the inn. That would, however, mean suffering more time with the deckhands.

'No,' Umishi said, using the word as if it were the tip of her dagger.

It was clearly not the answer the captain had expected, and he fidgeted a little before responding. 'Very well. If I can do anything further for you, you need only ask. I shouldn't be too hard to find: I'll be the one yelling the loudest. We will see us docked in no time at all.'

Umishi didn't answer, but he kept talking.

'For now, I have to get these lazy bastards into line, if you'll pardon my language, my lady. I don't want any of these fools cocking anything up and damaging my ship. I've never seen a tighter squeeze; it's a wonder they get any kind of ship into this place.'

Umishi glanced over to the warship, waiting there.

'Unless of course, they have another dock for supplies. I

saw that one time, I think it was in Yamahdrel or some sunny place like that, a tiny dock for people and then about a thousand miles up the beach, in the back end of Gods bloody armpit a great big bloody thing for animals, sheep and the like. Now, they were a people who valued food.' The captain laughed. 'Anyway, I can't stand here yammering when these men need their arses whipped! Look at them, standing around as though they have nothing better to do than gawk at us! Nice to see you topside, by the way; a bit of sun will do you good, I think.'

With that, he *finally* set about his tasks.

Umishi released a sigh of relief. It had seemed as though his prattling would never end. Setting her gaze towards the land again, disappointment sank heavily into her gut. She'd believed her summons to the deck was a sign there would soon be a feeling of dirt between her finger like toes, instead of the splinters of the ship's deck. That seemed to be a while off yet, though. Deciding not to waste time repeating her journey up the stairs, she sat between three barrels, out of the sight of any curious crew member with time to glance her way.

Umishi scanned the shore of the unfamiliar land for any hint of the Domvalkia she once knew. The buildings were the wrong shape, the waters too empty, and the *smell*. The smell was too *clean*. Glancing back to the activity on deck she was permitted a glimpse of the past through a blur of motion and memory. For a mere moment, she saw an echo of the land she used to know: the soldiers marching up and down the piers, children playing on the waterfront. Then she blinked and the ghostly past was gone. Umishi looked back at the stone pier and tried her best to re-conjure the moment. The wave of nostalgia ebbed, though, washing away the phantoms of familiarity it had carried. Umishi sighed and waited.

To be fair to the captain, he was true to his word. The sun had hardly moved in the time it took the *Queen's Memory* to enter the dock. After feeling the ship bump to a stop, Umishi moved silently to port, where a number of sailors were busy tending to the gangplank under the captain's focused scrutiny. She moved to his side.

To see how things were going, she would first have to announce herself to the preoccupied captain. However since they had spoken, Umishi's tongue had become heavy with age and memories; it was no longer easy to form the words she needed. She sniffed loudly, hoping that the noise would start the talkative captain off. It did.

'Look at that,' he said, pointing to the edge of the dock where the gangplank was being set.

Following his finger, she found twenty or so soldiers standing on the pier, uniformed in scaled dark grey armour with long blue cloaks wrapped around their shoulders. Masked helmets covered their faces, each hammered with intricate details, and the weapons held in their hands were Nalraka, spear-like weapons with barbed tips, used only by the imperial guard. They stood in two rows, as motionless as the stone buildings surrounding them.

'Looks like they got us an escort,' the captain said. 'I wouldn't mind so much, but for what's stood next to them.'

Next to these metal-clad soldiers stood figures wearing dark blue robes, the shadows under their heavy hoods rendering them faceless and sending a chill down Umishi's spine.

'Mages,' the captain said. 'Never seen a mage alongside good news.'

Given her occupation, Umishi was forced to agree, her mouth twisting at the sight of them.

'Would all passengers and crew of the *Queen's Memory* please make their way to the deck of the named vessel,' a male voice said from nowhere. The spell was a common enchantment, called the Voice of Saiallan. It allowed the caster to communicate directly with those they wished, whilst remaining silent to all others. It was most useful when setting up ambushes, or speaking over long distances.

'You heard them,' the captain bellowed. 'Everyone on deck!' He wiped his face with a hand in a bid to remove any visible evidence of his mounting stress. 'Bloody mages; that's all I need.' He muttered to himself and spared Umishi a glance before going to ensure his men were in check. It did not take long for the crew to assemble and the voice to speak again.

'Please be warned, our mages are now scrying your vessel to check for any possibly dangerous magical wards, artefacts or weapons. Please remain on deck while this is being performed.'

The scrying felt like a watery mist passing over the ship, and Umishi shuddered. She felt naked before the magic. Clutching at her chest, she was relieved to find her dark leather tunic still beneath her claws. The captain's expression suggested he shared a similar discomfort. After a few moments, the voice came again, 'The scrying has found no undesired magic. Ready your vessel and prepare to be boarded.'

Umishi allowed herself a smile as she tapped the hilt of her blade.

'By all the bloody gods! What shit hole have you brought me to?' the captain growled through gritted teeth. 'If you'll pardon my language, my lady.'

She granted him a guilty half-smile, as his thoughts echoed her own. Why had she accepted this assignment? Why had she permitted herself to return, after so many years of avoiding this place? The task was not beyond others in her order, yet she had been drawn to it by a force she could not explain. It was the first time Domvalkia had requested assistance in the many years since her joining the Order of Alpharus. When she had been told about the islands cry for help, it was as though its plea was for her, bidding her to come back, begging her to return and lend aid before the tragedy that befallen Malhain was repeated.

The clunking of iron on wood drew her attention. As the mages had finished their turn, it seemed that the soldiers were to be allowed theirs. They walked up the gangplank in double file, and in unison, a sequence that seemed perfectly rehearsed. Once aboard, they wasted no time separating to search the ship. One, however, marched to the captain and removed her helmet. She was young, younger than Umishi had expected, with short dark hair that her ears kept back from her gaunt face.

'I am Commander Isolda Vallis of the Kingdom of Fendamor, and I welcome you to the city of Hanaswick. I apologise for the inconveniences my people have caused you,

Captain. We hope to have you on your way as quickly as we can.' The commander was a statue, with only her eyes and lips moving.

'Thank you, Commander, but I haven't seen this high a level of security since I docked at Valshia just before the war broke out. Though they didn't have mages: they had Salvian Warhounds. Those things were as big as horses, jaws the size of your arm! These creatures, they could sniff out anything, and not just what they were supposed to. You can imagine the damage those bastards did to my ship!' It seemed to occur to him that he was comparing the soldiers to dogs. 'Your methods are much cleaner though, that's one thing in your favour.'

'Quite,' the commander answered with a clear lack of interest. 'Which among your number is to be our guest?'

The captain gestured to Umishi. 'That would be the lady here,'

The commander looked down at Umishi, her face unmoving. 'It is an honour, Lady Inquisitor,' she said coldly, nodding. 'Ready yourself. As soon as my men have finished their work we will be departing for the shore, where you shall be processed and briefed on our predicament. I imagine you're eager to begin your work, so we will try to keep it as painless as possible.'

Processed; Umishi disliked the sound of that. Words that clean were often used to mask murkier pursuits. Next to her, the captain shifted his weight, colour draining from his face.

'Processed eh?' he blurted, 'Never heard of that but I'm always up for new experiences. There was a time on the islands of Lintals wh-'

'Not you,' the commander snapped, tone sharper than any cold blade. 'I am sorry, Captain, but I must ask you to depart as soon as me and my men are ashore.' Her threat was as clear as her apology was hollow.

'Wait a moment!' the captain protested. 'With all due respect, my lady, we can't be shipping out just yet; it would be impossible. My men haven't set foot on land for three weeks! We need supplies and rest.'

The commander regarded him with unsympathetic eyes. 'My apologies but Domvalkia is a closed island, hence the security measures. None are permitted to enter or exit without clearance granted by King Edwin himself.'

'Wait a fucking m-'

'Were it up to me, Captain, I would see that you were well-stocked and rested before setting off. Unfortunately, it is by his majesty's orders that you are to be clear from these docks by sundown,' the Commander granted each soldier a glance as they reassembled on the deck. 'If our guest is ready, we shall move out.'

Umishi shuffled uncomfortably as eyes bore down on her through slit helms with the pulverising weight of expectation. They were waiting for her to affirm her decision to step off the ship, onto a land that she struggled to separate from her nightmares.

'I'm ready,' she stammered, her voice as hesitant as she was.

'Excellent!' the commander said. 'You will be brought to our guardhouse, where you shall be updated on what you need to know. We are anxious to see an inquisitor at work.'

Turning back to the captain, the commander spoke with chilling calmness. 'Once again, thank you for your understanding, Captain. We apologise again for the inconvenience we have caused you and hope that we have not given you too much of a bad impression of our kingdom.' Leaving no time for a response, she turned her back to the captain and fell in line with the rest of her men. They began their descent down the gangplank, along with the *Queen's Memory*'s former passenger.

Under Umishi's bare feet the cobblestones felt as cold and unwelcoming as the island itself. Umishi looked back at the captain's defeated expression, his anger dampened by helplessness. He turned to his crew and cried out orders in an attempt to retain authority even while conceding to his ship's inevitable departure. Umishi was to be left alone in this strange land. She only hoped she knew what she was doing.

As she was ushered further from the ship, Umishi felt some unseen force squeeze at her heart, shortening her breath. For an instant, her lungs stopped, heart beating faster as if to compensate for its constriction. With a strained cough the moment passed. An uneasy, almost unbelievable realisation set in: she was back in the land that haunted her, the place she had spent a lifetime avoiding. She was there, really there. Half of her wanted to run away, to return to the *Queen's Memory* and continue believing the island was just a bad dream. The rest of her knew that she was, for better or worse, already there and with a job to do. The guards, oblivious to her internal conflict, led Umishi deeper into the island.

There, the city's buildings all but overwhelmed her, with their size and strangeness amplified many times over a short distance. It was almost impossible to believe it was the same land she had fled; that in her time away, the people of the city had already built higher than any human settlement had the right to be. It was as though these structures were ashamed of their once humble size, and had begun to become castles. Gone were the practical and uniform, stone-built hovels, replaced by expertly carved statements of beauty. Black clouds billowed from the rooves of some, spewing from cylindrical mouths in scenes which reminded her of the tales she had heard about the great forges of the mountains, with their huge furnaces and unrelenting industry.

Umishi's escort tightened around her as crowds began to appear. The guards positioned themselves close, sacrificing manoeuvrability for a formation designed to defend her and obscure her from the gazes of curious onlookers. The arrangement worked well for Umishi, even if it did mean that the guards were uncomfortably close. Their proximity did allow for one curious observation: their armour was not nearly as thick as she had expected.

The suddenness of exiting the claustrophobic alleyways that branched away from the docks towards the city centre was jarring, as though turning a corner in a corridor and finding the openness of a garden.

This had once been the heart of Domvalkia's former empire, with armies marching through the square in extravagant, terror-provoking parades designed to crush any doubt of the empire's iron might. Instead of that will-breaking, oppressive awe, Umishi's senses were assaulted by the sights, smells and sounds of bustling trade. Where there was once an ocean of swords and steel, Umishi found a market: hundreds of stalls among huge tents, most of which contained some form of livestock. She raised her hand under her nose, hoping to block out the stench.

A sudden chime rang through the hustle and bustle, drowning out all other noise, causing Umishi's heart to lurch and her bat-like ears to jolt upwards. Her head whirled sharply toward the source of the sound. Glancing towards the far side of the cobblestone clearing, she expected a town hall or some kind of temple, but instead found a giant tower, burdened with a massive sundial.

'The Pillar of Fendamor,' the commander said, clearly noticing Umishi's expression. 'The great clock that gives time to our city, the crowning achievement of our formidable engineering skills, and worthy tribute to the late founder of our great kingdom. The building at its base is our destination.'

Umishi did not understand what a clock was, but it *was* impressive. The commander was still facing her, silent. Did she expect a response? Umishi offered her an awkward smile and hoped it was enough. To her relief it seemed to be.

The commander continued through the market. 'This is Fendamor's finest market, the largest of its type on the whole island of Domvalkia,' she said, as they passed through 'We receive wares once every month and the majority of them are sold right here. Should you be interested in acquiring goods, foodstuffs, clothes and the like, the market is open in two day periods and closed for four days in between; there are no exceptions to this.'

Umishi gave her a look that she seemed to take as a question.

'The system works well to accommodate the limited

supply. We even receive trade from your kin, should your tastes be for home.' She gave Umishi a sharp glance, as though remembering who she was talking to. 'Of course the relevance of this information is directly related to how long your business detains you in our fair kingdom.' It was clear that, however short Umishi's stay, it would not be short enough for the commander's liking.

Hindered by curious crowds and stubborn customers, it took longer than expected for the soldiers at the escort's head to navigate their way through the flood of flesh, to their goal. The posted guards bowed their heads in salute as their commander approached; opening the doors permitting them entry. Smells escaped through the open entrance and into Umishi's nostrils: ink, burning oils and sweat, all failing to hide under a mask of perfume.

'Please, come in my lady. We have much to discuss,' the commander said, gesturing to the building. Umishi pulled at her hair as she entered.

The floors were covered in a dark blue carpet and framed by panels of redwood. The foyer connected a network of corridors, separated by lavish timber doors. Two guards within saluted the commander as she entered, while a third approached her. 'Commander,' he said, with some urgency.

The commander scowled at him. 'Speak.'

'We received word this morning from the watchmen at Fort Jimmarah. They have noted a continued increase of Dhal-Llah numbers at the borders of Nalador and are requesting orders.'

Dhal-Llah was not a name Umishi recognised. When last she resided on the island there was only one people, ruled by one emperor. Had these Dhal-Llah arrived from somewhere else, claiming ground the humans had lost since the empire's collapse?

The commander released a sigh reminiscent of a forge venting steam. 'I don't have time for this,' she muttered under her breath, then addressed her underling. 'This is neither the time nor the place for such talk. You shall be summoned after I have formally welcomed our guest.'

'Yes, Commander,' the guard replied bowing his head.

'I may as well do everything myself,' the commander muttered as she led Umishi through hallways lit by glass covered candles. The guards lined up along the corridors stared forward as though not noticing their passing, their obedience unsettling. She was relieved when they reached the commander's office

'Please, sit,' the commander said, gesturing to an empty chair in front of an oak desk.

Umishi felt the eyes from beyond the desk scrutinise each move she took to ascend a chair built to fit no other form but human. Blood rushed to her cheeks as with each moment the struggle lasted. Finally mounting the seat, she twisted her body and tucked her legs under herself. Umishi took a deep breath before facing the commander, who took her own seat in silence, with a stoic expression that made a poor hiding place for her mocking smile. She took some papers from one of the desk drawers. Even they seemed strange to Umishi, for the paper was whiter and smoother than any normal parchment.

'I hope your trip here was a pleasant one,' the commander said, talking more to the papers in front of her than to Umishi. 'The waters around here can get a bit choppy this time of year, or so I am told.' She glanced up from her papers to scan her guest for a response. When none was forthcoming she turned back to her pages. 'Before we begin, I have been advised to go over some of the background on our community. The unorthodox nature of our fair kingdom has a tendency to leave outlanders... a little overwhelmed.'

'No need.' Umishi said. As alien as the island had become she had no desire for a history lesson. 'I'm not an outlander, I lived here... when there was an empire.'

'Oh really?' the commander said, taken aback enough to offer Umishi her attention. 'From which township did you hail? Surely not the city, not back then.'

Umishi's tongue rebelled against saying the name aloud, her throat closed and, heart froze. She took a breath and spat the word out as swiftly as she could, 'Malhain.'

'Malhain?' Commander Vallis echoed, testing the name on her tongue. 'I can't say I have heard of the place. I'm afraid many of the smaller villages and towns were unable to survive the transition into the Kingdom of Fendamor.'

It was no surprise the human had not heard of the village, since it predated anyone alive on the island. It had been over a hundred years since Malhain fell, devoured by a nightmare far more devastating than a change of rulers.

'In any case, you'll notice a great deal has changed since you were here last, Lady Inquisitor,' the commander continued. 'The dark days of the empire are long gone. Never before have the people of Domvalkia been as free or as safe as they are now. Despite the impressive military presence we hold here in the capital we haven't been called into any significant action in quite some time. You see, Ms Zaimor, for a great many years, violent crime has been all but abolished, and *murder?* The word had almost fallen from our vocabulary.'

'Until now,' Umishi interjected, eager to both direct the conversation toward some kind of point and deflate the commander's seemingly ever-bloating pride.

'Yes, until now,' the commander agreed, her voice oozing with stifled irritation at having been interrupted. 'There has been a murder, and we suspect a mage's involvement. However, the magic that was used is beyond anything we have seen before. Believe me when I say that Domvalkia rarely asks for outside help, but there's not a mage in the kingdom who can explain how it was done.'

'I wish to begin as soon as possible,' Umishi said, done wasting time with this commander. Besides, her curiosity had been piqued; it was a rare thing indeed to hear of a mage who abandoned their delusions of infallibility and had admitted defeat, let alone so many of them.

'That is excellent news,' the commander said. 'His Majesty will be quite pleased indeed. However, there is one more thing we must discuss first. Domvalkia is a closed island. Foreigners... and those who have been estranged from the island for over a human lifetime, are not permitted to just wander about the place. We need to discuss the kind of access you have been awarded for your visit.'

What 'access' she had been 'awarded'? Umishi pushed herself back into her chair and folded her arms tight against her chest. The true meaning behind those words was all too clear; she could predict how the rest of the conversation was going to go.

Ignoring her guest's reaction, commander Vallis continued. 'The king has awarded you free access to the whole of this great capital city. You are permitted to speak to and interrogate any and all residents, in relation to the crime you are investigating, of course. Naturally we expect some decorum while you conduct your interviews so as not to lead the public into any kind of panic. The act of murder is a rare and frightening one for our people, as you can imagine. During your stay in Hanaswick, you are to be granted free food and lodgings within the city's guard-house and an escort, for your safety '

The thought of baby-sitters and boundaries set Umishi on edge; such restraints rarely made for a very productive atmosphere. Even without them, the task was going to be difficult. However, she had worked with paranoid and isolated peoples before, she knew how hard to push their rules and how far she could bend them.

'Do you have any questions, Lady Inquisitor?' commander Vallis asked with a tilt of her head. 'Anything you wish me to clarify?'

'No,' Umishi answered, thankful that this procedure had seemed to reach its end. There was no reason to extend this aimless prattle any further. If there was something that she was unsure of, or if she were about to overstep some arbitrary bounds, there was little doubt that her assigned carers would be on hand to lend their aid.

The commander granted Umishi a slight grin before getting to her feet. 'With that out of the way we may start. I, for one, am eager to see you in action.'

TWO

THE DEAD, PHANTOM FIGHTERS AND PORK

Umishi was led into the corridor again. The same stationary guards greeted her, the eyes beyond their masked helms still as vacant as they had been when she first moved past them. They were so lifeless they could be replaced with empty suits and no one would likely notice, but she could feel them, taking the measure of her, passing silent judgment. Ignoring their stares she turned away and continued following their commander. They soon reached a flight of stairs leading down into a cellar. Umishi paused for a moment, watching as Vallis reached the bottom.

'Is there something wrong?' she called up.

There wasn't, not really; at least, nothing a human would consider. Stairs had always been a problem, as humans rarely designed them to accommodate other races. Due to her height and digitigrade limbs, Umishi had never been able to tackle them with any kind of dignity. Ascending them, she would often fall to all fours, but was forced to resort to childlike hops to descend. Sighing and tugging at her hair, she tackled the obstacle. When she reached the bottom Vallis congratulated her with a bitten back smile. It was an expression that she had seen countless times, so she reacted to it in the same way she always had: with cold indifference.

'After you,' Vallis said.

As the door opened, Umishi felt herself being drowned by a rancid aroma that flooded her nostrils and oozed down the back of her throat. Despite how repugnant the smell was, she had spent a great deal of time breathing it. It was death's perfume, and it had been freshly applied.

She brushed past the commander, into the room. Had she not been so familiar with such places, Umishi would have mistaken the drab looking dungeon for a torture chamber. Her eye took the measure of the shelved tools associated with the embalmer's trade. There were knives, saws, pliers and needles, all forged with the skills of a master smith, and all cleaned to a loving shine. After reviewing the implements on display, her attention fell upon what was lying in the dungeon's centre.

Upon the cast iron table, a body was prepared in the same way a royal chef would lay out a grand feast. It was more a decoration than a corpse: stripped, cleaned and positioned with a clear amount of care. A sheet covered its lower half to retain its modesty, a sentiment Umishi cared little about. It had once been a male, human and young, and looked surprisingly alive despite the smell. A great deal of respect had been shown to this corpse, this boy. Looming above it was a human who looked more dead than the corpse laid out before him.

The human lifted his eyes to Umishi with a frown that seemed to have been etched into his face for centuries.

'What is this?' he asked, as though presented with an impossible puzzle.

The tone was enough to force every muscle in Umishi's body to tighten, so that even her teeth ground against one another. Recognising his kind had become second nature to her. It was no coincidence she was as familiar with mages as she was with death.

'Lothrum, we have a guest for you,' the commander announced as she walked into the room. 'This is Ms Zaimor, a—'

'I don't need you to tell me who she is, woman. I'm not blind yet,' the elderly human barked through white whiskers. 'She is an inquisitor, of the Order of Alpharus, a mage hunter. I'd be a fool if I didn't know her kind, given my line of work. It is your timing, not your guest, that confounds me. Leuvigild said you would be here in the day's latter half, but here you are, earlier than arranged. Do you have any idea what state this room, this boy, could have been in? You may want to demonstrate the courtesy of knocking before showing a guest in here in future.'

'Uh... yes, I suppose you're right. I apologise,' Vallis said, clearly taken aback. 'However, she's here to—'

'To examine the boy's body, obviously. I hardly took him out of the ice house for a bit of fresh air or a pleasant walk in the park,' he snapped. From under heavy eyebrows, he cast his gaze back to Umishi. 'So, you're the expert? A walnorg from the continent? Haven't seen your kind around here in a while. I thought your kin were all fruit-pickers rather than oppressors of knowledge.'

'Fruit comes in all shapes; I tend only the rotten,' Umishi answered, her eye narrowing.

The old human grinned. 'I am Erik Lothrum, Head Alchemist of His Royal Highness, King Edwin the First's Court of Wizards, and right hand of Fendamor's arch-mage. Regarding my ripeness, I may resemble a shrivelled prune but, before you get any ideas of the witch-burning sort, know that I sleep with your little rulebook under my pillow.'

Umishi found herself wondering just how true that was.

'Moving on to the issue at hand,' the alchemist said, 'has the good commander explained what we're doing here?'

'No, I thought you might want to,' the commander said.

'Good girl, it's probably for the best.' Lothrum displayed the typical arrogance of a mage, turning his back to the two women, and ignoring Vallis' obviously building ire. Umishi found herself regretting the fact that the commander wasn't armed.

Lothrum moved with purpose back to the centre table where, with a stiff arm and flat hand, he rested his weight. 'This is.... well the name of this child eludes me at present,' he began. 'His mother, though. Helen Vandabolt saw brilliant things in him; the rest of us saw him as a fool who was doomed to fail as a travelling merchant.'

Umishi cared very little for this corpse's backstory. The context of his life might have once stirred something within her, made her feel something. Now though? She had felt nothing for the dead since Malhain; since she fled this island. It had been so long ago and she had seen so many dead since, this boy was no different. Death had become her job, the dead meaning nothing more to her than an anvil meant to a smith. There was no need to know where the iron came from, nor who shaped it. It was there for her to work with, nothing more.

Lothrum, picking up on his audience's lack of enthusiasm, hurried his tale along. 'My point is, Inquisitor, that this child was as harmless as he was foolish, yet was found face up in the streets two weeks ago, wide-eyed and staring to the stars, lips an icy blue. He was brought to me in the early hours of the morning and... well, I don't know. He was killed with magic far beyond my understanding, and I'm no common hedge mage. I just can't... well, come look for yourself, mage hunter.- after all this is why your here.'

With both sets of eyes upon her, Umishi walked to the table and took a sniff. There was something other than rot in the smell; her nose could sense it. There was alcohol, dry but pungent. Over two weeks old he had said, yet the body didn't look over a few hours dead. Magic must have been used to preserve it, and preserve it well. The boy was no more than sixteen or eighteen years old; young, even for a human. There were no marks of note on the chest, pelvis or legs, but the head was another story. The back of it was bruised, dented and there was dried blood inside its ears. He had fallen backwards and cracked his skull, killing him in moments. Umishi noticed something about the angle of his jaw as well: it was dislodged. She let out an exaggerated sigh as she pulled a medallion from her tunic and placed it on the body. It vibrated, but only slightly, no doubt detecting the residual magic from the spell used to slow its decay.

'You've wasted my time,' she said. 'The boy was in a

fight outside a tavern; he lost. No mystery here, no magic.'

Lothrum's eyes widened as though he had just been slapped. His jaw dropped as he tried to form a sentence. 'Your kind live who knows how long? Think how much this has wasted *my* bloody time.' With movements uncharacteristic of a human so old, he whirled to face the commander. 'This girl is a finite commodity that I cannot afford to lose. You haven't bloody told her; she hasn't got a clue what's going on here, has she?'

'The arch-mage made it clear he wanted her to see the body first, before she knew about the Ward,' the commander answered.

'I do not like being played for a fool, and I doubt our guest does either,' Lothrum snarled.

'What's going on? What's he talking about?' Umishi's anxiety started building in her gut. She imagined this was how a child felt listening to its parents argue about taxes for the first time, grasping its importance but not understanding its content.

'Murder, Lady Inquisitor, simply can't happen here,' Lothrum answered, twisting himself to face her. 'We abolished it, snuffed it out. Through our pioneering magical knowledge, such a thing as tavern fight should be impossible. Our magic would take effect before a single blow was landed.'

Umishi could see the mage's pride ooze out from beneath his anger. It was a sight that turned her stomach. She tried to make sense of his boast, unravel any clue she could about the information that had been kept from her. In order for a spell to protect someone in the manner that Lothrum suggested, a mage would have to be assigned to every tavern and street, warding each and every patron and passer-by. Using magic so frivolously and on that scale would not come without obvious and dangerous side effects. With a shake of her head she dismissed the images of cowled mages patrolling the city streets from her mind. No, there was something else at play here; something subtler, something that raised the hairs on her arms and sent chills down her spine.

'What's he talking about?' she snarled at the commander, frustrated at the games which were being played.

'I was told to show her the body without context,' the commander explained, ignoring Umishi's question. 'The arch-mage thought this would give us new insights.'

'Pointless!' Lothrum exclaimed. 'The only insight we gained was into the limits of my already stressed patience. Now, if we are quite done here, I think I need to turn my attention to more meaningful things, like taking a *shit*.'

'I'm done here,' Umishi added. She had quite enough of this farce and had grown tired of being treated like a child; besides there was no need to linger, the job was done, at least as far as the murder was concerned. A mage was not the cause of the boy's death, despite what Lothrum had said. She knew the markings of a fist when she saw them. With no renegade mage, there was no reason for her to be the one conducting the investigation.

'Very well,' the commander replied. 'Lothrum, if you would be so kind as to remove the body?'

'Of course, I forgot I was the only bastard who did anything around here.' He began to roll up his sleeves. 'Here

I am, the most powerful human mage in Fendamor, and I'm left cleaning up after some bright spark at the top decided on some elaborate and pointless scheme to get his point across solely for dramatic effect. They couldn't even be bothered to let me in on the joke!'

With those words, the room went silent. Lothrum closed his eyes and started breathing deeply. The silence lasted only a moment before he spoke again, not in the frantic, irritated tones of before, but in a way that was both more sombre and monotone. His words were not in Valitchnee, the language of the mainland, but rather, a language that had become known as the Elder Tongue, the language of magic. The spell worked quickly; Umishi could feel the air around her lose its heat as Lothrum drew the energy from the room. Her medallion shuddered violently between her collar bones as ice formed around the body on the table. In moments, it was done; the corpse had become preserved under a thin layer of ice.

'That should keep him fresh for another day or so,' Lothrum said, emerging from his trance, 'and give you enough time to get the inquisitor up to date so we can start this investigation for real, and not just have a dress rehearsal. Meanwhile, I'm not going to waste my time any further, so I bid you ladies farewell.'

Umishi watched him leave with no small amount of jealousy. 'I shall give my report to your king,' she said, turning to the commander.

'I understand your eagerness, Ms Zaimor. However, His Majesty is currently bound to equally pressing matters of state and will not be free until the small hours of the morning.' The commander smiled. 'Fear not, I have no doubt he is as eager to meet you as you are him, and I shall arrange a meeting as soon as possible. If you'd be so kind as to follow me, I shall take you to the room we have prepared.'

Although the brevity of Umishi's task seemed to diminish every time the commander spoke, she found herself too weary to argue. 'No, I have arranged a room for myself.' The idea of staying in the guardhouse made her stomach twist. There were too many eyes and too many swords. She would be in a cage when, in a tavern, she could be invisible.

'I assure you, Inquisitor, the chambers we have set aside for you are more than accommodating. What's more, they are *safe*. I strongly suggest that you take the offer presented to you.'

The words 'or else' were all that were lacking from the commander's threat. The corner of Umishi's mouth twisted at the thought of conceding to Vallis' poorly veiled demands. 'Wasn't I granted full access to your great city?' she asked, 'If a rogue mage is among your people, that's where I need to be too.' While her argument wasn't entirely strong, she could see there was little fight left in this commander; the day's weariness was clearly readable on her face.

'If you insist,' Vallis surrendered with an exhale of breath, 'I shall escort you there myself. It would be remiss of me if I did not offer such a service.'

Umishi had already spent too much time in the company of the commander and her lackeys, but it was an acceptable and understandable compromise; whatever got her to the inn fastest. All she wanted was rest, to rejuvenate herself from the weeks she had spent at sea and maybe have a drink to wash away the day's irritations. She pushed herself forward, tugging her hair tightly against her ruined cheek. In the corridor, the commander followed, ready to overtake her and lead the way. Before she could, a guard hurried towards her.

'I am sorry to disturb, you, Commander,' he said. 'I have news regarding events at Jimmarah.'

The commander barked, 'I already told you that—'

'The topic has been brought up at the palace and His Majesty wishes your presence.'

Based on Vallis' expression, that changed things. The commander wet her lips and took a moment to regain her composure. She turned her attention back to Umishi. 'I'm sorry for this, Inquisitor, but I am needed elsewhere. If you would kindly wait here, I shall promptly arrange an escort for you.' With that, Vallis followed the guard down the hall and out of sight.

Umishi had no intention of waiting and even less of being escorted. She ignored the commander's orders and headed for the door. Truth be told, she expected to be stopped, for at least one of the guards posted along the walls to stand in her way. They instead looked down at her, perplexed, as though they had no idea what to do without being ordered. The thought of their lack of will and blind obedience sent a chill down her spine as she made her get way to the exit.

Outside, Umishi took to the less used pathways as she entered the shadows. Away from the eyes of passers-by, she recalled the maps that had been sent to her. Throughout her journey she had looked over them with great care. Although they did little to prepare her for the alien appearance of the buildings, she took comfort in one certainty: all buildings had shadows and within them she was safe. She rolled up her baggy black sleeve, speaking an Elder Tongue word into a bracelet. While Umishi lacked any magical ability herself, she had long made up for it with enchanted items that facilitated her tasks. The bracelet allowed her to become almost indistinguishable from shadow. The talisman around her neck reacted to the energies that magic displaced, making it useful for tracking down the source of spells. The last item was the most important: the blade issued to all agents of Alpharus. She kept the dagger at her side at all times. It was large, with red runes forged into the blade to protect her against any hostile magic. It and the others were essential tools when facing foes who could weave weapons with words.

Away from the hustle and bustle of the main streets, the Spinning Dagger Inn was not hard to find, despite the efforts of whoever had stolen the sign's letter 'P'. Umishi grinned; its new name was a decided improvement. The stagnant smell of spilt alcohol hit her first, closely followed by the sounds of merriment. Upon stepping into the light, the bracelet's enchantment was dispelled. As her image became clear, a feeling of nakedness took the illusion's place. She quickly grasped for her hair, checking it was in place before, having found an empty seat, she disappeared into a corner.

Umishi went unnoticed. The inn was full, but no one spared her a glance, at least yet. At any moment, though, a pair of eyes could stray from their tankard and fall on her – a stranger in their midst, an intruder – making the inevitable attempts to see the ugliness under her hair. The thought forced Umishi's clawed hands to her face again. To make matters worse, like those in the commander's office, the inn's chairs were not made for people of her stature. She folded her legs under herself, as allowing her feet to dangle made her feel like a child.

Sitting there, Umishi took measure of the inn's clientele. The patrons of the Spinning Dagger Inn were much as she expected from its type of establishment: yelling abuse and rude jokes at each other, as they drank from steel tankards and slipped on ale drenched floors. The sight of the chaos lured her mind from the notion of wandering eyes. Umishi found herself relaxing further, as even a fool could be invisible in a room full of blind drunks. Stumbling into her view, a large man fell into another, knocking him to the ground. A sly grin moved across Umishi's face as she anticipated the predictable, and violent, outcome. The man stood, cursing the clumsy instigator, and throwing a punch that caught him across the chin, except… except there was no collision. The man's fist seemed to have gone straight through the other's face. Umishi blinked, and rubbed her eye in disbelief. The man's aim had been true, yet the other man was unharmed. Perhaps she was mistaken? The voyage had tired her, and what else could it have been? Drunken, fist-fighting phantoms? The idea seemed ridiculous, but she managed a smile at the thought.

'Oh, I'm sorry… uh, I didn't see ya there,' came a voice that pulled Umishi's mind away from the confounding events. She turned to face the intrusion and found a large, bearded man wearing a white sleeveless shirt and an apron: no doubt the inn-keeper. 'I was just cleaning up. I, well…

thought this table was.... Never mind. What can I be getting you, little one?'

'Little one.' The words made Umishi grind her teeth. Pressing herself back into the chair, she bit out 'A room. Wine, white, and pork.'

He stared for a moment longer, then realised she would not elaborate. 'Eh, right, yes,' he stuttered. 'You can have the last room on the right, upstairs.'

He trotted back off to the kitchen. Umishi's attention wandered back to the fight that never was, and continued to contemplate what had happened. At a loss, Lothrum's words finally found her. *'Our magic would take effect before a single blow was landed'*, he had said, but that was impossible. She lifted her eye from the table of the two drunkards and searched the crowds for robed figures; there were none. She was exhausted, the vexing words of pride-filled mages had scrambled her thoughts and played with her imagination, nothing more.

The pork arrived overcooked, and the wine was watered down, but it was good to have something in her belly that wasn't fish. The weeks spent on the *Queen's Memory* had lowered her standards for all foods not from the sea. As she finished her meal her 'protection' arrived. Umishi sighed to herself; that was something she did not need. The inn's atmosphere changed instantly: rowdy cheering turned to anxious whispers as curious eyes followed the four armour-clad guards as they moved their way around the bar area in their search for her.

Umishi trailed around the walls to the staircase that provided access to the floor above. She bit her lip, a knot tightening in her gut with the realisation that she would be forced to traverse the steep steps. There was no choice, so she did the best she could without resorting to all fours or making too much of a fool of herself. It was dumb luck her embarrassing ascent went unnoticed, dumb luck and the wall that offered its support. Barefoot, she padded across the corridor and to the last room on the right, her room.

The room was simple: a cupboard and a bed with reasonably clean white sheets, no less than expected. She made her way to the bed, climbed on top, and waited until the inevitable knock on the door from Fendamor's finest.

'My lady, has all been well?' one asked, as she reluctantly drew open the door.

'Yes,' she snapped, hoping it would be enough to have them go away.

'Good,' the guard replied. 'We can assume you have suffered no hostility?'

Umishi suppressed a groan at the stupidity of the question; surely the first rendered it redundant. It didn't matter. 'Yes.'

'This is good news,' he said, in a patronisingly cheery tone. 'We have your bag, my lady, from the ship.' She watched as a second guard placed her luggage on the floor; beside her. The other remained silent, awaiting a response that never came

'We will be stationed outside your room, and two of us on the stairs. Should you require anything, my lady, you need only ask,' he continued.

'Anything else?' she inquired flippantly.

'No, my lady. May you sleep well.'

'Yes,' came her answer, as well as the door, slamming , just inches from the guards faces. She made sure the lock was in place before empting her lungs of the day's frustrations, pressing her back against the door, allowing herself to slip to the floor. Finally, she was alone; no interruptions, no eyes, no one's company but her own. She checked her belongings, pulling out the smaller of her two daggers from the sack and nestling it under her pillow. Despite the guards outside, she would sleep easier knowing there was a blade in arm's reach.

A heaviness was lifted from Umishi as she freed herself from clothing befouled by the journey's grime and sweat. She washed the rest of the day away with a sponge dampened from a water bucket, a pleasant luxury she had not expected to find. After drying herself, Umishi slipped under the heavy blankets and felt her muscles shaking off all the stresses of the voyage and her taxing return to Domvalkia.

She closed her eye, finding a darkness that allowed long forgotten ghosts to ambush her. In the black, their translucent faces found her, phantoms her mind tried struggled to exorcise. There were those of friends and strangers alike, from whom she had fled without even granting them a backwards glance. They were faces that the slaughter over a hundred years ago ensured she would never physically see again; her family among them. She refused to face them, she couldn't. Instead, she buried her head under her pillow and begged for exhaustion to take her, drag her away from memories conjured by the island and into a dreamless sleep. To her relief, her wish was granted and the night was merciful.

A pounding at her door woke her. As she opened her eye

the sunlight gliding through the window forced it to seal again. The pounding returned, louder. She forced herself to move, pushing the covers aside and climbing off the bed.

'I'm awake,' she grumbled while rubbing the sleep from her eye.

'Lady Inquisitor, when you're ready, your escort awaits you out side,' a male voice said from beyond the door. 'The king has requested an audience with you.'

An army at her door, waking her in what she assumed to be the early hours of the morning, did not sound like a request to her. Regardless she had no choice but to obey. It took little time to dress back in the blacks of the Order of Alpharus. If she was to perform her duties she should at least look the part. Her guards were outside the door, but they stood there to let her pass, before following her down into the inn, and beyond.

Outside, the city was abuzz, humans busily brushing past each other with an air of urgency she had only seen in refugees fleeing war zones. She caught herself smiling as she watched, their strange clothes amusing her. The men wore hats that looked like black barrels with a rim at the bottom, while the dresses the women wore made them look like wine bottles.

Her joy was quashed, however, when she spotted her escort: four more grim-faced soldiers ready to fall in line with those already assigned to her. Umishi greeted them with a simple nod that they returned. 'If you are prepared, Lady Inquisitor, we will head to the palace. We will be taking the main streets, so stay close, if you please.' With those words Umishi took a step toward the guards, allowing them to close ranks around her.

The paths and alleyways twisted and spun, each corner branching off into some endless labyrinth. As she entered a clearing something screamed at her; the sound was tremendous and she felt the ground tremble with its approach. Instinct saw her body drop into a defensive stance and her hand reached for the dagger sheathed at her hip. After two heartbeats her mind caught up with her body, lungs relaxing and releasing a sigh. The horseless wagon and its cacophony passed her, the people within peering from its glass windows, faces mirroring her curious expression. After the moment had passed her focus fell back to the guards around her. She pulled at her hair picturing the smirks that hid behind their helms.

The speeding metal thing was not her only surprise as she entered the square that had housed the magnificent market the previous day. The stalls, the tents, the hollering and the smells, were all gone, the square empty. People seemed to gravitate to the walls of the surrounding buildings as opposed to walking through the clearing the market's absence left, as though fearing they would trip or bump into its spectre. Something Umishi could not identify made the formerly bustling centre of commerce eerie. Perhaps ghosts *did* linger there.

At a deliberate pace, they made their way under the shadow of the Pillar of Fendamor, past the guardhouse and toward the royal palace. It was clear that the word 'palace' was used in ceremony more than fact, as it was a building that could only generously be called a mansion. With no more than perhaps five floors, it supported a tower on its northernmost corner that granted a decent view over the waters and city walls. It stood upon a staircase of gardens overlooking a river that coiled around the eastern edge of the palace and out towards the city walls. It was no place fit for anyone of true importance. Where were the guards? The walls? The watch towers? Umishi had broken into bath houses more secure. Even the windows seemed large enough, and low enough, for anyone to infiltrate. The whole city seemed to be a plump sack, just waiting for a bandit's knife, with the guards only interested in protecting Umishi and the docks.

As they entered the palace through lavish doors, the garden did not end; it had invaded the foyer with an army of followers and foliage. Scabiosa bloomed from every corner and were engraved in every banister. Blue carpeted staircases flowed from the upper levels like waterfalls spilling into the main hall. As the door slammed shut, a page rushed to greet them, and they were ushered into the throne room.

This room, at least, was as Umishi expected, drowning in extravagant opulence. It was clear that the artist responsible was permitted to go wild with any designs they could conjure. A madness of tangled vines that sprouted blue flowers plastered almost every surface and glass pillars fell into waterless streams. It was more a lunatic's greenhouse than a ruling chamber. In the centre of it all the king sat on an ivory throne. The man on the throne was large with a form suggesting a strength ill-fitting the over indulgent luxury he surrounded himself with. Instead of the armour Umishi expected such a man to be wearing, he wore a black tunic with a fine white shirt erupting from its collar. He smiled through a well groomed, ginger beard at his new guest. Umishi found it difficult to reciprocate the king's attention; instead, her focus was drawn to a slender figure standing behind the throne, adorned in the hooded robes of a mage.

She watched as the page made an elaborate show of the introductions, an extended performance of bows and long-winded titles. The king rested his chin on the back of his hand as the page continued to ramble, making it clear that he was just as uninterested in the formality as she was. After the page was finished the king dismissed him with a wave. He was not the only one to exit; the guards followed. A cold trickle of unease slithered down Umishi's spine. It was one thing to be lax in the defence of a palace, but to leave their king unguarded in the presence of a stranger? Something was deeply wrong.

'Umishi Zaimor,' the king boomed as he rose from his throne. 'I welcome you to the Kingdom of Fendamor... personally that is. I know a great many people must have already done so on my behalf, but I rarely get the privilege of doing it myself nowadays. I hope you're finding our fair city agreeable.'

'I am, Your Majesty.' She said, her attention sweeping to the man who demanded it.

He laughed at Umishi's answer. 'Your Majesty? I am a king true, but I am not yours. I don't know how the fancy pricks on the continent do things but I treat my guests as guests. You have sworn no oath to me, taken no vows, I have as much obligation to bow to you as you do to me. My name is Edwin Randell, and here Ms Zaimor, you are my guest. As such I extend to you every pleasantry that it is within my power to grant: food, drink, we have the greatest spas and entertainers on the Vendican seas, from what I am told. Speak your pleasure and it will be yours. Anything that'll make your stay more welcoming.'

'Your ear, Your Majesty,' she said, with a joyless smile creeping along her face. 'I have my report for you.'

'Of course.' He laughed again. 'I have been warned of your stubborn professionalism. It is, however, a trait I respect. We, the citizens of Fendamor, are a proud and private people. While we prefer to handle our own affairs without drawing the attention of the outside world we are not so pig-headed that we will not reach out for aid. However, when we do, we make sure our call is swift, concise and to the right people. How many of these bloody bastards have you captured? These mages who think themselves beyond the law? Sixty, seventy, more?'

'I don't capture,' Umishi corrected him, momentarily throwing her eye to the hooded figure. 'I apply a more permanent solution to their threat.'

'That is exactly why we need you,' the king boomed, pointing an excited finger at her. 'The crime this magic-using bastard has committed is murder, Ms Zaimor, an act of villainy that is known only to us through historians and scribes dustier than the tomes they scowl over. No one in this kingdom has a better understanding of what must be done than you. That is why I'll be giving you full authority over this matter and looking forward to you tracking down the wand waving-prick, before enacting whatever justice you see fit. I understand you've seen the body, yes? What did you think?'

She thought it was a waste of time. There was no need for her to investigate any further. The simple truth was there had been no murder. 'An accident, likely from a fight outside a tavern by the smell of him, a jab to the jaw, the victim fell and cracked his head on the sidewalk. No magic was used. Drunken rage more than murder, I think.'

'How can that be?' asked the robed figure. 'You are absolutely *sure* there were no traces of magic? Nothing strange, out of the ordinary?'

'The woman knows what she's talking about,' the king answered. 'After all, it's why we consulted her.' He turned to Umishi. 'Ms Zaimor, I hope you'd be kind enough to speak with my arch-mage and my Court of Wizards. Discuss theories, perhaps stumble upon something of an explanation for how this could have happened ?'

'There is no need,' Umishi replied. 'You have my report. This boy was not killed by a mage. My skills will not benefit you.'

'But he *was*, Ms Zaimor,' the robed arch-mage said in a tone suggesting he had revealed some great truth. 'You see, on this island, with the exception of yourself, there are none who can be harmed. Years ago, the great mage and beloved founder of this kingdom, the late Vulfoliac Fendamor, placed all of Domvalkia' people under what is known as the King's Ward. It is a spell that has since protected us and prevented violent acts such as brawling, murder, even war. Each fist thrown or dagger thrust with malicious intent will pass through the subject safely, as though the victim were made of air. For numerous decades both the people of Fendamor and the neighbouring Dhal-Llah have enjoyed the security and stability the spell has granted us. This harmony was assured by the spell's diligent and steadfast nature. The Ward, you see, is impossible to break, bend or bypass, and yet... '

The spell that the arch-mage was describing was impossible. It would take a hundred mages chanting to keep such a ward from dissipating and even then, even with every mage focusing their power into this Ward, the damage it would cause would be unimaginable. Speaking the Elder Words for but a moment was enough to freeze the air and fills rooms with the taste of death. The arch-mage said the ward had been in effect for decades. It could not be true.

That being said, if this King's Ward did exist as the arch-mages said it would make sense of many oddities she had come to notice on the island: the lack of guards, the poor security, the flimsy armour, they all granted validity to the impossible spell that was being described. While she had little reason to doubt that some magic was at play it was equally clear to her that trickery was the primary ingredient of the King's Ward. Perhaps there was an enchanted item at work? Umishi had seen it, though, had seen the Ward at work, could she real doubt her own eye? It was impossible, her mind twisted inside her skull, her thoughts tied in knots. It had to be an elaborate joke. She wanted to storm out from the throne room, collect her things from the Spinning Dagger and leave the thrice cursed island forever. However there was something she could not ignore, despite the lies, the fanciful tale that the arch-mage conjured, there was still one truth...

'There's been a murder that you can't explain,' Umishi said, her voice trembling with renewed resolve.

'Precisely,' the arch-mage answered. 'And with this kind

of ability we can only fear what this killer will do next. I cannot... it should be impossible. At first, I thought it must be some kind of weapon enchanted to bypass the Ward by disconnecting itself from its wielder's malicious intentions. Days I spent looking, scrying the weapon we found at the scene for any hint of the magic used, but there was nothing; it was a blunt instrument one could easily find anywhere. You have no idea how much dread this revelation fills me with, Inquisitor, It should be impossible, I don't believe... I cannot believe. But if I am wrong, Inquisitor, then... I fear no one in this room can understand the forces we are dealing with, what this hypothetical mage has at their disposal.'

Umishi knew the dangers of such knowledge all too well. Mages were, at their core, megalomaniacs scrambling and clawing for any amount of power which could elevate them over their peers. Being the only person capable of killing in this land would make them very dangerous indeed.

'I beg you, Ms Zaimor,' the king began, 'we need to find out how this murderous fuck managed to bypass the spell. I will not have this kingdom plagued by murder, not under my rule. I shall grant you any resource you wish, but I need him found.'

Umishi bit down on her tongue. She wanted to say no, she wanted to leave. Every moment she stayed here the shadows of her past grew stronger, threatening to take hold of her mind and drag her into an inescapable darkness. Even so, she understood what the consequences would be if this rogue mage conducted their business unchecked. She had seen and felt the terrors of such an event herself. She raked her hair over the ruined side of her face and sighed. 'You said there was a weapon. Show me.'

THREE
A BLUNT WEAPON

Once more Umishi struggled down the staircase of the gardens. The arch-mage, despite his large strides, consciously kept pace with her, a respectful gesture that few offered. From just a glance it would be easy to mistake him for human. He was tall, slender, his movements elegant and calculated. However, under closer inspection his Nal-Tiran features become clear. His skin was akin to milk in both colour and texture and seemed to resonate with magic. Gaining the title of arch-mage in a kingdom of humans must have been child's play for such a creature. With every glance she gave to him, his smooth features, his sapphire eyes, his perfect golden hair, she became more aware of the ugliness hidden under her hair.

'Where are you taking me, Arch-mage?' Umishi demanded.

'The guardhouse. It is the only reasonable place to keep such a weapon,' he answered. 'And please call me Leuvigild. There is no need for such formalities outside His Majesty's throne room.'

She nodded in response. Leuvigild was a strange Nal-Tiran name that seemed almost designed to get caught on her tongue. She would repeat it in her head, study its phonetics, before making any attempt to say it aloud.

'T'is good to see the flowers in full bloom,' Leuvigild said with all the elegance attributed to his kind. 'I tend this garden myself; a hobby my father indulged in and one I inherited. I take pleasure in helping things grow, but I am almost ashamed to admit, I am not half the gardener he was. I am now struggling to keep his more... unique creations alive. Take the Lapus Lathanum,' he said, as he pointed out a large blue, thorny plant in the centre of the lavish garden. 'It was my father's pride, he called it the eye of the kingdom. No matter how much I try; I find it weakening with every year. It is now but a shadow of its former beauty.'

This Lapus Lathanum was just like any other flower to Umishi. It was clear the arch-mage used the word 'unique' too liberally. The guardhouse wasn't too far away, and she hoped she wouldn't have to suffer the fool's wittering much longer.

'I get the impression you have little interest in botany,' he said, with a sly smile crawling up his right cheek as he stated the obvious. 'Pity, I hoped you may have had some insight, given your people's famed aptitude for cultivation. That being said, while you were born to the villages of your own, you did not stay in those trees for long, did you? I hear that you once called Domvalkia home. Is this true?'

'Many years ago, yes. I was very young.' she admitted, knowing full well the course this conversation was taking.

Leuvigild smiled. 'Good. It will do the people well to

know it is one of their own leading this investigation. They are afraid, Lady Inquisitor, having never had the threat of death held over them. They think there is a mage out there somewhere who can turn their world upside down with a few words and a snap of their fingers. They need reassurance, need to know someone trustworthy is looking out for their interests, protecting them from this ambiguous and terrifying new danger.' He paused for a moment, assessing her reactions. 'You, of all people, should understand how they must be feeling, given your line of work... and the fate of Malhain.'

Umishi's heart lurched as he uttered the name of her former hometown. She felt the shadows of that day, the day she ran, grasping at her like barbed tendrils pulling at her lungs. She couldn't breathe. She closed her eye and swallowed in an attempt to force down the memories that clawed towards her chest. She dragged her thoughts to the present, to the task at hand, the impossible murder, the arch-mage who was now staring at her. She couldn't lose her head, not here, not now. As her breathing returned to normal she fought echoes of the past back into blackness within her mind. This was no victory, however; the names and faces of those she left behind would be waiting for her that night, waiting to greet her when her defences were at their lowest.

'I am sorry,' the arch-mage said. 'I miss-spoke, I have a terrible habit of releasing my thoughts without the correct mitigation sometimes.' He paused for a moment. 'I fear I have done enough talking and I am sure you would prefer we move onto discussing the investigation at hand, rather than listening to me speaking of tragedies I have no place mentioning. So, what would you like to know? Is there any way I can be of service to you?'

'Is there more you're keeping from me?' she spit out.

'Ah,' he answered, pondering over his next few words. 'We are sorry that we had to keep you in the dark about the Ward during your examination of the body, but it was necessary. You see, what you knew, or rather, did *not* know, would have had an effect on how you approached the case. You see, we concluded that you were more likely to find something unusual were you not looking for it.'

Leuvigild's response was more riddle than answer. Either way, it didn't matter; whatever nonsense games they were playing seemed to be over. There was only one puzzle Umishi wanted to solve: the murder laid out before her.

'What is this Ward?' she asked, figuring that if she were to find out how this spell was bypassed, she would at least have to know what it did. 'In the inn, I saw... I think I saw a man punch another but hit only air.' She tugged at her hair, words bumbling and malformed next to his.

'What you saw was the truth of it,' he answered with more than a sliver of pride in his voice. 'The Ward detects violent intent and displaces the victim for a moment, long enough for the danger, in that case a fist, to pass.'

His answer made no sense to Umishi. From what she understood, a spell could not remain active indefinitely; a mage had to speak the words, make the air cold... *do something*. No spell lasted forever. She was reminded then of why she disliked magic so: its blatant disregard for rules, even its own rules. It seemed that, the more a mage explained their art, the less she understood it. Still, this lack of understanding had yet to prevent her from carrying out her duties.

The guards opened the giant oak doors as they approached the guardhouse. Umishi ignored the stares of their steel faces, she just wanted to be inside and out of the reach of the merciless sunlight.

'Good day, gentleman,' the arch-mage said from behind her. 'Just starting your shift?'

'Yes, my lord,' one of the guards answered.

'I do hope the weather holds up for you, I fancy there's a chill in the air.'

Umishi rolled her eye at the Leuvigild's cheerful prattle, preferring Vallis' stern silence. She quickened her pace, hoping to bring their tedious excursion to its ultimate point.

'I don't know why we do it, honestly,' Leuvigild said, catching up to her. 'The guards, I mean. These poor men and women, standing for hours on end outside doors, or wandering the streets in the bitter cold. There is simply no need. But then, I guess we both know how odd humans can be with their funny little traditions, saluting birds and refusing to cross paths with cats and all. Whatever makes them feel safe and happy is fine by me, I suppose.'

Umishi remained silent. Of course, Leuvigild was wrong. It was clear that he had devoted his unquestioning faith to this Ward, to this magic that he believed kept them safe. It was symptomatic of a problem she was all too familiar with, common in cultures that allowed their mages to run unchecked. The problem here was not too many guards, but too few. The magic that was supposed to protect the people of this island had failed, while the security of this city was more lacking than any township Umishi had ever visited.

The people of Fendamor were in clear denial. They were so blinded by their faith that they did not see how much danger they were in. No, the arch-mage was wrong; there was more safety to be found in good steel than in any kind of ambiguous spell, a lesson that this king would do well to learn.

The doors opened into the guardhouse's prisons. 'The dungeons?' Umishi asked as she stared into the darkness down the corridor.

'The weapon the rogue mage used is kept down here,' Leuvigild said. 'We found him wandering the streets the night of the murder. Our more traditional methods of investigation pointed this young man out as the killer. Of course, by the time things got to myself and the Court of Wizards the mere idea of such an accusation was laughable, but one could not deny the evidence. There were witnesses, even the man's own account. It is now presumed that this boy was a tool used by the mage, that the mage took down the Ward and this child brought down the killing blow. A hired assassin perhaps? I have not questioned him myself, having decided that it would be more prudent to wait for someone with more experience in that field.'

His assumption couldn't have been further from the truth. Umishi had no notion of diplomacy or formal interrogation. She could get words from those she questioned, true, but her ways were dirty and violent, ways this cheery Nal-Tiran would not stomach. Still it was the only lead she had, and she thought to follow its course whether through words or blood. Despite her discomfort, she pressed on.

Even from the entrance, Umishi could pinpoint the cell holding the man they were about to visit, the 'weapon' this monster had used. From the third cell down came the repugnant and unmistakeable odour of human sweat laced with urine and tears, hardly the smell of a personified instrument of death. If not for the arch-mage beside her, she would have left and returned with her report. Her senses had told her enough about what she would find in that cell, and about the type of person it held. There was nothing magical about him. From the fear in his body odour to the sobbing under his breath, the man seemed more confused than anything else. Umishi had more interest in the victim; she could use a body, examine it with fresh eyes. Mages were arrogant, sloppy. For them, killing was fuel for their ego, thinking as little for the lives they took as they did about wood thrown on a fire. When people thought so little of their tools, they rarely spent much effort disposing of them. That was when most mistakes were made.

Regardless, Leuvigild led her down to the prisoner's cell. Through the bars Umishi saw what she had already surmised, the prisoner was a balding, malnourished human, in tatters literally and figuratively. It was clear from his appearance that he had not been treated well, likely thrown in this closet made of stone and abandoned. There was no sign of food, nor any trace of bedding. Standing in front of his cell, Umishi could practically taste the evidence of his neglect. For a brief moment, something tugged at her heart: a pity that she had long forgotten how to feel. They feared him, of course they did, the first murderer in a human lifetime. They couldn't possibly fathom his crime, too afraid to address it, so instead they left him here to rot. This poor, wretched fool was no killer; he was very little of anything at all.

'Hello, Osbert, how are we doing today?' Leuvigild chirped as though oblivious to his surroundings. 'You're probably better off in here; it's starting to get rather cold out there. I have brought you a visitor. This is an inquisitor named Umishi Zaimor of the Order of Alpharus. She is here to ask you a few questions.' Leuvigild looked down at her with a warm smile.

The man cowered in a corner of his cramped room. As the Nal-Tiran spoke, the man drew himself tighter, so much so that it seemed like he was trying to burrow into the very walls that trapped him. His eyes were wide as they fell on Umishi, huge empty plates that seemed blind despite how they gorged on her.

'What happened?' she asked, already knowing the answer. The man, this Osbert, had struck the victim lying dead elsewhere in the building, forcing him to the ground where he cracked his skull, but maybe there was something else? A man in this clear a state of guilt was likely to deflect blame to something else, something perhaps that would lead to the mage who undid the Ward.

'He fell!' Osbert screamed, directing his words at no one in particular. 'He fell, his head smashed on floor like a porcelain tea pot, shattering... there was nothing I could do... there was... it spilt everywhere! I used cloth! Cloth to plug the cracks and clean the mess... but his head, it was broke and there was nothing I could do! I didn't mean to... it wasn't supposed to...' As he trailed off, the mad man's eyes fell to his curled hands with horror, lost in a terrifying image only visible to him. He screamed.

'Calm yourself now, Osbert,' Leuvigild sang in his soothing tones. 'No one blames you for what was done and the mess has all been cleaned up. No one would know an accident ever took place.'

Umishi sat on the floor as she waited for the prisoner to regain a measure of coherence. There was no way of telling whether Leuvigild's relaxed demeanour was helping, but, either way, there was little information to be had here. As she waited, she drew faces in the dust covering the dungeon floor. She had one more question before she would put an end to this spectacle and ask to go back to re-examine the victim. The dead made more sense.

After a while the Nal-Tiran stepped back and gave her a nod. The prisoner looked at them as though they were going to eat him whole, but he was calmer. She approached the bars with a question between her lips, she knew her words would be poison to him, likely driving him back into madness, but they were words that needed to be said. She tried to voice the question as softly as she could, but tact had never been her strong suit. 'What made you... why did you two argue?'

The human's gaze drifted, his focus drawn to the featureless wall, then beyond it, at something else that terrified him. He closed his eyes and swallowed his fear. 'He just came from Fort Jimmarah. He was at the bar, slamming drinks and running his mouth, flapping his fat lips. He told me the Jimmaron guard were more likely to fill their breeches with shit and piss than protect us from those corpse worshipping Dhal-Llah freaks. Prick told me, yelled it out to the whole tavern. Said that, when he made his delivery there, they spent more time digging the snot from their nose than performing duties! The shit! My brother... my brother is posted there and is twice the man he was, twice the man I am. The little pedlar shit, knew how to talk, he did, knew how to insult his betters! Thought he had brains bigger than all of ours, looked like nothing special when they spilled on the ground... looked like... He fell, how could I have known he'd fall? It shouldn't have happened... couldn't have... it wasn't me.' He looked at his hands again. 'His face was so soft and the crack.... there was...'

This was enough, the name Dhal-Llah set off alarms in Umishi's head. It was a name mentioned the previous day, one that had drawn Vallis from her charge and duties. Umishi pulled herself away from the bars and turned from the lunatic. She marched to the dungeon's exit, passing the speechless Nal-Tiran. She headed up the stairs and into the light.

After a few moments, Leuvigild appeared with a bewildered expression. 'What happened?' he asked. 'What have you gleaned?'

'The victim visited this Fort Jimmarah,' she answered. 'Yesterday the commander, Commander Vallis, I overheard her and a soldier. She was told that a people called Dhal-Llah were gathering there. Maybe the Ward was removed from more than a single person.'

'What are you suggesting?' the arch-mage demanded, words laced with panic. 'Impossible! The very notion that the Dhal-Llah are behind this! The very idea-'

'Is my conclusion.'

'I do not think you understand how absurd your

conclusion is,' he continued. 'One cannot simply *undo* the King's Ward. It is a singular spell that encapsulates the entire island. Do you not understand what this means? Even if there were a mage who understood the Ward and its intricate workings, the energies that would have to be drawn to edit it with such precision, to cut people from the Ward while keeping it from collapsing altogether, would have to be immense. We would have felt it; such an act would have left the lands dead and hollowed them from the fort to the lake. It would be like holding back the sea to pluck out a fish. No, such a feat is impossible.'

'Such power wouldn't be wasted on one petty merchant,' she snapped back.

The arch-mage glared down at her. His breathing became slow and powerful, his sapphire eyes filling with something that was not the start of tears, but something more elemental. He stood, unblinking, for a few moments. A few moments to her, at least, as she couldn't guess how long they may have been for him. Finally, he sighed and rubbed his forehead. 'I cannot deny your logic,' he said, defeated. 'I shall speak with the king and tell him the theory you have pieced together. He should at least know your thoughts, no matter how fanciful.'

He turned to leave.

Leuvigild's words seemed to seep into Umishi's every muscle, pulling at them, tugging relentlessly as the burning feeling of irritation consumed her body. They had called upon her for her advice; she would not have her conclusion ignored in the same manner one would a flight of fancy from a child! Although she would be the first to admit that she knew little of the world, magic especially, she knew people; she was good at connecting actions to motives. The strings that led from this murder to the Dhal-Llah were as clear to her as the sun. 'The boy's murder ends at these Dhal-Llah,' Umishi growled. 'I was asked for my opinion and I've given it. The task is done, I'm finished. I can't fight a war.'

The arch-mage froze for a moment before he spun, robe twisting around, in a way that bore all the theatrics of a dance move. However, when he faced her there was rage in his eyes, 'I am sorry, Inquisitor, but your task has yet to be completed. Regardless of whether the Dhal-Llah are involved, there is a monster on this island, a mage capable of the impossible. This is why you are here; it is your responsibility as an agent of the Alpharus to find this monster!' All the cheer had left him, sapped by her words and the fact that this 'Ward' the people of Fendamor worshipped was not as perfect as they had thought.

She disliked his tone. It seemed Leuvigild was grasping at straws to avoid the horrible possibility that she might be right. A thought came to her: if the spell, this 'Ward' was as powerful as he said, it likely wasn't a single mage. It could have to be a cabal, a legion, a whole fucking army of power-crazed monsters. 'The order polices rogue mages, we don't fight wars,' she insisted. If a kingdom was foolish enough to permit such people to become organised, it was on their own heads.

'The Dhal-Llah are not starting a war; they can't be.' He took another deep breath. 'We shall have to look into the King's Ward, make sure all the cogs and gears are in place, that all the workings are as they should be. Make sure they haven't been interfered with. We will have to... No, never mind, I need to think.' He wiped his face, 'I shall present my report to the king and you shall be sent for in the morning, to hand in your own findings. I am sure that is not *too* far beyond your duties.' His smile did a poor job of masking his anger. 'There is much I have to think on, much I have to do.' He brushed passed her without so much as glancing back.

She made no attempt to hinder his exit, she had pushed him enough and to do so any further would only serve to increase his ire. Besides, she had spent too much time in the company of others, long enough for today. The idea of returning to the solace of her room almost brought a smile to her face.

It wasn't long before she was slipping into the Spinning Dagger, where she was welcomed by the sound of loud, boozed up patrons too distracted by their own revelries to get involved in anyone else's business. It was another advantage of seedier locales. Not a word or nod was offered to acknowledge the stranger in their midst. Without anyone so much as glancing in her direction, Umishi managed to find her room. She changed into her black, knee-length night shirt and wasted no time in finding the puffed pillows and yellowish sheets.

Umishi sighed as her head found the pillow. She closed her eye and tried to push all the day's thoughts to the back of her mind. She lay in silence, waiting for sleep to take her away from, this nightmare, away from her own self-damning mind.

FOUR
THE HAUNTED STREETS OF HANASWICK

A cold blade slid through Umishi's skin. Waking, she lay paralysed by pain and terror. Three intruders loomed over her. She had to remain calm, resist the urge to hide, run, scream, fight. She must *remain calm* and find her moment to strike. One of the figures stepped back. There. Grabbing her knife, Umishi attacked.

'Shit in hell! She's awake!' someone cried. Her blade had already slashed at the throat of the first, stumbling foe. She spun, slashing another across the chest, expecting to feel his blood spray against her own flesh. Nothing. Terror gripped her. The dagger had passed through her target. She turned back to the first, who stood unharmed and was lunging at her.

'Stop her! Quickly!' With frenzy's tight grip on her mind there was no way of telling where the order came from. Desperate, Umishi lunged with incredible speed, taking her foe off guard. Her every attack was futile, finding no resistance of flesh or bone. One of them spoke and her whole body froze, warmth torn from the room.

'No!' Umishi cried. How could this be happening? Her eye widened as a panicked realisation flooded Umishi's mind. The King's Ward. As her blade fell from her limp hand, she cast a hopeless glance at her bag, where the tools that could at least counter the spell gripping her lay useless.

'Got her.' The invisible force crushed her chest and held her stiff in mid-air.

'She has fight in her, I'll give her that.'

'Exactly what we need,' said a third, by the authority in his voice, their leader. He approached and, as her body rose to match his height, stroked the hair from her face.

Even through the blackness of his cowl she could imagine him staring at her hideousness, her hollow eye socket, missing nostril and the ravaging scars that made her cheek look like a crumpled parchment. She wanted to cover her face, hide herself away, scream in embarrassment and rage, make him pay for the presumption, the *violation*.

'I am sorry for this, I wish there were another way. I wish I could undo this, all the suffering our efforts caused you in Malhain. I take no joy in this and, while the lives I have saved have done little to wash away the blood spilt that day, it does go a long way towards solidifying the necessity of their sacrifice... and yours. '

Although his voice was a whisper, distorted by magic, 'Malhain' screamed out louder than the pain that flooded from her arm, louder than the humiliation she was being subjected to. It raged through her mind, tore at logic and... that name, this mage... they fused into an echoing nightmare of the monster she fled, who later dragged her back through a vow made over empty graves. But he couldn't be... he could *not* be the Mangler of Malhain.

Blood slithered from her wrist and dripped from her fingers, gathering in a crimson pool beneath her. 'I want her bagged up,' the leader continued. One of the others jumped to attention at the sound of the command and started muttering an incantation. Umishi tried to scream in hopeless defiance as the heaviness of sleep started to settle on her eye, but even that freedom was stolen from her.

'Pack up the candles too, we will need them. This place has been compromised. We have to st...' Before he could even end his sentence, the pull of sleep dragged her deep into slumber, and the waiting blackness.

Warmth re-entered Umishi's body as the bindings of slumber unravelled and hate poured in to take its place. Umishi fought back the urge to scream. Closing her eye, she drew a deep breath, hoping that the cold air would cool her rage. Dragging herself into a sitting position, Umishi searched for the men who attacked her, but found no one. They had left her alone on a bed, in an empty room. She licked her dry lips and slipped from under the blankets. She pushed up her sleeve and found that the blood on her nightshirt was the only remaining evidence that there had been a wound.

Rubbing her now healed wrist she took stock of her surroundings. It was all too clean to be the Spinning Dagger; it looked more like someone's house. Running to the door, Umishi tried the handle; it was open. It was some kind of trap, it had to be. Why had they left her here, unguarded?

Doubt made her hesitate, allowing the coldness of the door handle to creep up her arm. They wouldn't have just left her with the door open; it didn't make sense. Was it possible that she had been rescued? Had someone found her after the attack? It would explain the care she had been seemingly granted; however, it would be foolish to accept the most optimistic scenario as fact. Deciding that it was safer to err on the side of caution, Umishi released the handle.

Moving back to the bed, she sat with her legs folded beneath her. She tried to make sense of the situation. It was possible that her investigation had drawn these mages to attack. If that was the case then it seemed Fendamor's king had a larger problem than he thought. He was not just dealing with one rogue mage, but an organised cabal. Perhaps, as she had speculated, it was one linked with these Dhal-Llah? Or was it just about inciting war? Why hadn't they killed her? They'd had every opportunity. Had they taken her blood? Much dark magic could be done with someone's blood. Once more, her trail of thought fractured into too many avenues.

One suspicion festered in the back of her mind like an angry spirit conjured by haunting memories and visceral dread. The monster of Malhain was there. As illogical as the notion was, it was impossible to ignore with his words echoing in her head. Malhain. He'd spoken as though he had been there, as though he had been the one who tore the village apart and reduced it to nothing more than a word. Umishi's heart pounded. She had gone in search of a mage, a murderer, but had never hoped... was hope even the right word? Her body quaked with... anticipation? Fear? Hate? She took a deep breath; it was not the time for that, not when more present riddles demanded her attention; not when it was likely that she was still in danger.

She moved to the window. It was still night. She was high, at least a storey from the ground, and she could see the sundial tower. That was good, since it meant they hadn't taken her from Hanaswick. With at least some notion of where she was and how to get to safety, her attention returned to escape. She tried the window first. Locked, and smashing it would risk alerting someone to her escape. The spell that had robbed her of her consciousness had failed to keep her from awakening, and she could only presume no one else knew about it. If possible, she would keep it that way. Bracing herself, she tried the door handle again. She held her breath, pressing down on the lever. Not even her heart dared to beat as the door inched forward and she risked stealing a peek beyond.

The way was clear, with nothing but an empty landing and stairs leading down to the ground floor. Umishi let out a quiet sigh and listened for any clue as to where her captors might be: nothing. She checked her arm again, not for wounds but for her bracelet; it was still there. Although grateful to find it, the question was why it had not been removed. They were mages, so they would easily be able to detect an enchanted object. Her kidnappers' apparent incompetence was starting to unnerve her. It was almost as though they *wanted* her to escape. Activating the amulet, she stepped into shadow, through the door and continued down the landing. There were no sounds and looking over the banister revealed no signs of life. What was happening?

Creeping down to the ground floor, Umishi found it just as lifeless. She was alone. None of it made sense. With each step she expected a trap, for something grizzly to spring from the floor boards or pounce from some darkened corner. However, there was nothing but hungry shadows and a deafening silence. Moving to the kitchen she searched the drawers, finding a butcher's knife. As her fingers caressed the grip, a smile ran across her lips. Regardless of how ineffective the blade would be, there was some comfort in being armed. Her gut twisted at the thought of leaving in just her nightshirt. Grabbing a rope from the kitchen surface she created a makeshift belt before clawing her hair into place. It would have to do; social dress codes were low on her list of priorities

The guardhouse would be her first port of call, with the offer to her of a safe base to gather her thoughts and determine her next steps. The attack had been planned, even if their detainment method clearly hadn't. She needed to be prepared; her foes could still be anywhere. She required help getting back to the inn, and with any luck, the sack of belongings containing the tools of her trade. With those in hand she would begin the job she was best at: tracking and eliminating mages. Umishi marched to the exit with conviction and opened the unlocked door. With the knife tucked between the rope and her hip, she took a deep breath and exited the house.

Outside, Umishi was struck by the silence of the city, a silence that implied death rather than slumber, and the darkness... the darkness was almost tangible, like a wall of fog that smothered any light that dared approach. She had been in empty, quiet streets before, preferring them over any hustle and bustle, but these seemed different. They were not empty, but hollow.

Moving into the street, she shifted her gaze to the sundial tower, in an attempt to gain a better idea of her location. It was northward and it wasn't too far away. She started down one of the side roads, unable to escape the silence, the emptiness. She tugged on her nightshirt. There were no lights in any of the buildings she passed, no warmth from any of the homes, but surely someone was awake? How late was it? It couldn't be too long before dawn. The shadows continued to play on her mind as even the strange, flameless lamps seemed to be struggling against the encroaching void.

The pattern was holding true as she peeked into a few more windows. There was only blackness, with every single one empty. The marketplace was as deserted as the alleyways. Where was everyone? It was as if the night had come to life and devoured every being that it encountered. The nightmarish tales of it happening were famous, recounted by bards and minstrels throughout the northern lands, where light was scarce, and days dark. Those stories couldn't be more than campfire stories, could they? Between the clouds the frozen skies opened into an endless void, one that would surely swallow her were she to remain in the open. While these notions were fanciful and childish, her caution was valid. There were truer monsters beneath the skies capable of horrors worse than any of those in stories. A chill forced her shoulders to jerk as it ran down her spine, reanimating memories of the attack, the crushing grip of the magic used to bind her, the helplessness, the mages' gaze. Umishi pulled at her hair, there was no time, she had to focus, had to reach the guardhouse.

As the streets led her towards the tower, there was something else, something her heightened senses normally took for granted. The air, there seemed to be no sign of it by taste or smell, not even a breath of wind. The place was still, a corpse of the land in which she had been put to sleep. Umishi felt her gut tighten at the sight.

Moving into the town's centre, she found it as hollow as the rest of the city, empty of light and sound, as if she had entered a large, abandoned warehouse rather than the market place from the previous day. The clock-tower came into full view. It was truly a marvel. With each glance she gave it, she was more convinced magic was involved in its construction. Each delicate mark and beautiful detail made it hard to believe the structure was crafted by human hands alone. Her gaze moved down to the building that lay under it. As she approached her eye widened.

A strange, blue dust emanated from the vague, misshapen silhouette of the guardhouse. Mesmerised, she walked to it and reached out with the edge of her blade. Despite seeming like dust the blue particles dripped from the knife as though they were floating raindrops. A mix of wonder and trepidation tore through her. Her mind cried out that, whatever it was, it wasn't meant to be; it was somehow very, very wrong. A loud crash came from inside the building. Umishi gasped and her body instinctively fell into a defensive stance, but the moment passed and silence was restored. Blue mist escaped the building's windows and seeped to the ground like a gaseous waterfall.

As she pushed open the door a flurry of tiny droplets escaped through the gap. Startled, she pulled her hand back, but it was too late; she could feel the wrongness dampening her skin. Franticly, she rubbed at her arm where the dust had landed. To her relief there seemed to be no effect, no burns, no pain. Despite what her instincts told her, there was nothing that indicated it was any more harmful than water.

She slipped inside the building now, silently brushing her way through the cold liquid specks. Much like the world outside, the guardhouse was empty. The blue droplets were everywhere, drifting through the air like ash or snow, colliding against each other and clinging to walls. It made no sense, what purpose did the dust serve? There was no logic to the chaotic scene she was now a part of; it was as though she had somehow fallen into a madman's nightmare. Umishi cast her eye to where the guards should have been, where they had previously stood so diligently. Even they had been evacuated from this vacant world. Their absence was more unsettling than their presence had ever been.

Their absence meant something else as well, meant that there was no help to be found. Whatever was happening had made the guards move elsewhere. Was the city under attack? Had it been evacuated? How long had she been unconscious? There were no answers in the guardhouse. As she turned to leave a bang escaped from the dungeon and found its way to Umishi's ear. Her heart raced; there was someone else there, something else moving in this city turned dead.

Clutching her knife's hilt and holding her breath she inched to the top of the stairs. Below her, through the open door, more blue dust formed into a dense fog. From its impenetrable shroud a stifled groan beckoned.

Umishi licked her lips. If there was someone down there then they would likely have a better idea of what was happening. With bare feet and light steps she descended, step by step. With each awkward step she took her mind conjured reasons for her not to take another. She did not know what was down there, there was no way of knowing if this was a trap, the building was filled with magic, did she truly expect there not to be a mage lurking in the darkness? Her fingers tightened around her blade's hilt. Her desire for answers drove her onward. The blue mist smoothed her face with moist strokes as she reached the bottom. Beyond the iron bars, she could make out a figure in the darkness of the cell's furthest corner.

Mindful of her breathing, she approached the bars. It was the prisoner. Of course it was; during evacuations such people were seldom considered a priority. While this made sense to her, something in her gut told her it was not him, that something *else* had taken his place in the iron cage.

She was right. The closer she came, the more the human shape devolved into something else entirely. While darkness obscured its head, she could make out its naked skin: black and glistening as though composed of ooze, barely stretched over its skeleton. It lacked any symmetry, with shoulders and limbs mismatched, the left side longer than its right and somehow... somehow its left arm was fused to its knee. A lapse in composure let Umishi take a step back, her blade scraping against the wall.

The creature's head inched around, revealing a warped face. Its eyes were sunken white orbs. Its open mouth was a crack from chin to forehead filled with white, finger-length fangs. Its tongue slid between them, falling from its maw like blood from an open wound. It screamed at her, attempting to stand despite its weird structure. The thing shambled towards her.

A knot twisted in Umishi's stomach as she backed away. The creature slammed itself against the bars, screaming as the iron failed to give way. It tried again and again, throwing itself at its cage, with no concern for self-preservation. The stone floor vibrated and the metal groaned with every assault by the creature upon its prison. It screamed again, blood spewing from its malformed and battered shoulder as it launched its gnarled arm through the bars, barbed talons reaching out for Umishi.

When Umishi looked upon this creature it was as though she was seeing rage for the first time. The monster's hate poured from its frenzy-filled eyes and caused Umishi's heart to pound against her ribcage in response. She moved to the dungeon's exit, her eye not leaving the creature until she slammed the door at the top of the stairs. Upon exiting the building she drew a deep breath, eye searching the emptiness of the dead city for anything – any movement, glimmer of light, dust stirring – *anything* to indicate that the wind was blowing, that she wasn't alone, that there was still life somewhere. In her desperation, the continued silence felt crueller. What had happened? Where was everybody? Had Hanaswick been invaded? No. She looked again. There were no bodies, signs of blood, weapons, defences... *nothing*. She tried to breathe as panic coiled tightly around her lungs, and her mind raced as her questions mounted. If it had not been invaded, evacuated then? Why? How long had she been unconscious? What was the creature in the dungeon? The questions were becoming too heavy; they forced her down, so that she could feel her legs buckle and her bare knees hitting the ground, hands catching her before her body could follow.

It was all wrong. Something had gone wrong in Hanaswick; while imprisoned in her cage of slumber; something had gone terribly wrong. Umishi screamed, windows vibrating with the strength of her fear and confusion. Then the sound ebbed, and the dead city was silent.

FIVE
SHADOW AT THE WINDOW

In the distance, above the fog, a light shone in defiance of the night's tyrannical rule. It bled from the palace windows, escaping into the streets. It emanated from the corner tower and had even been obscured twice as she approached. It could only mean one thing: that there was life within. Doubt clawed Umishi with jagged hooks as she recalled the beast in the guardhouse. Life did not guarantee salvation. Monster or not, though, exploring the source of the light and movement presented a hope she couldn't ignore.

The strange blue dust spilt from the palace windows and made ethereal rapids of the layered gardens as it drifted down. Umishi padded forward, each step synchronised with her heartbeat. The blue mists surged around her as she rose to the first step. Panicked at being surrounded, she whirled around but the way back was obscured by thousands of floating droplets. With clenched fists and no other options, she turned back to the palace. If she was to unravel the mysteries behind this nightmare, she had to press on.

Memories of the world she was once in faded as the drifting blue rain distorted the path ahead. She could no longer see the palace or the light that had called to her. More than the blindness, it was the silence that unsettled her. She had never before experienced such smothering soundlessness. The mists all but suffocated her senses, forcing her focus to the ground so that she didn't risk losing her way.

The climb seemed much longer than it had been when it was bathed in the warm glow of sunlight; a glow she was beginning to miss. Around her, the strange droplets rose, fell and lifted, bending to the will of a wind that wasn't there. Taking tentative steps she pressed on, shadows manifesting just beyond her sight: shambling things obscured by the twisting haze. Umishi blinked, straining her eye to gain some focus, to discern whether the encroaching figures were truly there or merely a by-product of a worked-up mind.

Refusing to take any risks, she maintained her distance, gripping the knife kept at her waist. A booming sound made Umishi stop. She froze, heart racing, flinching when it happened again. It took several moments to identify it: merely a bird, chirping, from somewhere far beyond the veil of silence. Still, every time the sound broke through and was amplified by the quiet, her heart skipped. Although her sight was still obscured, she risked increasing her speed. The chirping shifted into screams. Umishi recognised those all too well. The creature from the dungeon had escaped. No, it couldn't have. The monster seemed wild, too bestial to pick the lock or find another way out.

Her brisk pace turned into a run. Shadows stalked in her peripheral vision, clicking at each other and confirming her fears: there were more of them. She launched herself up the stairs on all fours, heart pounding with each step. Near the top, the palace emerged from the darkness, its pale grey walls promising sanctuary. A scream called behind her; they were coming. Umishi fought to regain control of her breathing. Everything had changed from the previous day, twisted. There had been a door, there must be a door, a window, a way in. The stairs wouldn't just lead to *nowhere.* Her mind spun dizzily through memories clouded by panic. With shaking hands she pressed against the cold stone and followed it to the left. Her eye searched for an entrance. She didn't dare look back. It was pointless; she knew they were there, and close. She scrabbled; there was no time. Her fingers finally found glass, but not respite. A cacophony of inhuman screams came from within. She knew what was in there, what she would find, but she looked anyway.

The mists had flooded the palace interior and the silhouettes of malformed creatures filled the halls. There were so many of them, fighting against their own uniquely deformed limbs as they tore apart furniture, ripped through carpets and wall hangings, searching and squabbling over anything they could fit in their mouths. What had happened while she slept? What had happened to this city and its people? Where had these creatures come from? Was she truly alone?

Talons scraped on stone behind her, urging her to find an entry point. Her heart pounded at her ribs; they were getting closer. Hastily examining the brickwork she found an opportunity. Her thin fingers slotted between the stones. With her grip assured she heaved herself towards the light above her, and, with any luck, a safe way inside.

Halfway to her goal, Umishi's heart jumped at a crash from below. Among the shards of glass ejected from the lower windows a creature stumbled. Like the one in the dungeon, its skin was an oozy black and its body was just as twisted, but it had notable differences: while its arms were free, its legs were hideously melded together. Umishi gripped the wall tighter and reached for the bricks above. Biting her lip, she climbed at a more deliberate pace, trying not to make a sound. It would only take a scream from the monster below for its more able bodied brethren to be upon her. The beast thrust its misshapen nostrils into the air, sniffing wildly, like a predator catching the scent of a rotting carcass. Umishi held her breath and climbed higher, her fingers now finding the window ledge. Releasing her breath she lifted herself up. She had made it.

However, reaching the window ledge was not the victory she had hoped for. She was instead presented with another problem: it was closed, a pane of glass between her and possible salvation. Biting her lip she fought back the urge to scream as rage and hopelessness made a battlefield of her mind. Was she to smash the glass and hope the creature beneath her paid her no heed? Or was she to wait and hope it wandered off, while more might come? She chose the first option.

As the butt of her blade smashed through the window, an explosion of sound rebounded from the palace walls, restoring temporary life to Hanaswick's corpse. Countless specks of glass rained onto the ground below, where the creature tilted its head at a freakish angle, its frosted white eyes finding her. Biting down on her lip, her body tensed in anticipation of its ear piecing scream. Time ground to a halt, until the beast jerked its head back toward the city. She was surprised as it dragged itself away toward the guardhouse. Did it see her? It had looked right at her. She considered its frosted eyes, and wondered at the strength of its sight; perhaps there was another reason it didn't want to pursue her: perhaps it couldn't? There was no time to search for answers. As the monster vanished from sight, she slipped through the window.

The commotion below became a cacophony of screaming creatures and smashing glasses. Inside, Umishi found a bed, a guest room of some kind. Further examination revealed the wardrobe was full of hanging clothes, everything untouched, undisturbed. What happened to the people? There were no bodies, no blood, no signs of fighting; the city had been emptied and the palace filled with these beasts.

An unsettling picture began to emerge from these clues, a theory that connected the fate of the city folk with these monsters. It was surely impossible, the stuff of tales made to scare children. She had heard, even witnessed, mages twisting or enhancing the bodies of their servants, but never to this monstrous degree, not to the point where they had become unrecognisable, and never on this scale. Not a whole city. No, this was nonsense, her mind leaping to grotesque fantasies driven by the night's events. Even so, her gut refused to let go of the possibility.

Without fully understanding what was going on she could still reasonably conclude that, with the timing of the blue mists sudden appearance and the overwhelming evidence of magic's involvement, the mages who attacked her were somehow at the core of it. A large crash from the floor below brought her heart to her throat and her mind back to the current situation.

Stepping out, she found the corridor empty of all but the blue mist. It emanated from downstairs and slithered from another room's door. This blue mist seemed to only develop where these creatures were. That would make them easier to avoid in future.

On all fours, Umishi moved silently to the bottom of the hallway, towards its exit. Checking to make sure no mist spilled from under the lavish double doors, she carefully pushed them open and slipped into the palace's great hall. The palace was rife with ornamentation, from leaf-engraved doors, to bronze branched candelabras. The expertly woven, thick, blue carpet that led to every door and trailed up the central staircase was especially prominent. Fortunately, although the colour featured often in the decorations, the blue mist was nowhere to be seen; this level seemed to be devoid of the creatures, at least for the moment.

A scream tore through the palace, shaking everything with its unchallenged energy. Umishi froze, her heart pounding in her chest as the vibrations ebbed. It was not the shriek of one of the monstrosities that occupied the floor below, it was a sound of helpless terror, from a female voice. Racing to the staircase, Umishi's heart pounded; she no longer cared about her human act, so she took once more to all fours and scaled the staircase with haste. Rising back onto her two legs she regained her bearings and guessed where the scream had come from: the door ahead of her, which held more sounds, weeping, sobbing, a voice; a *human* voice.

Umishi reached up and pulled at the door handles with all her strength. As the doors flew open, the blue mist within burst forth like a flood, floating, liquid tendrils coiling around her body and grasping at her hair. Umishi gripped her knife as she prepared for combat.

She entered a massive dance hall. Archways and domes spread over its ceilings in a way that, seen in other circumstances, might have been delightful. To her eye, they made her think of pox-infested skin attached to the archways, with pillars spreading down to the floor from between the boils. It was only after her eye was drawn to the room's centre that she found the source of the screaming.

A human in a torn ball gown lay pressed to the floor, half her face covered in blood, the rest twisted in fear. Umishi slipped into a guarded stance, as three monsters circled the poor woman, long tongues dangling from twisted mouths. One of the creatures held the human down with a skeletal hip and cupped the back of her head with long, talon-tipped fingers.

As Umishi inched toward them, their frosted eyes locked on to her, croaking and hissing with every step she took.

'Help,' the woman choked, all her strength seemingly lost from energy used to utter her last scream.

The beast that held her croaked angrily at its victim. It thrust her head downward, into the marble floor. Blood spilt from her mouth and the monsters claws sank in deeper.

Umishi darted forward. Before the first creature could react, she plunged her knife into its throat. Crimson liquid spilt from its wound as it rolled limply from its captive.

The second creature launched itself at Umishi. She withdrew her blade and dodged the onslaught of talons. It was slow, its movement restricted by its malformed limbs. Regardless of its failed attack it managed to place itself between Umishi and the human.

The woman's luck had run out, the third creature sinking its teeth into the back of her neck. Her eyes opened wide, the glimmer of hope they once held snuffed out as the beast gurgled triumphantly.

'Strange, very strange,' a soft voice said behind her. 'I ask for one, yet I have two. How did that happen, do you think? No, no, this is wrong, not what I'm looking for, not what I need.'

She glanced back and saw it, only for a moment, but it was there. There was a blur of black feathers, the size of a human; could it have *been* human? Then it was gone, dropping into the open air. Umishi attempted to wrestle her mind from whatever she had just seen, what had *spoken*. She had to maintain her focus on the creatures, or she would join their victim on the floor.

As she readied her blade, a golden beam rose from the woman's body and exploded with a blinding flash.

SIX

DANCING WITH MADNESS

Umishi blinked. The blinding light subsided, the world flickering back into focus. Shapes pirouetted in front of her, spinning and twisting. People, humans – at least fifty – were dancing. They wore extravagant clothing, ball gowns and bucket hats. They swooped and swirled around her, as they replaced the creatures that had vanished, along with their victim. Where once blood had sprayed, confetti now bloomed. It was taking too long for her eye to adjust, the colours overpowering after the muted shades before the flash of light returned their radiance. Neither the music nor the voices granted her mercy, instead beating her senses into a daze. Her head reeling, Umishi spun to leave the room and reclaim her faculties, but she found no reprieve.

Back in the main hall she saw large numbers of nobles milling around or chatting to each other. Guards stood at their posts flanking the door, helms tilted down to look at her as she stopped between them. Her hands rushed to her hair, pulling it as tightly over her face as she could.

'Where did you come from?' boomed a powerful voice, echoing from under one of the helms. Umishi reversed through the door. Panicked, she stumbled into a pair of dancers, dragging them with her as she fell. The female dancer screamed in surprise as her head hit the floor.

'Guards!' yelled the man rising to his knees. 'Guards!'

Her movements and muscles finally following her commands, Umishi attempted to scramble to her feet, and failed.

'What is this?' the man shouted. 'Who let this lunatic in here?'

Umishi dragged herself into a corner. Eyes threw judgemental glances at her; so many eyes, all bearing down upon her, some with amusement, others with anger. She pulled her knees up to her face. What was going on? Where did these people come from? Was she going mad? The was *so much* noise. The crowd parted for two guards.

'...lunatic...'

'... doing here...'

'... not even dressed...'

The clattering of approaching armour blocked out the voices.

'Who are you, girl?' a guard demanded, looming over her.

The pounding of Umishi's heart echoed throughout her body. Her mind rejected the guard's question, processing it as background noise. There was too much to grasp, too many sounds; she needed somewhere dark and quiet where she could think. First, though, she had to leave; she had to get out, away from the gazes of these slack-jawed, pompous jesters.

With her focus anchored to the ghost of a plan, Umishi shot to her feet, startling the people around her and making the guard step back.

'Calm down, miss,' he said. She offered him nothing more than a glance. The sounds he made seemed more like the grinding of iron along gravel than anything she could register as speech. The nobles retreated to the other side of the room, their whispers and gasps lingering behind them. Her gaze met theirs and she ground her teeth, anger overcoming embarrassment and confusion.

'Now calm down girl, I...' The guard was calling her 'girl' as if she were some small child; Umishi had no time for his patronising tone. Umishi ignored him, heading for the exit. As expected, the nobles in their fancy clothes didn't move against her; didn't dare try to stop her. Instead, everyone moved away as if she were diseased. There were guards ahead of her and, when one tried to grab her shoulder, Umishi dodged. They were slow, they were all too slow, but they were not really trying to stop her. Most were moving aside to let her pass, content as long as she was out of the palace and out of their hair. She made her way down the staircase to the grand hall, ignoring all those around her. Her head buzzed with questions. None of this made sense; she needed to get away, back to the inn. She had to evaluate what was going on, what had just happened.

Amidst the chaos, Umishi could make out distinctive footsteps on the stairs behind her. Although rushed, the footsteps were orderly and rhythmic. She knew that they were not human.

'Ms Zaimor,' came the calm but urgent call from the arch-mage. 'I implore you to wait.'

It was a simple enough request. However, anger and embarrassment drove her to ignore it. Besides, she needed to see the outside world, to make sure that it too had sprung to life in the wake of the flash of light. As she approached the entrance, guards pulled the doors apart like curtains, and before her lay exactly what she had hoped for: a cloudless sky, fireless lamps burning darkness away, steel carriages moving through the main streets while guards patrolled. All was in order; no great calamity had befallen the city, and no monsters hid in blue mists. A mix of awe and bewilderment held Umishi frozen. The world was alive again, moving like it had always done, like nothing had happened. A hand landed on her shoulder, reminding her to blink, to breathe.

'It was all empty,' she whispered. 'There was... no one at all.'

'They are all there now,' Leuvigild assured her.

It was a simple statement, but one that held so much weight. They were all there, *everyone*. She released a sigh of relief. Had she hallucinated everything? Had it all been a dream? No, it couldn't have been; surely it couldn't have been. As inept as they seemed to be, the guards would not have just allowed her to sleepwalk into the palace. It *couldn't* have been a dream.

'You need rest,' Leuvigild said. 'We'll have one of the guest rooms prepared for you. You'll sleep here tonight, and in the morning we can find out what this is all about.'

Umishi couldn't fault his logic. The night had left her mentally and physically exhausted, so she surrendered herself to the arch-mage's lead and followed him to a staircase that crossed into a separate wing. While walking, Umishi's mind began to fade in and out of focus, so that the corridors and hallways all merged into one until they reached a door the Nal-Tiran would not enter.

'This will be your room, Ms Zaimor,' he said, gesturing through the open door. 'I will have a guard posted at every inch of this corridor, supported by one of my wizards. I will ensure nothing further happens to you. Your things will be brought here in the morning, If I may be so bold, I also think it might be more prudent for you to base yourself here for the remainder of your stay.'

The logic seemed sound, or perhaps Umishi lacked the energy to fight, but the promise of a comfortable bed and undisturbed rest seemed too tempting an offer to refuse. Like the rest of the palace, the guest room he presented her with was lavish, with steel vines and blue roses stretching out from corner, to wall, to window. As she proceeded deeper she felt the cushioned textures of the carpet between her toes, like walking through balls of wool.

'Sleep well,' Leuvigild said as he closed the door.

Alone again, Umishi's eye fell on the shadows loitering between cupboards and amassing at the edges of the chamber. Silent and still for now, they awaited the opportunity to gain ground. They waited for the flameless candles to die. She would deny them that chance. The light would guard her slumber. Pulling herself onto the bed she sank into the warmth and comfort it offered. Reaching for the blankets, her attention was drawn to her wrists. They seemed completely healed here in the waking world. It did not make sense.

Sleep wouldn't come, despite her weariness; no matter how hard she tried there was no escape from her conscious mind. With her eye open she could not help but watch the shadows for her attackers, the mages who had made a toy of her mind. Closed, she would revisit the barren streets of Hanaswick in memory. She would find herself back in the bloody ballroom, surrounded by monsters and death. It had all seemed so real. Was she going mad? She *had* to have been going mad, yet her wounds had been healed and she had somehow managed to sleepwalk into the palace.

No, it *couldn't* have been real. The shadow she saw at the window, the soft voice it spoke with, had all been part of a nightmare she had been having for over a life time. It couldn't have been real... the Mangler was dead. But the mage who attacked her, he had spoken as if he had been there... as though he had been at Malhain. Was that part of the dream too? Was she going mad? She hoped that she was, hoped that Leuvigild was right, hoped that the Mangler still lay in his grave. Yet her mind kept finding the shadow at the window.

A knock on the door pulled Umishi from a slumber she hadn't known she had fallen into. Sunlight invaded her room and assaulted her eye. Although she blinked to stay the attack the burning glow was relentless. After a second, a louder set of knocks followed she finally had to submit and accept that day was upon her.

'Lady Inquisitor, His Royal Highness, King Edwin the

First of the Kingdom of Fendamor is ready to receive you in his throne room. He waits anxiously and requests that you do not delay.' The voice was frail, filled with weakness; it came from someone who spoke a lot but thought very little: a chamberlain or page.

The king could wait. After the inefficiency of his guards the night before it was the least he could do. Clothes had already been laid out for her; whether this had been done before Leuvigild ushered her into the room or while she slept, she could not tell. It did not take Umishi long to get ready; all the while she listened to the continued knocking on the door. She smirked at the sound as she tackled the final button on the neck of her black tunic. How long would he wait? What would he do if she never opened the door? Deciding to put the page out if his misery, she opened the door to find a very surprised human.

Umishi followed him from the guest wing to the throne room. With each step down the familiar corridors, shades of the previous night stirred, causing Umishi's attention to focus on the shadows they passed. The opulent doors opened and her name was announced. From his throne, the king fixed his gaze on her through fiery hair, clawing at his chair's arms as the page muttered in mind-numbing ceremony. Beside the throne, the arch-mage looked sombre; all indications suggested that this was not going to be pretty.

The chanting of titles and honours seemed endless, so much that the king lost his patience. 'Enough!' he bellowed, leaping to his feet. His voice made the chandeliers tremble. 'For fuck's sake! I shall have you out of this palace and down in a shit filled ditch should you utter one more puffed up word of bloody adulation! Now leave! The inquisitor and I have a great deal to discuss.'

Within moments, everyone vacated the room, leaving Umishi alone with the king and his arch-mage. The king turned to Umishi, with darkened eyes. 'Do you know what the hardest thing about being king is Ms Zaimor?' He didn't wait for her answer. 'Sorting through the shit to find the truth of things, and that dig, Inquisitor, it takes more than a shovel and a good back, I can tell you.'

He sat back down, the anger on his face, unchanged. 'My arch-mage advised that I summon you to my kingdom, told me you were the best the Order of Alpharus had to offer, that you would unearth the truth of things within a week. Now imagine my concern when your report came to me last night. A report telling me, not of a mere murderer, but of my neighbours plotting against me, the Dhal-Llah readying themselves for war! My wizards say this is impossible, that the King's Ward can't be undone in such a manner, that the fact it had been removed from a single person seemed unlikely enough. Regardless of this I saw logic in your findings, I found it explained much. I am king, and I have a duty to my people.'

He shifted in his chair. 'So, against the judgement of men I have trusted for years I sent a bird to Fort Jimmarah, advising them to shore up their defences. I sent a bird to the lakes town, telling them to prepare the bridges for destruction to hinder the progress of any advancing army. I did this all on the faith I had in your report. Then I was awoken in the early hours of the morning with reports of you breaking into one of my balls, half-naked and raving as though you were on bloody fire, guards and friends calling you a lunatic! So, I ask you, Ms Zaimor, what am I to make of this?'

Umishi could not hide the pinkness that rushed to her cheeks, could only tug at her hair. She understood what the king was saying, but she was there, she must have been, before the flash. No, he hadn't seen what she had: the looming shadow at the window that seemed to delight in the death the monsters fed it. She had seen him. It was him. It must have been him, he must have been real.

Clawing at the arms of his throne while he waited for her answer, the king gave an impression that was more like an angry bear than a human; beneath fur covered lips, his teeth were grinding, as though struggling to hold back a roar. While she had hunted bears before, this one seemed quick to anger; she would have to choose her words carefully. She wet her lips and took a breath. 'I was…' she began, hating the shrieking of her own voice. 'While I slept, I was ambushed. It must have been a pre-emptive attack, to stop my investigation. They put me under some kind of spell I…' with one glance at his eyes she could tell that a report filled with empty streets and strange blue mists would only serve to further his rage. She would skip ahead to the point. 'When I reached the palace, the ballroom, I saw him and his creatures. The mage, it had to of been him, the Mangler of Malhain, he… '

'Who?' the king growled, turning to the arch-mage. 'What is she talking about?'

'The Mangler was a name the common folk gave a mage who ravaged a small village just before the rebellion that brought the previous empire to heel,' Leuvigild explained. 'I can only speak of the aftermath, but reports from the day state that he performed acts that contradicted everything we understand about magic, demonstrated a power that is almost inconceivable. I can see how the inquisitor came to her conclusion.'

'Previous empire? You're talking about Ghaldail's empire, which fell over a hundred fucking years ago?' the king snarled. 'This is the very shit I was talking about! Never have I heard such madness! First, an invasion by our neighbours, which you fooled me into believing. And now what? An undead mage who apparently tip-toed through the bloody city gates with the intention of attacking you and then attending a ball with a bunch of monsters? Does this make sense to you when you hear it spoken aloud? If I had the privilege of a lesser position I would have you dumped in a cesspit somewhere so you could drown in your own piss and madness. Luckily for you, I am a king burdened with the lives of thousands. The claims you make regarding the Dhal-Llah at least have a horrible taste, and no matter how much I try, I cannot help but think that there may be a crumb of truth to them. It may be only a crumb, but I do not have the privilege of dismissing it, not with so many lives at risk.'

'If I may interject,' Leuvigild began, 'Your Ma-'

'No, you may not!' the king roared.

Silence flooded the room as the king drew a deep breath. It was a silence different from the one Umishi had found herself drowning in the previous night: a sombre but calming silence that was necessary after the king's outburst. The king himself had fallen deep into his throne and even deeper into contemplation. He pressed two fingers to his lips and turned to and then away from the arch-mage. With the king's silence and subtle movements, the atmosphere in the room became almost tangible, electrical, like the build up to a storm. Umishi and Leuvigild waited, breath held.

'Perhaps you are right,' The king finally said, with a calmness that made the oncoming storm dissipate. 'Perhaps it is time I brought the tone of this discussion back to a civil level. Please arch-mage, continue.'

'Your Majesty,' the arch-mage said, bowing. 'It is my belief the inquisitor was the victim of an attack. In the last few years, we have seen an increase in the use of poisons that bypass the Ward. Many of these are designed to attack the minds of victims. The fact that the inquisitor was attacked within our walls lends credence to my original theory: that this was the act of a lone wizard, a powerful one, perhaps even the inquisitor's Mangler. If you would permit me to offer my opinion I think it would be most prudent to review Ms Zaimor's account of what happened last night. I wish to understand what she saw, or rather what she *thought* she saw.'

'Perhaps the inquisitor was poisoned,' the king agreed. 'She seems quite calm now, at any rate. And perhaps this Mangler has, somehow, found a way to cheat death and now strikes at us from his grave, as insane as that sounds. I do not have the luxury of ignoring two supposed experts in the field of magic. So, for the sake of Fendamor's security, I shall ignore the events of last night and these claims of monsters.'

Umishi started to breathe a sigh of relief, but it seemed that the king wasn't done.

'That being said, however, before I can fully endorse you

two to start running here and there, chasing ghosts around my city, I shall be moving your investigation in another direction. To put my mind at ease and to at least cross one of these bloody theories off the list, you will both go to Fort Jimmarah with a new objective. You will inspect the Ward there. I need to know whether our borders are safe, that there are no cracks in our defences. I want you to unburden me of the terrifying thought of a foe protected by the Ward readying themselves to wage war while the same protection abandons us. After that, we can refocus our attention to whatever happened last night, and you can hunt your phantoms. Regardless, I want you two to find this mage who seems intent on tearing my kingdom apart, and I want neither of you to rest until the task is complete.'

The Order of Alpharus were not investigators or mercenaries for hire; they policed mages, ensured they did not step out of line, and the Order did not stray far from its duty. Under normal circumstances, an inquisitor would never agree to the king's command and risk being dragged into any kind of political upheaval, especially one that might lead to war. However, for Umishi, these were not normal circumstances. She had to find out what had happened the night before, to make sure she was not going mad, that it was real. If it was, despite how mad or impossible it seemed, then it was an opportunity she could not ignore. If so, fate had granted her a second chance to stop running and fight. She had vowed that the fate of Malhain would not be repeated, and she had spent most of her life fulfilling that vow. The Order of Alpharus would have seen him imprisoned and studied, but she would see him *dead*.

Yet part of her hoped that the king and arch-mage were right: that these nightmares were brought on by some toxin that caused fever dreams of vanishing people and hideous monsters. That explanation seemed more logical, as the coincidence of the Mangler being alive and behind the very murder she was investigating seemed unlikely at best. However, there was a lingering fact that made her doubt Leuvigild's theory: Umishi knew poison – by taste, touch and smell – and she knew that, whatever caused the madness of the night before, poisons had nothing to do with it.

SEVEN

DARK TRAIL OF THOUGHT

As Umishi approached the city's primary gatehouse, she couldn't help being in awe. The massive structure towered over most of its buildings while refusing to conform to the city's aesthetic. Freed of the need to be pleasing to the eye, this structure was built with a singular function in mind; presenting itself as the epitome of strength and intimidation only as a by-product of its functionality. Its cold, black stone reached up from the ground with purpose, not a brick out of place and not a gap between the stones. Its clear and singular goal was to protect the city, with crenulated ramparts and machicolations. There was little doubt that the formidable defence was more than capable of preforming its duty.

It was a part of Hanaswick that Umishi recognized. She only recalled seeing the city's gatehouse twice before, when she and Richard had first arrived from the mainland, hoping to build a life together. It was the gatehouse that had greeted them when they disembarked, along with its heavily manned garrison and the crossbows they pointed toward the city. It had been their first indication of the empire's cruel regime. Her second time was a blurred haze, barely a recollection at all, just the pain and the ship that took her away from the monsters the place held.

'Quite amazing, is it not?' the arch-mage said, jolting her back to the present. How long had he been there? How could he have snuck up on her? The answer was simple: she had been locked in her memories. It had always been her weakness.

'…kind of barbaric beauty,' the arch-mage was saying, 'A relic of an era that did not understand the protection that the mind could provide. Vulfoliac Fendamor decided to keep it intact, as a reminder of the monstrous things we used to create in the name of safety.'

She turned back to the wall. The faith Leuvigild placed in magic made her skin crawl. She had seen that kind of faith before, and how it could be used to control people.

'When can we be on our way, Arch-mage?' she asked, wanting to shift the conversation to something, anything, else.

'Arch-mage,' he repeated as he lowered his hood, allowing his expertly braided, liquid gold hair to run down his right shoulder. 'Please, as I have already stated, outside His Majesty's court I am merely Leuvigild. Hearing my title so often, as great an honour as it is, gets tiring. And, as we are to travel together I think it would be fitting to discard such formality.'

Umishi shrugged, not offering an answer. The arch-mage kept going anyway.

'I have arranged a carriage to take us to Fort Jimmarah. It shall be with us presently. I am trying to convince His Royal Majesty to grant his permission for a tram line to be installed, connecting our closer villages and townships. It would optimise excursions such as these exponentially.'

'Tram-Line'. The phrase meant nothing to Umishi. A mage had once talked to her about ley lines, so she could only guess that these were similar things.

Time passed in silence, at least for her. Leuvigild may have said something, but whatever it was did not interest her. The carriage eventually arrived, and, to her relief, horses were attached; she disliked the idea of being dragged along by something with alien motives. The driver jumped down from his seat, wearing the same strange barrel hat as most of the townsfolk. Umishi had to bite her tongue as she watched the poor fool try to keep it on while he bowed.

Slouched and almost dozing within the carriage lay the elderly mage – and Leuvigild's opposite – the mage from the dungeon, the one she'd met the day she arrived. 'Good day mage hunter,' the human said, exaggerating the effort needed to contort his mouth into a smile. 'Do you need a hand up? These basic carriages only adhere to the forms who make them which, in this case, seems to be a giant with legs as powerful as those belonging to the mules pulling.'

The question sent a jolt down her spine. She shook her head in answer, while rolling her eye at the human's observation. Using the wheel forks as a foothold, Umishi jumped into the cabin with the effortlessness of habit. The cabin was larger than any she had seen before, more than capable of seating six people of human size. The blue silk chairs stood out against the black wood panels. The indigo farmers must be some of the richest people in Fendamor, judging by all the blue that went into the city's decoration. She sat in one of the cabin's corners opposite the human, tucking her legs under herself, and granted the wizard a nod.

'I hope you do not mind,' began Leuvigild as he practically floated in behind her, bowing his head so as not to hit the roof. 'I invited Lord Lothrum to aid me in this expedition.'

'Lord?' she repeated with a raised eyebrow and a grin at the thought that he'd only just told her to avoid titles.

He returned the smile. 'Sorry, this is my good friend and colleague, Erik Lothrum, I hope you do not mind that I requested his company?'

In all truth she did not care; he could have invited a whole army for all that it would bother her. All she cared about was determining what had happened to her the night before, and more importantly, finding the monster responsible. It could have only been the Mangler, it had to have been. He'd said... he'd spoken as though he had been there that day. She was *not* going mad.

Lothrum scoffed at the arch-mage's correction. 'Good friend? A good friend wouldn't have dragged me out of my bed and ordered me to do field research halfway across the bloody kingdom!'

'Come now,' Leuvigild laughed. 'It will do you a world of good to get some fresh air in your lungs, clear out the cobwebs.' He knocked the ebony wall with the back of his fist, ordering the driver to set off.

For a time, the only sounds were those of iron grinding against stone and the odd snort from the horse. As the three passengers sat in silence, Umishi directed her gaze through a window, watching as Hanaswick's guards tended the winches that operated the city's massive doors. Through the yawning gap, the greenery of the outside world presented itself. She licked her lips, looking forward to a backdrop not crafted by human hands.

Upon exiting the city, the stone floors came to an abrupt stop, as though the enthusiasm of the builders failed upon completion of the city's walls. Where stone ended, fields began, slowly transforming into woodland as they reached towards the horizon. The only legacy of Hanaswick's oppressive masonry was a small dirt road that transformed into a bridge crossing a narrow river.

'What a lovely day it is,' said the arch-mage, breaking the silence. 'It is rare that I venture outside the city walls. I almost forget what the leaves of spring look like.'

'Lovely, I'm sure. that is if the very grass did not make your nose run and your skin itch,' The elderly human remarked. 'But still, at least we are out here for a reason, yes? At least I'm being kept away from my work for a greater good?'

'Absolutely, I shall waste no more time,' Leuvigild said as the joy he had been brimming with slowly dimmed. He turned to Umishi. 'There has been a development.' His tone became dark and weighed down into a whisper. 'This morning, it was reported that a young lady who attended last night's ball has gone missing. The guards, when questioned, stated that she had not left the palace. She was last seen retiring to the palace garderobe.' He noticed Umishi's raised eyebrow. 'An indoor privy, of a kind. Only, she did not return. It is as though she just vanished.'

Umishi fell back into the chair and clawed her hair over her face. The knowledge gave way to a flood of questions. How much of last night had been real? Did everyone actually vanish? What were the creatures? She knew she had not been poisoned, but what magic had caused it? Questions aside, she recalled the woman's face, the terror on it as the monsters tore into her, how helpless she was to their whims. She wished she had been wrong; she wished the king was right and that it had all been some vivid nightmare.

'The king is taking time to process this,' the arch-mage continued. 'It would be difficult for anyone to call this a coincidence but, out of respect for the hope the poor lady's husband still holds, we cannot dismiss the idea that she is still alive. Either way, I thought that you should know that evidence has begun to mount upon your words.'

Umishi was glad someone was starting to believe her.

The arch-mage sighed. 'Although our mission remains the same, I cannot help but feel we are going in the wrong direction. As I attempted to explain to His Majesty earlier, what happened to you last night should be our primary focus. The mage who attacked you – who perhaps took this girl's life – is still at large in Hanaswick; I have little doubt of that.'

'Him and his creatures,' Umishi said.

He raised his hand to his mouth thoughtfully, his words falling to a hushed tone. 'You said you saw creatures? That worries me. My father used to warn me of shadows built from the violent acts of men. Perhaps his warnings were not as fanciful as I thought, perhaps while you were there... I mean last night, you saw... my apologies, I am rambling, my thoughts scattered. The night has taken a lot out of me as well and, we have enough to think on without the inclusion of bedtime stories from my childhood.'

The arch-mage's mention of shadows was unsettling. There seemed to be something deeper behind those words than a random tale regurgitated by his subconscious. No, it was not the first time Leuvigild had allowed his mouth to run with his thoughts, and it was not the first time he had withheld significant information. His slips of the tongue were something to take note of.

'So we are placing merit in the theory that the palace was attacked in the night by a long dead mage along with a handful of monsters?' Lothrum sighed, stroking his whiskers. 'If I'm to believe what you're saying, that your mage is alive, what has he been doing for the last hundred years or so? Other than making plots to kill a sub-par merchant and kidnap a girl from a party? On the other hand, I suppose I don't know of a ghost that has done anything more meaningful. Perhaps I should be more impressed.'

Umishi ground her teeth at the mage's attempt at humour. At best, he was mocking her, at worst, he was belittling two needless deaths. No matter how many times mages demonstrated their inconsiderate nature, it seemed she was always taken by surprise.

'But, in all seriousness,' he continued, 'the only certainty we can draw from last night's events is that the inquisitor was attacked, and as for this girl, I dare say she may have found a little too much merriment in her drink and maybe the company of lordling other than her own. The girl will show up by nightfall; they always do.'

'So, you believe the Dhal-Llah are responsible for that poor boy's murder?' the arch-mage said 'I think not. Last month, I spoke to their latest prophet, for as long as civility would permit me, and from what I could gather advancing their magical knowledge seemed low on their list of priorities.'

'No,' the human growled. 'What I'm saying is, despite how sprightly I may seem, I can't jump to conclusions without all the facts. And, at least for the moment, the facts point to the Dhal-Llah, even after considering what happened last night.'

The arch-mage looked away from him and over to Umishi. 'Please, Ms Zaimor, as we make our way to Jimmarah, would you be so kind as to recount what exactly you remember from last night, in as much detail as possible? Anything you remember, no matter how fanciful it seems. I will not judge you; it is not my job to judge you,' the arch-mage begged with true sympathy. 'Perhaps together, with all the facts, we can discern whether it was a hallucination as my colleague believes... or something else.'

This was not the way mages spoke, not really. They didn't plead, or beg; they demanded. It was odd how this arch-mage valued her words over that of his colleague, his king. She tugged her hair and ran the arch-mage's question through her head again. There were no traps, no mockery – his words and tone had offered sincere interest. With puzzled reluctance, she began recounting all she could, from the time she had awoken in the Spinning Dagger to the mysterious silhouette in the ballroom window. They listened intently, ignoring her stammering over words. When finished, she looked to the window, not needing to see what their faces said.

They were passing through a small town, more a village, not unlike the ones on the mainland, with its little brick houses and thatched roofs. She could point out the stable, smithy, inn and the rest easily. It was getting dark and torches, the kind that were lit by fire rather than magic, were dotted along the road.

'Well, "insane" is the right bloody word for it.' Lothrum said. 'I have never heard such a tale outside the twisted ramblings of dribbling madmen, no offence. But then... there *is* something... something a layperson such as our inquisitor friend could not have fabricated.'

Leuvigild studied Umishi's face. Did he expect some kind of reaction from her in the wake of what the human said? She pulled at her hair again, ensuring he would not find one. He turned back to Lothrum.

'The blue mist,' he said to the mage.

'Yes, very interesting indeed,' Lothrum replied. 'That alone has made this trip worth getting up for. Of course, it could only be a Narsandles residual effect; that's what it sounds like at least, can't say for sure without having seen it myself, but the blue droplets, as the Walnorg put it, well, it's the only explanation.'

'It does sound very much like it,' the Nal-Tiran answered.

'I've only seen it once or twice in my lifetime, though

never in the quantities the mage hunter is describing: three or four drops at most, enough to fill a bottom of an egg cup, maybe. I didn't get chance to study the effect as much as I wanted thanks to our benevolent protectors, and their rulebooks.' He cocked an accusatory eyebrow at Umishi.

Umishi ignored the glance and addressed the arch-mage. 'What is a Narsandles effect?'

'And this, Leuvigild, is why the Order of Alpharus has no ri-'

'You are in danger of being rude to our guest,' the arch-mage snapped. It seemed as though the carriage rocked, and the air grew colder.

Lothrum folded his arms like a scolded child. 'My apologies, Inquisitor. As you're no doubt aware, the older us humans get, the less we think on the power our words may have. I meant no disrespect.'

She didn't care; she just wanted the answer to her question. She gave him a slight nod and hoped the conversation would start down a more productive path.

'The Narsandles residual effect refers to something that is left after a very complex spell has been cast,' the arch-mage began. 'By this I mean an existence changing spell, one that meddles with the reality of the world we live in. If reality were this cabin, then the spell I cast would be me installing another door, while the "blue mist" you described would be the... sawdust. Do you understand?'

The arch-mage's explanation was worrying to say the least. This was a new magic, a kind that Umishi had never encountered before. Was there a limit to that kind of power? How could it be countered? Her chest tightened as a thousand questions ravaged her mind. Was that what happened? Had the city been altered, its people changed into horrible beasts?

'Who is capable of such magic?' she asked drawing closer. There was a silence full of apprehension, a tension that slid into the carriage and suffocated those inside.

'Only once has a Narsandles residual effect been observed on this island,' Leuvigild whispered as though he was afraid of being overheard. 'I feel you can both hazard a guess as to when this happened and who was responsible.'

Umishi didn't need to hear the monster's title; it had been echoing in her mind for years. However, since setting foot upon this island the chant of it had been growing ever louder. At first it had been hidden, barely audible in the wind, then it had turned into a whisper, then a voice that taunted her when she was alone, but there, in that carriage, it began to *scream*. She turned to the window in an attempt to escape, but to no avail. Beyond the trees, in the darkness of her mind, she could see him waiting for her: the Mangler of Malhain.

'Forgive my scepticism, but to what end?' Lothrum queried, his head tilted to the side. 'I understand the power it would take to remove the Ward, and I understand that it might result in a Narsandles residual effect, but why would this mage do such a thing? If you believe the intention isn't war, isn't connected to the Dhal-Llah, why would this immortal magical genius commit a massive amount of skill and energy to a crime as lowly as murder? I do not mean to trivialise the death of that boy, but with such power it his command, with the very fabric of reality laid out before him, why kill a pedlar? Can either of you answer me that?'

They could not. With a glance outside, Umishi saw that they had reached a giant bridge and darkness had taken the skies.

'Ah, we have arrived,' Leuvigild said, joy seeping back into his voice. He knocked on the cabin wall to signal the driver to stop. 'This is the town of Jimmarah. We are still about a day and a half's ride from the fort itself but we shall freshen up here, enjoy the hospitality and rest until the morning.'

Umishi would have preferred riding through the night. However, she understood that the horses needed rest more than they did, and the feeling of dirt between her toes would be welcome.

'Hospitality?' Lothrum said. 'All I smell is fish.'

The night's chill wrapped around Umishi as she dropped onto wet, wooden planks. At a glance, it was obvious that Jimmarah was no ordinary town. Wooden roads led out into a complex network of bridges that spread over the lake, like a giant spider-web, connecting ship-shaped building as though they were cocoons. It was evident, from the washing lines strung up and the decorations arranged outside the doors, that people inhabited these ships, as homes, shops, inns. Umishi sensed movement from the cabin behind her as the arch-mage shifted.

'Quite tranquil, is it not?' he said, floating down from the carriage. 'I keep meaning to bring a canvas up here, try my hand at capturing the place. Shame, I keep telling myself that I am too busy. Then, of course, there is the question of which season. Can you picture the snow on the lake? Or would it be sweeter with sun skipping across its surface?'

Umishi didn't care; her mind preoccupied with translating the buildings into something she recognised. From their distinct shapes, she had identified two inns and a town hall. She also noted that the lamps, as with the town they passed through, were the more familiar sort, lit with flame caged in iron and glass. She watched the wooden roads for signs of life, for any kind of movement, and once or twice spotted the odd cat stalking the shadows. Leuvigild slipped in front of her and she tugged at her hair.

'I am not surprised you do not recognise it. I guess, back in your day, this would have been a trading post of some sort, with ships used to transport people, goods, beasts, all manner of things across this lake. It was quite lucrative in the days of the empire, or so I am told.'

Umishi tried to picture it.

'Of course, when the great bridge was made it spelled doom for their trade. But, as is often the case with humans, they adapted, turning their boats into buildings and transforming the bridge into a fishing village. Remarkable.'

Umishi had not asked for a history lesson; it didn't matter why the place was built nor who built it. The only thing she required from it was a bed to rest in until morning, until they had the daylight to move on to the fort. There was a reason the Dhal-Llah were waiting, were not attacking, and that reason had to be the spell – the King's Ward – not being completely removed. That would imply that the wizard responsible could be there, and she could stop him, putting an end to whatever works he was weaving.

'Are you not joining us, Erik?' the arch-mage called to

the mage with them.

With barely the effort required, the old human peeked his head from the cabin door. 'I think I shall be spending the night in here, if you don't mind, but you two feel free to experience all the... flavour this backwater town and its zoo of local bumpkins has to offer. I fear I don't have the taste for country life, not when I can smell it from in here.'

The arch-mage gave Umishi a knowing grin before pressing onwards. She followed, her eye jumping from window to window, distrusting this strange town. Light and noise resonated from each of the peculiar homes, offering a friendly warmth to passers-by, a glow Umishi remained suspicious of. By turning left at each crossroad they encountered, they reached the first inn, 'Ethel' the sign read. Umishi cocked her head at the plaque for a moment, before concluding it must have taken its name prior to being repurposed from a trade ship.

The jubilant singing and laughter they heard from outside fell away as they entered. Grizzled patrons turned to take the measure of their new guests. Much to Umishi's rather pleasant surprise, most of their focus seemed to fall upon the arch-mage. It swiftly abandoned her, however, as realisation took its place. It was obvious his visage would be granted more attention than her sorry form; after all, he was much kinder to the eye, with his golden hair and divine appearance making him almost glow in the drab, depressing-looking place. As more eyes fell upon him, Umishi took the opportunity to melt into the shadows. She slipped against the wall closest to her and followed it into a corner. Leuvigild seemed oblivious to the attention he was garnering. She watched his eyes dart back and forth, absorbing every fraction of the tavern's interior with the excitement of a child in a toy shop.

The inn's interior resembled a ship's hull, with little effort made to disguise its origins. There were makeshift tables and chairs scattered across the decking, with no discernible pattern. Under their feet lay tattered mats of some colour Umishi didn't know the name of. The place was lit by oil lanterns dotted on tables and nailed to the ceiling, casting gloomy shadows over bedraggled human drinkers. She sat on a stool made from a lock box and coiled her legs under herself. Her eye joined the direction of every other there as the Nal-Tiran approached the bar. She found a grin etching up one side of her face as the arch-mage spoke to the gruff looking innkeeper in his soft tones and scholarly vocabulary. It was obvious that the poor human was having a hard time understanding all the big words the arch-mage said.

As time drifted past the townsfolk seemed to grow bored with the new comers and turned their attention to other distractions: mainly the bottoms of their tankards. Umishi tapped her fingers on her knee without rhythm. Would it be possible for her to head to the fort alone? While it was true that the horses were spent, it couldn't be far from its namesake town. Her tapping grew. She did not need the arch-mage, or his agent, to interfere. She closed her eye to steady her breathing. They were wasting time. At any moment, the Mangler could perform his spell, allowing the Dhal-Llah to begin their attack, then leave, with murder and suffering in his wake. Umishi swore she would put an end to it, that the horrors she had experienced in Malhain would not happen again, and if he, or whoever, tried, she would break them, regardless of law or privilege.

Leuvigild placed down two tankards with a thud, breaking Umishi's trail of thought and returning her to the water-washed tavern. She took a breath of ale-imbued air and wiped her mouth.

'The locals call this Harpy's Tickle, apparently,' the arch-mage declared as he sat. 'It is a local beverage, they say, engineered right here. It will make a change from the wine and port of the palace, I should think.'

Umishi took a swig of the blackish-brown liquid. She allowed it to wet her lips and roll under her tongue. There was nothing unique about the drink; she had tasted it many times, in many different taverns, under many different names. Whether it was called the Harpy's Tickle or Dwarven Snot, it was the same stuff: rum and peach. Regardless, the drink was still good.

'How was your trip here?' The arch-mage began. 'I hear the waters can-'

'Get a bit choppy this time of year?' Umishi finished with a smile at the banality of it.

'Quite,' he laughed. 'I am guessing that someone has regaled you with this line before. Yes, the oceans beyond this island have become somewhat of a fairy tale, echoing from the lips of child and adult alike. Harsh storms and violent waves are pretty much all we know of it. No one has left Domvalkia since the fall of the empire.'

'So your people are trapped, then?'

'No, Ms Zaimor, not at all. Anyone is free to leave

whenever they want. There is... an apprehension when it comes to abandoning the protection of the Ward. I should like to, one day, see the seas, explore the continent, experience the things that this island cannot offer. But that is some time away yet. First, I would have to train someone to take my place as caretaker of the Ward. I thought I had someone in Erik, but human lives are so fleeting...'

'Wards caretaker?' she asked, cocking her head.

'Yes. The Ward needs a designated caster to uphold it. While I did not cast the spell, heaven knows I lack that kind of ability, it was passed to me as an architect might pass on a house. I weave words to maintain it, make sure it does not fall into disrepair. Alas, this means that I am unable to leave this island: the Ward would fail.' He offered a sad smile. 'But it is a duty I take pride in, much like you, I have no doubt.'

The so called indestructible Ward had a weakness, and there it was, sitting in front of her. She fell back into her chair. The existence of this role brought forth numerous questions. If the Ward had to be maintained, was it possible that it could be done wrongly, in a way that would leave people out of its protection? If so... could mistakes be made intentionally? She took another sip from her mug as she mulled over the possibility.

'Which brings me to a question I have been meaning to ask since our first meeting,' Leuvigild began while examining the contents of his tankard. 'I would like to hear your opinion regarding what we are doing here on Domvalkia, what you think of the King's Ward.'

She closed her eye and savoured the refreshing taste of the so-called Harpy's Tickle, trying to get as much enjoyment as she could before answering the question. 'You're sure you want me to answer?'

The arch-mage smiled at her response, 'I did not ask you to flatter our lands with gushing praise, Ms Zaimor. I am curious as to your opinion. I doubt you would be in your line of work if you did not question the benevolence or honesty of every spell you encountered. On the other hand, you have seen what the kingdom was, witnessed the brutality of the empire that reigned before the Ward was erected.'

She bit the inside of her cheek as her body tensed. The Ward was another means of removing control from the masses. Although she was no advocate for any method, it was Fendamor's that unsettled her most. The empire had used the sword and the fear of death to rule its subjects, but the Ward was something far more sinister. It was an invisible, ever present force that invaded the thoughts of those under it to decide how they were able to interact with the world. How did it decide what a violent act was? What if the spell somehow went wrong? Could it stop someone from eating or drinking? The threat of being put to the sword was terrifying but at least there was a mind behind the blade and an understandable logic to guide it.

The tavern door flew open and the clanging of armour rebounded through the repurposed ship. Three Fendamor guards stood in the doorway, drawing the attention of the patrons with their cold demeanour. 'Ladies and gentlemen,' the first boomed, 'we apologise for the disruption, but we require that you leave the premises and follow a guard or official to the western side of the village.'

The men and women erupted into a choir of disgruntled

mumbling. Chairs and tables scraped against the floor as some of the drinkers obeyed. Umishi shared a glance with the equally puzzled arch-mage. His eyebrows tilted down as his breathing slowed and deepened.

'Ladies and gentlemen,' the guard continued, 'we recommend that you leave in an orderly and prompt manner. The Dhal-Llah have begun their approach, so Jimmarah is being evacuated. This is an emergency, and your cooperation would be greatly appreciated.'

Confusion and chaos seeped into the room, washing over those closest to the exit at first, since they were close enough to hear what was happening outside. However, with each person it overtook, it grew more powerful. The murmuring escalated into rushed chatter, then yelling. Furniture scraped as it was dragged and then pushed over. As the humans made their way to the exit, the arch-mage stood.

'Under whose authority?' he demanded, voice raised with a force that commanded everyone to be still. 'I am Arch-mage Leuvigild, head of the Court of Wizards, Caretaker of the Ward, High Lord of Hanaswick and First Adviser to His Royal Majesty King Edwin. I demand to know by whose authority you carry out this evacuation!'

Surprise and awe locked Umishi in stunned silence. Within a heartbeat the arch-mage had transformed from the meek man she had spent the day travelling with, into this goliath of power and authority. He spun around launching his cold gaze at the poor fools who dared to carry out orders he did not sanction.

The guards recoiled, each offering the others nervous glances.

'The order was given by General Vorx, my lord,' one said. 'He received a report from the fort under an hour ago. There is an army, my lord. The report said that there are hundreds of them.'

'Where is this Vorx?' Leuvigild snarled as he circled the guard, his blond hair having fallen loose and wild, casting menacing shadows over his statuesque face. 'Take me to him so that I may nip this act of recklessness in the bud before it gets too far out of hand.'

From beyond the open door, behind the gawking guards, a roar tore through the ship with a volume and rage of some savage and unimaginably large beast. Whatever the creature was, its voice alone was powerful enough to reanimate the tavern into the sailing ship it had once been. Wood cracked as the ship rocked in the wake of the explosions outside. Screams soon joined the chaos and Umishi's hand fell to her blade.

'No!' the arch-mage shouted as he flew out the door, the guards following, clueless as to what else to do. They left Umishi alone.

Sliding from her seat, her heart racing as her fingers tightened around her dagger. Her mind found the Mangler. No, it was impossible. There was no reason to suspect magic responsible for what rocked the ship, no reason to suspect him. Even so, his silhouette crawled out from the depths of her mind, infesting every shadow, every sound in an announcement of his presence. Another bang cried to her from outside, summoning her. Was it him? Was he in the village, waiting for her? She closed her eye and stole a breath before exiting the tavern.

Outside, peasants and sailors alike fled westwards. Some of them held bundles of belongings, while others wore little more than nightshirts, running barefoot in desperation. One of the bridges had been destroyed, with only a ledge of splintered wood and the smell of fire as a clue as to whatever had happened. In front of her, the arch-mage argued with the guards.

'... taken a band of militia to the fort,' one of the guards was saying, 'to see if they can be of help.'

The arch-mage turned away from them, pinching the bridge of his nose. With his eyes closed, he faced Umishi. 'It would seem we have a problem, Ms Zaimor.' He gestured to the guards. 'This fool, Vorx, has placed us in quite a situation. The excitable child believes that we are being invaded and has taken it upon himself to command that the bridges be destroyed, turning the lives of all those who live here upside-down.' He looked over at the fleeing people. 'I need to stay here and oversee the evacuation, make sure every soul is safe before this whole village is destroyed. I will send you and Erik ahead to...'

Something twisted in Umishi's gut, forcing her attention away from Leuvigild. A coldness began spreading from her chest, through her veins, into the rest of her body. She fell to her knees.

'Ms Zaimor?' the arch-mage called out, but the sound was muffled, as though down to her though an impossibly deep well. Something moved behind him, then again, in the corner of her eye.

'Ms Zaimor?' he yelled again, in panic.

She was surrounded. With unnatural movements, they

stalked her peripheral vision. She blinked and saw them. The shadows were alive, launching at her with black fingers. They were everywhere, oozing from every ship, building and object. There was no escape. The darkness had devoured most of the village and approached her in a wave. She covered her head as the nothingness rolled over her.

EIGHT

RENDERBRIM

Her eye closed tight, and her body tighter, an almost tangible silence coiled around Umishi, numbing her to the world. Her senses had failed, turned their back on her. Even after the years of training they were useless, they told her nothing, not what had happened, nor if she was even still alive. She was forced to open her eye, forced to see what had become of her, what had become of the world after the darkness had washed over it.

She found the planks of wood – the floor of Jimmarah – damp, encased in shadow, but still there. She was still there, she was alive.

Umishi lifted her head; she hadn't moved from outside the tavern. With shaking arms, she pushed herself, acutely aware that Leuvigild and the guards were missing, vanished. It was not just them, but the villagers, the sailors; they were all gone, taking all their yelling and chaos with them. There was something else since opening her eye: the air had turned stale, and the darkness had grown thick, into a shroud denser than any night.

She wanted to scream, as a burning anguish built up inside her, crushing her throat. Her heart raced as she held her breath to keep her cry from escaping. It was not the time for such things. It had happened again – whatever happened the night of the ball, the night the mages attacked – had happened again. With a deep breath, she swallowed her apprehension and forced herself to focus. No one had assaulted her, not this time, not physically; whatever it was had been triggered by something else. Her mind found the Harpy's Tickle, the drink she had so happily washed down. The arch-mage had previously suggested a poison could be responsible for the situation she had found herself in. If that was the case then there was no better or easier way to poison someone than to hand the poison to them and ask them to drink it. If it was a dream, however, it was the most vivid one she had ever experienced.

Above Umishi, frozen in the icy sky, a pale moon loomed over her. Despite its unsympathetic gaze it granted her light with which to scan her surroundings.

A detail caught her attention; something that gave merit to her being in a dream. The bridge that had been destroyed was there, fully restored as though the events of a few moments ago had never happened. She took a step towards it.

If this was a dream or some hallucination, then nothing could be done about it, other than lasting it out and waking up. However, if this was a mage's work, he'd have to be close. No mage could stray too far from the spell they were holding, excluding the Ward, it would seem. Dream or not, there was no point in sitting idle and, if there was a mage to hunt, she would hunt him to free this village of his magic.

She held firm and breathed in the stagnant air that lingered around her as she consulted her instincts and prodded at her knowledge. Where would he be? That was the mystery that had to be unravelled. Where would *she* be were she orchestrating an attack on a town? On the front lines, directing the flow of battle as one wave crashed against the other, but mages were cowards who thought themselves better than those who fought for them, believing themselves almost divine. She opened her eye. He would be high up, somewhere he could survey the town from a safe distance and direct his monsters. Searching her memory, Umishi placed herself at the summit of each of the town's buildings. The temple would be the place she would use, that *he* would use.

The lamps tried to fight the darkness, struggling to aid her in seeing the way back. The buildings loomed over Umishi as though remembering what they once were and, at any moment, would come crashing down. Her heart stopped when something wet hit her cheek, then again on her hand. Tiny blue dots floated in the air in front of her. She took a step back; the drifting liquid came from behind the corner of the building beside her, no doubt gathering into a mist beyond. To avoid confrontation with the creatures she would not walk blindly into the mist: she would climb. Turning to the building, she took note of its construction. It was wood, of course, old wood, she leapt toward it, digging her claws into the welcoming oak.

Climbing was second nature to her, easier than walking the human way, on the flat. The smell of the wood reminded her of the treetops she had once called home. She loved the feel of it on the tips of her fingers, the fibres folding before her weight. Thomas had loved to climb. He would have loved the village she grew up in. He would have still been alive had they stayed, had they refused to go to Domvalkia. As she reached the top, the memories of her village crumbled, with blue, gaseous tendrils and the chilling shrieks of reality reaching up for her. She was safe, at least for the moment. It seemed neither the mist nor the monsters within could claw their way to the roof.

From her vantage point, Umishi took the measure of her surroundings. The mist seemed to be rolling in, flooding the town, but not in from the lake, as she would have expected. It seeped from the wooden floors in the form of massive blisters, then exploded into spore-like clouds. Her shoulders tightened to resist the chill running down her spine. She had to find this mage, had to find a way to push back the darkness so that everyone could return.

Ahead, not far from where she was standing, a building jutted free from the surface of the mist, its outstretched masts buckled and broken. In its crow's nest there was the symbol of some human god whose name was likely long and unpronounceable. From there, from that height, the mage would have a complete view of the town.

Using the masts as tree branches, Umishi climbed from one building to the next, without having to venture into the dangerous streets below. As she made her way to the third house, however, she felt the medallion around her neck thump at her chest, her heart pounding in response. She froze as she waited for an answer. The talisman thumped again and began to hum and crackle with the sound of magic.

She pulled it from the neck of her tunic, held it still and listened. There was sound coming from beneath her, within the building she was standing on, not the hissing or screaming she had gotten used to in this darkness, but laughter: someone was laughing.

Lowering herself from the roof to the building's balcony, Umishi carefully slid in through an open window. Inside, it was as though she had been transported to a different world. A blinding light lured her towards a wooden staircase, stealing from her all memories of shadow. She took a breath, drawing her larger dagger from its sheath, then tackled the stairs with stealth and trepidation. At the bottom, she found the light's source.

An open door lay at the end of a corridor. Through its slim gap, Umishi could make out shelves and a well-stocked wine rack. A kitchen? A storeroom? She wet her lips as she snuck forward. A figure stepped into view, the silhouette from the ballroom's window, the black feathers of his robe shimmering in the candle light. He was hardly the vision out of nightmare she was expecting. He was frail, his skin sickly and pale. He was not the Mangler of Malhain; he couldn't be. He was too young, lacked so much of the presence and power that the Mangler exuded. Preoccupied with picking his beverage of choice, he hadn't noticed her. Once he had chosen a bottle, he turned and moved back into the room. Umishi followed, the runes on her blade glowing.

She entered a world of madness: a lunatic's parody of a royal banquet. A table stretched the length of the room, covered in broken glass and spilt cuisine. Instead of guests, two misshapen beasts lurched over the table, gorging themselves like starvation-crazed wolves.

In that instant, the feather-robed human turned to her.

'Who are you? How are you back? Are you his? Did he send you? You must be! He must have! How else could you... could you be here?' The robed human choked on his questions. Using the table to steady himself, he approached her, face twisted into an expression between terror and joy. His eyes were open inhumanly wide; he was not the enemy she had been expecting at all.

Still, Umishi stepped back and fell into a defensive stance, bringing up her knife to guard her chest. If he took another step towards her, she would be ready to face his advance with aggression.

The stranger staggered away, showing her his open palms. The creatures raised their heads, interested in the interaction.

'Please, please,' he said, panicked. 'I didn't mean to... I... I was rude, forgive me, I am sorry.' With a flutter of feathers the strange creature spun, running back to his seat with movements mimicking a jester. 'We will start again, yes? So? I... I am returning to my chair, ready to enjoy a fine glass of the red tickle, oblivious to the fact anything strange or out of the ordinary will happen. Then... then, yes! Then, you walk through the door... not in my mind, but real, and there!' He gestured to her.

The human's mannerisms were eccentric and unpredictable. Without knowing how to respond, Umishi lifted an eyebrow and watched.

'Hello, my dear,' he said, voice warm as he stood with outstretched arms. 'I am Ashendale Renderbrim. I welcome you, humbly, to my holiday home! Please, please come in. Sit, be welcome! Let me introduce you to the others.' With unreserved excitement and open arms, he presented the creatures at the table. 'To the left here we have Mr Spooky, and on the right Peewee. Peewee has just joined us, so we gather here to celebrate his good health!'

Umishi ignored the madness that was spilling from the human's lips. 'Undo what you've done,' she demanded, striding towards him, her dagger ready. Mangler of Malhain or not, it was this madman whose silhouette had haunted the window back at the palace of Hanaswick. It was clear that, even if he was not fully responsible, than he at least had a hand in what was going on.

'Undo what I have done?' he said, pressing his fingers to his lips. 'I apologise, but I cannot uncook this beef or unpour this wine. But here!' he burst, spinning back to his chair. 'Eat, drink; get absorbed in the rich, diverse flavours of our feast; become as intoxicated as one could possibly get through our banquet of liqueurs! We are not here to be in dour spirits! The very point of this feast is to help us forget the pain that brought us here. Come, help yourself, there is plenty to go around!' With this, he swept his hand over the table. The beasts shifted their focus for a moment, cocking their heads at his grand gesture before returning to... whatever it was they were eating. 'I am rather eager to learn your story. Where did you come from? What brings you here? How did you get here?' he asked, filling his goblet with red wine. 'Did you come from the capital? Did you come here with others? Were you on the island before or after you got here? You really must tell me everything, my dear; between mouthfuls of course, I do not want you choking.' He took a large gulp from his cup.

Umishi's body shook as confusion's ice cold fingers traced her nerves. The fool was talking nonsense. Shifting her grip on her dagger, the blade's red runes glittered and shone. 'Take away the darkness, bring everyone back and we'll talk,' she demanded, trying to gain some control over the situation.

'Take away the... the darkness?' He said. 'Bring everyone.... Oh no, no my dear, oh no, you're not... No one has gone anywhere, well not really. They came, they went. Not you though, I guess they left you, and me, of course they left me, I've been alone here for a while now... well, I have the Kalsakian, I suppose, they're not big talkers, though.' He pointed his tankard at the beasts. 'They're more likely to gnaw their own hands off than engage in anything close to stimulating conversation; not like you.'

'Left you.' The words echoed in Umishi's head. Her heart raced as she tried to swallow the implications of those two words. 'Left me?' she muttered, not really wanting to hear a response.

'Oh, my dear girl, it... It shouldn't be me who... I mean not here, not like this... I am so sorry, I truly am. You're foreign, I take it? It has been quite a while since I've seen a Walnorg... well, since I've seen anyone, I suppose, but your kin especially.' His tone turned sombre. 'Where do I start? Have they even told you about the Kings Ward yet? How it works?'

Her guard slipped away as she was lured into conversation, was this his plan all along? Was he trying to distract her? Trick her?

'I…' she tried, shifting her stance.

'They haven't, not really. I can tell.' He licked his lips before he began to explain. 'Hanaswick is a city run by monsters, who enjoy using information to entangle the ill-informed in all manner of cruel and spiky traps! The worst of them is the one responsible for you and me being here and now. He, you see there is… was… *is* an arrogant mage who wanted to conquer all, whether land, men, women, life or death.'

'I don't understand,' Umishi said.

'He created a spell that would be placed upon all his subjects. Through this spell, the little darlings were granted a hiding place from harm, a place to dodge death's attention, the place where you and I, my dear, now find ourselves. He called this spell "the King's Ward".'

Umishi felt a shiver run through her.

'When under the effect of the Ward, it… well… kind of senses if that person is going to be stabbed in the belly or whacked over the head and, for the brief moment that the violent act threatens them… well, it seems to them, and all the other on-looking fools, that the sword that was about to slash them just goes through them as though they are ghosts or air.'

'I know that,' Umishi said.

'But , but no, no that does not happen at all, my dear, not at all. In truth, they are brought here, only for a moment, a blink of an eye, until the danger passes. They are brought to the safety of this hiding place. Then they are, well, normally, pulled back to the original plane by a kind of magical tether, with such speed that they are left none the wiser that they were ever even here. However, this does not seem to have worked for us. No tether pulled us.'

At last, things were starting to make sense to her: the men in the bar, her captors. She understood why her blade never touched them, the instant it would have, they were taken here by the King's Ward. But what did it mean for her, in this moment?

'How do I get back?' Umishi asked.

All joy left Renderbrim's already drawn face. 'I am sorry, my dear, I don't yet have the answer. I... I've been working on it, thinking about it, maybe I'll have it soon, maybe? It would take a far greater mage than I, I'm afraid.' He quickly turned to one of the monsters at his side, a Kalsakian, he'd called it. 'That being said, your brother managed it, didn't he?' The creature gazed back at him, confused, with drool dripping from its mouth. 'Yes, yes, he did, tied him to a tiny thread, watched as he was whisked up and away. It's happened once or twice now, not sure what shape they're in when they reach the other plane... if they're alive or not.'

No way out? The pace of her heart quickened. This wasn't true, couldn't be true. Isolation had broken the mind of this poor fool. Were his words truth or fallacy? A tempest of thoughts all grappled for Umishi's attention. The night at the Spinning Dagger, and the mages there, had cursed her to this world, trapped her here, but why? With shaking hands Umishi took a large sip from the wine. She closed her eye and focused on wrestling her mind from panic. The idea of being trapped in this place, this realm, was a bottomless pit, one that if she explored it too deeply she would be lost forever. She took one breath, then another; she had to focus on a solution.

She took another sip and sank into her chair. There had to be a way out. She had already escaped once. What had been different in that ballroom? What condition had been met there and not here? Something had happened which had pulled her back from this... shadow plane, but what? There was music, dancing, laughter, love... maybe it was love? There were lots of stories about love being a sort of magic, weren't there? Could that, ridiculous as it sounded, be the answer? After all, the whole situation was ridiculous, so why not?

Her clawed hands massaged her brow, attempting to get her mind to work, lamenting over how little knowledge she had in the field of magic, how even a small amount might have made her task easier.

'You said you know who did this,' she whispered. 'You said "arrogant mage". Is it the Mangler of Malhain? Is he... have you seen him?'

'Mangler of Malhain? No, it's Fendamor you seek,' Renderbrim answered. 'Fendamor trapped me here, and he's the only one with the knowledge to trap *you* here.'

There was one problem with that, for Umishi. 'Isn't he dead?'

'Dead?' the madman snarled, his voice darkening. 'He's not dead! He's everywhere! All around us, in the faces of every fool on this island! He's not dead; I would know if he were. Each time his heart beats it feels like a spear is rammed into my ear! You know, all this talk about that black-hearted bastard and his poisonous Ward has spoiled my celebration.

I am really in no mood for it now.' He pushed himself out of his chair. 'So, what of you, my dear? Perhaps we can figure out why, or how, you got here; why *he* would want you here. What do you last remember? What were you last doing?'

After his outburst, her hand had slipped to her daggers. 'I was... I was heading to the fort.' Umishi's floundering tongue stumbled, did she sound as mad to his ears as he did to hers? Closing her eye, she continued, 'The Dhal-Llah were attacking and-'

'No! Liar! You're a liar!' he yelled, whipping his feathered robe into a wild frenzy, as he jumped from his chair. 'They are not attacking. Why would they attack? I made it clear when they had to attack, when they could attack! Years, I spent *years* making it clear! You, you...' Suddenly his frantic motions calmed, and his hands began caressing his face over his eyes.

His change in tone forced Umishi to her feet, her blades flashing to her hands.

'I'm sorry to have startled you,' Renderbrim said then, once more showing her his palms as his jade eyes found her blade. 'I get confused sometimes, my mind fuzzy. After all, why would you lie? You wouldn't lie to me, no, not you, my dear. You don't know, didn't know. I am sorry, so truly sorry, my dear, sorry, please forgive me. I must go, I must leave, I have to. I can't be late if I'm going to bring down the Ward.'

Her head buzzed and screamed as anger replaced pity. She had been right: he was the source, and the Dhal-Llah were readying to make war. He wasn't trapped here; he'd lied to her! He had to know a way out; he was aiding the Dhal-

Llah, communicating with them, giving them orders.

'You're bringing down the Ward?' she demanded.

'Yes, my dear, Fendamor has to be held accountable for what he has done to me, to you, to everyone on this island. He has poisoned it with a vile corruption that can't be allowed to spread. Fear not, I have set events in motion that will bring justice down upon him, upon them all. I'd best not be late; the Dhal-Llah will be so discouraged if they start without me. The fort would be reinforced. Perhaps men have been switched I cannot afford... they would be disappointed, so disappointed.'

Umishi's heart battered her ribs as she saw that he was the monster they had been searching for: not the Mangler, but this creature. Her mind buzzed as it overloaded. She had to stop him, before he reached the fort or... she lunged for him, blade darting for his shoulder. She wasn't fast enough. Her large dagger skimmed a feather on his cloak before it was intercepted by a wall of flesh. One of the creatures had thrown itself between them, shielding its master. The creature made a pained clicking sound as the sharp edge penetrated its oozing skin.

'I see I have upset you. I am sorry; hopefully my other guests can make up for it? They cannot dance as well as an Order-trained inquisitor such as you, but I am sure they can put on a rather entertaining show.'

Umishi took a moment to recover from her failed attack; a moment too long. Before she could regain her senses, the creature threw its arm at her with an unforgiving ferocity. As she fell she caught a glimpse of the cloaked madman stepping out onto Jimmarah's wooden streets.

NINE

Between the Trees

The beast ignored the wound in its shoulder and extended to its full height. Umishi scrambled to her feet and took a moment to fall back. It asserted itself in a way that none of the others had, rising on legs that seemed stable and powerful. From its intimidating height, the monster's cold, hollow eyes bore down at her as though to make her understand how small she was; to remind her that this was not her world. It jerked its upper body in a grotesque way that made its bones scream in defiance, twisting itself into a position to pounce.

Umishi was ready. She spun from the Kalsakian's mass, then slashed at its grasping claw as it missed her. The feel of steel against bone made her grin. The creature fell forward, its head crashing against her former seat.

Umishi's ear twitched as a clatter of porcelain on wood broke her focus. The other creature was moving. She faced the room. The first monster was struggling with its own limbs, twisting them into hideous shapes and causing them to crack angrily with each movement they were forced to make. The second, this 'Pewee', having been distracted by its food until now, raised its head. Umishi's stomach turned as she saw that its long, skeletal arms were fused to its face, covering where its eyes sockets should have been. It fell from its seat and screamed with all the hate it could muster.

The fight was pointless, a distraction. The mage was getting away, heading to the fort. She couldn't lose him. A myriad of thoughts flooded Umishi's mind. His ramblings about Fendamor, the threads, Pewee's good health and how discouraged the Dhal-Llah would be; all of them competed for her attention, distracting her from combat. Taking a deep breath, she fought to regain focus.

With her larger dagger extended between her and the creature, 'Mr Spooky', Umishi reached for the door handle. The monster faced her as she slipped from the building.

The landscape outside remained unchanged. A bleak, all-consuming darkness bore down on her from every direction, with hints of the blue mist weaving through the shadows. Despite the keenness of her eye, Umishi could barely make anything out in the unyielding black. The streetlamps were too weak to aid her. Fort Jimmarah was to the east, at least that much was certain. In the sky the moon gave her a sense of direction, pointing its cold light northwards.

An explosion of sound shook the door, causing Umishi's heart to lurch against her ribs. The whole world seemed to shudder as splinters erupted from the wood. The Kalsakian were not giving up; the world trembled at the force of their unchallenged screams. There was only one way to stop their pursuit of her. The door buckled as one of the monsters pounded it again. There was not much time.

With nimble movements, Umishi climbed the door frame and readied herself for an ambush. Within two more heartbeats the beast smashed through. The smell of blood invaded Umishi's nostril and its twisted form insulted her eye. It hissed in confusion, swinging its head back and forth, it did not expect her to attack from above.

Dropping, Umishi pressed her full weight on to her larger dagger, plunging it deep into the creature's back, forcing a bloody stream to bubble up through its black tar-like skin. It screamed in pain and surprise as she hooked her smaller blade into the side of its neck. It flung its spidery arm at her, attempting to pull her away. As she rotated the smaller blade arteries burst and tendons twisted. The arm fell back to the ground as its whole body collapsed. It cried out again as she gave her blade another twist for good measure. Through the blade at its back, she felt its breath; it gasped once, then twice more, before it fell still. She jumped from the creature's body and tore a part of her sleeve from her tunic, wiping her blades with the torn cloth before returning them to their sheathes.

Umishi allowed her body to relax for a time before making her way back on to the building's roof. As she climbed, the other monster screamed. There was a moment where she felt a twinge of pity pull at her chest for the poor creature blind and trapped within its own twisted body, but it was only a moment.

From the rooftop, the way was clear. She would use the masts and rigging as she had originally planned; the ground was unsafe. The mists licked and clawed at the buildings on her route and the beams reached out to her like branches as she jumped from one to another.

Above her, the skies remained frozen, a reminder that this wasn't her world, that she was not meant to be here, that she was as trapped as the moon and the clouds in the sky. Was she to become as mad as the mage and hold parties for the ghoulish monsters? No, she pushed the thoughts to the back of her mind, she would not succumb to despair.

She tried to focus on jumping, climbing, but, with each leap, each glance at the sky, dread and fear clawed at her heart There was no escape, no way out of this world of shadow. She would be lost, left to wander aimlessly in an unending nightmare. The thought grappled with her lungs, almost pushing her from the rigging and onto the ground below. Shaking her head, Umishi fought to refocus, to address a new, more urgent problem: she had run out of masts.

The structures ahead started to look less like the ships she had been navigating and more like the buildings of more common human villages. The gap between the one she was standing on and the next was easy enough to jump across, but beyond that she would have to find another way. Below her, wooden walkways fell to grey waters. Swimming was not an option, not when there was no clear sign of the shore and no way to guarantee that water worked the same way here as it did back... back where everyone else was. She would go through as many of the houses as she could, instead. The narrow corridors would provide her with cover and decrease the possibility of an ambush.

As Umishi's feet found the wooden walkways, it seemed as though the mist had lost her. Her path to the next house seemed clear, so she ran to its door and rammed her shoulder against it. The wood was weak, rotten through from years of damp air; it did not take too much persuasion to open. Within, her fingers fell to the hilt of her larger dagger. Although it seemed the Kalsakian stuck close to the blue mists, it would be foolish to throw caution to the wind.

The house was like the others: dingy and small. She paused to regain her breath, but there was no time to linger; time was a resource Umishi could ill-afford to waste, one she had little doubt Renderbrim was taking full advantage of. How had this happened? How could she have *let* this happen? How could she have let him escape so easily? His distraction with the Kalsakian shouldn't have delayed her so. Many mages had tried to confuse her with another target, a servant or some kind of hireling. She had never before allowed it to crack her focus. She moved through the building. Her lack of focus was unacceptable, even with the insane situation being laid in front of her. She pushed herself through the door and back into the streets, the silence and the dark. How had she let him get away?

The way was clear; she could see no signs of the mist or the creatures it concealed. She climbed atop another building and, from there, the edge of the town revealed itself. With her goal in sight, Umishi wasted no time in reaching it. She had grown weary of the sight of water and ships, weary in general, truth be told. Her muscles ached, and each joint seemed to plague her every movement with painful resistance. She regretted not taking the opportunity to rest in the carriage. Images of Lothrum sleeping darted across her mind. Regardless, she had reached the town's end.

With a few more steps her feet finally found the wooden planking and, before her, lay grass and a dirt road. Umishi bounded off the wooden decking, eager to dig her toes into soil and feel the glorious sensation of dirt under her feet. In time, it would become just as tedious as the wood but, in that moment, she focused on enjoying the sensation.

The trees awaited her, leaning forward in welcome, but the shadows that lingered beneath their outstretched branches suggested their motives were not benign. She trod cautiously under their massive forms. The trees were as alien and monstrous as the Kalsakian. They were not those of her homelands; the trees of home used to dance and sing in the winds, nurturing all manner of life under glowing green leaves. These, though, nurtured only darkness, allowing nothing but shadows to grow. They were so silent, so still, that they could have been mistaken for stone. Umishi did not want to linger. She marched along the dirt road that led from Jimmarah, a road that would guide her to the fort.

She must have walked for hours, yet the sky never changed, and the moon rarely had a chance to offer her its light. It was obscured by endless nests of branches that conspired to hide its pale face, depriving her of even that hollow comfort. Her legs were begging her to stop and her eye was beginning to join their protests. In this world, day never came, and night never ended. It was a world where shadows made their permanent home, where neither light nor hope belonged.

A tree vanished, though it had been ahead of her only moments ago. Umishi rubbed her eye. Perhaps it had always been a stump? She hadn't truly been paying too much attention to her surroundings. Upon approaching she touched its flat surface: it was ridged and full of splinters. In the time it had taken for her to blink, and without a sound, the tree had been cut down and removed. Around the stump, the earth was freshly pressed, as if the tree were laying on its side but invisible. Umishi's hand hovered above the flat greenery to see if it was there, but it was not. Perhaps exhaustion had confused her, prevented her from thinking straight? Perhaps she had somehow fallen asleep without noticing, and this was all some mad dream inspired by the nightmare she found herself living?

As the possibilities swam through Umishi's head, another tree vanished and, this time, she was sure. One after another disappeared, each leaving marks as though it had fallen. Was the forest haunted? Was there a new, invisible enemy? Not wanting to wait for an answer, she ran, and the ground beneath her started to change shape; Umishi fell, tripping on the changing terrain. The ground looked as though it was being ravaged by an unseen force pounding massive indentations into the earth, like something huge and heavy being dragged along the road. She scrambled to her feet and darted off the dirt trail, into the bushes. The bush crumpled as another tree next to her vanished. Creatures screamed in the distance. The only option was to run.

As Umishi broke through the trees and into a clearing a massive stone wall came into view. She drew a breath as her eye was drawn to the wedge-shaped structure that lay under its shadow – a fortress with a single cone tipped tower – the fortress of Jimmarah. With her goal in sight, she sprinted to the fortress doors. They were closed; of course they were closed. There had to be another way in, there had to be. More screams echoed from the forest behind her. She would climb. The windows of the tower were a considerable height above her, but there was no other option. Adjusting her tunic, Umishi began her assent.

Pain ran through her exhausted limbs as she scaled the stone wall. The window seemed so far out of her reach, a distance that would have seemed easier early that morning. How long had she been here in this world? It felt like days. Her aching fingers dug into the mortar and pulled her body forward. Why, why was she doing this? What did she expect to find when she reached the top? The mage? He had to know how to escape this nightmare, he *had* to. How else could he communicate with the Dhal-Llah? Umishi gritted her teeth; the window was in reach. She would find him, she would make him talk, make him tell her how to escape. With a final push she was there, at the opening. Holding her breath, she squeezed herself through and into the fort itself.

TEN

CRUMBLING WALLS

Renderbrim was close, inside the fort. His footsteps, his breathing, echoed from the walls, bringing life to an otherwise dead world. Umishi moved deeper into the courtyard, aware of the looming tower above her. She extended her blades, their runes glowing with a blood-red hue to reassure her of their protection. These runes would stand between her and the mage's twisted spells; without them he would make a puppet of her, with the ability to bend her to his every whim. She pulled her hair over her scars, knowing full well what it was like to be at the mercy of such power.

A yell reached out to her from across the courtyard. She glanced to its source before reapplying her focus to the direction of the fading footsteps. The yell had come from a guard standing at the other end of the courtyard, another soul trapped in this lifeless realm. Her heart leapt to welcome the hope offered to it.

That glimmer of hope was so easily stolen from her. Surprise tore the air from Umishi's lungs as the ground vanished from beneath her feet. She stumbled into the large indentation that replaced the soil, managing to catch herself in time to avoid a face full of mud. Whatever was happening outside was happening in here too. Pain rushed through her leg and up her spine. She cried in anguish and threw her hands down to find the source: a wooden spear had somehow managed to rip its way through her, just below the knee. She drew a breath through her teeth; where had it come from? She hadn't felt it when she fell. Glancing down, Umishi tried to assess the wound but failed; her leathers were intact, undamaged, merged with the wood, melded together as if they were always meant to be. As panic tried to burrow its way into her head, she cut open her breaches. Her skin, like the leather that covered it, had fused with the spear. The entry point was shallow and the spear hadn't passed through anything important, just flesh.

With her eye closed and taking a deep breath she knew what she had to do. The mage could not be allowed to get away from her again, however much it was going to hurt. Umishi placed her belt in her mouth, gripping it between her teeth. With deep and slow breaths she took a moment to focus her resolve. It would be quick, at least. Her heartbeat drummed in her head, speeding to a bloody climax as she plunged her blade into her leg. Pain tore through her body as she cut through the flesh around the spear. She would not let him get away! Her screams were muffled as she bit down into the leather. Tears swelled in her eye as she tried to keep her hand steady. The steel was cold, but her leg felt as though it was on fire. With a final, deep breath she tore her blade outwards, freeing it from her skin and herself from the spear.

Dropping her dagger and grabbing as her wound, a scream exploded from her mouth while her leather belt joined her blood on the ground.

Umishi pulled herself to the wall, pressing against it and watching as pikes and spears continued to appear. Long grooves also dug into the ground, as though a massive, invisible worm were dragging itself through the courtyard. Before her eye, siege engines formed on the fortress's walls, facing the forest beyond. Huge trebuchets and bolt throwers assembled out of thin air. What was happening? What magic was this? Umishi had seen nothing of its kind. The soldier, however, was gone, vanished, along with any company he may have offered in this empty world. She inhaled through her teeth as pain and hopelessness took hold.

Umishi tore the lower leg of her breaches off and wrapped the leather around her wound. There was more blood than she had expected; a lot more. Sitting, she watched for movement, for any more structures forming from nothing. In the time it took to catch her breath and familiarise herself with her pain, whatever was going on stopped, or at least seemed to.

She struggled to her feet and limped towards where the human had stood, in a space that had been replaced by stone. A bloody arm launched itself from the newly formed rubble: the soldier! Hope and panic twisted in Umishi's gut as she pushed herself towards the loose rock. She saw his face first; his helm had fallen off and his expression had contorted into one of true horror. He screamed in a way no human could, his eyes open far too wide. Umishi rushed to remove the rubble as he cried in pain. She would save him, she told herself, she would save him and then, together, they would figure a way out of this thrice-damned world.

'What's your name?' she cried, clawing the stones away from him. It was the first thing that came to mind; she was panicking. She couldn't let him go, couldn't be alone again.

Blood spilt from the guard's mouth as Umishi came to terms with the full extent of his grotesque predicament. Removing more of the debris, it became clear he wasn't just under the rubble: he had somehow become *one* with it. Jagged stone emerged through his legs and waist, yet no obvious wounds were visible; his armour was undamaged as if he and the stone had always been there, always been part of each other. He reached out for her with his one free arm, his eyes filled with desperation. Umishi grasped at his hand tightly, as though she could pull him from the brink of death. His expression was filled with such terror that there was no way to know if he could even feel the warmth of her touch. He gasped one last time, before joining the rest of the world in silence.

Umishi fell back as the guard's hand limply fell from her fingers. There was nothing that could have been done, and whatever magic was responsible had made his end a painful one. Pushing herself from the ground, the world twisted around her. Drums pounded in her head as overwhelming dizziness took hold. She reached out for the stone to steady herself. A bolt of blinding light erupted from the corpse, stealing her sight.

Her breathing sped up. Swallowing the air, Umishi instantly recognised a difference in it, a freshness. Sounds started to explode around her: shouting, yelling, the buzz of conversation. No amount of rubbing at her eye cured her sight, but there was little doubt what was happening, to the world, to her. She had returned to the world of life. There were people, humans, all around, their pungent smell filling her nostrils, their clumsy footsteps sending tiny tremors through the ground. She was free of the other world's blackness. Removing her hand from her eye, a blurred silhouette manifested before her, awash with gleaming armour and strong, feminine, features.

'You?' Commander Vallis exclaimed, with just as much surprise as Umishi.

The courtyard was busy. Fendamor soldiers were running back and forth, climbing ladders and barking orders at each other. Umishi tried to restrain the laughter building inside her by biting her lower lip, but it was no good. She covered her mouth with one hand, trying to contain her hysteria. She was free! She had escaped!

Cold, iron hands gripped and shook her shoulders. 'Where in the bloody hells did you come from?' the commander thundered. 'Answer me!'

'Commander!' another voice called down from the walls. 'Towers! Towers are approaching.'

'Keep an eye on this one,' the commander ordered a nearby soldier as she pushed Umishi towards him. She then marched in the direction of the shouting. 'We need archers on the wall now!' she barked. 'Get me bloody flame arrows! We'll torch the buggers before they reach us!'

'Aye, Commander!' Once more, the soldiers on the ramparts fell into chaos, running back and forth, as though lost.

'I find it funny,' Vallis snarled as she turned to Umishi, 'that the Dhal-Llah are beginning their assault just as you appear out of nowhere. An odd coincidence, don't you think? Where are the mages?' she bellowed to her men, making Umishi flinch. 'Fetch me a mage this bloody instant. How am I supposed to direct this defence without a fucking mage?'

She was too late; it had begun. The war between Fendamor and the Dhal-Llah was about to start, breaking the legacy of peace held by this land's people since the forming of their kingdom. Umishi's throat felt dry as the magnitude of what was happening sank in. The guard in the other world was just the first of many deaths that would occur before the day reached its end.

She watched as the archers took to the wall and, within moments, unleashed a hail of arrows at the unseen enemies beyond. It did not take much effort to wiggle herself out of the preoccupied soldier's grip. The human seemed lost, his mind already retreating from what soon would become either a battlefield or the site of a massacre.

With as much speed as she could muster, Umishi limped forward, catching up to the commander and, with a great deal of effort, matching her pace.

'You need to withdraw,' Umishi said, her voice frail with exhaustion and barely audible over the sounds of panicked cries and clambering armour.

'I need more logs to brace these walls!' the commander yelled into the air. 'I thank you for your concern, Inquisitor, but debating the situation is the last thing on my list of priorities right now. I assure you, after the Dhal-Llah have been repelled, I would be very interested in having a little sit down and a chat.'

There would be no repelling the army, and no amount of shoring up the walls would be able to stop them. It was clear the commander didn't have any understanding of what was happening, or what was *going* to happen. Vallis must have read about sieges in books or heard about them from scribes and scholars. She was checking all the boxes, giving all the textbook orders, but this wasn't a siege, at least not by any conventional meaning of the word. With the Ward still protecting the Dhal-Llah, the siege would fast become a flood. A whistle rang through the air as the glowing tails of arrows reached for a flaming siege tower that could barely be seen above the wall. Any moment, it would reach them, and the killing would begin.

'They have the Ward, you and your men don't,' Umishi snapped.

'We just have to hold the line, prevent them from entering the fort. A good defence will break their resolve and make them flee,' the commander snapped. She stopped in front of a gruff-looking, hairless man. 'General Vorx, I need your men at the trebuchet, we'll make these buggers think that the sky is falling on their heads!'

'Yes, Commander.' he said, with the eagerness of a child allowed to take a swing with his father's sword for the first time.

Umishi clawed at her hair as Vallis stormed away, continuing her pointless preparations. Umishi regretted that there was no magic word to convince them to retreat, nor some clever way to make them understand that their defences would fail, and they would be overrun. Neither wit nor charm had ever been a tool she had wielded with any kind of skill. Licking her lips, there was no choice but to concede that there was nothing to be done; that nothing *could* be done. With two daggers, Umishi couldn't defend against an army, and the mage responsible for this wasn't even in the same world!

There was no reason to bear witness to this senseless massacre. It was a scene that had played out a hundred times before, in books, in history, and it wasn't one Umishi cared to have etched into her memory for the rest of her days. While these fools were too blind to see the death that was at their door, the people of Hanaswick, the people of the lake village, *they* still had a chance. Umishi turned to the fortress's entrance. Doomed soldiers laboured through the courtyard with the logs Vallis had demanded. Umishi turned, dragging her wounded leg as she struggled towards the fortress gates, back towards the forest she had so recently escaped.

Fighting this war would not help them. They had to strike at the heart, the mastermind pulling at the strings. Umishi rolled her eye at the thought of the madman in the other place as a mastermind. However, with Renderbrim concealed in the shadow world, she would need the help of someone who could understand the magic he used: the archmage.

A thunderous boom roared towards her, followed by a scream that was not from any man. She turned and saw... a Kalsakian, crawling its way up one of the towers, unnoticed by the defenders. Umishi paused, staring at the beast. How had it gotten here? Did Renderbrim send it here? Wood smashed against stone, and the terrified screams of men filled the air. The mouth of the siege tower opened, spreading forth the flood that would overtake the fort. Over a dozen creatures came from the blackness, wearing robes made of shadows and featureless white masks. They tore into the front line of archers with cold apathy and an eerie silence, using barbed blades that darted from their sleeves. The Fendamor forces slashed at the robed figures, but their swords passed through as the Ward carried out its work, protecting the Dhal-Llah.

Screams rebounded from the walls as the fort's defenders fell into desperate panic. With the archers dispatched, the ramparts fell, allowing the Dhal-Llah to assault the wall with ladders. The men and women broke into a stampede with each participant clawing, clambering, crushing their fellows to get ahead. All the while, behind them, their blood-drenched foes increased in number.

Umishi fell to all fours. With as much speed as she could muster she threw herself ahead of the tide of terror crazed humans. It was not enough. Ahead, the fort's gate exploded as a thousand stones came hurling toward the fleeing masses, toward her. She collapsed, blood racing from her head. Dirt filled her mouth as she faced the ruined gate house, and the gigantic boulder that had reduced it to impassable rubble. They were trapped. She turned to her other side to greet the endless tide of human feet. A boot found her ribs, a knee slammed against her temple. Her vision blurred as each blow landed, then blackness.

ELEVEN

CAGED IN IRON

In the blackness, Umishi could smell the blood, feel the table's splintered wood poking at her wrists. The screams came from all around her, some crying out tales of pain, others of hopelessness. Umishi herself remained silent. She had to: her son lay on the table next to her, she had to be strong for him. She could hear him; even through everyone else's cries, she could hear him. His was a gentle sob. She had told him it would be fine, she had told him everything was going to be okay and when it was all over they would go climb trees with Richard, see grandma and granddad and find the biggest tree they could. Life made a liar of her.

The explosion woke her so that she could experience a pain like no other, like a thousand tiny fishhooks digging into the left side of her face, all pulling, twisting, tearing in impossible directions. The pain was too much; she wasn't strong enough, she... she couldn't hear him, she couldn't hear Thomas anymore. The physical pain was replaced by something stronger and more primal, something so strong it overwhelmed everything else. Each moment stole her breath and drove a dagger through her heart. Nothing around her mattered anymore, not the agony of her skin being torn apart, the screams, the taste of blood, the fear. It all fell into numbness. Through it all, his silhouette twisted into focus: the man responsible for everything. He was the one they had trusted, the one Richard had told her to trust, a shadowed figure who would haunt her nightmares forever. It was the creature that would be known as the Mangler of Malhain.

Umishi felt the wind against her skin, tugging at her hair while a dull ache gnawed at her head. Sunlight thwarted every attempt to open her eyes. Her mouth felt dry and her lips cracked. Lifting her hand to her forehead she found some kind of fabric. She groaned and made another attempt to peel open her eyelid. This time a blur came to her: black and white streaks and shadowy blobs. One of the shapes moved, gaining size and definition as it lumbered towards her.

'Easy now, girl,' came a withered voice. 'There's no rush, not when rushing could cause you a great deal of harm. Well, probably; it can't be good for you anyway.'

Umishi tried to blink the fuzziness away; it worked to a degree. She could make out that the blob peering over her was human, elderly and wearing a long blue robe. With that, coupled with his voice, she could guess that it was Erik Lothrum, the court wizard. Umishi's heart skipped and panic ran through her veins, across every muscle in her body. She recoiled, pushing herself back into something. A wall? No, she drew her knees to her chest and clawed at her hair. She blinked again, but everything remained in blurred haze, as though a raging waterfall flowed between her and everything else. Her head hurt. Where was she? What was she doing there? The fort was being attacked, but what had happened after?

'Stupid girl!' the mage growled. 'I told you not to move! Was there any point to saving your head? It seems there's nothing of any importance in there anyway!'

Despite her lack of vision, there was no mistaking the thick iron bars that pressed against her back. There was something else... at first, she had thought it was dizziness, a feeling of displacement as her mind tried to refocus, but as time passed, it became more apparent: the cage she was in was moving. She tried to speak, tongue feeling strange as it twisted in her mouth 'Wha-'

'What's going on? Where am I? How did I get here? Those are the normal mumbles that dribble out of the mouths of those recovering from your condition, so let me save you the bother of asking. In the siege some debris must have smashed against your head. That, or someone managed to give you a whack, but I stand by my first assumption.'

That explained some of the pain, at least.

'It almost killed you too. You're lucky I noticed you when I did, and that you look lighter than most, else you would have been reduced to pre-mashed worm food. I managed to heal all the superficial injuries, your arms, your leg but I wasn't about to touch your head. The mind is a delicate and complex thing and even with my not inconsiderable power, I'd be risking causing more damage than good without the proper equipment. These bars don't help much, either.'

Umishi's head throbbed with the kind of pain one

would expect from the injury that Lothrum had described. Her sight was clearing, The old mage's face emerged from the haze, as did the forms of the others who shared their cage. There were five of them, excluding her and Lothrum, curled up asleep on the floor, still wearing the uniforms they had been captured in: thin armour, dented and bloodied. The mage spoke the truth about her wounds. It was as though nothing had happened to her leg, making her trip to the other world seem all the more like a dream. But it had been real and, this time, she could be sure. She had seen it, a monster that belonged in the shadowed world, a Kalsakian, on the fort wall. Hadn't she? Everything seemed so hazy. Just moments ago, she could have sworn she was there, with her son, in the cursed building that lurked in her memories, the one that housed all her nightmares.

'We lost, of course, if it wasn't painfully obvious from our choice of transport. Not much we could have done against a foe we couldn't harm. I did my best: tended to the wounded, threw as many rocks in their path as I bloody could. I wasn't even meant to be there. Leuvigild sent me looking for you.'

The cart rolled on a few moments longer.

'And where were you, Inquisitor? So-called "defender of the powerless"? Lying on the ground after failing to flee, blood running out your nose, while all about you were killed or captured!' He paused. 'I'm sorry, I... well, it doesn't matter now, we're all stuck in the same bloody boat.'

Beyond the cage, rolling hills went by, the sun beamed down on green grass and a whole choir of birds sang; it was strangely comforting, even through the bars. Life seemed to be doing its best to show Umishi that she was back in her world.

'I didn't mean literally,' the mage said, noticing her gazing at the scenery. 'I can assure you that we are very much on dry land. We're heading to Llanvurgist by my reckoning, so that's going to be a glorious treat for everyone involved.'

Outside, another carriage passed, dragged along by around twenty human-shaped creatures, masked and bound by chains. Umishi could not trust her eye, but there was something odd about them; something not quite right about how they carried themselves, how they carried their chains. The cage they pulled was filled with more soldiers from the fort. Theirs was fuller, about ten maybe twelve humans crammed into a cage no bigger than hers.

'Ah yes,' he was speaking so much, it made a miracle of the fact the others managed to get any sleep at all. 'I should congratulate you. More than likely due to your curious looks you have been promoted to the officer's cage. Lucky you. Look around. There you have General Vorx; that's Captain Williams huddled next to him, of course you've met Commander Vallis there and Captain Briggs next to her. I forget the other one, but I'm sure he's just as important as the rest of these blade-wielding dandies. You are truly in the company of Fendamor's finest. Are you feeling privileged yet? Look over there, so important are we that the Dhal-Llah have even given us a slop bucket with a fixed lid in case we go over bumps. I grant you it isn't quite to the standards of the arch-mage's personal garderobe, but sill it makes me feel quite la-de-da.'

The sight of the slop bucket forced Umishi's mouth to

twist and her already weak stomach to turn. 'What's at Llanvurgist?' she asked, through bloodstained hair. Umishi was almost sure the mage was about to choke after hearing her voice; his eyes grew twice the size and he visibly flinched, as though he would have been more comfortable talking to himself.

'More than likely death for the poor fools in these other carriages, I fear,' he answered, a distant expression falling upon his already weary face. 'As for us, well, I hope to be traded back to Fendamor. That's the way these things normally go, isn't it? It's what the history books say, although you probably know more about that than I.'

The idea that all these people knew about murder, death and war came from books chilled Umishi to the core. They didn't know what to expect; what was at the end of this journey, what torture and pain that came with it.

Umishi had no intention of dying in a cell. In her life, she had escaped more dungeons than she knew numbers, and this one would be no different. Besides, there were more important concerns. One thing that truly mattered was finding the source of all this chaos; somehow it was all connected: her shifting from one world to the other, the Dhal-Llah invasion, the Mangler's supposed resurrection. It was all somehow connected, by the one person at the centre of it all. 'Renderbrim,' she whispered.

'What did she say?' Vallis snapped, as though the very name had stirred her awake.

The scorn in Vallis' eyes gave Umishi a reason to pause. It was as though she was a child saying something scandalous in front of her parents for the first time. It was the kind of reaction that could be expected from uttering the name of a warlord or tyrant, but this man from the other world seemed like neither. He seemed sickly and weak, barely holding control over his own mind, let alone his monsters.

'I don't know,' Lothrum replied. 'Damn girl's light in the head. I don't think even she knows. Leuvigild must have mentioned something about him, and now through this head wound it's popped out.'

Umishi pushed the rage caused by Lothrum's comment to the back of her mind; it was not the time for anger. 'Ashendale Renderbrim is the mage who broke the Ward, not the Mangler... He's in the other place. Renderbrim, the mage... and the Kalsakian... There was one on the wall, so it has to be real.' She clawed at her hair as they looked down at her. They regarded her with a familiar expression of tired annoyance and dismissal, the kind offered to a child blaming the mess they had made on flying Narfwells or invisible friends. 'There was a soldier in the other world, like the woman... he died and I...' and there it was. 'There was a flash of light' she muttered, more to herself. Of course, it could have been a coincidence, but after both humans' deaths, a flash had brought her back to this plane. It was the deaths, in both instances; it had to have been.

'I don't understand a word of what you're saying, girl,' Lothrum said. 'As for this "Renderbrim", I don't doubt you saw someone who called himself by that name. That would make a certain amount of sense, in a morbid kind of way.' He paused, as if trying to judge what to say. 'Ashendale Renderbrim is something of a legend here: a campfire story used to frighten children, a child the Ward didn't take to.

He was the first to officially receive the Ward. During the revolution, the boy was stabbed and lost, vanishing with a blood curdling scream, they say. Of course, as with all such tales, it ends with the promise of the lost lad coming back to claim vengeance on those related to the revolutionaries. I would guess this mage considers himself witty, taking on this name to bring down the Ward, especially when considering the Dhal-Llah's relationship with the Renderbrims.'

Umishi did not care for Lothrum's tale. This character from the past didn't interest her. Her focus remained on her trail of thought, how, if death was truly the answer to leaving the other plane then *why* was it so? If it was true, then it could only have been intentional, done by design. Of course, there was a problem with her working theory: if this 'Renderbrim' was behind all this madness, how was he orchestrating this war? When he had told her he was trapped in the other plane, had he lied? His words had seemed sincere, and her gut told her that there was something more sinister behind the Dhal-Llah. She could practically see the hands of the Mangler pulling the strings; it was he who attacked her at the Spinning Dagger, he who trapped her in the shadow in the first place. Why her, though? It didn't make sense. She was missing something.

'Why are we even talking about this?' the commander exclaimed, standing up, towering above the others as she walked the few steps to them. 'Doesn't she understand what's going on? Didn't she see what happened? We didn't... and the blood.' She gazed at Umishi, eyes filled with rage and loss. 'Look, Inquisitor, I don't understand much of what's going on, but what I *do* understand is that I was stabbed yesterday. It shouldn't have... but it happened and there was blood and pain and... When you turned tail, I stood, I saw them... I saw my men... my brave men... and they were so still, stiller than anything I had ever seen.'

Umishi could guess at some of the horror running through the commander's thoughts. It wasn't that far from that in her own, most nights.

'It wasn't right! It wasn't how it was meant to be! And they lay there! They were dead! Don't you get it!?' She wiped her nose. 'If we get out of this... this whatever, then I'll be happy to talk all day and night about your fairy tale mage!'

'I'm trying to keep an open mind here, girl,' Lothrum added, sympathy in his voice. 'After all, the arch-mage puts weight in some of the things your saying, but I have to admit I am finding it rather difficult. Perhaps it's the décor? I've heard it's healthy for thought to have specific colours and objects around you to help you better retain and make sense of ideas. I don't think brown bars and slop buckets are listed high amongst those that are helpful.'

The situation did not worry Umishi, though. If their captors wanted them dead, they would have killed them on the battlefield. No, the Dhal-Llah wanted them alive for some reason. It was an expensive thing to transport a prisoner, let alone as many as they had. The cages would have cost a great deal of work to create and, on top of that, they were giving out bread and water to keep them alive. They also had to provide the army with extra provisions, as hauling the cages would slow them down. No, the Dhal-Llah would not simply make that kind of investment just to kill them at the end of the journey. She did not know where they were being taken, or for what reason, but Lothrum's theory sounded likely. Back on the mainland, it was a common, and lucrative, practice to sell hostages.

'You're a mage; can't you just magic us out of here?' Vallis asked with a tone of impatience.

Lothrum scowled. 'You're a soldier; can't you just fight your way out? No? Didn't think so. Have you noticed what these bloody bars are made of? Iron, that's what. Don't you know anything about alchemy? Of course not. If you had any kind of intelligence, you would not be in command of protecting a people that can't... or rather *couldn't* be harmed! Iron has a tendency to affect magical energies in unpredictable, and often unfavourable, ways. There's a reason most cell doors are made with the stuff.'

Everyone jolted forward as the cage came to a stop. Vallis fell against the bars in a way that seemed painful. While they had been talking, the grass had turned to dry earth. The soil had a strange reddish hue, and it was clear they had been making good time. Umishi listened as footsteps approached.

A creature dressed in a hooded black robe and wearing a white porcelain mask approached the iron bars. The mask lacked any detail, just two black holes that betrayed only unblinking, bloodshot eyes. The creature's heavy breathing echoed deep within.

The hooded creature held a long, thin sword: a blade fit for piecing rather than slashing. There was something odd about the way it handled the weapon, though. As the creature's arm lifted and its sleeve fell away, it was clear the blade had been fused to the beast, buried deep into a stump that grew around it. It stared from the black pits of its mask as though calculating how much of a threat they would be if they managed to escape. The answer, of course, was none. The creature was obviously one of the Dhal-Llah Umishi had heard so much about, and their death-like visage clearly lived up to the dread that the people of Fendamor had of them.

It pushed its blade towards Umishi in a slow, exaggerated stabbing motion. She recoiled, and the creature tilted its head to the side. It withdrew its bladed arm and silently walked away, towards the convoy's head.

'What was that about?' Vallis asked.

'It was making sure I was alive,' Umishi answered.

TWELVE
THE DHAL-LLAH

The shadows grew longer as the sun crept behind the mountains ahead. Umishi had spent her time studying the Dhal-Llah through the bars. With her vision restored she could take the measure of her enemy, at least. The beasts that pulled the cages were resting on their knees. They were masked creatures whose unnaturally large muscles distorted their form. With the haze cleared from her eye, Umishi could see what was wrong with them: the chains the poor creatures used to pull the carriages were not bound to them by leathers or rope. The chains had been placed *in* them, fused as the blade was to the hooded Dhal-Llah she had seen earlier. These creatures would pull the carriage or tear themselves apart trying. Pity stole a breath or two away from her, but now was not the time for such things. With the Dhal-Llah establishing a campsite, an opportunity to escape was likely to present itself.

Umishi moved to the cage door, taking advantage of the chance to assess her situation and how to improve it. At this point, she didn't have much of a plan, more just a list of goals. The fact that, at any moment, she could be torn from this world into a waking nightmare of shadow and monsters loomed forebodingly at the back of her mind. It felt like a thousand spiders running down her back. She felt naked without her blades and, were she to fade back into that realm without them, she would be all too vulnerable to the horrors that awaited her there. There was no doubt her captors had claimed them.

Each time the Dhal-Llah stopped she was granted the chance to keep track of them, observing their behaviour and taking mental notes of their activities. It did not take her long to realise there were strict roles allocated to these robed creatures. The larger Dhal-Llah pulled the wagons, that was obvious, but the differences between the bladed and unbladed were subtler. Those with swords fused to their bodies never left guard duty. They remained at their posts, around and between each cage. Those who were gloved handed out rations. It was through this that they betrayed themselves.

Umishi was able to work out that the supply caravan was in front of them, which made sense as, if the convoy were attacked, it would be from the rear. Each time one of the bladeless Dhal-Llah passed her cage, she would count their steps, determining that their supply caravan would be about four wagons ahead. Umishi grinned. With her bracelet still around her wrist, it would be an easy enough distance to traverse undetected and, reunited with her daggers, she would keep the fears of falling into the other world at bay, freeing her mind so she could focus on escape.

Her chance arrived when they made camp for the night.

Unlike the shrouded world of the Kalsakian, the shadows were her allies here. Pulling a lock pick from a concealed pouch stitched into her tunic Umishi turned to the cage door. The lock itself was basic, as they always were on portable cages. She had hoped to get some entertainment from it, a puzzle to keep her mind awake. Instead they might as well have left the door open. After a few precise movements, the lock responded with a click no louder than a bat's, but it was enough to stir the others.

'What's she doing?' hissed one of the humans, general Vorx, if she recalled correctly. 'Gods, she's gonna get us all killed,' he said. He stood, trying to intimidate her with his height. Umishi offered him a grin; the tactic had been tried on her many times before, and by creatures far taller.

'Stop it, you vile little imp'

'Are you trying to put words together again, General?' Lothrum asked. 'I'd rather listen to your madness-inducing snores than be forced to tolerate the annoying hum of your attempts at speech.'

'Perhaps you need to unclog your ears, mage!' Vorx snapped. 'As soon as she opens that bloody gate, they'll see it. You think they aren't watching us? They're out there right now, watching every move we make. As soon as this little bitch opens the cage doors, we'll all be slaughtered thanks to her failed escape attempt!'

The general's words managed to stun the mage into silence. He didn't know the general was wrong. Umishi had monitored the shifts the guards took, memorised their patrols, and taken note of the limitations their masks put on their sight. Although their formation was tight, she had seen tighter; the holes were small, but they were there. Also, he had not considered the amulet she wore on her wrist. The shadows would have granted her cover from the Dhal-Llah's prying eyes as she slipped by them. It was, however, pointless trying to explain this to the humans – they were too big, too loud, too much of a liability. Hers was not a rescue mission. Her task was clear: a monster controlled the Ward and the beasts of the other plane; she would find him and bring justice down upon him through the tip of her dagger.

'Lady Inquisitor,' Vallis said. 'Maybe you are able to escape, maybe the Dhal-Llah won't kill any of us, but wouldn't it be better not to risk it? If Lothrum is right, then we'll just be ransomed and be on our way back to Hanaswick faster than you can walk anyway. They've already shown their power, and there is no reason to kill anyone else.'

'Are you all mad?' said Williams, pushing himself against the bars. 'Take me with you, Inquisitor! We'll achieve nothing sitting around here, trapped like dogs! We need to get back to Hanaswick, warn them before the Dhal-Llah continue their invasion!'

'Shut up, boy!' the general growled. 'As soon as I received word these bastards were on our borders I ordered every bridge, every walkway, every wooden plank of Jimmarah dismantled or set ablaze. I have already given Hanaswick all the time required to prepare, to get the Court of Wizards off their fat arses and find a way to combat these bastards. Besides that, didn't you see the cowards run before the battle began: the clerks, the scholars? You can bet every hair on your arse that they have given Hanaswick an account of what happened. I doubt the Dhal-Llah are foolish enough to try to swim their invasion across. The rest of Fendamor is safe, for now. It's your own skin you should be worried about.'

Umishi fell back to her corner. Any chance of escape had been rendered too risky by the inability of the humans to keep silent. She tucked her legs under herself and clawed at her hair. The humans continued their bickering well beyond the point of relevance. Umishi tried to ignore them as she rolled one of her lock picks between her fingers and kept her eye on the shadowy figures moving in the dark.

Screaming came from one of the carriages to her left as a group of the creatures moved towards them. They began to speak with those within, but their words were lost due to the noise of Lothrum and the rest. She dragged herself closer to the opposite side of the cage and of course the others followed. Umishi gritted her teeth as the fools clambered over each other, clutching at the bars as though thirsty for the same attention those in the other cage were being given. The breathing of the humans began to accelerate, and panic started to infest the cage.

'Oh God, God,' Williams cried. He was making too much noise.

Umishi moved away from the others, back towards the cage doors. She would make sure she had a way to get out should events escalate. A louder scream came from the other cage, a scream that tugged at Umishi's gut: a cry of pain. The boy, Williams, stumbled away from the bars and vomited.

'Why would they do that?' Vallis gasped. 'Why would they do that to his arm? He didn't... why would they do that?'

'Hush, girl, or it'll be us they toy with next!' Lothrum whispered, understanding the need for silence.

It was too late.

One of the Dhal-Llah approached, one that lacked swords growing out of scarred stumps. The creature wore its hood down, so its mask was fully on display. The mask encased its head in such a way there was no obvious way to remove it and, unlike the others, this one possessed no eyeholes. Instead, there was a single hole for the mouth, which bore painted black lips. The cage fell silent. Umishi couldn't hear a single breath from those within. The creature on the other side of the bars wheezed and snorted.

Vallis approached it then. 'I am Isolda Vallis of Hanaswick, Commander of Fendamor's foreign defence forces,' she said with a confidence similar to that of their first meeting. 'You have our full cooperation, we will comply with any commands you may give us, so long as we are kept safe. Please, the people of Fendamor have always been close friends with the Dhal-Llah; our trade deals have always been-'

The creature smashed its arm against the iron bars, silencing the commander. It tilted it's head downwards to Umishi. Swaying its head back and forth, it seemed to be assessing her, in the same way a cat might a mouse, staring at her with eyes that were not there.

'One is a mage, the others soldiers of high rank, but you... you are different,' came a voice from the mask's slit. It was not the kind of voice Umishi had been expecting. She could not tell if it belonged to a male or a female, but it sounded beautiful, with a talent to make every sentence a song. 'A child returned. A soul on this island untainted by Fendamor's corruption, his poisoned words. A lost child who may yet return to the breast of the emperor. You ooze power and shine with such beauty. Such a rare curiosity you are; a precious stone dropped carelessly into the slop and defecation the enemy's kingdom has produced in the years you have been away.'

Umishi remained silent, her tongue too afraid to move, lest her clumsy words offend this beast. Even if she had mustered the courage to speak, what would she say? She knew nothing of this strange race that hid behind cold, ghoulish masks. She knew nothing of their temperament, but the fact one of the soldiers in the other carriage had just had his arm torn from him was a warning best not ignored.

'You remain silent. You refuse to pleasure us with your words,' sang the eyeless Dhal-Llah. 'A pity indeed. The emperor wished to hear you sing. He wished to hear your voice reverberate through these bars, rebound from the trees. It does not matter, however. There will be time for such glorious song later. For, you see, you have been blessed. The emperor wants you brought to the temple, before the altar. He wants to speak with you; a rare privilege indeed, an offer never granted to a person of foreign descent since the emperor achieved godhood.' The Dhal-Llah straightened and twisted to face the others. 'As for the rest of you, children of Fendamor, you shall be granted the honour of being voices. The emperor prays you are of stronger stock than those in the other cages.' With deliberate motions, the masked speaker turned its body and marched to the convoy's head, out of sight.

'Did you hear that?' Williams sobbed. 'We're dead! We are fucking dead! You heard that thing! We should have listened to the inquisitor. We should have escaped when we had the chance. Now? By the gods, now we're gonna be voices! Do you know what that means?'

General Vorx fell into a stubborn silence, while Vallis tried to put on a brave face. Everyone else seemed to understand what it meant, the gravity of the phrase. Umishi did not; not in this kind of context, not in a way that generated such dread. She could only surmise that their fate would be worse than the poor fool in the other cage.

Lothrum turned to her, a grim expression stretched over his face, 'I hope you're not expecting anything in the way of good conversation with their emperor,' he said sombrely. 'You of all people should recall that the emperor of Domvalkia has been dead for decades.'

The emperor? The thought made Umishi raise an eyebrow. The same emperor who ruled when she and her family... when they lived here? She did not understand how that could be, what was going on, how could he be dethroned, dead, and still ruling? Who were these Dhal-Llah?

As though reading her mind, Lothrum continued to explain, in dull tones. 'These morbid fools think they can use the dead as conduits, through which they can speak to him. The most unsettling thing is that they delude themselves into believing he talks back. That's what that thing meant by "voices"; it meant the poor dead buggers they use in this insane ritual.'

Lothrum's explanation was received with expressions of

distain, the others doubtlessly upset that their sorry fates were being spoken with such flippancy. Taking in his audience's wordless criticism, Lothrum joined them in mournful silence. After all, he was set to be among the 'poor dead buggers'. The silence did not linger too long, though, as it was quickly quelled by the sound of the wheels under them turning, creaking as the Dhal-Llah bound to the carriages hauled them into motion.

As night turned back to day, a nervous silence reigned over the moving prison. Black, naked trees loomed overhead as they passed, some even attempting to reach in and claw at them. Umishi sat, wondering. What did these strange beings have in store for her? Why had she not been dealt the same fate as the rest, doomed to be some kind of mouthpiece for a dead ruler? She thought it inconsiderate to ask, given the nature of their fates, yet there was a part of her that could not shake the feeling that hers might be worse. To her knowledge, there was only one possible way to be granted an audience with a ghost, and it was certainly not to her liking.

'There it is,' Lothrum whispered. 'The Dhal-Llah capital of Llanvurgist.'

The mage's voice made Umishi's heart skip a beat or two. He had been awake. There was something else that had escaped her notice, too. Above them, bursting from the twisted trees like blisters, were grim-looking huts. From their centres, bridges spread like spider webs. Umishi felt rage growing within her. It was as though this village in the trees was a personal attack on her, a mockery of the homesteads of her kin.

'Not *there*, girl,' the mage whispered. 'The trees are

where these lunatics keep their dead. Look to the ground; that is where you'll see their cities.'

She followed his directions and found a massive pit opening up on the horizon. Once more, the island surprised her with how alien it could be; the underground city looked bizarre and wholly unnatural. It was as though some catastrophic event had drained an entire lake and, in the water's absence, giant maggots had made their homes. Regardless of what it looked like, it was their destination, and there was nothing between here and there to stop them being carried into the open maw of this lightless void.

THIRTEEN
THE ALTAR OF GHALDAIL

The Dhal-Llah dragged their tormented prisoners into the chasm's open maw. Umishi pressed herself against the bars as the disturbing wonder of the subterranean world was revealed to her. They descended via ramps and bridges carved from the earth that was once contained in this massive, open, mine-like structure. These pathways spiralled ever deeper into the island, surely deeper than most seas. As they were led down the mud-covered, spider web-like pathways, they could see giant maggot holes opening, revealing corridors that dug further into the earth to form the streets of the underground city. All this was lit by torch fire, giving the place a smoky orange hue. The most unsettling thing about this Llanvurgist was the silence. Apart from the grinding sound the carriage wheels made as they crushed the soil, there was nothing; not even the normally vocal captives dared risk a whisper. If not for the foulness of the air or the prisoners around her Umishi might have believed she had been drawn into Renderbrim's shadow world again.

They finally levelled off at a junction and headed into one of the burrow-like streets. Umishi couldn't tell how deep they had gone, but they were still high enough for roots to break through the ceiling, invading the passageways like the dark tendrils of some giant, burrowing beast. Umishi held her breath as they moved through the claustrophobic tunnels, protecting herself from the vile odour of rot and decay as it assaulted her from all angles. It did not improve as they passed into a massive cavern.

The carriage jerked violently, stopping and throwing all within the against the cage's floor. The Dhal-Llah who led the convoy began unloading the portable cells, hurling the captives out onto the hard ground. Everyone in Umishi's cage watched in silent horror as they awaited their turn. She watched as soldiers from the fort were dragged down tunnels, screaming, sobbing and pleading for mercy. The empty carriages were pulled in the opposite direction, their rattling chains and grinding wheels echoing as they went. Umishi braced herself as their carriage moved forward.

Footsteps proceeded shadows, heralding the approach of the faceless, bladed Dhal-Llah.

'Please,' Williams pleaded as they grabbed him. 'I beg you, please.'

They ignored him, dragging him from the carriage and throwing him face down onto the hard floor.

'Bring him to me,' said another sweet voice from beyond Umishi's sight. 'The small one too. The emperor wants them both. Also, make sure the mage is gagged. It would be catastrophic were he permitted to speak within these halls.'

They reached for her next, but she would not allow these creatures the satisfaction of seeing her thrown to the ground. Dodging their clumsy attempts at capture, Umishi jumped down from the carriage. Blades rushed towards her, stopping at the skin of her throat. The threat rang loud and clear, so Umishi raised her hands to show them she had no intentions of resisting. The creatures twitched their heads at her and stayed their blades. Motioning with its arm, the Dhal-Llah in front commanded her to follow. Williams was not treated with such respect: they pulled him from the ground and pushed him forward. He continued sobbing as he spat out dirt and blood.

They were brought before a stone desk that, until then, had been obscured by the other carriages. An impressively large tome rested open upon it, its pages yellowed and torn. Above it, another mutilated Dhal-Llah hung from chains, its legs missing and its mask granting holes for both mouth and eyes. It gazed at Umishi as she approached, its hazel eyes trying their best to escape their sockets, hungering for every detail Umishi offered it. She clawed her hair tighter over her face.

'Yes,' the creature asserted as if in agreement with itself, the chains that bound it rattling as it moved. 'This is the one. The emperor wishes to speak with this one.' With its dangling arms, it scoured the pages of its tome. 'The soldier too; he needs to be there. There is much His Imperial Majesty wishes to know, a great deal he has to ask.' Five, maybe more, of the bladed, mouthless creatures fell in around her and Williams. With a sharp shove they directed them back the way they had come.

Umishi tried to maintain her composure as she was led through into the central pit again. She took an opportunity to glance upwards at the sun, to get some grasp of the time that had passed since she had been driven down into this hole. She also took the opportunity to fill her lungs with fresh air and empty her nostrils of the smell of damp and rot that seemed to spread from every crevice the pit offered.

The broken creatures were a mystery to her, the fate they had devised for her even more so. Umishi swallowed the urge to resist, as outward panic would achieve nothing except to antagonise them. Instead, she distracted herself by trying to memorise the bridges she crossed and passages she walked. She tried to keep her mind busy by taking note of possible landmarks and, more importantly, possible ways to escape. Williams, however, screamed and fought every step of the way. The bladed Dhal-Llah ignored most of his attempts at resistance, but it did not take long before their patience appeared to wear thin. With a powerful blow to the face they brought the Fendamor soldier to the ground, after which he only offered quiet whimpers as they scraped his face along the stone and dragged him deeper into Llanvurgist's bowels.

As they passed through a numbered gateway she took note of the winches working it. It appeared the gates could only be opened from the inside, leaving those outside completely dependent on those within to grant them access. It was a system likely put in place to hinder invaders and implied that there was someone inside each locked room at all times.

Tunnels led to corridors and corridors led deeper into

the earth, until they reached a room larger than any they had come across. A water filled chamber lay before them. The water was a mix of greys and greens, while its smell was pungent rot, but not of the kind that came from plants or fungus: it smelled of death. In the centre of the putrid subterranean lake rose an island of bronze and iron. It was clear, from the direction they were heading, that it was their destination.

Umishi and Williams were forced onto a rope bridge that swayed with every step. She could not take her eye from the murk beneath her and her heart pounded each time a wooden plank twisted. Behind her, the bladed Dhal-Llah pressed them ever on. She should have escaped when their carriage stopped; she should have ignored the other fools. Williams sobbed again. Her pride had made her hesitate, her pride had told her there was no situation that could hold her captive, no scenario that she couldn't escape from. It was this pride that would be her downfall, here, miles under the earth; a grave she had freely walked into.

Her feet found the cold metal of the island's floor. A robbed figure sat in its centre as a spider might sit in its web. The creature's mask was open at its mouth, just like the one who had spoken to them on the way here; however this mask was not nearly so plain. On what would have been the forehead, painted in golds and reds, was an ornate eye, etched with a great deal of skill, surrounded by gems and jewels. Not only was it the focal point of the mask; it seemed to be the centrepiece of the whole room. Umishi could not take her eye from it. The creature sat with its legs crossed, its hands lying flat to the floor. 'You came,' it said in its hypnotically beautiful voice. 'He knew you would, he predicted this would be so. I am to welcome you to his altar. I am to introduce myself as the speaker of Ghaldail. He has been interested in you. He has taken an interest in you ever since his shadow masters sent word of your arrival, ever since you landed on Domvalkia. Our great emperor has been very curious to see what the world has made of his wayward lamb, how you have fared without his wisdom and guidance. He would like to speak to you, if you would permit me to summon him.'

Umishi remained silent. What could she say? What was she *expected* to say? She would wait to see what this creature wanted from her. She tried not to breathe, tried not to draw in the smell of death that surrounded her.

Once more, Williams had other plans. He fell to his knees, his eyes wide, his face stained and bloody. 'Please,' he grovelled as he approached the creature. 'Please I... I... don't.'

The speaker cut the pitiful human off with a wave of its hand, but its command was not for him. From behind, one of the bladed Dhal-Llah approached and, with swift motions, planted its steel through Williams' back. Blood ran from his chest as the blade tore through armour, cloth, skin, muscle and then finally through his ribs. His limp body slid down the sharp edge, down to the warm, crimson puddle it had created. His head fell to the side.

His eyes were wide as he stared at her, tears escaping only to find themselves lost in the blood pooling below. He tried to say something: his lips moved, uttering soundless words, yet... yet she couldn't make them out. His mouth fell still and whatever he had attempted to say became as lost as his tears.

The Dhal-Llah unsheathed its blade from the soldier's back and flicked the blood away. Tiny droplets made the stagnant waters move. As Umishi watched the life fade from the human's eyes, the speaker raced towards the corpse on all fours. With spider-like movements, it crawled over the body and pressed its mask against the cadaver's open mouth. The speaker's breathing grew heavier and heavier until there was silence. It threw its head back and screamed; the sound was inhuman, more akin to a thousand tortured birds shrilling out a final, morbid crescendo. The monster twisted itself into unnatural position after position before turning its jewel-encrusted eye back to Umishi, breathing steadily.

'The emperor wants me to express that he deeply regrets how poorly you have been treated,' the speaker cooed, its voice distorted and dreamlike. 'The manner in which you have been welcomed back to Domvalkia, back home... He wishes you had come here first, wishes he could have met you before Fendamor made a plaything of your mind. It is such a waste, what you have become, such a cruel waste.'

The creature circled her, crawling on all fours. The intensity of its attention bore down on her, held her fast, its jewelled, blind, cyclopean eye taking the measure of her. Its breathing echoed through its mask in long, focused breaths.

'I don't serve Fendamor,' she managed, not sure quite what to say, not sure what words would allow the conversation to continue or which would land her with a sword through her chest. 'I am an inquisitor of the Order of Alpharus.'

The creature twisted to face her again, in a grin filled with blackened teeth. 'Yes, he knows you, Umishi Zaimor, knows you like he knows all his children. You were one of his subjects. Before you fled, before you succumbed to the temptations of free will, and who could blame you?'

Umishi could only stand there, staring.

'He does not blame you for seeking a new master after his lips fell silent, after his body broke. He was your emperor, you and your family surrendered yourself to him, and he failed you. As a mortal, he did not anticipate Fendamor's betrayal, could not see the horror that would rise from Malhain. Now, he has transcended. He is capable of seeing the situation with a clarity far beyond that of a mortal man. He regrets that he did not take action to defend Malhain all those years ago. He knows now, had he done so, he could have prevented all this suffering, this war.'

Umishi closed her eye and shook her head. Nothing the creature was saying made sense. It was all gibberish. 'What's Malhain got to do with this?' Umishi whispered.

'He can sense your confusion, child,' the speaker said, its words laced with its own joy. 'The emperor is not surprised you don't know that the master you serve is a pretender. He wants me to tell you what kind of beast you have been blindly following. Fendamor is a monster who sailed here from distant shores. He crawled into our emperor's service, his mouth filled with treachery and lies. It started in a small village north of Lake Jimmarah, this was the birthplace of his insurrection, the birthplace of the Ward, and a bloody birthplace it was. Through experiments on loyal subjects he perfected his weapon. Armed with this

"Ward", with a narrow mind and overzealous confidence, he destroyed our emperor's body and proclaimed that he ruled the empire, dividing it in two as he vainly forced his name upon the lands. This is the atrocity he laid upon us, but the emperor's spies say you know him by another name...'

'The Mangler? He's not dead?' Umishi gasped feebly. Had she been right all along? Was this creature telling her that he was somehow alive, here on this island? Her body trembled, a hundred thoughts spinning in her head as she fruitlessly struggled to process the implications of what she had deduced: the Mangler and this Fendamor were one in the same. She felt numb, her mouth dry. He was here; he had been here all this time.

'Dead?' The creature laughed like a child, frantic and high pitched. 'Death is a shallow concept driven by a narrow mind. As our emperor has shown us, no life just *ends*, it merely changes. However, whereas the emperor transcended to godhood, Vulfoliac Fendamor became a plague, a corruption that now fills his son and spills out through his words, onto his kingdom.'

It was hard for Umishi to tell, but the creature looked almost... regretful.

'If only you had understood this lesson before you fled, understood that our master would not have abandoned us, you would never have bought into the illusion of free will. You thought that, without the emperor's direction, you were capable of making choices for yourself, that you were the master of your own destiny, that you understood the direction of your life better than a god.'

It made it sound like an accusation, rather than the most

fundamental basis for the life Umishi knew. It kept going.

'Leuvigild Fendamor has taken advantage of your naivety in the cruellest way. He picked up your strings and, with the elegance that comes so naturally to a monster like him, he manipulated you, forced you to protect the very spell seeded through the blood and death of your neighbours, your friends, your family. Poor, lost child, the emperor pities you,' the speaker continued, its eyeless mask tracing invisible phantoms that circled around the chamber. 'Armed with the Ward created from the experiments on your family, Leuvigild rules. The emperor wants you to understand that the greatest lie Leuvigild has told the people of Fendamor is that the Ward is a shield. In truth, it is a blade he holds against the kingdom's throat.'

'And you're better?' Umishi asked.

'Only we can stop him, only we can break the Ward and reunite this island once more under the banner of its one and only true ruler: Emperor Ghaldail.'

'No,' she gasped, her ribs tightening around her lungs. Her fingers were numb, her legs frozen. The lives of those of Malhain, her neighbours, friends, family, Thomas, Richard… they had all been sacrificed for this 'Ward'. It was a spell created from their torture, a spell used to conquer, placing the power of life and death in the hands of the mage wielding it. Umishi's head spun as she struggled for air. This was the exact kind of spell Umishi vowed to defend people from yet, here, on this island, she was defending it, fighting to keep it in the hands of the Mangler's son. It couldn't be. It had to be lies.

'The emperor tells me he mourns for the boy who

wasted his life for this conversation,' the speaker went on. 'It saddens him every time his children die needlessly, even if that child has betrayed him. Today, he has witnessed two children lost, confused, lied to, tricked into chasing the dream of free will - a dream they have neither the ability nor the right to obtain. Know that, before the end, he will lift this curse from you and, once more, offer you glorious purpose.'

Umishi welcomed the cold hands that fell upon her shoulders, the force they applied to get her to her feet; the implication that her time with the speaker had drawn to an end. She longed for the dark, for a place that the horrors and carnage around her could fall into, leaving her alone.

'Before you leave,' the speaker sang through blackened teeth. 'The emperor has something he wishes for you to ponder, something for your mind to explore while your body is imprisoned. He wants you to consider your failings, to understand the errors in allowing yourself choice. That, while you chose to wallow for years in suffering, your Mangler lived here in comfort. That, while you made your vows to ensure what happened in Malhain never happened again, we will be the ones to end Fendamor's legacy, while you chose to protect it. He wants you to think on that before you become a voice. Think that, as his voice, you may at least achieve a semblance of worth before the end. Be humbled by the fact you have been forgiven, that you are blessed. Through the emperor's benevolence, his will, his wisdom and guidance, your wretched life has found meaning. Wait for him to call upon you, child. May you feel the relief of the crushing weight of choice and responsibility lifted from you.

May you now, in your final hours, find peace in his glory.'

Umishi could not say anything, could not speak, could not move. She felt her heart pound as the truth cut its way into her mind, and she was dragged from the speaker's chamber.

FOURTEEN
A DARKER CAGE

In the darkness of Umishi's cell, the Mangler found her. It lurked in the corner opposite, leering from the black, staring with its mocking grin. It sat in the shadows beyond her sight, a faceless spectre that no longer represented a single man, but something more: a poisonous evil that slithered through every town, city, village and homestead, infecting all it touched. It was a venomous thing that would corrode any good, leaving Domvalkia to rotten blackness. She tried closing her eye, tried turning away, but it did not leave her. Instead, it sat in her mind, gloating over its victory. Without sound, it laughed at her from beyond the grave, from every shadow.

The words of the Dhal-Llah speaker had burrowed into her mind like starving maggots that forced her to see the truth of things, to see the Mangler's, no, *Fendamor's* victory. It had revealed that her son was mutilated and tortured to grant Fendamor and now his son uncontested power. Instead of standing in his way, fighting against him as promised, she had wasted her time chasing shadows. She had chased any mage but the monster that tore her life apart. Why? Because she couldn't see the bigger picture, or because it was easier not to?

Her revelation did little to explain why Leuvigild had sent for her. The king had said it was her they sent for, specifically her. Had his goal been to torment her all along? Did he delight in the morbid irony? What had he been expecting her to do? How did he expect her to truly defend his Ward? Did he think she could somehow find a way to prevent the Dhal-Llah from removing it? Did he expect her to kill Renderbrim?

There it was, the answer. That was exactly what he had expected, why he so adamantly insisted that the Dhal-Llah were not the cause of the Ward failing, why he thought investigating her dreams was so important. He had known all along. He wanted her to do his dirty work, to kill the madman in the other world. But how? She could not cross over; he must have known that, must have known how his own Ward worked.

Of course, there was only one answer. Renderbrim, in his mad ravings, had tried to tell her. He had tried to explain that the only person who could have cast her into the other plane was Fendamor himself. At the time, his ill-formed words had seemed like madness but now, through the clarity the Dhal-Llah had granted her, it was evident he didn't mean the long dead founder of the kingdom. He meant *Leuvigild* Fendamor. *He* had sent her into that realm. A thousand scattering insects ran down her spine as the realisation set in. Of course it was Leuvigild who had attacked her that night in the Spinning Dagger, him and his Court of Wizards. That would mean it was possible one of those mages was...

'Are you okay, girl?' Lothrum asked as her thoughts returned to her cell. The cell was nothing more than a crack in the wall someone had tried to cover with an iron fence; cramped even for her stature. In a cell opposite her, the mage lay hunched, bound in iron, his hands cuffed, his neck chained, and the gates pressed to his face; they were clearly not taking any chances with his magic. 'Your expression is almost as blank as those faceless monsters.'

'Monsters? You mean humans; they're your kin,' Umishi corrected him with a sour grimace. Even as the words came from her mouth she could hardly believe the truth of them. They were humans who had twisted themselves beyond recognition. Their descendants had once been a part of the same empire that ruled over Hanaswick, had shared the same plight, tended the same fields. They were human. What madness had turned them against each other? Were the Dhal-Llah considered monsters before or after they had made themselves so.

'I'd hardly call them that, girl,' he sneered. 'What was human once, they've long abandoned, torn off and replaced with metal. Spoke to one, did you? Manage to find one that hadn't cut out its own tongue? What did it have to say? Are we as doomed as the fool Williams thinks we are?'

He'd called her 'girl' again. She drew a breath. Every word the mage spoke felt like a blade piecing her chest, to the point where she could no longer process what he was saying as anything but pain. 'They told me the reason they attacked. How Fendamor split the empire, how they were cast out.'

Echoes of Fendamor

'It wasn't that simple, girl. Fendamor gave them a choice but, where anyone sane would choose to be free, these fools chose to remain slaves to a dead master. It is astonishing the lengths they go to in order to deny themselves freedom, to prove their subservience, to reject their individuality. Surely even you've noticed how each of these creatures has mangled themselves in a way that forces them to perform one duty, so they are not tempted into thinking what else they could be. No, girl, it was not Fendamor who cast them out; it was their unwillingness to take responsibility for their own lives.'

'Why do you defend that monster?' Umishi growled, rage building within her, threatening to burst through her skin.

'What is this?' Lothrum snarled back, 'What are you getting at? Speak plainly.'

Speak plainly? Such a thing would be a novelty on this island; the request almost seemed like a monstrous joke, designed to suffocate those who heard it with barbed laughter.

'I know the truth about the Ward,' Umishi snapped. 'About your arch-mage. I... I know what he... what *you've* done to me!'

And there it was. With those few words, truth twisted his face into an expression of horror. Her heart felt alien; it felt like it had become alive, beating independently, trying its hardest to escape.

'It's true...' she whispered.

'The fools were meant to explain everything to you,' Lothrum stammered, his voice somehow cutting its way through her rage. 'I told Leuvigild that you di... This wasn't how it was meant to be.'

'Wasn't how it was meant to be.' The words were poison, burning as they entered Umishi's head and exploding as they seeped into her heart. He had lied to her, they had all lied to her, the Dhal-Llah were right! He had lied to her to protect the monster who sat in a palace, no doubt weaving political strings like a web, trapping all who stumbled into Hanaswick's throne room. Her rage took over her senses as she threw herself against the bars that separated Lothrum's cell from hers. She screamed at him, she had to let it out, she... she couldn't contain it anymore. All she had done up until now was pointless. He was right there and she had spent days going in the opposite direction. She screamed until there was no air left in her lungs, until there was no strength in her body, until she fell to the ground. There she sat, gasping, trying to replace the air she had lost.

'It's not what you think,' he whispered, defeat stifling his voice. 'Fendamor has protected-'

'He threw me into the other place. Into the jaws of those fucking monsters, the Kalsakian, blind. So, he could keep hold of his power, his Ward made from the blood of my *family*! My *son*!' She recalled what he had said to her: that the momentous day in Malhain had finally caught up with her. It made sense now: he had been talking about how she would help him preserve the Ward! She screamed again.

'I am sorry, that was not how it was supposed to happen,' Lothrum said. 'There wasn't... I mean, he told me there was no risk; that you wouldn't get hurt. There wasn't meant to be anything in the other place. We didn't even know what a Kal-bloody-sakian was. How could we have?

Please you must believe me, he... *we* didn't intend for any of this to happen.'

Umishi breathed deeply as the mage made his confession. It was him; he had been there when she was attacked. Which one had he been? The one who slit her wrist? Did she stab through him when she awoke? It didn't matter; what mattered was that the Dhal-Llah were right: she had been manipulated into serving the arch-mage and his monstrous lineage.

There was nothing more to say. The lies had taken their toll on her weary mind. Umishi took a deep breath and pulled away from the bars. In the dark, Lothrum explained what had happened to Vallis, what had seeded the rage, what he thought was going to happen. It didn't matter. Locked in this cage, her rage would do her no good. It would blind her to chances of escape... she had to control her breathing, slow it down, bring it back to normal. She closed her eye and focused on the air she was expelling. When it opened again, clarity grew within her, bubbling from the pit of her stomach like a newly sprung stream.

'Fendamor has protected.' The words ran through her head over and over, again and again. She recalled the promise the Mangler made before his spell tore her life apart: he had promised to save them from the emperor's brutal rule, promised the spell he intended to cast would grant them safety. The promise of protection was the same lie his son was using to justify his father's horrific experiment.

'... be okay?'

Umishi turned to Vallis. Her mind twisted in on itself as it failed to process the stupidity of the question. Despite the thousand answers her brain cried out, her jaw locked, refusing to release the incoherent scream of rage she wanted to throw at the fool in the other cell. No, it was not the time for anger; it was the time to regain control. Ignoring the question, Umishi closed her eye and retreated inward. To attempt escape, she needed to dispel this emotional fog and regain clarity.

There was no way to tell how much time had passed since she had been placed in her cell. It was possible that hours or days had gone by since Vallis had asked her question. Had she given the commander an answer? Was there a response? None of that mattered as Umishi approached the cell door. She traced the keyhole with a finger. Once more, the lock was simple. She pulled a lock pick from her hip and, with a few swift and elegant movements, the door clicked to announce it was ready to be opened.

'Wait! No stop!' The mage insisted from behind his bars. 'I know... well no, I don't know, I... Look, you're confused. Your mind is a hot pot of emotions, but now is not the time for you to do anything rash. There's a guard on the other side of that door, and I have no doubt he has a great set of lungs!'

Umishi sneered at the human as she passed him.

The breathing of the Dhal-Llah seemed to be amplified by their masks. Maybe the humans could not hear it as clearly as she could though. Even through the heavy dungeon doors, his breathing filled the room: slow and deep, close to snoring. To Umishi, it translated to one thing: this creature's guard was down. She had monitored the movements of the Dhal-Llah since entering Llanvurgist. They could be quick and powerful when they wished to be but, for the most part, they seemed to favour slow, often exaggerated, movements. The only risk she was taking was relying on the overly talkative humans to be silent.

'Wait!' Vallis gasped from her cell. 'Y... you don't know the way. You don't know how to get out. I've been here before, I visited their speaker... I know the way out.'

Vallis' words made Umishi pause. The commander was right: getting out of the dungeon was one thing, but out of the underground maze was another. She tugged at her hair and twisted to face the human's cage. There was no doubt the human commander knew more about the current situation than her, more about the monsters she would have to face and more about the layout of their city.

'Commander, I knew you were a fool, but to join in on this madness?' said Lothrum with dismay. 'You of all people should know what the Dhal-Llah are capable of and, between here and Fend... and our home, there will be an army of those creepy bastards.'

'I don't want to die,' the commander stated, 'If we stay here, that's what will happen. They'll have us killed so they can hang us from hooks to perform their... acts of madness. I've never had to question which way I'd rather die before, but it wouldn't be that way, not like that. Please, Inquisitor!'

Although Umishi's mind was trapped in a tempest of swirling hate, Vallis' plea resonated with her and found mercy in the squall. It was true that Vallis was a servant of her unmasked foe, but it was clear overcoming the current obstacle was at the forefront of her mind, despite her misguided loyalty.

Once more, the lock might as well have been a door

handle. The cage door swung open. Vallis passed over the threshold faster than Umishi could remove her pick. The commander gave Umishi a grateful, but nervous, smile as she held her hands out before her. Umishi pulled back; she didn't have the time or understanding to engage in human customs. She gave the dungeon doors a glance.

'Fine!' the mage grumbled 'If you ladies will not heed my wisdom and continue to shun all logic then I guess I must come with you.'

Umishi ignored him and headed for the door. The idea of freeing such a knowing agent of the Mangler was laughable, and the fact he had yet to bring the truth of things to his lips only proved him a coward. Vallis, on the other hand, paused, clearly torn between escape and the fate of the mage. That was a problem Umishi had no desire to let linger. Vallis was to come with her or not.

'You're still not thinking clearly, are you, girl?' The mage barked. 'I have little doubt you will make it past those doors and do something very impressive and clever to make it out of the dungeon, but you seem to be forgetting a very important something: your weapons are still in the hands of the Dhal-Llah. So, before you rush off, I ask: do the Dhal-Llah use magic? I don't bloody know, do you?'

She gritted her teeth. He was right, of course he was right. She took a step closer to the door. For a moment, she considered leaving him there anyway, out of spite. Would anything the Dhal-Llah did to her be worse than his company, the constant reminder of her foolishness? She refused to meet his gaze as her fingers worked to grant him his freedom. There was no need to acknowledge the smug smile that doubtless engulfed his face. She clawed her hair over scars that seemed to grow in both size and ugliness with each moment that passed under his watchful eyes.

'You've made a wise decision, girl.' Lothrum said with a shallow smile in place of the smugness she was expecting. 'Now then, Inquisitor, what's the plan? Are we going to stick to the shadows? Sneak around on our tiptoes? If we are, then I shall have to borrow the young commander's shoulder; my balance isn't quite what it used to be. Of course, we could always break out of here in a cacophony of fire and explosions. Likely, we'd get caught quickly, but we'd put on quite the show.'

Surprise stole his smile as Umishi administered a swift kick to the knee. Lothrum groaned in pain as he hit the ground with a thud. Watching him writhe on the floor brought her little satisfaction, but it did bring him down to her level. She grabbed him by the neck and forced him to face her.

'You will do as I tell you,' she snarled. '*Exactly* what I tell you. If you don't, you will beg me to put you back in the cage.' She pushed his face away, tired of looking at it.

'I likely deserved that,' he sniffed, wiping the dirt and blood from his mouth. 'Probably worth the risk of alerting the guard... but your message is received loud and clear, girl. Even if I need to piss, I shall ask you first.'

'And do not call me "girl".'

'I...' he stuttered, pulling himself up. 'Yes, I'm sorry.'

'What's the quickest way out of here?' Umishi growled, turning to Vallis.

'There's a well in the chapel, just a little way away from

here,' the commander offered. 'It leads all the way back to the lake; at least, that's what I was told when they showed me around this place, but that was years ago and-'

'Seems as good a plan as any, I'd say,' Lothrum declared, offering Umishi a weary glance. 'Besides, we don't have time for a better one to fall into our laps. The more time we take dallying, the more likely it is the Dhal-Llah will ensure there is no safety to escape to.'

Once more, he was right. Between the revelations and being captured, Umishi had almost forgotten about the Dhal-Llah's impending advance. There was no time for doubting or delaying. Umishi had been still for too long; she had to move, had to *do* something. 'Stay here and do nothing,' she said. 'The screams will be your signal to leave.' She picked up a loose stone and set her plan into motion without further explanation.

FIFTEEN
THE COST OF FREEDOM

There was no time to waste. Umishi pushed the door open and squeezed through into the next room. Undetected, she assessed her new location. The main entrance lay just before her, an oil lamp burning above granting the room an oppressive orange glow. Her eye turned to a flight of stairs next to a small wooden desk. The stairs led up to a second floor and their escape but first, she would have to dispatch the guard. As monstrous as the bladed Dhal-Llah's appeared, it was still human and therefore cursed with the same flaws as any other.

On all fours, Umishi circled around the creature's back. The Dhal-Llah's breathing started to pick up pace. Could it hear her? She pressed herself against the dungeon wall. The guard shifted, twisting its faceless mask towards the door she had come from. With honed agility, her body slithered around the creature's legs as she began towards the dungeon's exit.

The Dhal-Llah took a step back, and she felt its leather boot brush past her tail. The guard retracted its original movement.

It twisted to face her, and Umishi saw a slight glimmer as the lamp above the exit cast light into the dark pits of the creature's eyes. She stood, her tail moving back around her ankles. It worked; the fool did not seem to understand it was being lured into her trap. The Dhal-Llah ran towards her, slashing at her with its bladed arm in a way that demonstrated its lack of discipline.

Umishi easily dodged, spinning away from the Dhal-Llah's bestial charge.

Stopping just short of the exit, it turned to face her. She could sense its rage as she threw her stone at the guard. The creature put its hand up in an attempt to catch the hurled projectile. The Ward performed its duty diligently, allowing the potentially harmful object to pass through the Dhal-Llah. Umishi grinned.

A violent crash made the creature look up. In that same moment, shattered glass and burning fluids rained from the struck lamp onto the creature's black robes, rage twisted into pain and confusion as the pitiless flame engulfed her foe with ravenous speed. She did not need to watch the Dhal-Llah strike itself with its bladed arm in a fatal attempted to put itself out. She got no satisfaction from the death of the human; there was no justice in its death, just necessity. Stepping back into the dungeon's entrance, she gestured for the others to come.

'What happened to the screaming?' Lothrum asked, emerging from the dungeon.

Umishi offered him a joyless grin. 'It must have cut its tongue out, I guess.'

The mage did not seem to find any amusement in

Umishi's quip. Instead, his focus was drawn to the burnt Dhal-Llah corpse, all colour drained from his face and his eyes seemed to grow, barely fitting his sockets, giving him a visage more dead than the creature that lay before him.

'Is it...?' Lothrum whispered, with a quiver in his voice.

It was not a response Umishi had expected. 'There will be more death upstairs,' she said, detecting a potential problem. Her plan relied on the mage's ability to fight. She watched both Lothrum and the commander gawk at the monster's body for a moment, realising how blind she had been while formulating her plan. These humans had never seen death before; not this kind of death. This would be a problem, but not one she had time to deal with. The plan was already in motion and there was no turning back. Umishi grabbed a box of parchment from the desk and lobbed it at the burning creature. The flames consumed the wooden box with an impressive hunger and lunged for the papers that flew from it. Set free onto the floor, the flames leapt at anything in attempt to satisfy their insatiable appetite, including the wooden frame of the dungeon's exit.

'Are you insane?' the mage cried, his focus finally torn from the corpse. 'Are you trying to roast us? Is this your plan to escape death at the hands of the Dhal-Llah? Burning us alive instead?'

'Up the stairs,' Umishi ordered. 'Expect more Dhal-Llah.' She tugged at her hair and cursed the stairs ahead of her. What did it matter? Now was not the time for caring about such indignities; now was the time for survival. Before the stairs, Umishi fell to all fours and ascended them ahead of the group. Vallis followed, tailed by the grumbling mage.

As expected, upon reaching the top of the stairs, she locked eyes with another guard at the end of an ill lit corridor. The Dhal-Llah raised its bladed arm and charged toward them with relentless rage. Umishi jumped out of the creature's way. It rammed its shoulder against the wall to stabilise itself. The beast's reach was long. She couldn't dodge it again. 'Mage!' Umishi cried as the monster readied its swing.

A biting chill filled the air as the wood around the creature grew, recalling its past life. Branches spurted from the floor, wrapping themselves into tangled knots as they reached up towards the ceiling.

Only a finger-sized space existed between the grizzly-looking blade and Umishi's ear. Cold terror infested the creature's eyes. The weaving branches encaged the beast.

'You are quite welcome, gir- Mage-hunter,' Lothrum gloated, standing aside for Vallis to continue up the stairs.

Umishi turned to the window behind her. Through it, thick black smoke rose from the floor below. The fire, it seemed, was doing its job.

'Are you not curious about what I did?' he continued. 'You see, it took a considerable understanding of dendrology and some guesswork to...'

Umishi blocked out his nonsense as she found a crack that seemed to lead out of the prison complex. The smell of smoke began filling the room. Umishi resisted the urge to cough. A crowd of Dhal-Llah gathered on the bridge beneath them, all enthralled by the growing fires. All was going as planned.

'You're not planning on going out there are you?' Vallis

asked. 'We'll be seen and-'

'Not if the mage tells the smoke to cover us,' Umishi answered. She shot a glance at Lothrum.

'You understand that there is only so much energy I can draw from one place without causing some rather ugly problems? But I suppose I can muster up enough for such a small spell. Let's see.'

As he started to speak, the smoke drifted over the crack, offering them enough cover to hide as they made their escape. The mage opened his eyes as the familiar chill froze the air around them. However, this time, it was accompanied by a strange smell: the smell of a catacomb or some other room left dormant for a long time. It was a smell that reminded Umishi of the other place. Biting her lip, she tried to shake off the cold, unpleasant feeling that clawed at her memories. She gestured towards the crack for the two humans to take their leave. They gave her apprehensive glances but followed her command. For them, the gap must have been painfully tight, but they made it onto the ledge safely and out of her sight.

Alone and beyond the range of human eyes, Umishi did what the humans could not, what they had no stomach to watch. Using a branch snapped from the prison Lothrum had erected, she took the fires that crawled up the staircase and brought them to the still paralysed Dhal-Llah. Fear filled the creature's eyes as she did so. Once more, she took no joy in this act, but she could not risk the mage's spell coming undone as they navigated the thin walkways. She could not risk this guard calling down to those below, drawing their attention from the flames. The creature's eyes were wide and filled with terror, but she did what had to be done so that those below had no reason to look up.

Beyond the thick smoke, more creatures gathered beneath them. They skirted across the wall of the great pit on a ledge that barely existed. The Dhal-Llah were distracted by the blaze rather than what was happening above them. It was a lesson she had learnt during the early days of mastering her trade: Walnorg, human or Nal-Tiran, people seldom took the time to glance upward.

Ahead of her, the humans were having a harder time of it. The narrow width of the walkway made it clear that the ledge was designed for maintenance rather than casual use. The larger, flatter feet of the humans were not made for navigating such precarious footing, and she doubted their footwear helped them either. A shiver ran down her back as she tried to imagine how the Dhal-Llah might have altered themselves to traverse these platforms.

Lothrum struggled the most, his teetering progress hindering her own. Umishi gritted her teeth, having to remind herself of the old mage's usefulness.

Vallis, on the other hand, seemed to be making good speed and looked to her for what to do next. Umishi acknowledged her with a nod before pointing at another nearby bridge, slightly lower down.

The bridge didn't seem to lead anywhere, and Umishi guessed its creation was incidental, or perhaps as a support of some kind. Either way, it would be useful in their escape. It was an easy enough gap to jump; the people of her homelands would jump gaps like that all the time, even the children. Surely the humans wouldn't have too much trouble with it? Thomas could jump gaps twice the size. She took a moment to push the memories back down.

Above her, Vallis jumped safely onto the narrow bridge. Without prompting, she lay down flat. Umishi smiled. There was hope for the scarecrow soldier yet.

'You have to be jesting,' Lothrum gasped. 'I am seventy-three; my jumping days are far behind me.'

Regretting that she hadn't taken the lead, Umishi bit down hard on her lip and took a deep breath. She could not help but cringe as the mage spoke the number as if it were an explanation for his inadequacies; she was over twice his age and complained less than half as much. Behind them, the smoke was starting to dissipate. The Dhal-Llah were starting to get the fire under control, which meant the three of them were running out of time.

'Take my hand, Erik,' Vallis said as she reached for him.

Umishi watched as the elderly human took the commander's help. With much dithering and posturing, the mage was aided across. Vallis then helped him to his knees as they waited for her. The mage was lucky this solution worked, as she had considered just pushing the old fool. Umishi jumped from the ledge onto the bridge with visible ease. She joined Vallis and the panting mage, who were as low to the roof as they could get. It was still not low enough for Umishi's liking; alone, she would have sunk below any possible sightline, rendering herself invisible. The height of these humans would be a problem should a wandering eye turn skywards.

Below her, there lay what could only be the chapel entrance the commander had told her about. The mouth of the tunnel looked more ornate than the others, decorated with symbols and writing Umishi didn't recognise. It was a short distance away after dropping from the bridge onto its lower twin. It would be a quick run, perhaps passing three junctions, before getting there. It would have been a simple enough task, if she had been alone. She glanced back at the mage. He looked as though he was about to pass out; his breathing was sharp and erratic, sweat streamed down his face. All that, and they still had a way to go yet. This wasn't going to work.

'Did you know about this platform?' the mage whispered. 'I'm fairly sure you were pretty focused on your brooding when you were brought here. I could be wrong; it's hard to tell with all the hair and, well...'

Vallis gave him a sharp nudge to the rib to shush him.

'All I want to know is whether we are being led by our single-minded friend here or following luck into the jaws of doom.'

Umishi had never believed in plans. To her, it seemed one could plan for years, analysing every possible scenario to find it all counted for nought, as there would always be some unexpected variable; something that found its way into well-oiled plans and ruined everything that had taken so long to build. The guards were disappearing through the dungeon's entryway now, meaning there would be fewer to hide from.

'Come on,' she grunted, as she slid from the bridge and onto the larger walkway below.

As her feet touched the ground, she resisted the urge to run for the well. Above her, Vallis was readying herself to make the jump, whereas the mage was sizing up the gap with dismay. Taking another deep breath, she waited.

Around her, life seemed to be going back to whatever this strange city considered normal. The crowd around the dungeon mouth had begun to disperse. Two guards took up positions outside the charred doorway.

Vallis' feet reached the bottom, her eyes ablaze with an anxious fear that Umishi understood perfectly. Above them, the mage was slowly getting down onto all fours; what was he doing? They didn't have time for this kind of silliness. They were out in the open, exposed; it was inevitable they would be seen. It only took a guard to turn its head, a passer-by to turn in their direction. Hell, someone could come out of the tunnel they were next to. They had to run; they had to go. They would be spotted, but they had to run.

Lothrum finally started his descent. Vallis offered her hand, and Umishi couldn't tell whether it was out of kindness or eagerness to get him down. Out of the corner of Umishi's eye a shadow moved. A faceless mask clicked as it turned in their direction, its eyes within wide, burning with a rage much akin to the blaze that had just been put out. The Dhal-Llah roared and two more jerked into a similar position. There was no more time for this baby sitting. Umishi fell to all fours. With staggering speed, she darted past several junctions and into the chapel's opening.

As she entered the massive, dome-shaped chamber, she was greeted by a familiar face. A towering statue reached out to her from the far end of the room. It bore an eerie likeness to the madman residing in the other plane: Renderbrim.

Behind her, Vallis practically dragged the mage along. Some distance away, the guards closed in. Her eye found a winch on her side of the entrance, which would no doubt release the gate above and ensure her escape. Of course, the consequences of that would be her reluctant companions' deaths. Her temptation to free the mechanism only lasted a moment; she still needed them; she didn't know this land, how far she was from Fendamor's borders. She gave them a glance before she headed straight for the well that lay between the knees of the open-armed idle.

From openings that led deeper into the place of worship, white faces appeared out of the darkness, with the sound of blades scraping against walls. They had found her. With no time to think, Umishi lifted herself onto the well's lips and, as she did, a blue cloud erupted from the stone mouth, spewing over its sides and spilling onto the floor. Umishi leapt back, her heart barely contained within her chest. She found no escape; from the corners of the strange temple, shadows grew towards her. The Dhal-Llah had vanished, her companions were gone, and the stalking darkness rushed in to consume her.

SIXTEEN

FALLING INTO DARKNESS

The shadows were relentless in their attack, merciless and unforgiving. Umishi fell to her knees as the cruel shades turned her world into blackness. With her face cradled in her elbows and her heart deep in the pit of her stomach, familiar sounds announced the beginnings of her recurring nightmare, heralding the monsters in the dark. They were all around her, their talons clicking against the stone floor, their breathing reverberating from every wall. The heat of their bodies pressed against her skin. The Kalsakian surrounded her.

'You?' enquired a familiar voice, the only other voice to haunt this realm of darkness. 'You're here again! Why? What is this? If you are not his, why are you here? Why are you moving stuff? Why are you moving *my* stuff?'

Umishi raised her head to behold the shadow plane again, to once more witness the lifeless reflection of her own world and its malformed denizens. She stood as the monsters gathered around her. Twisted things with ill-formed, skeletal limbs dragged themselves from the well and shambled through the temple doors. In front of her stood Renderbrim, his pale skin and soft features a stark contrast to the horrors that circled around him.

Umishi's lips remained still; she did not know how to respond to his mad questions.

With a swift twist of his heel the madman spun himself around. 'No, no I forgive you my dear! You didn't know any better after all, and no harm was done.'

'You tried to warn me,' she whispered, her mind twisting in a maelstrom of blurred worlds and loyalties, each one forever in motion and offering nothing tangible for her to hold on to. The more time she spent spinning in the storm of Domvalkia, the more these concepts started to meld into one.

'Shh,' Renderbrim replied, twirling and dancing around her, as though he were a ballerina in a dream. 'We will talk, my dear. Yes, we will have a great conversation, but not yet. I must focus; I need to concentrate if I am to see them. Do *you* see them? Like wisps in the air, spider webs on the wind. Thin, translucent cotton, each strand connecting to those on the other side. Threads which tether those with the Ward from here to there. Do you see them? We must be quick, my dear, I shall not lose them to the Dhal-Llah. To do so would be such a waste.'

Umishi watched, her eye tracing his erratic movements. Was *this* what she was doomed to become? Was this island, were its people, conspiring to break her mind, forcing her to share the same madness as this poor fool?

As he moved, his creatures followed, skulking at his heels. They were different from those she had seen before. The limbs of these monsters weren't just melded into them; most of them were missing limbs altogether. The more she looked at them the more her stomach twisted. It seemed as though they had been ravaged by some beast, or insane butcher. She cast her gaze back to Renderbrim.

'How do you command them like that?' She asked.

'Hmm? The Dhal-Llah?' Renderbrim asked, seeming to wake from his lucid dream. 'No, my dear no, no, no, they take their orders from *him*.' He pointed to the statue that loomed over them both. 'Although not really; he's dead of course. Still, they think they hear him. I don't understand it myself, whether their speakers lie to their people or truly think they are talking to a ghost. No my dear, I merely allowed them to start their war, herded them. I was always good with pets, that's what he said - my father - yes, good with pets. The secret to controlling both creatures is the same. You condition them with symbols and rewards. For the Kalsakian, a command followed by a treat, and for the Dhal-Llah, I send a Kalsakian into their world, into their sight, so that they know when I have cut the threads, brought down the Ward, and they can attack. It is really not that complex.'

Umishi's mind was adrift, clawing desperately for any strand of logic she could use to create a stable chain of thought, a raft in the sea of madness. Perhaps it was the state of mind she was in, but Renderbrim's words were making complete sense. She had seen it; had seen the Kalsakian on Fort Jimmarah's ramparts. It had been the signal that initiated the Dhal-Llah's assault and so much death.

'Ah ha!' Renderbrim screamed with childlike jubilance, a grin carved into his sickly face and raven hair falling to mischievously tease his eyebrows. His arm grew and twisted as it freed itself from his feathered cloak. Focusing on the transforming limb was painful as it distorted. Another arm burst through skin and cloth, in an eruption of blood. It extended outward, shaking and flailing, looking more like a tree branch than anything made of flesh. Umishi's eye widened with horror as she took a step backwards. Gnarled twig-like fingers sprang from its hands, grasping as if holding a fine teacup. With a quick movement of the wrist, a blinding flash exploded from between Renderbrim's fingers, making Umishi's talisman practically jump from her neck. The mad mage cried out in delight.

As the light subsided, her vision returned, as did the blurred forms of Lothrum and Vallis. Their heartbeats joined in a rushed pulse that offered a dramatic duet to the backdrop of rapid breathing.

Limp and visibly sapped, both humans were brought to the ground as Renderbrim twisted himself back around to face her. The grotesque extra limb shrivelled and receding back into his flesh. A grin stretched across his face, threatening to break his cheeks. 'There it is!' he crowed. 'Now, we have to keep it safe, we can't have it moving again, can we?'

It was not clear whether the crazed human was talking to her or himself. Umishi remained silent, either way. The Kalsakian snarled and clicked angrily at the new arrivals, their teeth only held at bay by stern, silent orders issued by their master. Vallis remained still; she seemed to be hardly breathing at all, her eyes fixed on the twisted monsters that drooled before her, too afraid to move at all, Lothrum did not seem to share her caution.

The old mage pushed himself to his feet, taking in the new surroundings with a voice eager to be heard. 'What?... How?' he yelled in sporadic gasps, 'The Dhal-Llah, these beasts.... where? What's happening?'

'No! No, no, no,' Renderbrim screamed. 'You don't speak! You're a puppet, a pawn, one of his *things*! You don't get to speak!' The monsters around them barked and chirped in an echo of their master's wild rage. 'You will walk, you will follow, you will do as I say. It is what your kind does, it's the only thing you do correctly.' With a reluctant glance, he cast his eyes over the fallen commander. 'Get that one to its feet, it'll need to stand, to walk too. They can't be here, they don't belong here, they can't... they need to... never mind, just make it walk!'

As the monsters wrapped their claws around Vallis' shoulders, horror and hopelessness bled into her face. Her eyes, wide and oozing with cold terror, looked at Umishi. What did she expect her to do? They were in the same predicament. Umishi had no more power over the situation than the commander. Renderbrim, despite his madness, was a mage. It would only take a single word for him to break their necks or turn their insides to ash, and she was just as naked before that power as everyone else without her daggers to protect her.

As the Kalsakian attempted to force Lothrum forward, the elderly human started to mutter. The words grabbed

Renderbrim's attention and froze him to the spot, and Umishi guessed that they were words that would normally invoke the energies that surrounded them. Lothrum's furious rambling stopped, though. His face contorted in horror and pain. Choking, the elderly mage seized his neck as though he were trying to squeeze the breath from his throat. His face reddened as he fell to the ground, blood dripping from his nose.

'A lesson learnt, I think,' Renderbrim said. 'This is not your world. The energies of this plane are already being taxed and spent elsewhere. Not here... the other place.' His tone grew softer as he approached Lothrum with an open hand, helping him to his feet. The Kalsakian gathered closer, their hungry eyes closing in on the broken mage. 'There are scraps left for those like us, but you need to know how to look, how to see the strings, the tiny threads that... ah yes, you'll see, yes.'

'What is this place? Where are the Dhal-Llah? I...?' Lothrum wheezed, still choking on the remnants of failed words. 'Why?'

'The inquisitor brought you here. You're not meant to be here, I didn't *want* you here,' Renderbrim replied.

'What!' Vallis struggled, her gaze fixed on Umishi. 'What's he saying? What is happening? What did you do?'

'Pointless, all pointless, no, no, your questions have no purpose,' Renderbrim snarled 'You need to be at Hanaswick. You have things there you must do. We have people to free and a monster to slay.'

Umishi watched as the deranged mage led his captives back through the temple. The Kalsakian made no effort to get her to follow, made no threats against her, yet she watched as the creatures tugged and lashed the humans, biting at their heels if they did not move in line with their master. They were leaving her. Renderbrim had already stepped beyond the temple's threshold. They would leave her in the dark alone, in this place, in a world that was alien to her and on an island that she had no chance of navigating.

Umishi was torn. Seeing them dragged away in such a manner sparked the urge to help. Her brain gave other commands, telling her to stand aside. Renderbrim sought to kill Leuvigild Fendamor and destroy his Ward; was that not her goal? The mage had lied to her, brought her into this world, into this mess, and the commander, although ignorant of the evils that surrounded her, was she truly blameless? She recalled Vallis' coldness on the docks, a cruelness the Ward granted her the confidence to execute.

The commander cried out as the teeth and claws of the Kalsakian dragged her forward. Every muscle in Umishi's body called for her to be merciful, begged that logic be tossed aside for sympathy. She needed time, needed to think. She cursed herself for being so stupid. Why couldn't she think faster? How was she taking so long to figure out who was right and who was wrong? Which of these two forces was the greater evil? She needed to *think*.

The drumming of her heart pulled her from her thoughts. Her attention fell on the progressing situation and the gate's open mouth. The captives were fast approaching the exit. She glanced at the winch drilled into the entrance's lips and pressed herself forward. Her limbs rejoiced at the order to move, her speed matching her body's eagerness.

Passing ahead of the Kalsakian and their prisoners, she leapt, her hands grasping the winch and pressing down on it with her full bodyweight.

With a single click, the chains that held the gate in place roared into action. The twisted metal came crashing to the ground, separating Renderbrim from the other humans with thick cell-like bars. The mad mage turned around and threw himself at the obstruction. The Kalsakian dropped their quarry and then, with upturned heads and confused expressions, searched the air for their next orders.

Renderbrim explored the gate with his fingers. 'Iron.'

'Iron,' Umishi repeated with a proud grin.

Free of the Kalsakian's grip, Vallis made for the nearest wall. The creatures croaked, her motions sending them into a rage. The monsters were upon the commander, then, her arms lifted, shielding herself from the onslaught of teeth and talon.

'Stop!' their master called from beyond the gates. 'I will not have them harmed, any of them, they must be intact, they must be able to move!' His words halted the Kalsakian as his eyes fell upon Umishi. 'What is this, my dear, you clever little bird? Why is it that you keep finding ways to delay me? If you are not his, why do you hinder me so?'

'You promised me a conversation,' she whispered, unsure of what she was doing. What did she even expect of him? Answers? The truth?

Renderbrim gave her a pleasant smile, white teeth shining from under stretched lips. 'Ah, yes, yes, you were listening, yes, you heard right,' he cooed. 'I did promise, my dear, and I give you my word, we will talk, but not now, no, no, no, not here. The setting, it isn't right, so drab, so ghastly,' he said, stroking the bars. 'And neither of us have the time, my dear, no, I fear I will not be able to make you understand, make you see. Even now, I am acutely aware of the motions of the Dhal-Llah: their strings, fluttering through windless skies, ever westward. No, we do not have the time.'

Umishi's mouth dropped open as Renderbrim pushed himself away from the gates. Was this a trap? A trick? Was he truly leaving Lothrum, Vallis, her? This wasn't how she had thought it would go. She needed answers, she...

'Wait!' she cried.

Lothrum started to push himself to his feet. His motions were slow, and not just because of his age. He was looking around at the monsters around him, with their clicking and croaking.

'Come on,' he whispered.

'Do not worry, I am not leaving you, my dear, not in earnest,' Renderbrim called back as the shadows started to engulf him. 'We each have places to be. I have duties to perform in Jimmarah, and Holsta. And you, my dear, you have presented a solution to a problem I had. I can't be in two places at once, after all. You shall take these puppets of Fendamor, and lead them where they should be far more effectively than I could. You'll take them to the place they need to be, and then we will talk. All will be ready and set, and from there you shall see, you'll understand. The mage will help you if you get lost. I have every faith in you, my dear. Every faith you will set the pieces in their right place.'

Umishi didn't understand. How could he know where

she was going, what she was going to do, before she even knew? She pressed herself against the bars.

'Be quick, my dear,' he said, nothing more than a formless shadow. 'My friends will grow impatient when I am gone, and I feel they are already hungry.'

Umishi took a breath and turned back to the inside of the temple, the well, the two humans and the many hungry mouths. Once more, she did not know what to do. Should she open the gate? Should she run after him? Would she be able to do it before these monsters attacked? It was all such a mess. How had it come to this? How had she *let it* come to this?

'We have to move!' Lothrum yelled.

Vallis did not hesitate. The human commander, with her eyes still locked on a misshapen enemy, dragged herself from their reach before taking to her feet. Likewise, Lothrum, still fatigued after his failed attempt at spellcasting, made his way over to the well's opening. Meanwhile, Umishi watched.

The well was big, big enough for a human, a thick iron chain running down, easy enough to climb. 'We'll lower Erik down first,' Vallis called to Umishi, without taking her eyes off the creatures. 'Please, come with us, you're the only one who... please, I can't... not alone.'

Umishi felt her heart once more call out for pity, at least for the commander. She shot another glance at the darkness beyond the bars, then bit her lip. She hadn't been given much choice and she likely needed them as much as they needed her. Umishi sighed, conceding to her own logic. Renderbrim was right about one thing: this putrid mausoleum was no place to linger. Vallis began to wrap the well's chain around Lothrum's waist.

'I can do it myself,' he protested. 'I am not completely useless!'

Vallis ignored his stubbornness and secured him before lowering him into the black. After they felt him reach the bottom, it was her turn. She braced herself against the stone walls, her feet locking to the weak mortar, and gave Umishi a silent glance of gratitude before she too descended.

Umishi took a deep breath and jumped into the darkness, through the blue mist, down the well's throat.

SEVENTEEN

LOST

Umishi allowed herself to fall. Falling was good, falling was fast, falling put distance between her and the monsters above. She counted to two before she grasped hold of the chain. Her hands screamed in pain as she brought herself to a halt. The chain swung back and forth for a time before she steadied it. The darkness reached up from beneath her, beckoning her into the seemingly bottomless void. Was this well still in use? Were Vallis and Lothrum safe? Had they gone on without her? Hand over hand, she lowered herself into the cold darkness.

There was no sign of how deep the well was, nor how far she had climbed. The sound of her heart echoed off the walls. Lowing her tail, she tried to use it as a warning for what would greet her at the well's floor, whether it was water, ground or anything else.

Finally, after what felt like an age, the tip of her tail felt wet, soft earth. Umishi let go. The mud reached her knees; it would take a great deal of effort to wade through.

'I'm glad you decided to side with us,' said Lothrum's

sarcastic voice, presenting her with his mud-sodden robe. 'I feel I would have missed out on this quite magical experience had you not saved us from that madman. I can't help but think how much I would have regretted not being up to my knees in mud and rat shit.'

'For fuck's sake, Erik, shut up!' Vallis said. 'Nobody cares. Don't you get it? Didn't you see those things? Those monsters? And we're without the Ward, down here in the dark. I can't see. I... I want to go home. I just want to go home. I... I can't... I can't move anymore.'

The human had made it this far, had done the hard part; why did she have to break down here, in the mud of all places?

'Waiting does good for nobody,' Umishi said to the commander. Despite her own fears she had to be stone, they needed leadership, direction. In the dark she bit her lip. 'We need to keep moving.'

With outstretched arms Umishi found her way to the wall.

'What? Why? Where can we go? Our homes are being invaded! There's nowhere left for us to go! The Ward has gone, and these monsters are after us,' Vallis cried. 'Do you even care?'

'I know how bleak things seem, girl.' came Lothrum's voice, his steps squelching as he approached the sound of Vallis' sobs. 'And I doubt me adding bullshit about hope and silver-linings would make the mess we are in feel any better. But you've got to get up, girl. Personally, I'd rather be in the light feeling miserable for myself. At least then I can take some comfort of seeing how much more bloody miserable everyone else is. After all, our leader here is a veritable ocean of misery.'

The truth in Lothrum's words burnt. Umishi held back her anger and took a breath. His words got the commander to stand, that was all that was important. She closed her eye and drew another breath before pressing forward.

For a time, the trio walked without uttering a word to one another. After a time, the silence was broken, not by tongues but by the cave itself: the sound of dripping water came from ahead. Of course, it was a well, after all. Umishi pulled her hair over her face. She'd have to be careful. She felt Vallis bump against her. The feeling of another living person felt alarming and alien, and she pulled herself away as fast as she could. 'There's water,' she said, regaining her composure. 'I'll need to go slower, until we find it.' Lothrum grumbled something, nothing constructive or positive she was sure. She continued to press on into the ever-blinding darkness.

It did not take long for the water's whereabouts to make itself known. Umishi felt the cold wetness as her toes dipped off into the water's edge.

'It's here,' she whispered to Vallis, without knowing why she adjusted the volume of her voice.

'Can we go around?' the commander asked.

'No,' Umishi answered after some thought. 'If we do, we risk losing the wall and getting lost ourselves; we're going to have to climb.' The walls were jagged, with no end of footholds and stones to grip onto. 'I'll lead the way.'

'Climb? You have to be joking, girl, I'd sooner walk on the bloody waters,' the mage said. 'There has to be another way.'

'I shall try to be as loud as I can, so you can keep close.' She didn't know how weak the hearing of humans was, but she hoped her plan would work.

'Wait,' Vallis said, with a strange amount of delight given the situation. 'We can use Erik's belt. It's long enough. We can tie it to each other, and you can guide us across.'

Once more, grumbling echoed from the dark as the mage accepted the commander's solution.

It was a good idea, a better plan than the one they had already, at least. It was not long before the makeshift rope was pressed into her hand. Umishi tied the lace around her own belt. The plan was going to work.

There was no true way of knowing if this was the way out, no way to guarantee that there would be anything beyond the stagnant waters but a dead end, death or, worse, a maze without end in which they would wander blindly forever. Umishi took a breath and, without any more pointless thinking, thrust herself against the wall, gripping hold of it with both hands and feet. She started climbing horizontally across. It was at moments like these that she was grateful for her claw like appendages. She felt the tug on the belt as Vallis followed.

'Are you okay?' Umishi asked into the blackness.

'Uh huh.'

Umishi waited for some kind of sarcastic remark from Lothrum, some statement about how he was loving the situation, how climbing was one of his favourite pastimes, but all she heard were indistinct grumbles muffled by exhausted panting and grunts of pain.

Her hands passed stone after stone, working her way

across. The waters seemed endless and her arms began to weaken. Stone after stone, she continued to cross and, unable to see, she felt for footholds with her tail. Her people were born to do this kind of thing, even here, under so much earth and stone. She smiled, recalling her and her parents manoeuvring around the branches of their treetop village. She recalled how much she wasn't like them, how poor she was at moving through the branches. It was at the age of nineteen that she decided to abandon that life of climbing up high, where it was safe; nineteen was the age where she had chosen to live her life on two legs and give herself to the hardships of the ground.

That was the moment that had brought her to the fate she would find in Malhain, the loss. Had she been a fool to give it up? How different her life would have been if she had managed to persuade Richard to live with her instead; persuaded him to climb beyond the worries of human life. Thomas would have loved life in the trees; he had always found his way into them anyway. Umishi closed her eye and pressed her head against the rough stone, cursing herself. Her thoughts always managed to find their way back to them again her lover and her son. 'It gets higher here,' she whispered back at the human, knowing full well the commander was having a harder time of it.

Each time her tail sought earth, cold wetness answered. There was no way to tell how long they had been climbing, but her legs and arms begged her to stop. The end had to be near, didn't it? She had seen it, hadn't she? Again, her tail reached out for ground and, again, liquid denial was the response. She could not give up, there had to be an end, the waters could surely not continue forever. A few rocks further on, a few more negative replies and then her heart skipped as, despite the water's shallow objection, she felt ground, stone. Jumping down, her feet joined her tail in the shallow waters. 'We've made it!' she said with sudden relief.

'Finally,' Lothrum wheezed.

The darkness surrounded them as they continued to follow the cavern walls. The stone was cold and cruel, cutting and biting at their hands any chance it got. Umishi had never liked being underground, so far away from what her people were accustomed to, and every breath of stagnant air reminded her of how unnatural it was for her to be there. The blackness felt like a vampiric mist that drained them of any strength they could muster, drowning and choking them with every step they took deeper into its lair. It wasn't long before Umishi heard Vallis break behind her. It felt as though they had travelled weeks in the unending darkness, and Umishi could not help but to agree that falling to the ground was the best option, for the moment. The ground felt as unkind as the wall she leaned on. Vallis' breathing turned heavier, her sniffing echoing throughout the seemingly endless cavern.

'I don't want to die down here,' the commander whispered from somewhere in the dark. 'Are we lost? Are we going in circles? I don't want to die... I...'

'We are not going to die,' Lothrum whispered to the commander. 'We'll get out of this, my girl. If even that... that madman had confidence in our escape, we'd be crazy to think otherwise. No, somehow, whatever way we can, we'll get out. Besides, I have already done my back in coming this far; I am not wasting this time and expended energy for nothing.'

Umishi listened in silence, wishing she could say something that would help to provide reassurance and comfort. It was a skill that had abandoned her when life abandoned her son. Lothrum's warm words came so naturally that she envied him. It was hard not to feel sympathy for the woman. It seemed that the stern commander from Hanaswick had completely dissolved. What was left, when the darkness stripped away all her armour, was a woman who knew nothing about the world, and who was just discovering the fragility of life. What were the qualifications for being a commander in Fendamor's army? Acting skill and blind faith? It all seemed like a cruel joke at the expense of everyone Fendamor called military. Renderbrim's deconstruction of the Ward and the inevitable war that came after was merely a punchline the Mangler had set up years ago.

'We'll rest here for now,' Umishi whispered into the blackness. 'When we wake, we will find a way out.' Umishi refused to die down here, *she would not*.

'Rest? How? I... With those beasts, those monsters, coming? They're coming and we are going to die, we are going to die down here in the dark! I can't see, I can't see!'

Umishi gritted her teeth, not knowing what to do. She must have known, at some point; she had been a mother once. Her words had slain invisible child-eating monsters and brought joy to the gloomiest of days. It had been so long since and the memory was so thorn filled that she pulled away. It would hardly be the same anyway. Vallis was a grown woman.

Echoes of Fendamor

'It'll be okay,' she managed and, as the words fell from her mouth, she knew how stupid they sounded. She could feel Lothrum smirking at her somewhere in the darkness. How could it be okay? The Dhal-Llah would likely win the war. With the time they had spent down here and in Llanvurgist, it might already be too late. Her efforts here certainly didn't work; the sobbing and sniffing continued. Umishi pulled at the hair in front of her face and brought her knees tight to her chest. For the moment, she would remain silent and try to ignore Vallis' weeping; she would close her eye and try not to let the sounds in as she tried to sleep. This was beyond her skill.

Opening her eye, Umishi could not be sure how much time had passed, whether she had been asleep for days or merely blinked. Behind her, the others were obscured by a curtain of blackness, and only their breathing assured her of their presence. Vallis and Lothrum lay close. She closed her eye again and pretended she was not in a sunless world, or in a dark, hellish pit. She pretended she was home, at Malhain, and that the sounds, the smells of those around her were not those of two strangers. She pretended, for a moment, that the Mangler, Vulfoliac Fendamor, had not come to visit, that...

A sound shattered the illusion she had created: clicking and croaking that carried its way through the black. Her stomach twisted into knots as the familiar smell made its way down the tunnels.

When the realisation fell upon her, it made her body tremble. She felt the warmth of her blood run into her limbs, jolting them to life. She leapt over to Vallis and forcefully pushed her shoulder. Their heavy breathing pounded at the walls, heralding their approach like war drums. The sounds, the smell, were unmistakeably Kalsakian. Had the beasts been sent by Renderbrim to ensnare them in the dark? Or were these monsters unbound by his commands? Had they been driven to them just by their primal need to kill and devour? She shook the human again and again until the commander gasped.

'We have to move,' Umishi whispered.

'Wha?' Vallis answered, still not truly wake.

'There's no time; we must move now!'

'What... What's going on?' Lothrum snorted as Vallis shushed him.

On all fours, Umishi ran deeper into the darkness, her heart pounded as fast as her feet. There had to be a way out; she would not be trapped down here. Behind her, Lothrum and the commander began to run, their footsteps calling back to their pursuers. The Kalsakian roared in answer.

The thundering sound of an army of feet was only magnified by the sound reverberating off the walls. They were increasing pace, closing the distance. Over her shoulder, Lothrum stumbled, struggling to keep up. Vallis braced him, steadying his balance and speed.

Ahead of Umishi, light broke the illusion that the cave was endless. There was a hole, a passage to the surface, a means of escape. The way was tight, made of earth and stone, but it was big enough for the humans to get through.

'Good girl!' Lothrum said as he reached her. 'I knew you could do it; I knew a rat like you couldn't stay buried for long.'

Umishi's muscles contracted as Lothrum spoke. His words were like nails on a chalkboard. 'You two go first, I shall follow behind.'

Lothrum did not hesitate. He dived through the hole with the eagerness of a man half his age. Umishi watched as the mage scrambled through the dirt, pulling himself through by means of the protruding rocks. She was impressed by his pace until the stones he grasped started to loosen. She watched in horror as the dirt above him started to stir and, before she could call to him, it came down. The light that had so boldly shone hope through to them was crushed. Umishi could taste the dust as it exploded in her face and Vallis gave a hopeless shriek from behind her.

At the new dead end, Umishi pressed her hands against the stone to examine it. She tried to block out Vallis' screaming and the roaring which attempted to steal her focus. There was nothing. She smoothed her hands across the stone. Nothing, but then a larger stone moved, and she felt something she had almost forgotten about: air.

She pulled at the stone, and it came loose. As it did, it revealed a way forward, a glimpse of light. That light rekindled the hope she had momentarily lost. With held breath and a racing heart, she pulled herself into the small gap. The stone gouged at her knees and elbows and tore at her tunic; the heat of blood ran down her legs. Her focus pushed through the pain, towards the hinted freedom.

'Inquisitor!' a scream echoed towards her. It was Vallis; her silhouette could barely be made out as she struggled to fit through the gap. The human was too big; there was no chance of her escaping. 'Please... I... I... don't want...' she cried. Her bloodied hand reached for Umishi's tail.

Umishi doubled her efforts and crawled out of the commander's reach, afraid the human would pull her back, would doom them both.

'Don't... please... please!' With each plea, she sounded weaker, hope fading from each letter.

For a moment, Vallis' screams got louder, until there was a sudden silence and something else came creeping up behind her. The sound of talons grating against stone filled the claustrophobic tunnel as a gnarled, skeletal hand reached for her.

The claws franticly moved from left to right, carving shallow scars on the cave walls. The creatures shrieked with frustration as they scraped their twisted faces against the stone in a vain attempt to fit through. Umishi sighed. She was safely beyond the reach of the Kalsakian. She had escaped the gaze of their lifeless frosted eyes, escaped the putrid and violent lands of Llanvurgist. Ahead of her were more stones, small stones, stones that struggled to keep the moonlight from seeping through their cracks.

With each rock she excavated, more light seeped into the narrow cavity, accompanied by a rush of air, allowing her to breathe deeply as though it were the first time. Tears of hope welled in her eye as she worked the stone, making the exit larger, until it was big enough to squeeze through at last. As she escaped, her heart and senses went into a frenzy. As stagnant as it was in this world, the air had a taste of its own, subtle and moist, refreshing to her parched lips. An explosion of manic laughter expelled the dust from her lungs. With all the willpower she could muster, Umishi gave herself one final, hard push into freedom.

She fell from the hole and on to dry earth. Her limbs protested; joints and muscles begging her to allow them rest, resisting any attempt at movement. Exhausted, her mind was all too willing to agree with their demands. Sacrificing the remaining strength in her arms, she managed to drag herself into a sitting position, her back against a wall. She was in the mouth of a shallow cave. Outside, there were gnarled trees, and a landscape similar to the one the Dhal-Llah caravans had carried them through.

Lothrum lay beside her, his body covered in muck and blood, his face bruised from the stones that had almost crushed him. He turned to her, his eyes barely managing to open. 'You made it. I almost surely thought that...' he whispered. 'By all the gods, Mage-hunter, you are harder to kill than a cockroach.' He laughed, still panting. 'And the commander?' he asked. 'Is she...?'

Umishi didn't need to answer. There was no point, as the realisation set into his face, the tears welled in his eyes. Saying the words would not make the conclusion any less painful.

'No,' he gasped. 'No, no. She... she is tougher than she seems, tougher than you give her credit for.' He struggled to his feet in a manner that reminded Umishi of the monsters they had just escaped from. He fell against the dirt wall they had just managed to claw their way out of. 'We have to get her, she... she won't last long under there if we don't.'

Umishi watched as the mage tried vainly to pull the soil way. Her eye burnt and her body ached, begging for rest. 'They took her,' she managed to whisper. 'She isn't there.'

'You should have helped!' the mage screamed, falling to his knees. 'Why didn't you help her, you cold-hearted bitch? Do you feel nothing?' He wept, his tears leaving his face in muddy streaks. 'I fucking killed her, bloody gods... I killed her.'

He was wrong. Umishi felt something: a dull ache wrenched her heart as doubt gnawed at her mind. Had she done all she could? Did she give up on Vallis too quickly? There had been no option to save the commander without being condemned to her fate, she told herself, but as the Kalsakian clawed their way toward them was it logic or cowardice that led to her abandoning the poor woman? She clawed her hair and rubbed her nose on her sleeve.

They had survived, that was what mattered. They had managed to escape the clutches of both the Dhal-Llah and Renderbrim's monsters. Regardless of the cost for better or worse they had survived.

It did not take long for the mage's body to win over his emotions. His futile digging slowed, and his angry cries fell into weak sobs. He slumped to the ground like a doll whose strings had been cut. There, he wept until his eyes gave up no more water and his mind could no longer cling to consciousness. After, silence was restored to this soundless world. It did not take long for Umishi to follow Lothrum into a darkened sleep.

EIGHTEEN
FINDING WARMTH

Umishi awoke, still trapped in a nightmare. The world stretched out before her in a maddening void, an emptiness that made her long for the sure walls of the twisted tunnels she had sought so desperately to escape, even though they had devoured Vallis. At her side, the mage lay, the sounds of his heavy snoring almost making up for the absence of bestial noises that would normally inhabit the forest that lurked in the thick darkness. His eyes were raw with tears, his fingernails broken and caked in blood. Vallis was likely dead; the darkness had taken her, and Umishi had been powerless to stop it. The commander's screams echoed in her head. The Kalsakian had taken her back deep into the well's caverns. They hadn't killed her, though, had they? There would have been a flash of light if they had; wasn't that how it worked in this world? It didn't matter. Vallis was gone, they had taken her and there was no getting her back.

Umishi convinced her body to stand, but her legs

protested. With what little light the frozen moon offered her, she examined what damage her flight had caused her. The leather at her knees and elbows was torn, the wounds under them mere grazes that would heal swiftly. Her parched lips began to crack as she licked them, and she knew there was a new enemy to face. Not since escaping their cells had they drank, and the ache in her throat convinced her over a day had passed since.

Once more, blackness lay ahead of her. Endless trees stood against Umishi in every direction, each one commanding its own legion of shadows. She bit down on her lip and took a deep breath. They could have been anywhere, facing any direction. Did north and south even work in this world? Marching forward without a plan would lead her nowhere. Next to her the mage lay, still asleep. She could use him; it was magic that brought them to this plane, magic that made the moon stand still in the sky. He had to have a better understanding of this world than she did.

Umishi shook Lothrum's shoulder. 'Come...' She began, before snapping her tongue back into silence. Her gaze moved upwards as her eye lid peeled open in horror.

Above, the collapsed tunnel had reopened, its maw yawning into the dark as though it had never been closed. She shook the human's shoulder again, this time with more urgency.

The hole led into a terrifying blackness. It was easy to imagine the monsters hiding in the dark, their twisted limbs unfolding with the fluidity of a waking spider, their long, skeletal fingers reaching out, their massive, barbed talons seeking flesh to rend. Her heart raced as she shook him again.

'Wha...' the old mage groaned as he finally came to.

She pressed her finger against her cracked lips and pointed to the hole behind him.

'Vallis?' he gasped as he staggered to his feet.

She shook her head and began to move toward the forest. Any direction, so long as it was away from there, away from that twice-cursed cave. It was with some reluctance that Lothrum followed, glancing back in a sign of disagreement.

The trees did their best to hinder their progress, jumping out at them with jagged branches previously hidden in shadow. Despite the blockade they seemed to be forming, the two of them managed to make considerable distance, somehow. The cave entrance they had fled from had long since been lost to shadow and the army of wood.

Seeing Lothrum start to struggle, Umishi called for a rest. She wanted it to be short, though, as, with each passing moment, her thirst grew. She allowed herself to rest against a tree as Lothrum collapsed to the ground like a marionette.

'Do you know these lands?' she whispered, clawing at her hair.

'No, not really. It is obvious we are still in Nalador. The trees are Nalvurta - ugly things that only grow on this half of the island, feasting off the dead remains of the Dhal-Llah, among other animals. Hmm... if the stars are the same in this plane as they are in ours, then we should have little to no problem finding Lake Jimmarah if we head west. At least, I hope.'

'And from there, to Hanaswick,' Umishi whispered, almost to herself. 'Then away from this rotten land.'

'Feel free to flee if you wish, girl, but I fear my skills shall be needed elsewhere,' Lothrum said. 'But, before that, I think a more productive use of my time would be to find somewhere warm, find some food, drink, maybe even something with a little kick to it, to get the old noggin' working. I need to sit for a spell, figure out how to command the energies in this world.' He pushed himself to his feet, joints clicking angrily.

'You'll be of no use anywhere,' she declared. 'Not on this island. We need to leave before Leuvigild and the Dhal-Llah tear each other apart.'

'This has to be a jest?' he exclaimed. 'Stupid girl. I have no intention of leaving! There are larger things going on here than our personal survival!' the mage stepped back. 'There's a bloody war on, if you haven't noticed! Thousands are likely to die if that shit-filled madman you call Renderbrim isn't stopped! There are people I must protect: women, children, friends. Do you care about nothing? Isn't the very *point* of your benevolent order to protect the powerless?'

Umishi pressed her lips together as her eye burned in reaction to the fires in her gut. He didn't see it! The arch-mage and the Dhal-Llah's war would make a wasteland of the island. It would engulf every village, town and city as indiscriminately as wildfire. The war was already in motion and there was nothing they could do to stop it. Umishi had seen it all before: mages locked in a tireless war of egos; it was always the weak who got burnt, the powerless who were trapped in the middle.

Umishi cursed herself when she thought of the lives that would be lost through the pride of Arch-mage Leuvigild Fendamor. It should have been obvious; all the signs were there. She had allowed herself to be distracted by a simple murder, by this plane shifting. She had spent too long chasing ghosts and shadows when she should have been helping the citizens to barricade themselves against the oncoming tempest. Should have forced them to see that the Ward they thought was keeping them safe was a poison that kept them blind to the building threat.

Umishi drew a deep breath and looked into Lothrum's eyes. Those were filled with so much fear, self-doubt and rage, but also with fire and determination. It was clear that he would rescue every man, woman and child if he could. The fact of the matter was, though, he couldn't. Lothrum had never seen war. She doubted he could even comprehend its nebulous nature. He was destined to learn the hard way. He was destined to fail, to see all his hopes and determination burn upon the pyre of his loved ones. He would learn, just as she had.

'You can't stop this,' she snarled. He was blind, she was doing the right thing! 'War can't be stopped as if it were a beast or some... some mugger. It's a flood, you can step out of its way or... or... I am not saying we don't try to save anyone, I am saying we go to Hanaswick, we evacuate as many as we can, and we-'

'And what about the rest, Mage-hunter?' the mage yelled. 'What about Holsta, Ghal-Talos, Lamvatzia and all the other villages? What about the armies, the soldiers, the men and women who joined the ranks without any intention of fighting, who have no notion of the ugliness of a violent death, who can't even hold a sword right, let alone use one? What about them? Are we meant to leave them, or flee without looking back? Pretend we did all we could?'

Rage built in Umishi's stomach, twisting with burning tendrils around her heart. His naivety was beginning to boil her blood; it was clear too many tales of heroes their valiant acts had warped this human's perception of war. Or perhaps it was ego, he was a mage after all, so it must irk him to be powerless in this conflict. Regardless of the reason he would fly into the jaws of battle to save all when in truth he would save none.

'What do you propose?' she snarled.

'I... I don't know,' Lothrum snapped. 'We head north! Leuvigild will be at Vianana without a doubt. We tell the arch-mage what we have learnt about the enemy, about this Renderbrim, about where he intends to attack next... fuck, that lunatic said Holsta. Leuvigild, yes, Leuvigild will know what to do. And then... then I don't bloody know. Perhaps he can send a whole army into this world to hunt down that monster before it's too late.'

'It's already too late, can't you see? The Mangler's son, your bloody arch-mage, his Ward, his pride; *that* was the problem all along,' Umishi said. 'Can't you see? His cure for war didn't cure anything; it was plugging a hole instead of dealing with the flood. He allowed the Dhal-Llah's hate to build up instead of talking. He tried to magic the problem away.' She tugged at her hair. 'It's already too late. The war has begun, and now we need to save who we can, and mourn the rest.'

'Mourn the rest?' Lothrum spat. 'How can you be so heartless? Save who you can, you say? Does that include anyone but yourself?'

'Did you know I would survive?' She growled. 'Where was your heart when you and your arch-mage attacked me in my sleep? Did you understand where you were sending me? You didn't know about the Kalsakian, or how magic here even worked! What if I didn't come back? What if I was torn apart before I even got there?' With both hands and hunched shoulders she pulled her hair back. The moon cast angry shadows at the ruined half of her face, muscles in her scarred cheek twitching and pulling at what had once been lips. 'The Ward almost killed me once, but instead it took so much more. Would you have sent others?' She asked, clawing her hair back into place. 'Had I died, would the arch-mage have sent more? So long as one survived to kill Renderbrim, you could mourn the rest!'

'I... I...' he stammered. 'The Ward was breaking; we could have prevented all of this! We had to, don't you understand?'

'I understand that you sent me towards what could have been my death!'

Lothrum flinched at that. 'It was a risk, and I am sorry for my part, that we didn't tell you. I wanted to tell you, for you to be a part of it! But Leuvigild, damn it, he said you wouldn't understand. The man knows what he's doing, most of the time. You must understand the importance of the Ward, girl? I didn't understand the risks, true, but the lives that were hanging in the balance. There were so *many* lives.'

She gritted her teeth. He'd called her 'girl' again, and for the last time. Turning she started walking away. It didn't matter where, or what direction, she needed to be away from him. She would find Jimmarah by herself. The island was too small for her not to. The mage would have just slowed her anyway.

Pressing further into the blackness, her thoughts turned to Hanaswick. What would she do upon reaching the city? What she had to do. Her first obstacle was the king. She would have to convince him to evacuate the city. It would be no small feat, as Leuvigild must have had his claws dug into him for years, forcing his obedience to the Ward. Even after getting the king's approval and, with any luck, the help of the guard, she would have to herd the people away… to gods only knew where.

As with all plans, a problem arose to tear the carefully thought out machinations down. She was trapped in this plane with seemingly only one way out. That thought brought her to a halt. Death was the only means to escape the shadow plane, to summon the light that would draw her back. She closed her eye and sighed as the solution came to her. Knowing what had to be done, she turned on her heel and headed back towards the mage.

He was exactly where she had left him. It seemed all his energy had been drained, leaving unable to move his body, as though all his good will and plans had crushed him. He looked at her, and there was something troubling about his face. His expression described an emotion between hate and sadness, yet more profound than both.

'There is no need to say anything, Mage-hunter, we both know why you're back,' he sighed, pushing himself from the ground, 'and I am half willing to guess you already know why I haven't moved a bloody inch. I'm old, in a world I don't understand. I can't cast a single fucking spell. Can you honestly see me marching across the miles between here and Vianana? You don't know where it is, but it doesn't matter. Hells, I am surprised I got up without help... let alone...' He shook his head and took a breath. 'I am not so proud that I cannot admit when I am beaten, and you've got me over a barrel. So, if you keep me alive, I'll work on figuring out how to escape this hell, yes?'

It would have been a lie to say that the thought of killing him had not crossed her mind. It was only for a moment, but that moment had lasted too long. She looked at the pitiful, desperate creature before her. Perhaps there was another way? A way without more blood?

'Neither of us has much choice,' she whispered.

'We'll save as many as we can, yes?' Lothrum replied. 'Maybe even the villages we pass through?'

Umishi nodded, although she did not have much hope.

They walked in sombre silence. As they marched through the trees, the shadows felt colder, heavier. The silence was maddening. Each twig they stepped on sounded like thunder. Umishi's legs ached for rest, there was little doubt the human's felt no better. After a time, Lothrum suggested there was a house nearby, something she could not recall passing as they had travelled in their moving cells. It wasn't long before they reached it.

The place was derelict. It had been for years, Umishi concluded through its lack of furnishings. Her throat ached at the sight of an empty cup. They needed to find water, and soon, but for the moment, a fire would do. At least her joints would find some comfort. With a few twigs found on the ground it did not take very long to get a fire lit; she had made many in the past on the road. The mage scrunched his face at the flames, no doubt jealous that the blaze had not been forged by his words. As they waited, time seemed to make no advance; the moon stood its ground with no intention of submitting its dominance. They would make a fire, allow themselves to warm and plan out their next move.

'The fire's wrong,' Lothrum said.

Umishi raised an eyebrow. There was nothing different about this particular fire than any other that she could see. It danced in front of her as though basking in the attention. She reached for it with her hands, and a comforting warmth greeted her. Lothrum's face offered her no answers.

'Wrong because it's right, Mage-hunter,' he attempted to explain. 'This is the only thing, apart from you and I, in this world that seems to be behaving correctly. Everything in this world is hollow, but this... this is real.'

He was beginning to sound like Renderbrim, his words detached and meaningless; was this world leading him into madness? Perhaps that's what this place did to the human mind?

The mage pulled at his whiskers in contemplation, then licked his lips before he started to speak the words his kind used to control the elements. Those had previously failed him, but the fire before him danced and twisted, then lifted into the air and his outstretched hand. The light shone upon his face as he released a triumphant laugh.

'When you created this flame, you awakened - revived - the energy. That, Mage-hunter, that is what makes this plane so different to our own: all the energy here has been depleted, drained somehow. It it just needs to be kickstarted and... well, hurry, place some leaves into those cups there, hurry,

hurry now.' His words turned back to the language of magic as the flame danced in his hand.

Umishi did what she was told and watched as the magically controlled fires landed in the leaf filled cups. The glow died and the leaves became transparent. Her eyes widened as she greedily grabbed one of the cups. Water! It was filled with water. She pressed it to her lips and the cold droplets fell down her dry throat, brought her insides back to life. With a grin, she silently thanked the mage for this miracle. She did not understand what Lothrum was raving about; however, it was clear a spell had been cast. It also was evident that the mage had reached an epiphany.

Lothrum leapt to his feet with an energy he had never displayed before. 'I see no more reason for us to be sitting around here. I am eager to see what more this world has to teach me, but I can figure that out along the way. Come, we head southwest; the Dhal-Llah are not going to wait for us, after all, and we have lives to save!'

The joy he radiated was almost visible. She had not considered what being without magic must have been like for him. Regaining it must have been like having a limb reattached. His joy was something she could understand. She offered him a respectful nod.

They walked for some time in silence. The landscape was too stubborn to change and the shadows around them grew ever hungrier. Lothrum's energy from the camp seemed to have sapped quickly, or had it? With the world looking the same, and the moon refusing to give any hints of time, they could have been walking for moments, half a day, all day… there was no way of telling. If they did not find Lake

Jimmarah soon, they would have to make camp again, if only for the mage to regain his breath. He would need it should they stumble across the blue mists that, up to that point, they had avoided.

The wall came from nowhere. A giant monument lurched from the shadows, stretching far beyond Umishi's view. The moon granted the smooth stone an icy shimmer, a potent illusion that forced her to shiver at the sight. Umishi approached it, unable to shake the feeling that something was watching her from atop the battlements of the colossal structure. They had reached the borders of Fendamor. Something turned in her stomach as the name echoed in her head. It was a true act of vanity to name an entire kingdom after oneself.

Behind her, the mage stopped in his tracks. A grim expression fell over his face as his eyes lay siege to the stone fortification. 'Ghastly sight, isn't it?' he murmured, his words dripping with disdain. 'Before now... well, before the Dhal-Llah made their move against us, I only ever viewed this thing as a line, a thick lick of ink on one of my maps. I never thought of it as a wall made to keep people out. It did a piss poor job... may as well have just been a line of ink after all.'

She clawed at her hair, ignoring Lothrum's musings. Close enough to touch the wall, she reached for it. It was not what she had come to expect from Fendamor's architecture. This was not like the buildings of Hanaswick. Contrary to what Lothrum had just stated, the wall here was far more formidable than any other on this island. Whatever held the stone together was of greater quality than the soft mortar that held the brick of buildings like the Spinning Dagger or Hanaswick's palace. It could have only been made by a people who understood defence, likely a relic from the former empire. She had to take a number of steps back before the wall's apex was visible. Regardless of how ineffective these walls were to the Dhal-Llah war machine, they would pose as quite the obstacle for them.

'We can't climb this,' she stated, 'We'll have to find another way.'

'Thank the gods,' the mage sighed. 'As soon as I set eyes upon this blasted thing, I thought you'd be having us make rope ladders or start digging under the damn thing. Seems you have some wits at least, Mage-hunter.'

'If we made a fire, would you be able to command the stone away? Maybe make a small hole to climb through?'

'Listen, this world is completely drained of the energies I require, and the tiny amount that is granted to me by awaking dormant energy through fire is barely enough to light a moth's fart. For me to perform the miracle you request, we'd have to burn this forest to the ground.'

'Would that work?' Umishi asked with a sly grin.

'What if I say yes, Mage-hunter?' he snorted. 'It would not surprise me if you did. I can almost picture you screaming with glee, running through this miserable place with a flame in your hand as everything around you turned to ashes. And, to answer your question, no, the energies awoken by a fire so grand would be wild and unpredictable, far too chaotic for any single mage to tame.'

'You told me you were the most powerful human mage in the whole of Domvalkia,' Umishi said, smiling. 'It would at least be worth a go.'

Lothrum granted her a stern glance before they pressed on into the still darkness.

NINETEEN
SAILS ON LAKE JIMMARAH

The wall seemed to go on forever, while the lands around them seemed to be repeating themselves. There was nothing but the wall to the left of them and trees to the right, with the sky remaining frozen. Just as Umishi's thoughts turned to setting up camp, however, the wall twisted inwards. Without thinking, her slow march became a sprint. Turning the corner, she found the ruins of a massive iron gate, buckled as though a giant had thrown its fist through it. All around, huge stones lay; the corpses of fallen towers. Drawing a breath, she began to recognise the ruins they had stumbled upon.

'As I said,' Lothrum wheezed, catching up to her. 'The fort's defences may as well have been made out of paper for all the good they did.'

Umishi passed through the buckled gates and allowed the ghosts that haunted the place to play out their final moments before her. The burnt walls and fallen barricades made it easy to see the shades of the Dhal-Llah attackers flooding the empty courtyard, the armoured Fendamor soldiers running about the place like terrified children, trying their best to defend the fortress. The Dhal-Llah had left a mess in their wake. The ground was charred, while ash covered the barracks and the other buildings. Wherever the fires could not reach was left completely empty. The people here had broken before the walls had, though. Around her, armour and swords lay scattered, each cluster representing a soldier fallen, captured or fled. Taking advantage of the situation, Umishi helped herself to one of the short swords. Their owners no longer needed them, after all.

'Poor fools,' Lothrum sighed as he entered. 'They didn't stand a chance, did they? Gods only know what's become of them now; sometimes I forget it was not just three of us: you, me and Vallis...'

Umishi paused, but there were more important things to do than dwell on shades. 'Where from here?' she asked, turning to the mage. 'West?'

Lothrum was still lost among the spirits of the fort, his eyes following phantoms only visible to him. 'This will be the fate of Hanaswick,' he whispered to the emptiness that loomed overhead. 'I don't understand, after all my years of reading through books, after all my pondering on the horrors of war, after seeing this first-hand... I don't understand. Could they hate us so much? I didn't think it possible, but... how can an entire race lose track of all logic?'

Umishi rolled her eye. To her, the answer was obvious. The corruption ran through every facet of the island, an evil that lurked in every shadow: Vulfoliac Fendamor. The

Mangler had conquered the island and divided it between those who served him and those who did not. Neither he nor his son had addressed the hatred that grew in those they had chosen to ignore, those they had left impotent and cast into the forests while they hid behind a wall. They were a people lost and directionless, slaves without orders. It was no small wonder they had taken the opportunity to make their war against the people of Fendamor. Little wonder they had placed their faith in a madman who offered them justice. Years of living under Fendamor's rule and unyielding faith to the Ward had blinded Lothrum to it, and she would be wasting her breath trying to make him understand.

'West from here, you said?' she asked, moving the conversation on.

This time, Lothrum's attention fixed on her, although there was a distance in his face. It was almost as though he didn't recognise her. He blinked once, then twice. His eyebrows met each other at the pit of his nose. 'Sorry, Magehunter, I…' he stammered, confused. 'Yes, we must carry on. Yes, yes, we head west, west until we hit the lake. I think, at least.'

Lothrum's final sentence did not fill Umishi with confidence, but even in his current condition he had a better understanding of the kingdom and the stars than her. Even were the sun to bathe itself down on these lands, this island would still be just as alien to her. The lake was half a day's walk from here, but that was all she could remember. Perhaps she needed to stay longer with the mage.

The sight of the lake turned Umishi's stomach. The grey waters were still clouds, a vapid ocean with no end. Seeing it brought home just how alien this world was, how out of place she and Lothrum were. This was no place for the living. It was a dead land filled of coldness and monsters.

Wood littered the lake's edge. The remains of ships lay cast into rocks like toys discarded by angry giants, their hulls collapsed in on themselves, their masts bent and broken. Umishi pressed on towards the shore. It had been the site of a battle. Among the ruins lay siege equipment, some she recognised while others were strange: long tubes of metal on wheels. Nothing was right here; this wasn't her world. 'How do we cross?' she asked, trying to quell the quiver in her voice.

'How good are you at swimming?' Lothrum answered. 'I admit it's been a while but, if memory serves, I am pretty good for my age. I float, mainly.'

'Swimming?' she repeated, taking the measure of the mist-like substance that filled the lake. She hadn't even considered the possibility of attempting it.

'My, my, you suddenly look incredibly pale, Magehunter. More so than normal, at least. It was a jest. The truth is, I can't bloody swim at all,' he said with a smile. 'They did a great job didn't they? It's like this in the other world, don't you see that? It's as Vorx said: when the fort fell, they took out the bridges of Jimmarah. I daresay the Dhal-Llah like the idea of swimming even less than you. Can you imagine swimming with swords instead of hands? Is that even possible?'

Umishi's mood turned to irritation upon the return of the mage's confidence. She clawed at her hair. He would be less help to her now than when he was enraged. But he was right; it seemed Fendamor's puppet king had been true to his word. The lake town had been sacrificed so that the forces of the Dhal-Llah would be delayed. Umishi knew Jimmarah's destruction would only postpone the inevitable, though; she had seen their hate first-hand. They would find a way, just as she would.

She moved up the shore. There had to be a way. The mage followed along, his footsteps echoing hers as though they were in an empty tunnel. There had to be something left, something they could use. After a short walk, the answer rose from the shadows.

The boat was small, but still large enough for the both of them. It was a simple thing, made of wood, a fishing boat like the ones once harboured in Malhain. Richard had tried to get her into one once, threatened to take her into the sea with a net and rod. The waters had terrified Umishi with waves that were bigger than she was, waves that might have grabbed her and pulled her away from her lover's arms, into the cold depths. She had never gone fishing with him. Instead, he had brought the sea to her, tossing it over her head when she least expected it and laughing that mischievous laugh of his. She breathed deeply, swallowing the past. It would do. 'How good are you on the water?'

'I studied the waters of Jimmarah… why, it must have been when I was in my early twenties. Mage-hunter, I know every rock and fish that ever existed in this lake,' he stated, oozing with pride.

She grinned. At last, the magicless mage had a purpose. Together, they pushed the small boat onto the water. Umishi half expected it to fall straight through the grey smoke that masqueraded as liquid. Her heart pounded as she jumped in. For a moment, she felt as she had with Richard – felt the fear of the wave – but it passed as Lothrum fell in beside her. She passed him an oar.

'Me, row? You have to be joking!' he exclaimed, astonished at the mere suggestion.

'The boat is made for humans.'

'Oh, of course, your stunted size. What an excellent excuse you have crafted, easily devoured by any half-wit who hears it. I, Mage-hunter, am no half-wit. You are up against a master of knowledge and I know it is weight, not height, that makes the better rower.'

Umishi tilted her head at him. 'You're saying I'm heavier than you?'

'Well yes. No, I don't mean. You're not... muscle mass weighs far more than fat and look at me, I am a wisp. I...'

She threw him a stern glance.

'Fine,' he snarled, snatching the oar from her. 'I guess I'll be a gentleman for the sake of putting aside this argument. I guess someone has to be the bigger man, after all,' he said, tossing a sly grin her way.

Umishi felt a quiver run through her body as Lothrum made his first stroke.

It wasn't long before the omnipresent darkness devoured all traces of land, plunging both them and their little boat into a vast nothingness. It was an emptiness many times more isolating than that she had experienced in the dark tunnels under Llanvurgist. She tried not to look over the boat's edge, tried to avoid the riddle of what she might see lurking in the depths. Could the Kalsakian swim? Were there darker things in this world's waters? She didn't want to know. She craved distraction. Her restless hands clawed at her hair and picked at the leather hilt of her newfound blade. Lothrum's face was vacant, his focus given completely over to his strokes.

'I can try to take over if you need rest,' Umishi said at last.

Lothrum regarded her for a moment as she braced herself for a sarcastic quip that never came. Instead, he passed her the oar and cricked his neck. 'A little rest for these old bones wouldn't be unwelcome.' He yawned, stretching his arms. 'Nor would a little winter warmth, if you know what I mean. Back at my tower, there's always a spot of wine or a little gin to cure an old man's weary muscles, a quick spot of something to help me relax. What are your thoughts on this grey stuff?' he asked dipping his hand into the water.

'I wouldn't drink it, I...' before she managed to complete her sentence Umishi's heart froze noticing horror sinking into Lothrum's expression, expelling joy into the depths.

The mage pulled his hand from the boat's edge. His eyes were wide, his brow drawn inward, his mouth ajar. 'What th-' he choked, shifting to the other side of the boat.

Umishi closed her eye and breathed deeply. Judging from his reaction, there was a new problem to face. Images of giant sea serpents and things with enormous tentacles swam through her mind but, as she opened her eye to what lurked beyond their boat, the source of Lothrum's concerns became clear, and it was far more bizarre.

The water off the port side had been replaced with a

large trench. She blinked, but the strange-looking ditch in the lake persisted. From deep within her, something stirred: a dread, almost a voice telling her to back away, to get as far away from it as possible. She grabbed hold of the oar and pushed with all her might. She was too late. Within a heartbeat, a massive ship tore itself into existence, its wooden hull filling the void that opened in preparation for its miraculous birth.

Its creation thrust a wave against the tiny fishing boat, throwing it into a spiral of chaos. Umishi's senses failed her. For what seemed like a thousand days, she had no grasp of what was happening, where she was, which direction she was facing. Cold waters wrapped around her, bearing down on her throat and smothering her face, stealing her breath. As the wet abyss took her sight, it showed only a mass of blackness and blurs of grey. Sound blasted through her ears. She tried to struggle, she kicked wildly and threw her arms back and forth, but the waters resisted, pushing against her, doing their best to restrain her. Then, something pulled the shoulders of her tunic. Pain ran through her arms as the leathers dug into her armpits. Without thinking, she gasped in terror, allowing the liquid enemy a breach in her defences. The water ran into her mouth. She started to choke.

'Good, well done. Get it all out,' Lothrum said, pulling her from the water's clutches.

He dragged her onto their capsized vessel as water poured from her mouth and nose. She shivered as her senses were restored.

'I am sorry to be the one to tell you this,' Lothrum panted, 'but you're not half as light as you implied.'

Umishi's breathing slowly returned to a normal rhythm. She turned herself over, adjusting her tunic. Ahead, the massive ship ploughed past them. It was poorly constructed, more a platform with sprouting masts than a vessel. There was little doubt that, if it were to enter the sea, it would be destroyed by the first wave it encountered. What it lacked in structure, it more than made up for in size. The ship was big enough to fit an army, which was exactly its purpose. However, as with all things in this world, the ship's bridge was lifeless, with not a single soul on board. The giant platform was running wild on its uncontrolled propulsion.

'Shit!' Lothrum exclaimed in horror. 'They... Do you know what this is? This means...'

Before he could finish his sentence, another ship materialised alongside the first, hosting an identical ghost crew. Umishi's heart raced, she looked to the mage in the hopes that he had gleaned something, could see something that she couldn't: a way out. His face provided no comfort. It was as grim as death and twice as pale. With no clear answers, Umishi swallowed her fears, resigning herself to the inevitability of what was about to happen. She buried her nails into the boat, the wood buckling at the strength of her protest.

She closed her eye as the newly manifested ship collided with the first. They smashed against each other in a war of splinter swords and jousting masts. Umishi knew that whichever of these wooden titans emerged triumphant, a wall of makeshift javelins would be hurled at them as its foe shattered. Angry roars echoed over the still lake as the second ship's hull tore through the first, drawing wooden spears as it went. Opening her eye, Umishi was determined that she would face the countless oak daggers thrown against her. She would not die here; she would destroy all the spikes with her fury if she had to.

'Do you hear them, Mage-hunter?' Lothrum yelled with frantic excitement.

She looked to him and he rolled his eyes.

'Of course, you don't, it... they... I can... never mind.' he stood to join her in her defiance. He cracked his mouth into an impish grin and started speaking again, in a language that electrified the dead world and raised every hair on her body. The stagnant plane trembled as life seemed to erupt from the mage's mouth.

The mass carnage that ploughed towards them suddenly broke in its advance and twisted into a full retreat. As the ruin cowered under the mage's spell, it lost control of all the energy it had possessed. Umishi's heart raced as the planks of wood, which had seemed very much alive moments ago, fell into the abyss beneath them. The cruel waters no longer granted the two ships support and consumed them, dragging them down into the black. In the end, all that approached the small boat they stood on was sawdust.

'Did you see that, Mage-hunter?' Lothrum crowed. 'This is what makes me the most powerful mage in Hanaswick!'

Despite his vanity, she couldn't help but smile with him. They were alive, by some miracle she didn't understand, but they were alive. A tingling tore through her body as she bit her lip to contain her laughter.

'How?' she whispered.

'You wouldn't understand even if I told you, but I shall

try using the smallest words in my rather extensive vocabulary,' he said with his usual sarcastic glee. 'The momentum those ships had was brought with them from the other plane. The energy that propelled them was as alien to this world as you and I... or the fire you created. It was energy I could, *can*, bend and command.'

Umishi felt what remained of her left cheek twitch as his patronising tone caused her blood to boil. She may not have had a complete understanding as to when was going on, but she was not a complete fool. The energies born of the other plane granted him power, that was all she need to know, all that was important.

'Let us turn this boat over. I think I have earned a considerable break from rowing,' Lothrum said.

Umishi ground her teeth at the thought of returning to the water and, beyond that, the pulling and dragging of the oar. However, they were alive, and she would do what she had to.

It wasn't long before they were on their way again. As wet as she was, as tired as she was, she could not escape her own anticipation. While she did not understand how Lothrum was able to cast his spells in this plane, she understood its implications. It would not be long before he wouldn't need momentum or fire. Soon, he would be able to command magic in this world as Renderbrim could. Soon, he would be able to pull at the threads of the Ward and free them from this plane.

With aching arms and a weary body, Umishi managed to get the fishing boat to shore. Even here, in Renderbrim's world, the earth was a welcoming sight and an even more delightful sensation on the skin. She dug her toes into the ground and silently thanked the gods that they would soon leave Jimmarah behind them, swearing she would never get into a fishing boat again. From then on, she would walk. But first, she would set up camp and recuperate her strength.

'What are you doing?' Lothrum asked as she began to settle down. 'We have to move! We have no time for you to be sleeping on the job!'

Umishi raised an eyebrow at the mage's eagerness. She had expected he would collapse out of the boat the moment they got to shore but, since casting his spell, he seemed wild with renewed energy. He marched with a swiftness of a man half his age, carrying the tail of his robe as he went. Umishi rose from the ground and followed, if only to see how far he would get on the steam he seemed to have acquired.

Heading northwards at a pace Lothrum's recently found vigour set for them, it did not take long to find a road: a dirt trail that bore the hallmarks of wagons and carriages. It was well-worn, making it clear that there was a town ahead; this 'Vianana' maybe?

'Holsta!' The mage's silence broke as the adrenaline granted to him by whatever revelation began to wear off. He pointed at a silhouette in the distance. 'Come, Mage-hunter, we're in luck. Given the timing we should be able to gain a relatively accurate understanding of what is happening on the other plane.'

She raised an eyebrow. What did timing have to do with anything? Time didn't move in this world, at least not to her knowledge. Had he gone mad? Maybe it was an effect of trying to understand the illogical nature of this plane? For once she was glad that she didn't think too much.

'Once more, I don't expect you noticed what happened on that lake,' he called back. 'Your mind was no doubt either preoccupied with your own survival or dazzled by my boundless skills, neither of which I can blame you for. This plane, it was aligning with the other. That's where the ships came from, that's why... it must do it every few hours. This plane is frozen until, well, I am guessing until each time the world stands where it is frozen in this plane. Then, for those few moments, time seeps into this world and everything changes to what and, more importantly, *where* they are on our plane, the *original* plane, do you understand?'

She understood enough. It wasn't the first time she had seen something like that happen. She recalled the bridges of Jimmarah fixing themselves and, before the siege at the fort, a spear had merged into her leg. The painful memory granted her an awareness of how fortunate they had been to not be sharing the same space as either of the mysterious vessels when they arrived.

'However,' Lothrum continued, 'what you also neglected to notice was the flags flying on those two ships. The bloody things were flying the colours of the Dhal-Llah, meaning we do not have much time to-'

Umishi silenced the mage with a sharp nudge to his hip. She didn't care about the colours of flags that sank with the crewless ships on the waters behind them. It was apparent that, despite Lothrum's boasted abilities of observation, he did not see the dangers of this world. He didn't see the movement in the darkness ahead, between the trees, slithering between the blades of grass: droplets of blue.

TWENTY

SHADOWS OF MALHAIN

'By all the gods,' Lothrum gasped, 'We have to... come on!'

Umishi watched, almost dumbfounded, as the elderly human ran straight into the ruined village, his fatigue seemingly forgotten as he disappeared. With no small amount of hesitation, she followed him. She had very little choice. Without her, the fool would likely get himself killed. She followed the sounds of his footsteps against the stone slabs that formed a road.

The ruins of Holsta erupted from the ground; they were broken, charred and gnarled, their frames twisting to form skeletal hands with splintered claws. Lothrum was nowhere to be seen and his footsteps could no longer be heard. Umishi pressed on through the hollow buildings, and felt coldness radiate from the stones she passed. She ran her fingers through her hair. The chill against her skin felt alien, wrong. Something had changed, something was *different* about this place. This world had always treated her with indifference, never offering a breeze, never a harsh wind, the sun never shone, nor had it ever felt cold. But here, now, something had changed; something stalked her from behind the debris, shrouded in the dark.

Umishi gripped her blade as she resisted the urge to call out to the mage. The specks of pale blue dust twisted their way through empty windows. She listened for the tell-tale clicking and croaking of the Kalsakian, but silence answered her, laced with something else. It was a whisper, barely audible, so low she questioned having heard it at all. Umishi licked her lips. Her skin itched. The wrongness of the place persisted as she caught sight of movement ahead of her, its form obstructed by the darkness. Brief as her glimpse had been, she thought that whatever it was stood upright. A Kalsakian? Lothrum?

More of the blue mist danced around her feet like snow in a playful breeze now. A shape stretched from the shadows, bearing long gnarled arms that reached out for her. It was a tree. At the sight of it, Umishi's heart skipped, all hesitation and caution abandoned as she flew forwards and embraced the wood. Even in this world, its warmth awoke joy in her breast. Tears ran down her face as her finger traced the bark, down towards the mark she knew was there. Her fingertips found the letters carved into its skin: T and Z - Thomas Zaimor.

Umishi's legs betrayed her. She fell to her knees, pain running through her body as memories of her son threatened to tear her apart. She tried to cry out, but the scream threatened to choke her. The blue dust twisted around her and she did not care. She had found her way back to the place she had never wanted to return to, the place that had always called to her. She had returned to Malhain. She gripped the tree's root and squeezed it as tightly as she could. She prayed that, if she looked up, she would catch a glimpse of him, if only for a moment, but it was not to be. The branches greeted her with a tangled web of wood, gnarled arms that twisted and weaved around each other, forming patterns: faces of the long dead.

'Butchered, all of them,' a defeated voice stated from somewhere in the ruins.

The words electrified Umishi's body, every nerve exploding into a death-like numbness. The knotted twigs above her blurred as tears flooded her eye. 'I could... I could never get him down from this tree,' she whispered. 'My son, he... Richard always had to get the ladder, and...'

Lothrum's footsteps were heavy as he approached. 'Shit,' he exclaimed, the sound of boots on stone speeding towards her. She barely noticed his hand fall on her shoulder. 'Holsta,' he continued with genuine concern, 'Oh my... I forgot this was... are you okay, Inquisitor?'

The faces bore down on her, waiting for her answer. With a deep breath, she lifted herself from the ground. 'I'm fine,' she declared. 'I just need to...' She turned to face Lothrum and the cinder-filled city. The destruction was a dream, a memory of how she had left it. 'The Dhal-Llah?' she asked, her eye taking in the devastation.

'Yes,' Lothrum replied. 'They completely levelled everything. I doubt there would be any survivors. If there were, they'd have been taken to become voices. I didn't think so much time had passed since... I didn't think they would get this far, so fast.' He licked his lips, the memories clearly pulling at him too. The weight of death in this place was more powerful than any mage Umishi had fought.

'I am sorry, Ms Zaimor, I know... I too would like a moment, but if... if we are to have any chance of reaching Hanaswick before these monsters, we have to leave.'

'Leave,' Umishi said, recalling her original plan. Flee for Hanaswick, flee and not look back at the ruins they were abandoning. It was happening again: echoes of the past rippling through time. Her body quivered as it tried in vain to reject the feeling of déjà vu. She was running again, as she had from Malhain all those years ago, from Fort Jimmarah, from Renderbrim in Llanvurgist and when Vallis had so desperately needed her; running like she had vowed never to. Taking a breath and turning to the tree, she found a different shape, the ghosts of family and friends no longer haunting the branches. Instead, her mind managed to summon the thin silhouette of the Mangler. She ground her teeth. 'No.'

'What is it?' Lothrum asked.

'I will not let this happen again,' she snarled, approaching the tree once more. Her pulse throbbed through her blade's hilt. In the back of her mind, Lothrum stood there with an oversized eyebrow raised, but she didn't care. He couldn't see what she did. He only saw the shadows of history, not the events they so dutifully followed. He couldn't see what had awakened in her, but he would soon see. He would see that, although her own shadow had fled, this time, she would stand and fight. She gripped her sword, then she threw the blade at the tree with a blinding speed that forced the blue mists around her to flee. The sound of steel striking wood brought the dead village to life, if only for a moment, each battered building singing songs of her landed strike. The image of the Mangler collapsed back into patternless bark, the blade having cut deep where his neck had been.

A burning energy started to grow within Umishi as she pulled the sword from the wood. Her blood boiled, her nerves pulsed, she was frozen in time and her chest seemed like it was going to explode. As she drew another breath, the cacophony of emotion focused into a sense of liberation, a sense of purpose, a renewed sense of direction. She turned to face Lothrum.

'Have you gone mad?' he whispered, in a tone that was indistinguishable from concern or jest. 'I feel you've been affected by that water more than we thought.'

'You were right, Mage,' Umishi said, 'I've run for too long and far enough. I am an inquisitor, and Fendamor's poison has corrupted this land for too long.'

'Wait, what?' he gasped. 'Perhaps it is your inability to form coherent sentences, or maybe it's because your volatile emotional state, but I don't think I quite understood what you said. It sounded to me, and do not be shy in correcting me if I am wrong, these old ears clog up with wax more often than not, but it sounded as though you were implying you were going to kill Leuvigild.'

'Yes.'

'You are broken, Mage-hunter. Now is not the time for your order's shallow-minded nonsense. There is a war on, against the Dhal-Llah and this madman, this Renderbrim. People's lives are in danger! Don't you think that should take priority over Leuvigild's misuse of magic?'

This was the kind of answer Umishi had been expecting: Lothrum's blind faith in magic, his continued denial about his kin and country. It was understandable that he would hide from the facts; it was easier. With reluctance, she would educate him. After all, she still needed his aid. 'This war, is a symptom. We can't fight or stop a war, but Fendamor, the Ward can be stopped. If we want to save the people of Domvalkia, we have to tackle him first. We need to cure the roots before...' she stopped herself and clawed at her hair. Running her teeth against each other, she cringed at her attempt at metaphor.

'But killing Leuvigild? You think that will bring peace? You think the war won't continue? I will not be a part of this, this *murder*,' Lothrum protested; his arms crossed like a stubborn child.

'It is his ego, his lust for immortality and power that created the war in the first place! I have dealt with his kind before, with these situations before.' Umishi's tongue felt as though it were swollen but she knew she was right. 'You're right, killing Fendamor may not end the war, but it will stop it from repeating, stop all of this from happening again.' She gestured to the ruins they stood in.

Lothrum pulled at his thin beard, hand shaking. 'You're wrong about him, you know, Mage-hunter,' he said, his voice quivering. 'He isn't the monster you think he is; he is not his father. I have no doubt he wants to undo this as much as you or me. Please think with your head, Mage-hunter; not all answers have to come from a blade's edge.'

Umishi turned from him. How could he still not see? How could he still have such faith in the monster that had thrown her into this world without explanation, naked and unarmed? If Fendamor's intentions were good, then he had no idea of how to act on them correctly. She took a deep breath. Erik Lothrum, on the other hand, had at least given her reason to pause. Was he just mindlessly acting on his master's will? She couldn't tell, but he, at least, valued the lives of his own kin. In that, he was not trying to steer her wrong.

She turned back to him. 'Lead me to him. If you are right, if he is reasonable and he truly wants to undo what he has done, I shall listen.' With each word, her body felt sicker; each letter she spoke tasted of poison and betrayal. 'But, if I am not convinced, I shall not hesitate to do my job as an inquisitor of Alpharus, I will not turn away again.'

The mage's thick eyebrows darkened his eyes. 'Let no one say you lack compassion, Mage-hunter,' he muttered, in tones lathered with sarcasm.

As the argument quietened, the former village begin to stir. A dull rhythm of clicks echoed through haunted streets and, through broken windows, shadows moved. Umishi's stomach turned at the thought of the creatures that would soon be upon them. 'We need to move,' she said as the blue mists around them grew thicker.

Lothrum seemed mesmerised by the blue droplets, brushing them with his hands with dreamlike movements. He seemed oblivious to the increasing chatter that broke free of the ash-painted houses. Though seemingly ignorant of the mounting danger, a horror grew in his eyes, a fear that hinted at something more troubling than the beasts that surrounded them.

'Lothrum?' she snapped. Her fingers ran through her hair. The monsters didn't bother her, but not knowing what worried the mage set her mind racing. 'Lothrum!'

His name snapped him from his trance. 'The Kalsakian?' he whispered, 'Yes, of course, there'll be many of them, Mage-hunter, more than... yes, we need to make haste.'

Through the darkness of glassless windows, from behind corners and open doors, long talons and skeletal limbs emerged. Once more, Lothrum was right: there were so many of them. Umishi twisted her blade in her palm. It only took a blink for the misshapen limbs and bladed claws to be joined by grotesque faces that contained bulging white eyes and long tongues.

'Oh god,' Lothrum gasped. 'Leuvigild, what have we done? Inquisitor, I swear... I didn't know he...'

Umishi nodded towards their escape route: they would go through the temple ruins. It was the only route the Kalsakian had not blocked. Before them was debris containing steep, jagged rock and invisible shards of glass. Umishi was nimble enough to traverse the hazards, but Lothrum was having a harder time. His progress was slow, requiring her to help him overcome some of the larger structures. All the while, Umishi looked to the mist and listened for the clicking and croaking that accompanied those lurking within. Off to her left, they screamed, shrieking in anger at one another, no doubt fighting over some scraps they had found.

After she and Lothrum had climbed over what used to be the roof, they exited the temple through charred frames and broken doors. Ahead, between dismantled houses, the village gates had been prised open, allowing them exit to the northern road beyond. The road led them past fields as barren as the village they had just left. Kalsakian crawled through the crops, tearing at the corn as though they only half knew what it was. Watching them brought a chill to Umishi's spine. There was something about how they acted, how they moved; it was as though they were children pretending to be wolves.

TWENTY-ONE
THE SAWDUST OF THE UNIVERSE

They walked in almost complete silence for what could have been half a day, or even a full day, for all Umishi could guess. Lothrum had told her that Vianana lay to the north, and that was where they would find him: the Mangler's son and heir to the Ward.

'If I may make a suggestion,' Lothrum said, making her heart jump at the reintegration of noise into this world. 'I think we should probably be avoiding the road, rather than walking on it, maybe head into the mountains. It would probably be safer for us.'

Umishi closed her eye and stopped. 'Why?'

'I am not suggesting we go hiking for a lark, Magehunter. Believe me, rambling is not high on my list of hobbies. I'm guessing that, in the other world, the Dhal-Llah will likely be using the roads.'

'The Dhal-Llah?'

'Of course,' he replied with a tired sigh, 'why would I

expect you to ask yourself questions like, "where did these creatures come from?" or "what are these hideous monsters?" when you could just stab them and make them go away. You must have been aware these were not natural beings?'

Honestly, she had not even considered it. The Kalsakian were obstacles for her to overcome, nothing more. What they were and where they came from were irrelevant. She had never considered that the answer to such questions would aid in overcoming them.

'Bloody hell, Mage-hunter, can't you see? The Dhal-Llah's attack... shit, it turns out you may be right about the Ward... about its...' He shook his head. 'I think the longer I spend in this world, the more my mind unravels. I'll try to explain. I told you about Narsandles residual effect. I would have thought you would have gleaned something from that.'

She stared at him.

'The blue mist,' he explained. 'I guess it's difficult for such a small head to handle such large concepts. Narsandles residual effect. It refers to the bits left over when reality fixes itself after a hole has been punched through it. In this case, the hole is human-shaped. I guess reality doesn't know how to make humans very well because what we get instead are these Kalsakian things.'

She was growing irritated. It was as though the mage was purposely trying to confuse her, trying to show off how much cleverer than she he was while avoiding the point. 'So, why would these Narsandles effects be on the roads, and what's it got to do with the Dhal-Llah?'

Lothrum pinched the space between his bushy eyebrows. 'Perhaps I need to make myself clearer. It's the people, Mage-hunter, that's what we need to avoid. When someone with the King's Ward is faced with the threat of harm, they are brought here for less than a second, but, my dear, they leave a hole, a footprint if you will. Reality has a hard time dealing with things that are there one moment and gone the next. So, in its confusion, it washes over the footprint and tries to fill the gap. The holes those under the King's Ward leave behind become a mould and, from that mould, comes a Kalsakian.'

Umishi still didn't truly understand what he was trying to say, but she understood enough: the blue mist and the Kalsakian formed where people protected by the Ward were. With that knowledge, she accepted the mage's advice and allowed him to take the lead.

'Mount Ende should be a little east of here,' he said, although he lacked the confidence he held when describing the strange magic. 'It should be no more than a half day's walk from here. From the village we passed, anyway.' He looked about himself for a moment, then his face twisted. 'Gah! I am a mage, not a map. I could be wrong.' Despite Lothrum's self-doubt, it did not take them too long to find that he had been right. The fields they were crossing started to steepen and slanted upwards into hills.

The hardships of traversing Mount Ende filled the following day with problems, hindering them at every step. Most of the time, Lothrum had to be aided as he climbed over the more challenging rocks and, due to Umishi's short stature, helping him was difficult. The mage was undeterred however, resisting any offers of rest. Umishi admired his unfaltering resolve. He wanted to protect Hanaswick out of a genuine love or loyalty. Her own reasons seemed so hollow next to his but, hollow or not, it had to happen. Vulfoliac Fendamor could not be allowed to get away with what he had done to her, to them. He could not be left to be revered and rewarded for his sins instead of punished. Despite how futile or meaningless the task seemed, killing Leuvigild would at least give her some kind of resolution, wouldn't it?

As the ground grew flatter, shoots of greenery were smothered by red stone. It would be at least another day before they entered the lands of Vianana. 'How old did you say you were?' asked Lothrum after almost stumbling from a particularly large rock.

'One hundred and fifty-five,' she answered.

'Gods, do you know how much I hate you right now? You and your functioning hips and silent knees.'

'Do you ever stop complaining about how old you are?' Umishi sighed. 'You humans are given such short lives and you spend half of it complaining about how short it is.'

'Bah! In the course of our adventure, I have complained about a great many other things! At home, you should see me; I can knock out a complaint every other second! Things like "when I was a lad, we didn't have any of these fancy magic lights, we had candles we had to light every night" and "I remember when all this town was grass!" You haven't seen me in my prime, Mage-hunter!'

'Really?' Umishi said with a growing smirk. 'I've been known to complain about the clothes people wear and how they are so much more restrictive than the loincloths of my day. I get angry at trees that have carelessly grown where I used to picnic. I can go on and on about rivers that have become streams: "I remember when I used to fish here for hours!" When I was your age, I used to complain about all sorts of things. Now... now, I tend to focus on one.'

'Fine!' The mage said. 'We are both old; only someone truly ancient could make a complaint like, "When I was as old as you, I used to complain more about my age".'

'Talking of being old,' she said, her demeanour returning to its natural state. 'We should likely find a place to rest. I think I see a cave just over these few rocks.' She pointed to a heightened cliff face about half a mile away. Lothrum squinted at the horizon, and then turned back to her

'I'll have to take your word for it, Mage-hunter. I can't see a bloody thing. But, no, dear lady. I feel fine for now. I can press on a little further. After all, we do not have a great amount of time to waste.'

Once more, Umishi admired his commitment. However, this time, it was foolish. 'That is where we will rest,' she insisted. 'We need our wits if we are to carry on climbing this rough terrain.'

The mage nodded. 'Fine, I must concede to your age-earned logic.'

Once more, the fire went up quickly and they placed it just outside the cave's entrance. Were they far enough from the blue mists to be out of the way of the Kalsakian? Umishi did not know, but it had been a considerable amount of time since there had been any evidence of the creeping fog or the deadly creatures that lurked within.

Lothrum sat down and asked the flames stern questions with his gaze. The weight of his moustache drove his expression to a deeper frown than the one he normally wore. Umishi placed herself at the cave's mouth. She would keep her distance to avoid catching his ill thoughts. There was silence between them for a time, deep and cold. It did not last long before Lothrum reached out with his concerns.

'How many monsters do you think we've created?' he asked. 'I don't mean just the Kalsakian; the Dhal-Llah too. So many monsters created through our selfish need to live, just a little longer, to avoid the inconvenience of the pain normal people endure, are strengthened by. The more I think on it, after learning of the monsters we have bred here, the more I can't help but feel you're right, Mage-hunter, you and that madman. We've been fools. Perhaps we are the baddies in some over-the-top fairy tale, after all.'

'Baddies' was not the way she would describe them; not Lothrum at least, nor Vallis. After all, they hadn't *asked* to be part of Fendamor's power mad spell. They hadn't been aware of the suffering the Ward would cause, or what it had cost to make.

'You weren't to know,' she whispered, almost by accident. Only Fendamor knew of this world. Fendamor, who sought to further his father's legacy at the expense of everyone else, and who had to pay the cost of those injustices.

'I guess that makes it all okay then, doesn't it, Mage-hunter? I guess, like you, we can pin everything on the arch-mage?' It was clear from the bitterness on his face that he didn't want an answer. The fire before him crackled, as if in response.

'He'll face what he's done soon enough,' Umishi assured him. She would be ready for him; her mind focused, her body poised. She would find a way around his Ward, and she would break him. She would force him to face the harshness of her ninety years' worth of accumulated vengeance, a debt was owed, passed from father to son, much like the Ward itself. As her mind found the memories of his marble skinned face, she became aware of the twisted expression she wore. She quickly clawed her hair over her ghoulish scars.

'I no longer wish to wallow in this gloom!' Lothrum grumbled. 'I must do something, try something. There is a reason you've been dragging me around, after all, tolerated my prattling. Perhaps, if I can't fix a war today, I'll be able to do something about a war tomorrow. I've been thinking: that lunatic must be getting energy from our world somehow, he isn't getting it from here, that's for bloody sure. So, what if he's using the Ward, syphoning energy through the threads that bind us to it? It would be tricky but perhaps... I could do the same.'

'But you no longer have the Ward,' Umishi corrected him, cocking her head. 'I thumped you, remember?'

'Yes, you did,' he replied, his hand feeling his jaw for the past pain. 'But haven't you been listening, Mage-hunter? Even when something is removed, it's never truly gone, like with the Kalsakian. Maybe there is no tether linking me to our world, but there is a trail to lead me to it... and if I can just...'

Umishi drew closer, and the mage started to weave words with magic written into them. The fire turned blue and faded away. As the heat started to leave her body, dizziness festered inside her head. Had she not already been sitting, she would have fallen.

She tried to focus on the mage, but she could barely keep her eye open. With each letter Lothrum formed, his lips cracked and blood dripped from his nose. Then, with a sudden breath as though he had emerged from the bottom of some frozen lake, he expelled a final word and collapsed, blood oozing from every pore like sweat.

Umishi wasn't sure what she was seeing. It was a black dot floating, a hole torn into nothing. She held her hand next to it and something coiled around her fingers, an invisible force, a force that had a name: wind.

'I told you it wouldn't take me too long to figure out,' Lothrum choked as his head fell limp and his eyes fell shut.

The hole was not open for long, only a moment or two and, as it closed, a tiny droplet of blue fluid floated out: the sawdust of the universe.

TWENTY-TWO
VIANANA

When Umishi woke, she started the fire again. She glanced at Lothrum as he lay stirring in his sleep. He seemed so weak, broken. She watched as his chest rose and fell; it was slower than it was meant to be. Blood had clotted over his lips and stained his face in evidence that he had bled during the night. She placed her hand on his. It was colder than most corpses, and softer than she had expected. His skin felt odd against hers. Images of Richard swam through her mind; it had been so long since she had felt the touch of another person. She missed his smile, the way the corners of his mouth had pushed his cheeks tightly to his brown eyes. How had she lived so long without him?

Lothrum's hand jerked, drawing her back from her husband to affirm that he, unlike the man who visited in her daydreams, was still alive. She pulled away, retreating to the other side of the flames and pulling on her hair. She watched him for a moment, hoping he would wake up. This world seemed quiet without his complaining. It was a silence that seemed less familiar to her now, bitter after being parted from her for so long. The mage slept on and she waited.

'Not since...' Lothrum grumbled, his eyes flickering open and closed like leaves against the wind. 'Since... ugh, shit, I can't even think of a humorous tale of hangovers to describe the monstrous headache I am feeling. But it worked, Mage-hunter. It did, didn't it?' Lothrum's words were a whisper of their former selves, cracking and breaking each time they ended or a new one began.

'You almost died,' Umishi whispered back.

With a long sleeve, he wiped the blood from his mouth. 'Yes, it took more energy than I expected, but did you see what I did, Mage-hunter? I punched through the universe, something only.... look, look!' Making use of the stone around him Lothrum struggled from the ground, his legs barely able to support his trembling body. He took a step, then another and reached out for the blue speck of liquid that floated in the air, his hands shaking as he did so. It was still there; it had persisted through the night.

'I can only think of three or four others who could have done this. Well, who are crazy enough to draw energy from themselves to do this. I guess there's a reason, eh, Mage-hunter? But look, I've done it! Through that pinprick of a hole I made... that was our home!'

'Would you be able to remove Fendamor's Ward?' Umishi asked. The vanity of mages made her stomach turn, their insistence on making overdramatic speeches to boast of their power. She always made a point of cutting them off before they finished, usually by more physical means.

'No, all this time, I've just been talking about fishing

and how to spend a beautiful afternoon reeling in trout! Yes, I can get us out of this lifeless hell. In theory, if I can do that, cutting the measly tether that binds the arch-mage to the Ward would be child's play, but it'll take a lot of energy!'

'So, we make a bigger fire?'

'Bloody hell, I stand here performing miracles, pioneering unprecedented advances in magical understanding and the only one I have to witness these great feats is someone who thinks lighting a fire is enough to rewrite the cosmos!'

The word 'cosmos' meant nothing to Umishi; she could only guess at it being some kind of very big magic book. Mages always gave their tomes strange titles to lure their betters into humbly asking after the meaning. She understood the context clearly enough, though, and she knew an insult when she heard one.

'What is it we have to do, then?' she snarled from under her hair.

'We need to... I need to figure out how this "Renderbrim" is able to manipulate the threads he is siphoning from, where he is drawing energy from. I need to think; you said the lunatic "tugs" at the Ward's tethers to bring people here. The word *tug* implies that it is a physical act, which of course sounds absurd. At least, that was until I saw that tendril thing come out of his body. It was limb that could physically interact with the Ward, the threads. A somewhat twisted and rudimentary way of doing things, and certainly not something I would do but...' Lothrum's frantic rant came to an end as he turned to Umishi. 'You don't understand a word of this, do you?'

Tendril, tethers... the words pounded against Umishi's head harder than any fist.

'So, we have nothing then? You're saying this hole that almost killed you, has brought us no closer to getting out of this world?'

'Give me time, Mage-hunter!' Lothrum snapped back.

'We haven't *got* time!' she growled. 'And what of the Ward? You and the arch-mage spent days telling me how impossible it was to destroy. Now, you're telling me doing so is a meagre thing? You're making no sense!'

'From *this* side, Mage-hunter!' The mage snorted. 'From this side, cutting the threads is, yes, a meagre task. Hells, I could teach an infant to do it, perhaps even you! Doing so from *our* plane, however, would be like trying to paint a picture while being in a separate room from the canvas, and your brush was made out of...'

'Enough!' Umishi said, rubbing the bridge of her nose with the back of her hand. The rules of magic always seemed to be bending, distorting in an endless attempt to be incomprehensible to her. 'We need to move.'

She rose from the cave floor with the speed her purpose granted her and kicked earth at the flames. She didn't care to watch the fire die. She marched to the cave's mouth; they had wasted enough time there. The moon greeted her through stagnant clouds. There was no morning chorus, no welcome here.

Behind her, Lothrum clambered to his feet. The corner of her upper lip twitched.

The pair marched in silence over the jagged red stone under the moonlight. Their progress was slow. It was clear that the mage was still weak after his attempt to tear through into the other world. It was hard not to take pity on him, and Umishi considered slowing her pace, but that would place her within talking distance.

The wastelands seemed to go on forever, with no signs of the blue mist. However, there were also no signs of any kind of civilisation; no evidence of towns or villages, let alone any giant fortresses. Doubt started to seep into the pit of Umishi's stomach; doubt there ever was a Vianana and thoughts that this mage was leading her into the middle of nowhere just so his murderous ruler could live a few more days. They only lingered for a short time before being consumed by a deeper, more pressing, feeling: hunger.

The further they walked, the more pressing the hunger became. Memories of the mage making water from leafs wrapped themselves around Umishi's mind but, with every step Lothrum took, he seemed to grow sicklier. It seemed unlikely that he would repeat the miracle.

The only objects filling the horizon were mountains, sheer cliffs breaking through ground like jagged, bloody teeth. They were heading towards a dead end. Before Umishi could raise her doubts a loud thud resonated from behind her. Looking back she found Lothrum, face down on the ground, his eyes closed and his fingers digging into the soil. She strode back towards him. She couldn't have him die, not here, not yet, not like this.

'Don't you dare die,' Umishi said. 'I need you.'

'Ha!' he yelled again. 'I must confess to feeling a little embarrassed. Tell me Mage-hunter, am I blushing? I feel the heat in my cheeks, I must be. Did you just give me a complement? Did I just get elevated from hindrance to handy? Why, I feel positively weak at the knees, and it's not just because my ever advancing arthritis!'

He stood and plodded towards her.

'I don't know where this "Vianana" is and, in all likelihood, you'll die before me. If that happens, I may be lost here for at least a few days. Days during which you will provide me enough sustenance to keep my strength until I find a way back to a city, or town, or whatever.' She turned back to the direction they had been walking.

'Cannibalism?' Lothrum exclaimed. 'It seems, my girl, the more you open your mouth, the more worried I become.'

'It's only cannibalism if we're the same species,' she smirked.

'Lucky for me, your rather drastic survival skills need not come into play. Hidden within those mountains over there is the secret fortress of Vianana, well-stocked in food, drink and real drink, everything exhausted adventurers should need.'

Umishi looked in the direction he pointed. There were no battlements there, no gaps where windows might be hidden, no signs of any kind of entrance, but she had no option but to take his word. Dehydration and death would the only things to greet her if she were to turn around. Judging the distance and the rate at which Lothrum was walking, it would take them near to half a day to get to the foot of the cliff. She hoped Lothrum's fall was just an act to get some attention from her before they pressed on.

The cliff face seemed to have been built by insane giants who had slammed their bodies against the rock over and over until everything before them was flat. Umishi placed her hand against the even surface; only the walls of palaces were so smooth. She scraped her tongue across her teeth. As impressive as the structure was, it gave her no answers. Its dizzying heights made her stomach turn. It was a flat, tall wall, nothing more. Behind her, Lothrum approached. Despite his ill look, he grinned a toothy grin.

'Where is it? There's nothing here but stone,' she asked.

'Wonderful, isn't it?' he gloated. 'You can't tell even from this distance.' He pressed his hands against the wall, using it to support his tired joints. 'I guess I should be the first to welcome you to Vianana, seeing as the usual rabble of cheerers and grinning ninnies are indisposed. Oh, and Mage-hunter? Your lack of geological knowledge is showing. This isn't stone, it's dragon glass. Not the real stuff, of course, mages create far better art than some burps and farts from monstrous lizards.'

Once more she moved her hand along the wall. Glass he had said.

'How do we get in?' she whispered.

'Well, that, Mage-hunter, will take a little fire. While you get to that, I shall close my eyes for a spell, rest my knackered bones.'

With that, Lothrum slid down the wall and onto the sands. She couldn't tell if he was unconscious before or after he reached the ground but, either way, there was no chance his eyes would open any time soon. She set about the task of gathering as much kindle as this wasteland could provide. It was a laborious task. In the time it took to gather what she needed, she admired the location of Fendamor's secret fortress, with no apparent vegetation for miles. A siege would be almost impossible and would have to almost totally rely upon supply chains, with any kind of invading army sighted days before reaching it. She returned to the wall, where the mage still slept. Umishi licked her dry lips and took the opportunity to join him before they entered the fortress.

Umishi opened her eye to find the moonlight dancing before her on the ground, flickering and flashing in a rainbow of colour, as though the sand had turned into a frozen lake. She jumped to her feet to find Lothrum standing next to her. He nodded towards the wall behind her. A portion of the glass structure had shifted, revealing an entryway large enough for a horse and cart. Beyond unfolded an interior of stone walls and carpeted floors.

'I could not wait until you woke, Mage-hunter. I have a thirst that is now taking priority over my good manners,' he said, with a cough representing a full stop.

She couldn't argue with his reasoning; the dryness of her own throat was becoming almost painful and the skin on her lips was starting to flake. Umishi did not wait for any kind of invitation. She passed through the opening and into the fortress. She was greeted by a staircase that seemingly never ended, just led upwards into the beckoning shadows. With it, another wonder was offered to her. Although the inner wall was made of the same kind of stone she had come to expect of buildings made by the people of Fendamor, but the wall to her left – the dragon glass – seemed to be transparent from the inside.

'I forgot about the stairs,' Lothrum grumbled as he followed.

TWENTY-THREE
THE DAWNING OF JUSTICE

The stairs coiled upwards into the mountain, the fortress's narrow corridors offering an impressive choke point in aid of its defence. With each step conquered, Umishi glanced at the arrow slits along the walls. She couldn't help but visualise the slaughter any attacking army would face if they were to follow the same path. With its barren location and near invisibility, tied to its almost impervious defences, it was clear that Vianana had been built as an irremovable foothold on the island: a place where an army could withdraw to and attack from, leaving the Mangler's hands around the island's neck.

'We need food, water, supplies,' Umishi said as she pressed onwards. 'Any idea where a kitchen would be, or a storeroom?'

'These thrice damned stairs lead up into a nest of caverns,' the mage grumbled. 'Beyond that, I have no idea. This is my first time here, if you can even count being this side of our plane's dark mirror as actually being in Vianana.'

Umishi sighed. It seemed that they would have to resort to trying doors until they found what they were looking for. They ascended, until they reached what Lothrum had described. A massive cavern yawned ahead, as open and spacious as any town square. The sight was reminiscent of Llanvurgist, with its many long tube-like corridors spilling outwards like the tunnels of an ant colony. However, unlike the Dhal-Llah capital, the walls and floors were expertly smoothed, seeming more akin to the interior of a castle than the inside of a mountain.

The flameless lamps flickered as Umishi moved. Her nose, already on high alert, did not take long to detect something that forced a grin to her face. The subtle smell of spices slithered into Umishi's nostril and lured her towards one of the snaking corridors. Reaching a door, Umishi's imagination conjured all kinds of images of delicious foodstuffs, from soups and stews to sweetbreads and cakes. Even Lothrum managed to speed up as they headed for the door.

'It's her! She came, I told you she'd come! I did, and there she is, this is fantastic, wonderful!' screamed a joyous and familiar voice; the only other voice it could have been.

Umishi's heart sank as the room came into view. It was like a memory had been torn from her and warped in subtle ways. A grand table lay poised in its centre, covered with foods of all kinds, capable of seating thirteen, although only two of the chairs were occupied. Of course, the monochrome visage of Renderbrim sat at the head of the table, a pale hand slithering out of his black robes and coiling itself around the stem of a wine glass. To his left sat a monster; a twisted thing that forced a lump to surface at the back of Umishi's throat and the corners of her mouth to tighten. The thing bore a likeness to a Kalsakian that had human skin stretched over it, as well as being dressed in a Fendamor uniform. The pitiful thing's head clicked towards Umishi, its features all in the wrong places, its nose flattened and pulled to its forehead. Its mouth moved under a thin layer of skin as its exaggerated lips aligned more with where a human's ear should have been. Umishi couldn't see the eyes, if it had any at all.

Renderbrim stood and, with outstretched arms, said, 'Come, please come, come.' The red wine spilled from his glass as he once more made a grand, sweeping gesture over the table. His jade eyes fixed on her. 'You must be hungry, parched. I doubt the Vianan Desert has treated you with due hospitality, has it, my dear? Please, please sit. I owe you a conversation.'

Anger ignited in Umishi's chest, causing boiling blood to tear through her veins, setting fire to her mind. She found herself wrestling the urge to lunge at him, blade drawn and ready to indulge in its bloody work. Those fantasies would have to remain within, however. With only a few words, the mad mage could turn her insides to ash. With tentative steps and without removing her eye from him, she made her way to the seat furthest from her host. Her foe was dangerous and unpredictable; for now at least, complying was in her best interests.

It was clear, however, that Lothrum did not share Umishi's caution; his mouth widened, spilling the beginnings of venom-filled words. 'Warmon-'

'Don't,' Umishi warned, interrupting him.

'And there he is,' Renderbrim said in a tone he might have used to address a dog, 'our special little man, yes, yes, our special little boy.' With elegant movements, he returned to his seat, eyes once again finding Umishi. He offered her a generous grin as he watched her take her place.

'So, the plan's to play along?' Lothrum growled, his heavy eyebrows darkening his eyes.

'I mean you no harm,' Renderbrim returned, sparing Lothrum only a glance 'No, no, not either of you. I have been waiting, haven't I?' He slapped the mouthless creature on the back. 'Yes, waiting, three days I think. Three days, three meals? Yes, three maybe. I have been waiting here for you, my dear, you and... and him. Yes, so please eat, drink, you are perfectly safe.'

Waiting? The walls somehow felt closer than they had been, while the ceiling bore down on them. They had walked into a trap. Umishi glanced around. Apart from the table, the room was empty. There was only one exit, and there was nothing she could use, nothing that could aid her.

'Waiting?' she whispered. 'How could you have known?'

'Known? Known you would come? Come here?' Renderbrim smiled. 'No, no, I didn't, not you. I guessed, hoped, figured you'd come my dear, held my breath and prayed. Him, however,' he snarled, nodding towards Lothrum but keeping his eyes on her. 'He, I knew would come. I told you once before, I am good with pets and this dog is well trained. I knew full well this beast of Fendamor's would do anything to come yapping back to his master's heel. To be honest, I am surprised that I got here before him. If not for Happy's company, I surely would have gone mad with the boredom.' He gave the creature beside him a smile. 'Alas, I blame myself for how he came into this world. However. I shame myself with my weakness in the magical arts. I pulled him into this world and he got warped, wrapped, in his skin, but he smiles, smiles, happy he is here.'

Hate resonated from the corner in which Lothrum stood. She recognised the expression on his face; it was one she hid behind every time she found herself among people, in a crowd. It was an expression made from shame and hatred, an expression that told her he was aware of the truth: that he had been played.

'What is it you want?' Lothrum growled.

'What I want?' Renderbrim repeated, running his index finger over his lips, eyes still glued to Umishi, as though the question had come from her mouth. 'What I want is to help you understand that we are on the same side, Inquisitor. I want to continue the conversation we began in Jimmarah, when we first met. What I want is the same as you: I want justice, and not just for me, for my father, my family. No, no, my dear, no, I want justice for Domvalkia, for her people. A long overdue justice, yes.'

'What justice could you possibly offer?' Lothrum spat.

Umishi knew, because she felt Renderbrim's words resonate within her, feeding a desire that grew in her chest. He could offer justice long overdue, owed to Malhain, owed to her family, owed to Richard and Thomas. She tried to shut the feelings down, remember what kind of monster she was talking to, remember the lives lost in the war he had begun, but she could not shut out the voices that his words had awoken. They all screamed their agreement with the mad mage.

'Killing Leuvigild?' Lothrum continued. 'Are you in competition with the mage-hunter here for most narrow-minded point of view? People are dying. As we sit here arguing, the fiends you unleashed, the bloody Dhal-Llah, are crushing village and town, hundreds of lives! Where's their justice, boy? How will killing Leuvigild help *them*?'

Lothrum's question was one he had already posed to Umishi and she, even after so many days between the asking, had yet to find an answer that would justify murdering the arch-mage without first exploring what options he held to end the war. Umishi peered through her hair at the mad grin stretching across Renderbrim's face. He had an answer; it was obvious he did. He was ready to fire it against Lothrum as though it were a crossbow bolt, but she doubted the answer would offer any logical explanations, just further ravings. Perhaps it was her mind's unwillingness to address the larger question that enabled her to glean Renderbrim's true motives, the reason he had waited. He needed Lothrum, needed him for the same reason she did.

'You need Lothrum to get to the other plane,' she whispered. 'That's why you wanted him brought here. You can't... you don't know how.' She looked at Happy, the monster sat next to Renderbrim, the poor creature the mage had failed to bring to this plane intact.

Lothrum faced her, his jaw hanging open.

The mad mage's eyes widened as he threw himself to his feet. 'Yes, yes, but that was then, my dear. Not now, no, not now,' he sang. 'Now, you are here, able to pass from here and there, with little risk of consequences, unlike Happy here.' He approached her, bending to look her straight in the eye. 'With your help, my dear, with your aid, we can restore peace to this island and make Domvalkia the utopia she is meant to be, that she always should have been. Help me, Inquisitor. He's upstairs, above us, here, no, up there, poring over his strategy and maps. He is like a spider choosing his next meal, I have already removed the Ward from him, cut his tether from there to here; the rest is up to you. Please help me, do your duty and help me rid this land of Fendamor's corruption. Claim justice for all who suffered... *suffer* under his reign of madness.'

'Well, this has all turned out to be very romantic, hasn't it?' Lothrum growled, venomous hate dripping from every word. 'I do hope I get invited to the wedding. Do you think it'll be before or after this lunatic gets his Dhal-Llah puppets to raid and slaughter Hanaswick? I do hope it's before, as I imagine after, I would be very busy being dead!'

He turned the weight of his gaze on Umishi. 'Foolish girl! Can't you see that this lunatic hopes to use you? He gives not a fig for the kingdom, or the people of Domvalkia. Listen, girl, Leuvigild may be all you say, a puppet to the long dead Mangler of Malhain, spreader of corruption and evil, but all I see in this monster's eyes is hate and vengeance, while he spouts weak justifications for genocide! Please, all I ask is that you consider the lives that are bound to the archmage, the thousands who have done nothing to you or your kin. Just consider that there may be another option besides murder before you take this fiend's offer. Leuvigild must have an alternative plan. There must be another way.'

'You call *me* monster? Lunatic?' Renderbrim growled, driving the creature, Happy, to cower. 'These things may be true, but do not speak as though you and your people are innocent, as though you are without blame for all this! As if what I am doing isn't *just*!'

A fire built in his eyes as he approached Lothrum. 'It is a justice that has been a long time coming; a justice that has been building in the shadows for over a hundred years! I was there at the start. I stood there and watched as Fendamor walked past those who vowed to protect my father and me. I watched as their arrows and swords phased through him as though he were death incarnate. I watched as my father pissed himself and tried to flee. I watched helplessly as Fendamor rammed his sword down the emperor's throat! I watched as you all knelt to him, you all fell on your knees and crowned him your king!'

Umishi felt his hate reach out to wrap around her mind and penetrate her heart. Images of Malhain filled her head, along with the silhouette of the man who had turned her world upside down. Renderbrim's words set a thousand warm maggots wriggling in her chest. She knew his pain; she could tell from his face what he was feeling: that the Mangler had choked out all his light and made a victim of him too.

'That was his *father*, you fool!' Lothrum screamed.

'They are all part of the same evil! The name they share is what matters!' On his heel Renderbrim span to face Umishi. 'This dog is loyal, oh so loyal indeed. He would never turn on his master, never doubt his master's will, but do you see how loyalty has blinded him, sweet little mouse?

He's not like us, he is naive to how the world works, he can't see how this war will not go on forever. Despite their horror, all wars end. The island will be unified again, and more importantly, freed. Freed from the rule of magic and tyranny. Surely, you see now? Surely you can see, there had to be a war first for there to be a true peace, for Domvalkia to be reborn as a snake sheds its skin?'

Umishi closed her eye as her lust for vengeance started to crush her lungs. She searched her mind for anything that would quiet the drums of war pounding from her heart, a single reason she could use that would prevent her from killing Leuvigild Fendamor. Fendamor was at the heart of all of this. It was his corrosive influence that poisoned the soul of this island and twisted it into something unrecognisable and grotesque.

'I can't,' she whispered, her mind finding an answer that would at least stall things for now, until she managed to get her emotions under control, until she had time to think, to consider her options. 'I can't go to the other plane at will.'

Once more, a cold grin stretched tight across Renderbrim's sickly face. 'I think by now we all understand the mechanics of Fendamor's spell, my dear, and his intentions when he applied it to you.' With skeletal fingers, he snatched a steak knife from the table. 'You didn't bring the other one. The soldier... lost her way, no doubt. But Happy, Happy has volunteered himself in aid of our cause. Happy will do the job that the Fendamor dog failed to turn up for.'

With a flash of movement, Renderbrim's knife drew a stream of blood from the poor creature's throat. The monster spasmed in unnatural ways before falling to the floor. Lothrum released a mournful cry as blood started to pool around the pitiful beast's body.

'You're sick!' Lothrum yelled.

'His sacrifice will be remembered,' Renderbrim said. 'His parting is sad, so sad, but through his death, he has ensured so many will live freer and better lives.'

From the monster's wounds, a light grew, a light that Umishi recognised and Renderbrim had predicted. Umishi shielded her eye as the blinding glow engulfed her.

TWENTY-FOUR
THE COST OF ONE

Umishi allowed her eye to open and found the world alive. The brightness of colours once again dazzled her, to the point where she feared their definition would blind her. Umishi fell back into her chair, allowing herself a moment to recover. After spending so long in the other plane, it felt as though she had suddenly been freed from a sealed coffin. Taking a deep breath, she gorged greedily on clean, fresh air, allowing it to fill her lungs and expelling its dead, stagnant substitute.

Umishi's eye darted, surveying her surroundings. For the first time, this plane seemed to be the emptier one. Her breathing echoed from the walls, puncturing the silence. The massive table in front of her lay barren, dust taking the place of the once glorious banquet. Lothrum had not followed her; she hadn't expected he would, but Umishi had grown used to his complaining, and being free of it made her feel alone for the first time in a great many years. As her mind turned to Lothrum, she pictured him alone in the other plane and tensed. She feared what Renderbrim and his beasts had in store for the elderly mage, his situation made all the more dangerous by his loose tongue.

No, she couldn't leave him there; there had to be a way to get back. Pushing herself from her chair, she headed for the exit. Being in the same place as Renderbrim in this plane would draw her back into the shadow world. At least, that was how it seemed to work, how it had to have worked, if the pattern held. Throwing herself beyond the doors, she fell into the massive hall. It was as empty here as it was there, the flameless torches filling the room with a soft golden hue. Umishi's eye darted left to right, from door to door. Where would they have gone? Where would Renderbrim have taken him? She placed her hands over her face and breathed in deeply. Had they gone anywhere at all? She turned back, finding only an empty table. Were they still in there? Perhaps the spell took time after lifting her into this plane to pull her back into the other? Maybe it had to collect energies, or connect tethers, form the Narsandles effects Lothrum was so fond of? She closed her eye again and bit her lower lip, cursing the monster who weaved this spell and the magic that made it possible.

A loud bang came from the lower levels. It was the door, the main entrance, opening. Voices, loud and panicked, exploded upwards to her. Umishi attempted to slow her breathing and calm her heart. She had to move. Without knowing how these humans would react to finding her here, it would be easier to avoid the situation altogether. The sound of metal boots starting up the staircase reached her. With each heartbeat, her eye turned to a door. There were so many of them, six, with each presenting a different option and no sure right answer. Inhaling and strengthening her resolve, she chose at random and marched to it. Opening the door revealed more stairs. With a sigh, she fell to all fours and climbed.

Her body ached with each step she overcame. It took a while but the stone steps gave up their ascent and allowed a corridor to advance into the mountain. The walls were riddled with doors of different sizes and designs and, flying proudly above each of them, banners waving the colours of Fendamor, She felt herself recoil at the sight of them. Without knowing anything about the strange fortress' layout, Umishi allowed her senses to steer her direction. The sounds of humans reverberated along the full length of the corridor. Zigzagging between them, she allowed her ears to discern what lay beyond each, until silence answered.

Without a second thought, Umishi threw herself into what she could only guess was an alchemist's lab, carefully closing the door she sealed the room behind her. This lab was unlike any other she had seen. It surpassed any found in a common mage's tower and made her hairs stand on end. There seemed to be no respect for the laws of physics as coloured liquids flowed through portals, running like streams through the air, branching off into pots and cauldrons, bottles and barrels. Scrolls seemed to fly from cabinets and vanish into the air; even the smoke was directed and transported elsewhere. Umishi recalled Lothrum telling her how irresponsible it was for mages to use magic for prolonged trivial tasks and the dangers it could conjure. It was clear that Fendamor regarded himself as above all laws, magical ones included. Umishi's body shivered with anger, as though the very thought of the monster were a venom her body was trying to reject.

'-thing we could do, they were everywhere and-'

'The arch-mage will have to hear about this; he's in the war room. General Roberts has just arrived.'

The voices came from the corridor behind her. If she was quick enough, she could tail this human straight to Fendamor. Her hand fell to her blade's hilt. Drawing a breath, she closed her eye as her finger traced its pommel. She allowed the feeling of the familiar task to take her, to lead her forward into the shadows. She would stalk her prey and strike at the heart of this island's evil before he had a chance to utter a word, before he even suspected she was there. Fate had granted her an opportunity to end the Ward's corruption at its source. Why shouldn't she take it? It was her duty, if nothing else.

The way this monster used his magic to twist reality made him far more dangerous than any army, more threatening than any war. If knowledge of this Ward escaped this island, if the ability to use it was something any mage could do... no she could not ignore the opportunity. The bastard needed to pay for his crimes, justice had to be delivered for the dead he and his father had built their empire on, for Richard, for Thomas. As her anger grew, her grip tightened. For a moment, her thoughts returned to Lothrum, Renderbrim and the other plane, but what chance did she have of finding him now? She felt heat rush through her veins. No, she would not gamble this chance away.

Falling to her knees, Umishi watched the shadows move under the door and she listened as hinges groaned. Wood slammed against stone and the footsteps marched up the corridor. She kept still for a few moments to make sure the coast was clear before she exited the kitchen.

A soldier wearing a tattered uniform headed out through a door at the far end of the corridor. Umishi set down on to all fours to follow. She dashed across the passageway, her feet and hands barely making a sound as they made light taps against the ground. By the time the soldier passed through into the next room, she was at his heels.

Crossing through the doorway, Umishi found herself on a bridge overlooking a giant, artificial chasm – a chasm capable of housing an entire market. She couldn't begin to count how many humans were down there, though she could estimate there were more than a thousand. There were refugees, soldiers, families; most sat idle on benches, others talked or shouted at one another. At the back of the cavern, a giant mouth opened into the sea: a dock filled with hundreds of ships. The captain of the *Queen's Memory* had the right of it, 'a dock at the back end of God's bloody armpit.' She watched as the ships were loaded, as rag-wearing refugees were ushered into the holds. The sight of these poor souls permitted reality to sink its cruel claws into Umishi's mind. War had erupted on this once peaceful island, true war. She could not begin to imagine the dread that weighed upon the minds of those there, what it was like for a people who knew no violence to be fleeing for their lives.

A door slammed ahead of her, indicating the soldier had passed into the next room. Pulling herself from the impressive view, Umishi followed.

The war room was bigger than Umishi had expected it to be and resembled a hollowed-out cave more than the rest of the fortress. Like all the previous rooms, it was adorned with Fendamor's banners. They were hung from supporting wooden pillars and mirrored by torches that hung from parallel beams. In the room's centre, beneath a giant chandelier, lay a massive mahogany table, one that could easily compete with the dining table she had found Renderbrim feasting at. There was something engraved into the table, and she gazed in wonder. It was a map of Domvalkia, and it was beautiful, painted with a master's hand and a scholar's eye for detail. She climbed into a secluded alcove, where she gained a greater vantage point over the room. She whispered into her bracelet and allowed the shadows to hide her. A number of men and women stood around the table, all wearing their finest armour; armour which was designed more for heightening the wearer's grandeur than protecting them. On the battlefield, these fools would have stood out like parading jesters and would have been slain just as quickly. The efforts they had made to impress were lost on Umishi, as there was only one person she allowed her focus to fix on. The man at the centre of it all was a creature clearly not human and more impressive in appearance than all present: the son of the Mangler.

With wide, swinging arms, Leuvigild's hands danced over the northern half of the island, placing wooden markers on several little towns. '…coming from Trah-Rahel, surely Roderick's can hold another thirty or so more.' The words slithered from his mouth as a beautiful song and into the hungry ears of his listeners. 'You may enter now, boy, speak your piece,' he added without lifting his head.

The tattered soldier Umishi had entered with stepped

forward and bowed to the monster. 'Arch-mage, I am Alexander Fair, Commander of the battalion posted at Ghalsberg. We... the town was overrun. The Dhal-Llah killed them, sir, they killed them.'

'I had not expected them to gain ground with such speed...' Leuvigild said, mostly to himself. 'There is no more time, we can wait no longer.'

'They tore them apart like dolls and the blood I never....'

With every word the commander spoke his resolve seemed to decay. These people should not be in a war. Umishi doubted they even had the stomach for a brawl. They were children fooled into playing with real swords. Fendamor surely must have recognised this as well. She watched as the Mangler's spawn strode towards the commander and embraced him. He held him in silence for a great length of time before patting his back and releasing him.

'Be with your fellows and kin,' Fendamor whispered. 'There is warm food and wine waiting for you. We will get you all to safety, as many as we can.'

With shaking knees, the commander left the war room, allowing Fendamor to return his focus to the map and his pretty generals. 'You heard what the man said. We need to prepare, to cast off as soon as possible. I... we have done all we can. We owe it to those we could not save to see those we could to safety.' As he spoke, his eyes darted from one general to another.

'No one can question your character, Arch-mage,' boomed one of the fatter humans. 'There are hundreds of lives down in those caverns who would thank you for your heroism, hundreds of lives you have saved, myself among them.'

Umishi ground her teeth. She could hardly contain the hate that desperately wanted to explode into a scream powerful enough to bring down the whole mountain. There was nothing heroic in Fendamor's actions: he was fleeing, abandoning his kingdom, his people, sparing just enough to delude himself into believing he had done all he could, while he cast off all responsibilities. The people of Hanaswick trusted him, had placed their lives in his hands. How could he cast them aside with such little thought? How could so much faith mean so little?

Renderbrim was right. Although the mad mage triggered the war, it was Fendamor and the Mangler who had forged it. It was their neglect that had made the Dhal-Llah into monsters and had done nothing to temper their hate. The war would have come anyway and Leuvigild had done nothing to try to stop it. Renderbrim was right: there was only one solution to this, and justice had to be dealt.

'Thank you for your kind words, Tyrone,' Leuvigild assured them. 'But please, all of you, make your way to the ships; you are my hands. I want you to make sure everything is in order; that all the supplies are ready to be stored and every soul is aboard. The goal is to depart before nightfall.'

The polished generals bowed and exited, leaving the arch-mage alone; alone with her.

Umishi's breath slowed as she slid from her hiding place, landing on the stone floor without a sound. She pulled her sword from her belt and moved forwards to her target, who was fully absorbed in positioning small wooden markers on his grand map. Her heart pounded with an enthusiasm she feared would alert her foe. If Renderbrim had spoken the truth, then the Ward would no longer be protecting this monster. Finally, she would bring vengeance for those she loved – her neighbours, her husband, her son – by granting them his pain. She would make him suffer for them; would make him cry out each of their names before drowning him in his own blood.

She took another step closer. Her blade quaked in her hand as her whole body shivered. She took another breath, slow and easy, as silent as the death she was about to personify. She was close enough now to hear the monster muttering to himself about his regrets, about the people he was choosing to cast aside. What did it matter? It was too late for them, and what could she do anyway? She was an inquisitor of the Order of Alpharus; it was her duty to put an end to mages who misused their power, not to stop a war. No, she would do her duty. She raised her sword, readying to thrust the blade into the creature's neck. Her eye flashed down at the map as she did it; a model of Hanaswick easily recognisable by its pointed, pale faced tower. The model was filled with tiny blue blocks, which clearly represented the hundreds of lives the city contained. Beyond the walls, pressed tightly against them, stood dozens of green blocks, the Dhal-Llah. Lothrum was right: they were doomed. The people of Hanaswick were not prepared, could not defend themselves, and Hanaswick would not be the end, they would move on to the next town and the next...

Umishi's blade raced towards its target then froze, losing all its energy. If she were to kill Fendamor now, the people of

Hanaswick would lose their Ward and be slaughtered in the name of Renderbrim's justice. A realisation flooded her. Renderbrim was downstairs only moments ago; he had yet to remove the Ward from Hanaswick, or anywhere west of here. He couldn't have. He had followed the same course as her, from Jimmarah to Llanvurgist, then here. He did not have time to go anywhere else, remove the Ward from any other town, barring the ones he had walked through to get here. Hanaswick was still under the Ward. The image in the blade's reflection gave her a curious glance, wondering why she had stopped the knife.

Umishi took another breath while a thousand maggots wiggled in her belly. Why had she stopped? She had a duty; this monster could not escape justice. The voices in her head screamed for the blade to tear into him, called for her to rip arteries and sever tendons. He and his father had dodged justice for so long, built a kingdom atop the blood of innocent lives... her husband, her son. Lothrum was wrong; this man, this monster, was every bit the Mangler his father was. How easy was it for this coward to cast away the lives of those who had been so loyal to him? Justice called for his death. Her fingers tightened around the sword's hilt as she plunged the blade down.

'No!' she screamed. Her grip on her sword released; she didn't even notice it leave her hand, didn't notice the hollow clank it made against the floor.

'Ms Zaimor, you are alive,' Leuvigild Fendamor stated, without surprise. 'I hoped you would be. I had hoped to... that I would have chance to...'

'I will kill you!' Umishi cried out 'Why can't I kill you?

'I... I can't answer that, but I can only surmise you see it too,' Leuvigild whispered, his gaze shifting back to the wooden cubes laid on the table. 'I saw it when you stayed your blade. I see it reflected in your eye: you see what I see. No one else sees it, so sheltered from death have they been. This damned map, the people on it, the lives that are to be removed. Coloured blocks are so easily pulled from the board. I have removed so many these last few days, and yet so many more will be expunged. I wish I could replace them, put back the ones I lifted from Jimmarah, Ghal-Talos, Holsta. Instead...' He paused. 'Ms Zaimor, I can't be here when the time comes to remove them all. My heart could not take the pain.'

'You have a heart?' she snarled, stroking her hair over her face. 'Will you tell yourself that while you abandon them? You're every bit the monster your father was.' Although her accusation felt desperate and hollow, it rode a wave of pain and hatred. It didn't matter anymore; there had to be justice. Someone had to pay for all the suffering, for everything.

Fendamor's face darkened as he absorbed her bitter words. He steadied himself on his war table, eyes fixed on the blue blocks of Hanaswick. 'So, you know? I had planned on telling you, telling you everything, explaining the necessity of sending you into the Ward's workings, about Renderbrim. Things escalated so quickly, though, and I had to react. I regret I did not have the opportunity. Would you have even understood? Would you have lent Fendamor your aid if I had been upfront about the Ward, my father, his legacy?'

He paused, staring at Umishi as if he actually expected an answer. When it became clear that he wasn't going to get one, he went on.

'I think not, but this was not how it was meant to be. It was my goal to show you the good that came from the Ward, the peace that Malhain and her people brought to Domvalkia. I hoped that this knowledge would bring you some kind of peace too. I know you have been suffering for so long because of us, what you lost so that my father could perfect the Ward. In fact, your suffering has always been at the back of my mind when I regarded my father's deeds, and I hoped to one day-'

'You thought I'd forget what he did to them?' she snapped. 'What he... he tore them *apart!* Did you know? When his experiments failed, they were...' What remained of Umishi's left cheek twitched at the memory. 'You thought I'd *forgive?*'

'No, not at all. My father was unfeeling and cruel, but what he did has brought a lasting peace which our people enjoyed for decades. I thought that, if I showed you first-hand what the Ward meant to those who live on this island...' he looked over at the map. 'I thought maybe, if you actively helped maintain it, you too would see its necessity, the blessing and security granted to my people by your family's sacrifice. You would see that they did not die in vain, and the reason I maintained it. Of course, I was blind to the Dhal-Llah's resentment of my father's occupation, to the evil festering underneath. No, I was wrong, I know that now. The Ward was not the cure I thought it to be; it was a mask hiding infected wounds that remained unhealed. Now, it looks like fate has come to collect the debt for my hubris.'

'A debt you are fleeing,' Umishi growled. 'A debt the

people of Hanaswick will be forced to pay!' She glanced over to her blade; it was close enough for her to reach. She had fulfilled her vow to Lothrum, had listened to this snake spit his words. Despite Lothrum's claims, Leuvigild was a mage like any other, placing his own pride and survival above all others. While his attention was focused on the map in front of him, she reached for the sword. Its hilt was cold in her grip, and her eye made a target of his neck. So long as Leuvigild lived, the Ward still protected the people of Hanaswick; by killing him she would doom them all. But she could not allow another fiend to escape justice.

'On the contrary, Ms Zaimor,' he said, turning to her and pulling his robe open, baring his naked chest. 'I never had any intention of leaving. No, I intend to pay my dues in full.' He stared steadily, ready to accept justice.

TWENTY-FIVE

REFLECTIONS

They stared at each other for an eternity, their breathing and heartbeats mirrored. What was happening? This wasn't how she had envisioned this confrontation. It had to be some kind of trap. Leuvigild stood offering nothing but silence while he awaited judgement and death. Despite his statuesque expression, Umishi could sense something stirring within him: fear. His breathing increased, his heart pounded, she could smell the sweat seeping from his porcelain skin. It was clear, despite his noble gesture, that he was not yet ready to give up his life.

His eyes were filled with trepidation. She tried to rekindle her hate, tried her best to remind herself that this was the monster who had built an empire on the blood and suffering of her friends, her family. This creature believed he had the right to govern life and death. But, the more she assessed his slender, trembling form, the clearer it became this was not the Mangler of Malhain, nor was he some dark, corrupting legacy, fated to destroy the world. He was just a misguided man, a young fool who had this power thrust upon him with only the Mangler's dark example to follow regarding how to use it.

Her hand shivered into life. Her fingers clumsily fidgeted over the blade's grip. Misguided or not, she could not allow herself to be swayed from performing her duty, administering justice. Fendamor watched her actions as though they no longer mattered. Tilting the blade once more, Umishi saw her reflection. Her red eye was lost in the shadow her hate-filled expression had created, mouth twisted into a sneer and eyebrow arched deep into the bridge of her nose. Was this who she was fated to be? Was death to be the deciding factor in everything she did? Why did everyone's motivations seem so much nobler than hers? Was this truly justice, or was it revenge?

Umishi took another breath. There was only one option available to her, regardless of her feelings, her newfound insight. There was only one thing she could do, wasn't there? Lothrum had been right again and, she hated to admit, he had been right all along. Killing this man would not change anything; the war would continue, lives would be lost, Richard and Thomas would still be dead. There was no point to her vengeance. Renderbrim was wrong: all wars had to end, true enough, but not all of them had to end in blood, not when there might be another answer.

Umishi closed her eye. The lives of the people of Hanaswick were worth more than anything her futile vengeance could offer. The Mangler was dead. No amount of further death would heal the wound he made... but life? Maybe life could.

'Renderbrim has not yet removed the Ward from

Hanaswick,' she whispered.

'He has not?' Leuvigild whispered back.

'No,' she explained, clawing her hair. 'He... it seems he can only remove the Ward from people one at a time, by... he says he cuts their tethers, as he has cut yours. I met him in the Dhal-Llah city before here so, unless he has used magic to move faster, then he couldn't have possibly moved further west.'

'Which means all the towns and cities west of here are still under the Ward's protection.' For a moment, Leuvigild was silent again, absorbing the information and analysing her every word. He turned back to his map, tracing the roads with his fingers. 'He has to be stopped; there is no avoiding it.' Once more, thought made a mute out of him as he paced the hall, a finger to his lips.

'The Dhal-Llah will be heading directly for Hanaswick.' Leuvigild said, turning on his heel to face her. 'If, as you say, the Ward still protects those within the capital's walls, I should be able to force the Dhal-Llah to disband. I shall remove from them the gift they have so disrespectfully exploited.'

It seemed that he had a plan.

'Of course,' he continued in sombre tones, 'I will require your help. The people of Hanaswick need your help and I beg you on their behalf. If we are to reduce the lives lost, you will have to persuade the king to evacuate the city and, most importantly, you will have to...'

'Kill Renderbrim,' Umishi finished, knowing full well where Fendamor was leading her.

'Yes, if it comes to that. He needs to be stopped; of that,

there can be no doubt,' he answered, the words oozing regret. 'But there are other priorities. I ask that you make sure the people are safe, make sure the king understands the danger they will be in. After I have removed the Ward from the Dhal-Llah, it will be like making a hole in a woollen cloth, for lack of a better metaphor. Slowly, the whole spell will begin to unravel, but hopefully not before the Dhal-Llah have fled. After that... well, after that, the Ward will be no more and my father's dream... well, it is probably for the best, given the grief it seems to have brought.'

Umishi stood; she had heard enough. She was not about to console him, or tell him the time this land had spent under the corruption his father placed it under was somehow good. She knew what she had to do, and it would not be for his sake that she would complete her task. Her legs wobbled as she tried to push her hate away. She would take it one step at a time, and worry about finding her way after this war was over. At least, that way, there would be no more blood on her hands than necessary.

'Thank you, Ms Zaimor,' the Nal-Tiran creature said, climbing to his feet. 'Thank you for staying your blade. Thank you for helping all of us.'

She didn't want his gratitude, didn't want anything to do with him. She wanted him out of her sight. She nodded, because it was the only politeness she could muster. Leuvigild headed for the door.

'Feel free to rest here for a time, take advantage of our supplies, our armoury,' he called, as though determined to prolong her struggle. 'You are looking worn and you will need your energy. While you do so, I will have a horse readied.'

Umishi considered refusing the offer for a moment. She did not need charity from him, did not want to accept anything he had to offer her. Her body disagreed, though, aching in rebellion.

Umishi was given a room to herself. It was a small but reasonable size containing only a bed and a desk for a candle. Although comfortable, she found no rest there. Ghosts from her past took it in turns to visit her, faceless beings with the vague outlines of men and women. Some were old, some young, some too young. All of them died at her hand demanding to know why she had stayed her blade, why her vengeance was not realised. She didn't have an answer for them. She tried telling them, *herself*, that it was because he had trapped her, that she needed him to lift his curse from the Dhal-Llah, but she knew that was not it. There had been something in Lothrum's words, something she had seen in the madness of Renderbrim that awakened a kind of spark within her. The faceless ghosts continued to gather, haunting the back of her mind. Her quest to kill one man had already cost too much.

After her aches had subsided, she moved on to one of the armouries. Once more, Fendamor seemed to have sent a message ahead of her, as the supply captain welcomed her with over emphasised eagerness. Umishi hid behind her hair and ignored him. She was in no mood to take part in the games of society; she was there for one reason alone. Her eye led her down the weapon racks, fingers trailing over the hilts of swords and axes until she reached for blades more suited to her tastes. She took one of the daggers and ran parchment along its edge. The parchment fell in two. The blade would do.

From there, Umishi stood atop the stairs, staring out through the dragon glass. It was a strange sight to behold. Through the dragon glass, the land stretched out like an ocean of gold and diamonds, glistening under the desert sun. She pulled her hair and started her decent towards the fortress's exit.

True to his word, Fendamor had readied a mount for her; a fine horse at that. A soldier held its reins and looked down at Umishi with wide eyes. It was apparent she had never seen a Walnorg before.

'He'll get you where you need to be,' the soldier said, meek. 'You're... you can ride can't you? I mean, you can get into the saddle?'

Umishi ignored her. She didn't want to get into a needless conversation. With powerful back legs, Umishi jumped onto the seat of the horse. She looked down at the human soldier and gave her a grin. Then, with a quick kick to the horse's sides, she headed off.

Once she was on her way, her mood shifted. She began to have doubts about Fendamor's plan. She had seen the enemy, had seen the death-obsessed monsters and their talents for pain. Even without the Ward upon them, would they truly stop? Would they still throw themselves at the walls? Would the battle of Hanaswick be anything but a massacre? She took a breath to quell her anxiety.

She rode southwards, back in the direction she and Lothrum had come. It was a strange thing to see the flats so alive, to see the critters and other crawling things basking in the sun's generous glow. Here, it was the shadows that recoiled, hiding under rocks and trees like wounded prey.

Echoes of Fendamor

For the first time in years, Umishi found herself enjoying the sun's heat upon her face. It seemed to reinvigorate all her joints and push back the memories her mind had been harbouring about Renderbrim and his frozen world. For a short time, at least, she could take a breath and relax, before death caught up with her again.

The sun could not grant its favour to her forever, though, and, as she pressed her horse, darkness pressed against the light with the same determination. Umishi had no choice but to make camp. She had left it too late to do it properly though; the other plane had made her lazy. She lay on the ground with barely a sheet protecting her from the elements. She hugged herself, recalling the last time she had been there, how she and Lothrum could have slept on the sand with every faith they wouldn't be buried by a sandstorm and the night wouldn't freeze them. She was beginning to miss him, and company in general. She had been so lonely for so long that she had forgotten what companionship felt like.

Dawn came and Umishi moved on, continuing south. The ground grew lush and fertile and, as the day progressed, life bled back into the world. There were trees with leaves that stood bright and green, while birdsong gushed from all around her. It was not until evening returned that the fires on the horizon made their presence known.

TWENTY-SIX
FIRES OF GHAL-TALOS

The trees ended abruptly, bowing to the whims of the growing flames in the distance. Umishi's horse reared and whined, seemingly aware of the danger ahead, and that, if they charged in foolhardily, they would find their end. Umishi took heed of the beast's warning. With a sharp pull at the mount's reins, she tried to convince the beast to withdraw from the ash-coated fields. It was too late; as the horse turned, an explosion was expelled from the fiery landscape. It was followed by a high-pitched screaming that pierced Umishi's ears, as an ingot of spherical iron passed their right flank. The horse heard it too and, without warning, threw itself into a panic, jerking and retreating in desperation. Another explosion and more of the balls flew past at tremendous speeds.

The explosions burrowed through Umishi's ears and into her skull, followed by more terrible screaming. This time, one of the balls tore close past the horse, slicing through its skin easier than any bolt could have. The beast's panic heightened until it was beyond control. Umishi's heart seemed to stop as she felt a sudden sense of displacement. Time came to a crashing halt as she was thrown into the air and her lungs seemed to fill all at once, feeling as though they were about to explode. She didn't see the ground as it rushed to meet her, but cloudless skies and sparkling stars seemed to sing apologies to her for the pain she was about to feel.

Pain raced through every nerve and into every muscle as Umishi's back crashed against the solid earth. She groaned and rolled in discomfort, digging her claws into the mud and ash. She bit down on her lip and opened her eye to see the blurred form of her treacherous, cowardly mount fleeing in the direction they had come from. As she tried to move, another jolt of pain ran through her body. She grunted. Regardless of the pain, she had no time to lie on her back, the strange projectiles had not sprung from nowhere, after all. Her limbs protested as she pulled herself to her feet. In the distance, she could see humanoid forms approaching, outlined by the distant fires. It felt as though her mind was underwater, drowning in the pain that reverberated through her body. There was no time to think; she had to move, had to get away. She could not tell what direction she was going, just that it was away from the silhouettes pursuing her.

She stumbled away, using anything in reach to steady herself. Her breath was starting to fall back into a normal pattern, but the beating of her heart seemed to be getting faster and faster, louder and louder, until it was clear the pounding was not coming from her chest at all. Behind her, three horses were advancing. Straddling their backs Umishi could see the porcelain-covered faces of the Dhal-Llah. Two of them continued in pursuit of Umishi's fleeing mount, while the other turned to its side, blocking Umishi's progress north.

The robed figure pulled a strange-looking weapon from its cloak. It was long, cylindrical and smelled of fire. With steady movements, the creature slowly began to load it. The Dhal-Llah's motions were exaggerated but precise as its gloved fingers loaded the weapon with a ball of iron before ramming a stick into the mouth of the metal shaft. Umishi stared at the figure and ground her teeth. She was being toyed with. Although the mask was frozen with a stoic expression, she could feel the human's smile seeping through the holes.

With no choice, Umishi turned to the distant fires and ran. Behind her, she could hear the weapon's mechanism being cocked then, a hollow snap. An explosion launched at her from behind, pushing the iron projectile at her with astonishing speeds. She twisted her body in a way that would make her a smaller target. It worked. Whatever these weapons were, they didn't seem any more accurate than a common crossbow. An explosion launched at her from behind, pushing the iron projectile at her with astonishing speeds. Her heart slammed in her chest; it was close, too close. There were no trees to hide among; she had left them behind. Her only hope was moving forward towards the flaming ruins ahead, hoping that, there, she would find some kind of refuge.

Another explosion forced her ears to ring as the painful sound caused the land to tremble. The ball it unleashed raced for her, catching her shoulder. It passed through leather and skin easily. Warm blood ran from the newly hatched wound.

Umishi stumbled, clutching her shoulder. With dumb luck, she caught herself before falling, still hanging on, but barely. Behind her the other two horses thundered. She was not being hunted; she was being herded.

As she got closer to the village, Umishi began to recognise it. She had been there before: it was the village that she had passed through on the way to Jimmarah's lake town. Hanaswick couldn't be more than a day or two's ride away.

As she drew closer, it became obvious it was not the humble hamlet it had once been. The walls had been repaired and re-enforced with spikes and barbs. The perimeter was decorated with huge pikes which not only flew the colours of the Dhal-Llah, but also the bodies of flayed men. The rancid scent of death festered and seeped at the back of her throat as the town gates grew nearer.

One of the horses closed in on her side. The rider looked down at her, the black pits from within the mask showing only disdain. With a swift movement, the human raised its weapon in a signal to those upon the walls. The signal sparked a commotion above and, in what seemed like no time at all, the village gates opened. This would be the opportunity Umishi needed.

Umishi ran through the gates, leaving the Dhal-Llah riders behind her frozen in confusion, if only for a moment. Inside the town, she turned to the walls and jumped at the stone. She could hear the Dhal-Llah behind her. She did not know how many. They yelled wordless screams from tongueless mouths. What was she doing? Was there a plan? To these questions there was no answer; however her heart continued to pound. Her fingers dug into the pulp between the cracks. It was a good feeling and the gaps were more than large enough. It would be almost as easy as walking.

Above her a silent, cowled guard stood with one of the strange tube-like weapons in its hand and her head in its sights. The mechanism of his weapon creaked into action as its used pressed the trigger. The explosion which followed almost broke her from the wall but, with fortune on her side, her grip, with one hand, at least, held fast as she twisted her body away from the ball that sped at her. She threw herself horizontally from stone to stone, her heart pounding with each jump. She couldn't stay up here. Her luck would no doubt run out, rendering her nothing more than target practice for those below.

To the left of her was the door she had entered through, to the right nothing but endless wall. Another explosion sounded through the ruined village. Behind her, there was a ruined temple. Judging the distance, the jump to the temple window would be near impossible. Below her came the clicking sound of a thousand strange weapons as they were primed to fire upon her. In spite of the impossibility, Umishi took a deep breath and thrust herself from the wall.

As Umishi flew through the air, she heard the cacophony of explosions expel their charges towards her. With angry screams, each ball met their failure on the wall where she had just been. She reached for the temple's window ledge with such force that it felt as though her skeleton would burst through her fingertips. It was not enough. She almost reached it, one of her long talons almost managed to tap the charred stone. Her eye widened and her heart froze as the ledge grew ever further out of reach.

Her hand sped out, as though the wall would bend to her will and offer her rescue. It did not. She knew in that moment that she was going to fall, meeting her fate upon the blades below her. Then her fingers caught hold of something. Umishi gripped on to it as tightly as she could and swung towards the ruin, her breath stolen, her mind stunned with disbelief. The sea of white faces below cried up with wordless anger toward her as though their voices would pierce her in place of their iron.

Her helping hand was exactly that. Umishi almost let go when she discovered the nature of her saviour. Its skin was rotten and maggot-filled, its arm only holding her weight due to the armour that supported its putrid skin. With reluctance, Umishi grabbed the hanging corpse with her other hand. The grinning face of the Fendamor soldier looked down at her as she climbed up its decaying body. Below, the Dhal-Llah scrambled to ascend the ruin. Hand after hand, she climbed the corpse and hoped that, in the afterlife, he would forgive her for this indignity. Her muscles poised, she jumped from the corpse to stone.

Umishi climbed the temple's tower as high as she could. Reaching its pinnacle, the moon greeted her with a face that had become familiar to her, usually as one that greeted her every time she entered Renderbrim's shadow realm. Now it overlooked her world, instead. From her viewpoint, Umishi was able to see the doom that approached Hanaswick: an army of what seemed to be thousands of faceless soldiers, all ready to die for an already dead king.

The Dhal-Llah filled the fields of the humble hamlet, except they were not growing crops, but siege engines. This was no longer a Fendamor township, but a staging post where the invading army stoked the flames of industry using the surrounding trees as fuel and components. Here, they build catapults, battering rams and siege towers. They were preparing themselves for a long siege on the capital. She had to get to Hanaswick, had to stop Renderbrim before any of this could happen.

The sound of their leather boots pounding against the stone staircase reached her. They couldn't catch her, not now they had lost sight of her. They could only guess and, although their guess was right, it would be easy enough to persuade them they were wrong. Umishi had a few more moments before they reached the top. With all her might, she kicked a stone loose from the wall. Next, she wrapped one of the larger stones in a rag she had found lying on the burnt rooftop, unsure if it was a banner, a carpet or just a cloak someone left behind. It was burnt to blackness, but was still a tool for her to use.

Umishi threw the cloth-covered rock off the side of the temple and watched as its black tail fell upon the roof of an adjacent building. The town rang with explosions, none of the iron balls hitting the stone decoy. The footsteps stopped for a moment but only for a moment. It was long enough, long enough for them to question what it was, long enough to wonder if she had fled this tower. All she had to do now was prove to them she was not here.

There was not much time, the footsteps pressed against the stone as though they were pressing against her head. With doubt in their minds, the hiding place did not have to be good; it just had to be one, for a short amount of time.

The hunters were three or four floors below her and, within a heartbeat, Umishi spotted it. She quickly flew down the first staircase, then jumped upon the inner wall. With spider-like speed, she clawed her way into the ceiling's corner and waited for the masked fools to pass under her. They did not look up as they ascended the stairs. No one ever did.

She held her breath and watched them as they came to the conclusion she had engineered, watched them decide she was not there. With silent frustration, the soldiers marched under her and back the way they had come. Umishi grinned at their failure. As the last soldier left her sight, she slipped from her perch. Sticking to the shadows, she followed them down to the ground floor of the ruin and out the door.

Almost twice as many Dhal-Llah entered the building opposite, the building where her cloaked stone had entered. She was sure they would find it quickly, but that did not matter; they had lost her, and they would never find her. She snuck to the fields. Only a small group hunted her now, the rest seemed to scurry about, conducting whatever work they had been involved in before her arrival.

In the fields, she found herself in the open, but it would not be for long; she knew where she was going and darted eastwards. She ran towards a large siege tower. The tower was being tied to a small herd of horses and, without a doubt, being delivered to the walls of Hanaswick. Umishi allowed herself a smile. Direction was no longer a worry, with this mode of transport readied for her, she didn't even have to walk.

TWENTY-SEVEN
INFILTRATION

The siege tower ploughed its way through the plains of Fendamor, tearing apart the soil with its merciless traction. The Dhal-Llah drove their labouring horses with the whip, commanding them to achieve impossible speeds. Judging by the time they were making and the distance they had already travelled, Umishi guessed it would take them no more than half a day to get to the kingdom's capital. If Leuvigild's army was not already marching, then there would be no hope for Hanaswick or its people.

A thunderous rumbling sounded all around her. The tower's arrow-loop windows provided no clues to the source of the terrible sound. Umishi climbed her way to the top of the siege tower to get a better view of what was happening. A cold wind whipped at her as she reached the pinnacle of the massive construct. From her vantage point, she could see other towers being dragged behind her. The Dhal-Llah clearly aimed to overcome Hanaswick's walls quickly; this would be no normal siege. After the main force arrived,

Umishi imagined the siege would be over in perhaps a day. The Dhal-Llah had prepared everything before the battle had even started. The violent wind lashed at her again and again, until she could take it no more, conceding to its onslaught and withdrawing into the neck of the wooden siege engine.

On the third level of the siege tower, Umishi waited. The events that had led her through this island seemed dreamlike and unreal now, all culminating in the unbelievable fact she was heading towards a battle she had no stake in for a man she despised. Why was she risking her life? She had not asked for this, she had come to take a life, not to be some kind of hero. She did not want to have the fate of these people placed on her shoulders, but there it was. Even as she thought of the heavy hand fate had dealt her, it was hard not to see the pettiness of her vengeance. How many lives was her vengeance worth? Would Richard have wanted her to stay safe rather than fight on behalf of the Mangler's son, the offspring of the monster who had killed him? She would have given anything to have been able to ask him, to hear his voice again. She rubbed the dampness from her eye. Of course, she did not need to ask; she already knew what he would do. He was a good man, better than her. She shook her head in the hopes that all these thoughts would pour out with her tears. She had a task to do, wasn't that enough? She needed to stop thinking. She closed her eye, Umishi tried to expel anything her mind was trying to confront her with.

The earth shook and threw her consciousness back to the waking world. How long had she been asleep? How could she have slept? How *long* had she been asleep? She returned to the tower's roof. They had stopped; they all had. All the towers had positioned themselves in rows, falling in with those dragged before them. On the horizon, looming from the darkness, Hanaswick's wall came into view. The glow of the torches on the battlements and the fires below made the city's grand defences all the more impressive. Umishi licked her lips. She had to get in if she was to confront Renderbrim and stop this mess from getting further out of control. Beneath her, the Dhal-Llah forces gathered: those who came with the towers, those who rode the horses, but it was only a matter of time before the true army started arriving. She did not have much time.

From her window, Hanaswick's great walls stood firm in defiance of the growing army. Were this any normal army attacking, or any normal army defending, for that matter, the city would be impenetrable. Even a handful of well-trained archers and a mage or two could hold it. It was easy to imagine this city holding its own against almost any kind of siege. This trail of thought, however, led Umishi to her next problem: she had to find a way in. She took a moment to compose herself. There was a river on the eastern wall, running next to the palace; that would be her way in. With a new goal, her mind started to buzz with the thought of movement and her body gave in to the desire.

With keen stealth, Umishi slid from the siege tower's gate and to the ground that was soon to be a battlefield. She kept her eye on the masked soldiers who stood staring at the walls they were destined to mount. They stood as scarecrows, their soulless eyes completely lifeless; the fact they were human could have easily been forgotten. For a moment Umishi was tempted to stand in front of them to see if they reacted, to see if they would do anything without the say so of their fallen ruler. She kept going instead.

It didn't take long before she found the river that would be her entry point. The waters seemed just as dead here as in Renderbrim's empty world: no fish, no reeds. Even without touching it, she could somehow tell it was cold. The moon admired itself on the river's surface; it was half what it was in the other plane but it was still a white grin on the black ooze. She found herself recalling what Lothrum had told her about the other plane. When the moon reached the same point in this one, it would transfer itself to the other. She pictured the chaos the darker plane would soon be experiencing: the siege towers building themselves from nothing, as the soil behind them churned. The thought passed as quickly as it had come, and her attention refocused upon her means of entry.

Regardless of the river's appearance, it was her only option. Umishi took a deep breath and jumped in. The water surrounded her in its icy grip, so could that the sudden chill almost stole her breath. Her eye sprung open and the void stretched out before her. It took her a moment to regain her focus. She swam, faster than she ever had before, although she had never been good at swimming. The water hated her as much as she hated it; it pulled and tugged at her with a heaviness that was unsettling for someone meant to live in the trees.

Umishi pushed herself as hard as her arms would allow. Above her, the fires of torchlight signified the end of her plight, but she didn't see the grate that stood in her way. Hidden in the blackness, she felt a rush of agony run down her shoulder as she rammed herself against the iron bars. As the pain coursed through her, she felt herself let go of a breath. She watched in terror as bubbles escaped her mouth. She wouldn't be able to hold it for much longer, her cheeks beginning to burn as the pressure behind them became too much. This grid hadn't been there before; this tunnel had stood open. They must have sealed it in anticipation of the Dhal-Llah's assault.

Wait, but wait, the gaps between the bars were surely big enough for her to get through? She squeezed an arm through, a shoulder, her chest. But her head, her head felt like it was stuck. Umishi panicked; her lungs felt as though they were going to explode, she couldn't fit, she couldn't. She tried over and over, scraping her face against the iron until, through a cloud of blood, she burst free.

She swam upwards and emerged choking, coughing up all the water that had made it past her airway's defences. It didn't matter. She was there; she had broken through into Hanaswick.

With her head above the water, it was clear that the city had been completely transformed. The windows and doors were crudely boarded up, and there were poorly placed barricades throughout the streets. Behind every chained door and closed window, light shone through the cracks. There were people? What were they doing in their houses? Leuvigild believed the king would keep his subjects safe. It was clear that their opinions of safety differed from hers considerably. This was not how things should have been done. Were this a normal city, were this a normal siege, then the people would have been escorted behind the safety of the castle walls, protected under the keep. Of course, this was no normal city and its castle, its palace, was no more protected than a bakery. Ward or not, through Umishi's eye, the city was defenceless; the gates might as well have been open.

The city had to be evacuated but how? With the Dhal-Llah horde at the walls, escape through the main gates would be impossible, and she could hardly lead hundreds of souls through the same way she had come. No, there had to be another way. A clicking tore her attention from her thoughts, the all too familiar sound turning her blood to ice and forcing her to face the fact she was alone and out in the open. The clicking was followed by a scream that echoed from the alley behind her. Spinning on her heel, Umishi faced Hanaswick's haunted streets. She expected the lingering shadows to rush her, expected them to wrap around her and drag her back into the shadow plane, but they didn't. They waited and, shrouded in their darkness, a Kalsakian lurked.

The monster's clicking and croaking echoed off the walls of the houses as it charged at her. The world was still the same, which could only mean this Kalsakian had crossed into this plane as one of Renderbrim's messengers, the signal for the siege to begin. Umishi drew her blade from her hip and charged the blackness.

Empty streets swallowed her as she ran past buildings that reached out with weak shafts of light. It felt as though the monster's screams were coming from everywhere, burrowing inside her head with each shriek, but she knew that was not the truth of things: the Kalsakian had but one task, one destination. As the roads came to an end, she knew she would find it at the city walls. In the wall's entryway, she caught a glimpse of it before it slithered through the archway that would lead it up onto the ramparts. It was a mess of loose skin and skeletal limbs, crawling on all fours like a spider. If ever there was an embodiment of the suffering of war, it was the Kalsakian.

It would not achieve its mission. With every bit of vigour she could muster, Umishi darted forwards, throwing herself through the archway and into the spiralling stairwell. She caught a glimpse of its ankle as it shifted around a corner, and her heart sung a cacophony as she lunged for the creature's tar-like flesh. Her blade found its target as the creature's angry cries pounded at the walls. Regardless of its injury, the Kalsakian pushed itself forwards, ascending ever closer to the doorway above.

Umishi threw herself on top of the monster, stabbing at its back. She screamed with a fury equal to the creature's as blood erupted from its open wounds. The Kalsakian kicked back with inhuman strength, first at her knee, then twice into the softness of her belly. She groaned as pain exploded from below her ribs. Another kick and the creature freed itself. Umishi lost her grip on her dagger and fell backwards. Each step she tumbled down attacked her until the wall caught her head from behind.

The mangled, wounded thing dragged itself upwards, obstructing the light emitted from the door above. Umishi moved her arm and pain shot from elbow to shoulder. She wiped the blood from her lips; there was no time to cradle the wounds the monster had inflicted. Drawing another deep breath, she gave chase, grabbing her dagger as she rushed up the blood-lathered stairs and out onto the ramparts.

Cold winds attacked her as she lifted herself back onto

two legs and onto the walls. Beyond the battlements and stretching out towards the horizon, further than the night permitted her to see, were the Dhal-Llah armies. They were an ocean of black robes in textbook formation, their silence and stillness unnerving. Umishi caught her breath and turned back to her task. On the smooth stone pathway in front of her, the Kalsakian lay, drawing its final breaths. How pitiful it looked in the moonlight, broken, even before her blade had performed its grizzly work. Umishi studied the monster's twisted features, pondering over what violent act had created this poor beast, what cruel fate had moulded it into the misshapen thing it was. Her dagger twisted in her palm, and she readied herself to grant a final mercy to the broken soul.

As Umishi lingered, however, the Kalsakian filled its lungs. Stealing one last moment of life, it threw itself onto its hind-legs and screamed once more, this time not in hate or pain, but victory. Umishi's eye widened in horror. Its mission complete, the creature fell back, dead.

After the Kalsakian's cry, the world fell silent, its breath held, waiting for the Dhal-Llah to make their move. It didn't take long. A single robed figure moved with deliberation towards one of the cylindrical weapons Umishi had passed on her way here, weapons they had also brought to the walls of Fort Jimmarah. With morbid curiosity, she watched the Dhal-Llah soldier bring fire to the weapon's back, producing a sound that threatened to tear the world apart. She fell to her knees and clapped her hands against her ears. It caused the stone to tremble, and the air to stir: it was the sound of a thousand rocks being smashed together all at once.

Chained atop one of the siege towers, a Dhal-Llah mage shouted words that caught the iron ball thrown from the weapon's mouth and directed it over the walls at breathtaking speed. Fear overtook Umishi, crushing her lungs and twisting her body to face the city, and the damage the Dhal-Llah's first attack would wreak. The iron ball flew against Hanaswick's massive tower, cutting straight through it with a deafening explosion. Disbelief stole Umishi's breath and froze her face with awe; to her recollection, magic had never been used in such a way, nor to such devastating effect. The sundial tower fell like a tree to a woodsman's axe. It crashed down against the palace, scraping away walls and lavish balconies and crushing the gardens below. Umishi froze as the battle of Hanaswick began.

TWENTY-EIGHT
BEHIND HIGH WALLS

The city of Hanaswick awoke screaming, its people spilling into the streets, their panicked cries unifying in a symphony of terror. Beyond the walls, the Dhal-Llah prepared their ladders. Surely, though, the walls were too high to be mounted in that manner? Even as Umishi considered it, another of the cylindrical weapons was being loaded. Clawing at her head, she closed her eye and tried to steady her breathing as the sounds of chaos ambushed her from every angle. She needed to think.

There had to be a way to get the people from the city before the walls were breached, before the Dhal-Llah tore through, turning streets into bloody streams. Frustration built inside her as the Fendamor's citizens abandoned their crudely defended homes and fled, directionless and frightened. Every inch of Umishi's body told her to follow their example: to flee this city, to abandon it to its fate, as she had done before with so many other doomed cities, as she had with the Fort Jimmarah, as she had done with Malhain. The corner of her mouth twitched with the recollection, but what else was she to do? It was part of being a survivor to know when to fight and when to run. The ability, the courage, to rescue anyone other than herself seemed to be beyond her nature. Her shoulders fell as she took a breath, willing herself to be something that she was not. She wanted to save them, but she couldn't. She couldn't think of a way to lift them from their doom. She closed her eye and cursed herself, her nature, her cowardice. This was not a task meant for her; her skill lay more in death than in saving lives. No, this was a task more suited to Lothrum or Leuvigild; they would know what to do in this situation.

Her eye suddenly shot open with the realisation that Leuvigild had already *given* her the answer. He had indeed already been in this situation and shown her the solution. The ships! She recalled the massive warship harboured down at the dock. The ship was the biggest she had ever seen, capable of holding maybe a thousand souls. Was it enough? No, likely not, but a thousand survivors was a better situation than she had had moments ago. She would try. She licked her lips. Perhaps there were more ships, too? Maybe a fleet she didn't know about?

Even as she reached a solution for this problem, another crawled from the recesses of her self-doubt and into the forefront of her mind. She couldn't evacuate a city by herself, she would need help. To get word to these people, to tell them their salvation was at the dock she would need a hundred messengers; or just one, who could be heard loud and clear over vast distances. She needed a mage. Another explosion came as a second iron projectile was guided over the walls and permitted to wreak its devastation upon the denizens below. Another building crumbled to rubble in the explosion's wake.

On all fours, Umishi charged across the ramparts to the adjoining tower. With her shoulder, Umishi rammed against the wooden door, throwing it open with little difficulty; it was easier than wasting time attempting to reach the awkwardly high handle. Within the circular stone room, she found, cowering in the dim light, a guard. He was a human man clutching at his weapon as though it were a stuffed toy. Umishi released a sympathetic sigh. The pitiful scene only re-emphasised what she knew of the soldiers of Fendamor: these were no fighters; they could be scarcely relied upon to throw a punch, let alone kill. But, here and now, this human did have a purpose: he would be her guide.

'Where is Hanaswick's mage tower?' she asked the sobbing guard.

He looked at her as though she had grown an extra head. His lips and eyes seemed lost with a will of their own. Another explosion seemed to shake the world, pulling the human out of whatever trance he had fallen victim to. With quickening breath, he sprung to life as though waking from a nightmare, his panicked eyes darting back and forth. 'I... the walls... they, they...'

Umishi clawed at her hair, losing all hope this human would be of any use after all. 'The mages,' she repeated, slower and louder, 'where are they?'

'The mages?' he echoed, his attention unfocused, staring at phantoms visible only to him. 'They... they're... they're gathered, gathered in their tower, the mages' tower at the palace.'

The palace. Her skin crawled with the memories the building invoked, but at least she knew where it was and how to get there. Leaving the guard to his thoughts, Umishi descended the tower's staircase to the streets of Hanaswick. This time, the streets were alive with panic. She hoped that, with direction, these people would rally themselves into some kind of order. It was a fool's hope maybe, but one worthy of holding onto. If she could only save a few, a son, a father, a daughter, a mother, then, when she looked back on this moment, she would not find another Malhain. She opened her lungs, inhaled as much courage as she could from the air and pressed on towards the ruins of the once great Pillar of Fendamor.

Having navigated the way through the chaotic streets, Umishi approached what remained of the palace gardens. The massive chunks of rubble from the sundial tower had devastated the once perfectly maintained gardens. Jagged stone and mountains of marble tore up from the earth like the massive teeth of some gigantic creature. Umishi looked upon the largest of these pieces, which lay crushing the archmage's precious blue flower. She turned and pressed on towards the doors. The main entryway was guarded by two soldiers standing firm, weapons in hand and masked helms over their faces. Looking upon them sent a jolt through her body, along with the urge to avoid their attention. Within a moment, she had spotted an alternative route in: she could use the shaft of the fallen tower to climb up and jump across the small gap to the door that had once opened onto the now collapsed balcony. She shook the feeling out of her head, though. Now was not the time for unnecessary precautions;

the front door would do fine, and the guards would not stop her. They had no *reason* to stop her.

Umishi passed through the maze of destruction that lay between her and the palace entrance. The guards shifted their position, their Nalraka held towards her. Their stance was all wrong, their grip weak, their hands shaking. Umishi continued walking towards them.

'I'm sorry, we cannot let you go any further,' one of the guards stated, his voice quivering more than his grip. 'Only those... those with express invitation by the king may... may enter.'

A grin twisted on Umishi's face. She found herself both surprised and impressed that, as their world collapsed around them, these play soldiers still remembered their scripted lines. She clawed at her hair and took a breath as she prepared her own words. 'I am an inquisitor; the king will want to see me,' she said, her voice barely audible above the sounds of madness running through the city. 'Arch-mage Leuvigild has sent me.'

The guards faced each other, their confusion almost a visible cloud engulfing both their heads. After a few uncomfortable moments of staring, one of the guards nodded at her. 'Inquisitor? We... yes, the king shall want to... We will escort you to the throne room... at once.' The second guard opened the doors.

'Follow me,' continued the first.

Umishi complied, following the guard through the grand entrance and into the main hall. Around her, nobles floated in their fineries, talking, sharing drinks, laughing, as though she had slipped into a different world. As insane as the thought was, she granted it credence by taking into account the madness she had experienced since landing on this island. She had walked into some kind of party. As the city fell apart outside, as screams filled every alleyway, in here, they celebrated. A sickness stirred in her thoughts, threatening to suffocate her. Umishi closed her eye and swallowed. She would move on, she would find the king, would open his eyes, get him to use his mages, get them to cast the Voice of Saiallan. Hanaswick had to be evacuated; those outside had to be safe. The guard led her on, until they were standing before the ornate doors of the throne room.

The throne room was abuzz with activity. Umishi had never seen so many fancy suits and fine dresses; she felt as though she had intruded upon some extravagant gala rather than the nerve centre of a city under siege. One or two of the overdressed humans took the time to offer her a glance, but that was the limit of the attention granted to her entrance. As Umishi forced her way through the forest of colour, another tremor tore its way through the palace. This intruder gained far more attention than she had. The disgruntled nobility held on tightly to each other. Screaming came from those gathered there, but she couldn't see from whom.

'There is no need for alarm,' boomed a voice that emanated from a large, confident-looking man dressed and trimmed in silver and blue. 'Please, these kinds of vibrations are expected in circumstances like these but, like with any thunderstorm, it'll pass. Until then, we all but have to wait here, where it is dry and safe.'

His misguided optimism made her cock the corner of her mouth in disgust. She knew his kind: hired fools who spread optimism regardless of the facts. The worst part was that all the present jesters bought every one of his pretty words. Umishi pushed forwards, until the throne was only a few steps away. As she moved closer, the presence of the nobility lessened, replaced by soldiers in thick plate mail and well-suited generals who wore medals they couldn't possibly have earned. At their centre, the king sat with a bored expression as though he was as frustrated by this pompous charade as she was. She approached with steady steps, clawing at her hair.

' - and the rest of the merchants have been barricaded in the Spinning Dagger, sire,' one of the generals said proudly, glittering in his over polished silvers.

With her approaching footsteps, the king lifted his head and his eyes met her gaze. He raised himself out of his throne with the speed of a man less than half his weight. 'Well, fuck me, now there is a face I did not expect to see!' His voice was lined with regal power, a power Umishi expected from a ruler. He was the only thing in this room, on this island, which made sense. 'They told me you were dead. I thought by now those dickless Dhal-Llah would have made you a sock puppet for their bloody dead king!'

'You need to summon your mages, they need to... we need to have them...' Her words stumbled out of her mouth. 'We need them to send word, to direct everyone onto the battleship.'

'Calm yourself, Ms Zaimor.' The king laughed. 'Why would we do such a thing? My generals, my advisers, even the bloody historians, have been regaling me regarding the impressiveness of Hanaswick's walls. How, in the days of the empire, when you were a citizen of this very island, armies of hundreds of thousands crushed themselves against our walls. These Dhal-Llah barely number half that. I assure you, Ms Zaimor, we are perfectly safe. Now, please, get yourself a drink, wash that stress and stubbornness from your mind and loosen up a little, eh?'

The king's words had the opposite effect. She could feel every cocksure word the king spoke fuelling her anger. 'I have seen siege weapons out there more destructive than I have ever seen before,' she growled. 'Your walls are falling and the Dhal-Llah will... they'll...'

'They'll what? Come to kill me? An inquisitor and now a master tactician? I am surprised the Alpharus let you out of their sight,' the king said with oozing sarcasm. 'I have no intention of evacuating my people. They are safe here. The walls of Hanaswick are more than enough to hold back these dickless freaks! I think you overestimate their abilities and their conviction. Give it a few hours and those fucks will skulk off to the holes they dug themselves out of.'

'The walls are not enough,' Umishi insisted.

'Are they not?' the king snarled back. 'Let us say you are right, Inquisitor. Let us say the walls will miraculously crumble into dust. I think you're overlooking one very important thing, something that has slipped your mind despite being the very reason you were brought here in the first place: we still have the Ward!'

'Are you so sure the Ward still protects you?' Umishi whispered, her mind turning to memories of the sickly creature on the walls: the messenger used to signify to the Dhal-Llah that the Ward had been broken.

He took a glance at her, his eyes filled with contemplation. With a swift movement, he threw his arm at one of the guards' heads. There was no contact; his hand passed unhindered through the guard. Her theory was wrong. Renderbrim was yet to remove their ward. It also meant her warning had been revealed as toothless.

'Now, dear lady, we are all on the same page,' the king growled. 'I must thank you for your concern and for the advice you have offered, but we need to get you to safety. I shall have you escorted to a cell where…' The king froze, his focus turning to the centre of the room. 'What… what is…' There was a sudden fear to his voice that forced his words to tremble.

Screams erupted from behind her, panicked nobles crying out and running in different directions. She turned to the source of all the newly birthed chaos. There surely could be nothing more terrifying than the situation this city was already in.

'Fuck!' the king roared. 'Summon the mages! Fetch me the bloody mages!'

A storm of confetti blasted from the room's centre, from thin air, spilling all over the floor and then rising up as mist. The nobles fled from a wave of ash as it swept its way across the room, unchallenged. Umishi's stomach turned. She recognised this magic instantly, had seen it countless times since her arrival. It was blue.

TWENTY-NINE
VENGEANCE UNENDING

As the plumes of blue dust fell, raised and twisted around her, Umishi's body became as stone, her focus on the shadows. She waited for them to come to life, for them to take her. This was different, though; the mists had never escaped the other plane before. Something was happening, something that made Umishi's gut tighten and forced her teeth to grind. Around her, the world seemed to have frozen, her mind muting the screams of the king and his nobles. She inhaled, exhaled, then inhaled again, deeper. It was coming, the other plane began to claw and pull at her insides. In the corner of the room, the shadows began to awaken, to stir and shift. Cold sweat rolled between her fingers as her grip tightened around the hilt of her dagger. Her heart jumped as the shadows charged at her. Closing her eye, she allowed the black flood to envelop her, to wrap itself around her, to squeeze and drag her through the fabric of the world.

Released from darkness's grip, Umishi was left choking on her knees. With stiff joints and swallowing whatever anxieties she had, Umishi rose. There were no signs of Renderbrim or his beasts, but she was in his world of death. Around her, the eerie silence grew into a sound which could not be ignored. It whispered this world's emptiness to her: how alone she was, how there was no one here to help her. She tried in vain to escape its relentless mutterings but, from every wall and corner, lingering shadows threatened to ambush her. In the centre of the room where, in the other plane, the blue mists spewed forth, here was a spot of light: a small diamond floating in the nothingness. It was a portal like the one Lothrum created in the cave, barely the size of the tip of her finger.

The light that clawed from the pinprick hole drew Umishi closer. As her hand neared it, a faint wind reached back for her, the stagnant air around it coming to life, heat slipping through and twisting around her finger. Almost touching her ear to the tiny star, whispers from the other side managed to break through. Even though they were sounds of chaos, they were still a comfort; they still told her that the world beyond this one hadn't ended.

A desperate scream filled the empty palace behind her. At first, Umishi thought her short time in this place had already driven her mad, but the scream called out a second time. It did not come from the portal, but rather from the palace itself, from just behind the door. Her heart pounded hard against her ribs, making her chest sore. There was someone else there, with her, and there were few possibilities when it came to who it could be. She readied her blades and started for the door. Approaching, she listened for any hint as to what she would find. Raspy breathing and hard sniffling echoed from beyond the entryway, as though this mysterious person was suffering a terrible cold or some other ailment; he sounded wounded. She could only imagine it was a hostage, a poor fool Renderbrim had brought to the world to ensure he could send her back should he need to, or... maybe... Umishi pulled open the door.

As the way opened, a figure fell towards her. She jumped back and watched as the body fell. It was Lothrum. At least, what was *left* of him. He was missing his left hand, and two fingers on his right. He looked up at her with worn eyes and a face far more ancient than any human she had ever seen. Using his elbows, he pushed himself toward her. 'Zaimor?' he said, his eyes welling with tears. 'Zaimor...'

She moved towards him and helped to set him against a wall. There was blood all over him. His robes were torn, and it looked as though he had been dragged by horses for miles. 'Shit, what happened to you?' she whispered as she stroked the hair from his face. He looked up at her, his eyes wide with whatever horrors he had seen. His mind was gone. She did not expect an answer from him; his reaction to her voice was enough for the moment.

'Zaimor...' he repeated. 'I am sorry. I am so sorry. I... I... couldn't... he... Zaimor.' His voice was so weak and regretful, so distant from the sarcastic confident person he once was. 'He forced me to... the bastard! I... the portal... I couldn't... he made me.'

'I wouldn't bother, were I you, my dear,' came a soft voice from the corridor beyond the fallen mage. 'My interrogation drilled little holes in his head, allowing more than just the useful stuff to fall out.'

Umishi looked up while she set Lothrum to the ground, her breathing racing almost as swiftly as her heart. She would be no match for Renderbrim's magic, not while he had her at a disadvantage. She would bide her time, wait for an opportunity to present itself.

He glided into the room, his feathered robe dusting the floor with each step. Behind him, five or six of his beasts limped in. Drool and slime undid all the work his cloak had done. He faced her with a grin that threatened to burst into his eye sockets. 'I waited for you, you know, my dear. I thought you had the right to enjoy this too. I'm so glad you made it here to witness the sublime justice that I am about to exact.'

He waited? The army outside was waiting for her? It made no sense, it was madness. 'Why?' she screamed in frustration. 'Why me?'

'Because you're not like them!' he screamed. 'You are not like those mindless, pathetic drones who throw themselves at his feet. Because you care about justice as much as I do!' He granted himself a breath to regain his composure. 'I've been here so long, my dear, ageing only for a moment every day. I have passed the age of my father, yet I remain as young as I was when he was murdered, when that monster stole the kingdom! He tore it apart! I have been trapped here, soaking and bathing in this darkness. Not the shadows, I don't mean the shadows, I mean *his* shadow. I've been tortured here, frozen in time for so long. I felt like I was going mad. Then you came, from the other land, an authority on the evils of magic, a mind uncorrupted by Fendamor's poisoned words. You were a witness, a judge, someone who would understand, who would see the light in what I am doing, I need you to see that it'll free us! I... me... me and the others, we need not be alone anymore. Please, I am not mad, I am righteous!'

'The bastard's dead,' Umishi said. 'The Mangler, the Fendamor you knew, is dead. He's dead,' she whispered, trying to withhold a snarl. 'The only people you and your war will kill are the poor fools who don't even know you exist.'

'You still don't see, you still don't understand! He's alive still!' he cried. 'He is everywhere, in every plane, every city, every town, every street, every house, in everyone! He's in every breath I take, he's in the shadows. I hear him whispering when I close my eyes! This whole island is him. Please tell me you see it too. You hear it, yes? You knew it before you set foot on Domvalkia.'

Renderbrim gestured to the walls around him. 'Despite his body, his grave, you could hear him whispering and you were drawn to the possibility of his existence. He called you through Leuvigild's voice. You must see he has corrupted them all with his words, his spells, his lies, his beliefs. They're all a part of him on some level, in some way, whether they know it or not! They are all at fault, all culpable, all compliant in his rise to power! And now justice comes for them, for him and the people of Fendamor.'

Umishi took a step back, his mad ramblings still echoing. The words terrified her in a way she had never felt before. Every syllable felt like a worm permeating under her skin, greedily burrowing towards her heart. She had been so close to agreeing with these now seemingly insane statements, so close to thinking this way. Umishi recalled the fortress of Vianana, how quick she had been to overlook the craziness in his words, how quick she had been to buy into his blurred logic, how willing she had been to ignore the suffering of others, using words like duty and justice to validate her vengeance. No, that would not be her. Not again. She had changed.

'I've let him live. Leuvigild, I let him live,' she proclaimed, stepping forward. 'I didn't kill him. He will find judgement at the tribunal of Alpharus, not at the tip of my daggers and not by your hands.'

Renderbrim cocked his head as she took another step towards him, her hair flowing from her face.

'He's coming,' she continued, 'before I bring him back to the mainland for justice, he is coming, and he will rip the Ward from under the feet of your Dhal-Llah armies. They will run and neither you nor they shall steal vengeance. You've lost.' Umishi closed her eye and traced her dagger's hilt with her thumb, waiting with held breath for his inevitable retribution.

Renderbrim's joyous cackling filled the air and forced the room to tremble. His dark lips twisted into a smirk. 'Dhal-Llah?' He spat. 'Worms, leeches, dogs! I think you are confused, my dear. Do you think I expected anything more from them but to die at the walls of Hanaswick? It's what they were always meant to do; fodder is all I could ever rely on them being. They had already proved the weight of their loyalty to me after they abandoned me and my father to the whims of Fendamor.'

He took a step closer, his smile widening, his teeth

showing. 'Don't you see, it is as I said: wars always burn out. The Ward was always going to fail at this point in the war, at the battle of Hanaswick, whether it was by you or me killing Leuvigild, or Leuvigild himself destroying the Ward. Do you not see the inevitability of it all? It is as if it were all orchestrated by fate, as if it was all meant to be.'

From behind Renderbrim, a thousand clicks and croaks called out from the blue mist as it filled the corridors. Within the encroaching fog, silhouettes scrambled across the floors, against the walls, towards them, towards Umishi. Her heart pounded. She turned and fled deeper into the throne room; there was no other choice. She had to get out, had to escape, had to warn those in the other plane, but how? She looked to the tiny portal, then to Lothrum, barely alive at Renderbrim's heels. How much did the lives of Domvalkia matter? She pondered as the only plan available presented itself.

'Do you feel it? Any moment now, the planes shall align, and this little star created by Hanaswick's finest mage will tear its way into the other plane,' Renderbrim said as he approached the portal. 'At last, justice will be done. It will spill forth, sweeping away what remains of the traitors and cowards after Hanaswick have had their battle, and their Ward has bolstered my army. My Kalsakian friends and I shall at last be free to take what is ours by right! We will be victims no more. Do you not understand?'

He stared at her. 'How do you not understand? Have I... we... have the Kalsakian not suffered enough? Birthed from pain, trapped in a moment of violence, doomed never to see the light, never to feel warmth! Have they not earned their right to justice? Have *I* not earned the right to grant them that justice? Do you not see that, after the war, after the slaves of Fendamor and the Dhal-Llah fools have been washed away, a new empire will be born? Domvalkia will once again be united, peace and justice restored, a glorious land for the righteous! Can you see it, my dear? Can you see the new age dawning?'

'No, no, you're not righteous,' she declared, 'you... you use them for signals, for tests, for distractions. You're pretending it's for them, for justice, but it's not, it's for you. It's all for you... your vengeance, not theirs.'

Renderbrim's face darkened as his monsters flooded the room. 'No!' he shrieked. 'I am just... I am... I... why are you saying these things!? Why are you saying these horrible fucking things? Why do you refuse to see it! Why can you not see that this is good, is what needs to happen? You have to see, you must! I am not mad! I... I... no. I am sorry, my dear, truly, but I have tolerated your voluntary blindness enough., yes, yes, no, I can no more, you have stubbornly hindered me at every turn. I've given you chance after chance to see what I am doing, to see the righteousness in my cause, but now... no, I can't let you anymore, not now.'

Umishi could see a mixture of anger and pity spreading across Renderbrim's face.

'I was too late, he had you! He must have had you from the beginning! Poisoned your mind! Dissolved your understanding of right and wrong, good and evil, until... no!'

The words which followed were not those meant for speaking, they twisted the air and warped the space in the room. Umishi had felt magic before, felt how it chilled the air, but this was different: this made her feel sick. A Kalsakian fell to the ground, dead, sapped of its life as Renderbrim lifted his hands, then another, and another. At his command, the ceiling above him broke away and transformed into lances, their tips pointing directly at her.

Umishi ran, but she knew she would not be fast enough. With a lazy flick of his wrist, Renderbrim launched the stone projectiles at her. All she had time to do was react. She thrust her arms over her face and shrieked in a way which made her feel ashamed of herself. After a breath had passed, she lowered her arms to find the lances had not hit their mark, but had hit the ground instead. Ground that now hovered in front of her face.

'Run, girl!' Lothrum shouted, his arm reaching for the stone he was levitating, his other beckoning invisible forces from the portal's other side. 'Do what you must!'

A hate seeped from Renderbrim's eyes as he spun to face the wounded mage. There was nothing she could do; she knew he wouldn't kill Lothrum, not unless he wanted to free her from this plane. She turned back to the door opposite the one Lothrum sat at and ran.

The door opened into a staircase, a sight that brought a smile to her face. This was the right way. With each step she mastered, Renderbrim's words echoed in her mind: at any moment the planes would align, align as they had done in Fort Jimmarah.

She had reached the top before the blue mists claimed the bottom, behind it came the thunderous scraping sounds of countless talon-tipped feet. Her heart pounded, hoping her plan would work, hoping Renderbrim led his army of beasts. Umishi threw open the door in front of her and greeted the moon with another smile.

Stumbling onto the balcony, the city below stretched out before her, although she could see nothing of the floor, nothing of the wall or even the lands beyond, where the Dhal-Llah stood. All was black with the dark, oozing skin of the Kalsakian. The endless sea of flesh stretched out towards the horizon, all of them hissing, croaking and snarling, eager for their promised revenge. It was an army of darkness ready to lay waste to Domvalkia as soon as the portal was opened. Umishi looked to the ever-faithful landmark, the tower that had granted her guidance since she had set foot on the island. Standing tall, the sundial tower looked down at her with its marble face. It had to work.

Blue liquid dust slithered past her face as though suggesting that she turn back to the door to welcome the monster stepping out to greet her. She resisted.

'Beautiful, are they not?' Renderbrim's voice crept from behind her. 'An army of countless built from the selfish deeds of those it will soon cleanse; a poetic end for such monsters. Speaking of ends, my dear, I fear you have reached yours. You've strived for so, so long, run so far. It is your failure to accept, or even acknowledge, the truth which has brought you here. I'm sorry, but truth has caught you, little mouse, and there is nowhere left to run.'

To her right, her eye was drawn to something: a mound of Kalsakian falling away, revealing the wall underneath, damaged. It was beginning. 'You're right,' she whispered, 'I think it's time we both faced the real world.' With those words, she jumped, casting herself from the balcony, towards the white-faced tower and into the nothingness between.

Time seemed to slow at the very moment it was meant to move in this world. The leap didn't feel like falling; she had fallen many times throughout her life. This was different, strange. There was no breeze, no air pushing against her. For the first time, she was free and falling through a dream. Below, buildings shimmered and vanished into piles of rubble. The Kalsakians moved as the gardens beneath their feet were crushed by a not yet visible force, a force that soon appeared. The tower before her vanished while, at the same time, appearing, collapsed and destroyed, beneath her. With arms stretched out as far as she could, Umishi latched onto the ruin. The monsters below screamed. Umishi laughed.

Over her shoulder, she caught a glimpse of Renderbrim. For the brief amount of time he stood there, he held the most horrifying and pitiful look, an expression that was a mix of hate and terror as realisation tore the air from his lungs, ensuring the scream that followed was the last sound he ever made. Umishi had made a career from dead men, but the look on this one turned her stomach. She blinked, and he was gone, vanished along with the balcony that once held him above his army.

With Renderbrim's death, the light returned for her, pulling her back into the other plane. She watched as the Kalsakian shimmered and vanished. Returning to her own world, the sky above was a deep blue and alive with stars.

EPILOGUE

The Battle of Hanaswick

Leuvigild looked over the battlefield. His men were in position, ready to charge. He had mustered as many soldiers as he could, as many as would volunteer. He would not stand idle while Umishi, a foreigner Domvalkia had so wronged, *he* had so wronged, risked her life to save them. It was the least he could do. Around him, his soldiers sat upon the steeds which had carried them from Vianana. He was surprised how many of them there were who would offer themselves to fight a seemingly impossible war. Humans were an odd people indeed.

The Dhal-Llah did not seem aware of the approaching ambush or, if they were, they showed no sign of it. The countless number of their forces looked blankly at his city's walls, bombarding it from afar. He knew what he needed to do, and he needed to do it soon. The vanguard was about to charge into the Dhal-Llah's flank; if he did not do what had to be done, they would lose the crucial initial strike. He could not afford for that to happen.

He slipped from his horse and prepared his lips to undo

decades of hard work. Although the cavalry charged past him at incredible speeds, he could not help but think all their eyes were on him as he readied himself for the monumental task that he was about to perform. He formed the words in his mind, each letter taking the fullness of his concentration, each letter burning in his skull as though someone had taken a branding iron to his brain. He gritted his teeth and bore the pain. The more words his mind formed, the more pain he had to endure, the incomplete sentence pressing against his skull, trying to claw down to his mouth, down to freedom. It tore and scorched in an unquenchable thirst for release, but he couldn't allow it to be loosed, not yet. The phrase had to be complete. Each letter meant something - not to him, not to any mortal - but to the universe itself. Each sound was a carefully crafted command telling existence where to draw energy from and what to do with it. One slip could ruin this.

It took him only a moment but, to Leuvigild, it felt like more than an eternity. He felt he had aged a thousand years, his limbs weak with the passing of time. With the phrase ready to explode from within his mouth, he took a deep breath before he spoke. Then the words spilled forth, free. He collapsed to the ground, choking up blood. One or two of the men threatened to stop, to help him, but he waved them away. He would be fine; he had used crueller words than these in the past. Not many, but some.

He tried to envision his words above him, flying across the battlefield, cutting away the threads that bound everyone to the other plane. He watched as the spell he had maintained all his life fell to tatters before him. An immense force pressed against his heart as he brought ruin upon the only tangible thing left of his father. He coughed up more blood as tears started to run down his face. Of all the people his father had wronged, out of everyone who wanted him wiped from the world, Leuvigild found it impossible to believe it would be he who drove the final blow into the Mangler of Malhain. He'd failed, though. They both had.

He lifted his head as the brave men of his kingdom were about to crash into the opposing force. He watched as the battle of Hanaswick began. He had never intended this to happen, never intended for so much suffering to be enacted in his name. It was his desire, his *father's* desire to end conflict, not fuel it. They had intended to stop all this. He understood now, though, that this was not how it was to be done. War could not be ended with some great spell.

He turned as the screams of countless humans made the earth tremble. He turned away as humans he had grown to care for charged into the slaughter. He would not see this. He would not see man kill man; would not bear witness to the destruction of all he had strived to build. He started to walk away. He did not know where he would go, but it would be away from the blood, the violence: somewhere quiet where he'd live out the rest of his days, where none would see his face.

He knew the outcome of the battle already, knew what reward he would gain from his tactical victory this day. He would gain a new title, 'the Mangler' and, like his father before him, he would birth a vengeful child out to claim justice for the Dhal-Llah slaughtered in this battle. He did not need to see it; did not need to be here when it happened.

As he started walking, however, his forces stopped in their charge. The horrific screams turned to cheers. The battle could not be over already, though. The Dhal-Llah ranked in the thousands; even the most skilled mages would have needed more time to kill so many. Leuvigild turned around to witness the cause of this new, joyous hysteria, which seemed to be spreading to each soldier. It was then that one of the soldiers ran up to him and embraced him tightly. Leuvigild lifted his arms, allowing it to happen but not understanding why.

'We won!' she cried.

They'd won? But how could that be? He hád only just lifted the Ward; the battle should have only just begun. After the woman released him, he marched towards the vanguard again. Leuvigild weaved his way through the jubilant masses jumping, screaming, singing. As he pushed ahead, he saw the front lines. He saw the Dhal-Llah forces standing there, frozen in place. He saw his men dismounted, celebrating. He didn't understand; his mind could not process what was happening.

'They surrendered,' one of his generals said. 'The bloody cowards waved the flag of Zella's mercy before we could even get to them.'

They surrendered? He held his hand over his mouth and looked again. It was true. There was no battle; there was no murder or slaughter, no blood or violence. The Dhal-Llah had given up before the battle could begin. They must have felt the moment when the Ward had been removed from them, and when they saw the army...

They hadn't seen a real battle, any more than

Fendamor's soldiers had; they did not know how to react. Now that the situation had changed, the Ward undone, they were lost awaiting an order from their dead emperor. Without a command, there was only one option open to them: to wait until a new one was issued.

'We are rounding them up as we speak,' the general said. 'Gods only know what we are going to do with them... haven't got cells big enough for an army.'

It didn't matter. For that moment, Fendamor didn't care. He let out a laugh and bit down on his finger. The sight was unbelievable, a victory a without bloodshed? It was a more optimistic outcome than he could have ever predicted, a miracle birthed before him. He had been sure that there would be a massacre here. He had been sure human nature would compel them to slaughter each other now they had been given the chance, but he had been wrong. They were without the Ward and, still, no one had died.

'Maybe we could have them work on the city, repair some of this damage they have done?' the general continued.

The days following saw Hanaswick restored, its people falling back into their routines. The seafront had become a bustling marketplace and, with the Ward's removal, Domvalkia opened its boarders, allowing visitors and merchants from distant shores. It felt as though the mists of Hanaswick had dissipated and Leuvigild was seeing his whole kingdom for the first time. However, it was not *his* kingdom, not anymore. He no longer thought himself qualified to advise the king, and no longer had the stomach for matters of court.

He had a new goal; one that did not require the burden

of magic: he sought to reintegrate the Dhal-Llah with their Fendamorian brothers and sisters. After those who had orchestrated the war were brought to justice, Leuvigild found pity for the people he had once plotted war against. He would heal the madness that the Renderbrim bloodline had imposed on them.

Lothrum was a great help to him in the reformation of the Dhal-Llah. They had found him while the palace ballroom was being repaired. They found him wounded, tortured. He told them he had managed to escape the darker plane. He managed to drag himself through a portal he had created.

The world changed after the battle that never happened. Leuvigild Fendamor saw it filled with renewed promise and a whole host of options laid out before him. With the help of Lothrum and his own hard work with the Dhal-Llah, he would usher in a new dawn; he would mend the world.

As for Umishi, she sat above the rebuilding and watched. She already knew she would leave Domvalkia behind her. She was unsure if she would ever return; she had only one desire: home. But, before she left, she would visit Malhain, Holsta... she would find the stone of her husband and son. It was a monument she had not visited, one she had never even seen. She had always dreaded what her husband would have thought of her, an inquisitor, a mage-hunter, a killer, but now, now, that part of herself had gone.

She would leave for home, the village she grew up in. The village in the trees where her kind flourished. She did not know whether any of her family remained there, but she would find out. There, she would make a home for herself among her kin, a race yet to see war. Whether she would stay there or not would be another matter. She had a great deal of life ahead of her but, for now, all she could think of doing was finding a quiet spot and resting.

The End

CPSIA information can be obtained
at www.ICGtesting.com
Printed in the USA
LVHW021830280520
656844LV00004B/706